D1784885

BOURBON & BLOOD

Andrew J. Cole

TABLE OF CONTENTS

CHAPTER ONE

Saturday, August 13th, 1994.

Most people in the United States couldn't find White Wreath, Kentucky on a map if their lives depended on it. Come to think of it, a few people from White Wreath couldn't find it on a map if their lives depended on it. A tiny place in the southeastern part of the state, its nestled in the shadow of the black mountains. On a windy day, you can spit and hit West Virginia. Not a lot happens there. There's always semis and dump trucks on the road, hauling the coal non-stop from the surrounding hills. They never stop. Day and night, the trucks vanish into the ever-present fog of the 1789 highway, only to reappear with full trailers of coal. Being so far from the interstate, or anything for that matter, trucks need a place to stop for fuel or food.

That place is the Imperial Truckstop, a bustling 24/7 ballet of trucks flowing in and out of the pulverized gravel lot surrounding the lone building and its islands of pumps. At night, the multitude of halogen bulbs that cover the Imperial turn the night into day. Pumps always clicking, the metal on metal of the nozzles striking the pump or gas tanks strike an industrial melody that plays around the clock.

The constant rushing sound of the diesel flowing into empty tanks makes the place sound like it's a breathing entity of its own. Trucks like gassy titans, belch fumes into the sky as they approach and fade away into the distance to

1

be followed by another. Gary Burkich, the smiling man with the bushy, reddish-brown, "Wyatt Earp" mustache owns the place. People say he's not happy unless he's in the middle of it, playing conductor the diesel symphony. But outside, away from the chilly airconditioned interior, his adopted son, the skinny teen in the sleeveless black t-shirt with the white letters spelling "SIOUXSIE" across the chest was having a less than stellar time filling the potholes in the gravel lot.

Miles Burkich used the toes of his boot to kick larger rocks into the indentations before shoveling in a half scoop of smaller gravel after and then topped it off with a scoop of stone that was the fine consistency of flour. A few boot stomps smoothed it all out. Without an upward glance, he moved to the next closest pothole and repeated the process. He cursed himself for starting so late. The sun had been high in the sky and scorching everything in sight for hours. And just his luck, there wasn't a cloud anywhere in the sky to help him out. Son of a bitch.

Just as he finished the last of the spots in the smaller front lot, a faint rumble found Miles's ear. Recognizing it immediately, Miles closed his eyes, threw his head back, and grimaced in aggravation.

The rumble became an intermittent growl before morphing into the predictable hum of bass speakers rattling. He opened his eyes and followed the invisible path of something moving beyond their line of sight as it got closer. Just then, a tricked out, red Ford Explorer with tire rims almost too small to be work came speeding into the lot. The speakers blasted "Cop Killer" by ICE-T out the open windows, the expletives of the lyrics echoing louder than the rest against the aluminum awnings of the pumps. It rolled up fast and skidded to a dangerous stop, inches the curb of the building.

The engine and music died, and four males in their twenties piled out of every door of the SUV. Each one was dressed in oversized clothes and hats practically hanging off them. While three of them looked undernourished, the one that managed to pry himself out of the front passenger seat was easily 500 lbs. the whole vehicle shifting as he forced his girth through the frame.

"Yo! Where's my uncle?" the driver, his 'cousin,' JoJo yelled.

"Maybe he's in the back where he always is!" Miles replied, just loud enough to be heard.

"Well is he, or isn't he?!"

"I'm busy, go see for yourself!"

"Yeah get back to diggin' them holes, dipshit!" JoJo yelled back. The other three followed him through the door, the big one waddling more than the rest as he brought up the rear.

"Asshole," Miles muttered. He shook his black bangs out of his eyes before moving to the next waiting pothole. Ever since Gary's nephew, JoJo, got sent to the county jail two years ago for breaking into somebody's home, he'd fashioned himself some kind of hardcore thug gangster type like the ones on MTV and surrounded himself with a crew of three others as daft as himself. He only showed his face when he wanted free gas or money. Miles kicked another group of sizeable rocks into a divot before filling fine

3

gravel in around them and stomping it four times, pretending each time he stomped, he was stomping JoJo's face.

A small but welcome breeze slipped around him, carrying with it the shadow of a red-tailed hawk as it passed between him and the sun. It carried on to the southwest and Miles imagined it heading to New Orleans. New Orleans, the place he wanted to be more than any other place on the planet. But with no car to get him there, his hopes of walking the decadent streets of the French Quarter were as hollow as the divots he was patching.

"Maybe someday," he said to no one as he scanned the lot. "But not today." Miles hoisted the shovel over his shoulder to seek out the next concentration of potholes when the aging loudspeaker hanging from the awning of the store sent a wave of feedback in every direction. The voice that came through afterward belonged to Darla, the head cashier.

"Miles, come in here and help me for a minute, hun."

As Miles crossed the lot, he hiked up his jeans over his skinny hips as a diesel semi on the highway downshifted, filling the air with a sluggish, mechanical, rat-a-tat-tat. The crunch of the gravel under his boots was loud but not loud enough to drown the din of the cicadas in the tree line. He propped the shovel against the ice machine and threw the front door wide. Entering the cloud of conditioned air made the fine hairs on his arms stand endwise. Darla, the quiet woman who'd worked the cash register at the Imperial ever since he could remember, hardly ever said a word to him.

Strange that she'd call for him now when she knew Gary or Mr. Jenkins the night manager had him doing a chore.

"What's up?" he asked, leaning over the counter.

"JoJo's friends are in the store," she said in a voice just above a whisper without looking up from the receipts. "They're always trying to pocket something. Go stand next to them, so they don't think about getting sticky fingers."

"Got it." JoJo must've already ducked into Gary's office in the back, so Miles made a beeline for the three goons congregating near the beer cooler in the corner. Two of them were already pulling bottles of Corona out of the cardboard six-pack carrier as another played the role of lookout down the far aisle.

"What's going on, guys?" Miles said, knowing full well they were trying to heist booze. The bigger one looked Miles right in the eye as he shoved a longneck down the front of his shorts.

"Yo, be cool. We're just getting these for the road. JoJo's gonna pay for these." These assholes clearly thought he was stupid.

"Well, if JoJo is paying for them then you just take them straight up to the counter and wait." Miles pointed to the counter.

"Yo, don't be a snitch," said the skinny one with the poorly drawn prison '606' tattoo on the left side of his neck. "This place makes all kindsa dough."

"It makes 'all kindsa dough' because we don't hand out free beer to everyone who wants it," Miles said. The more massive thug looked angry as he jammed another down his shorts.

"Don't be a rat or I'll come back and fuck you up when your dad isn't here." To be fair, the big moose didn't know that Gary wasn't his dad, but it still pissed Miles off.

"Hey, Darla!" Miles yelled over his shoulder. "Is Sheriff Taylor still here or did he leave?"

"He's out back writing a ticket for a speeder," she answered without skipping a beat. The goons froze and looked at one another as they tried to figure out if he was bluffing or not. The funny part was Miles knowing that the goons probably didn't know the sheriff's last name was Wallace and that 'Taylor' was the last name of the lawman on the Andy Griffith television show.

The three looked at each other one more time to figure out if the stolen beer was worth the potential intervention of a police officer. Miles could almost smell the dormant gears smoking in their heads, attempting to work hard enough to create a solution. In the end, the bluff worked. Each one rolled their eyes, and their shoulders sagged as they began pulling the bottles from their respective pockets and underwear.

Yuck.

Just as the big one was pulling the last one from his pants, JoJo appeared to survey the scene.

"Yo, what the fuck are you doing? I told you I was coming here to get money, so why are you trying to loot a six-pack?" He waved a handful of twenty-dollar bills in their faces. "I can't take you bitches anywhere."

The three shrank like scolded children and placed the bottles back into the carrier before putting it back in the cooler. JoJo stared Miles down. Miles hadn't noticed it before, but his cousin's face looked even paler than any time he'd seen it before. Something looked "off" this time. The tight lines of JoJo's neck and collarbone poked out from beneath the t-shirt in an unhealthy gauntness Miles hadn't seen in the seventeen years he'd known him.

"The fuck you staring at, homo?" JoJo said. "Shouldn't you be digging more potholes?"

"I'm *filling* the potholes in the lot, not digging them," Miles corrected him. JoJo's expression changed in a flash from annoyance to aggression.

"What's that?" JoJo stepped forward and shoved Miles in the chest, pushing him back a foot. "You think you're smart?" To Miles's relief, Gary appeared, surprising them both.

"Miles?" the man said. "What are you doing in here? I thought you were told to take care of those spots in the lot."

"I-I was just," he stammered.

"You were soaking up the air conditioning. The sun is getting higher, and you're gonna be hatin' life if it's not done before quittin' time like I told you. Now get a drink of water or take a leak or whatever you need to do and get back out there and do as I asked."

JoJo must have sensed that Gary, standing directly behind him, had no idea what was going on. He made a mocking face at Miles and had the gall to stick his tongue halfway through his teeth just to mock him and piss him off.

It worked.

"You mother f-" Miles began to say.

"I said outside, now!" Gary shouted as he pointed to the door.

Miles bit his tongue to turn on his heel and trudged out the door. It took too many steps to get there. He could still feel JoJo's smirk burning through the back of his head as he threw the door open and snatched the shovel from the ice machine.

JoJo's attempted thievery and taking advantage of Gary's good nature ate him up from the inside out.

"Lying, cracker ass, worm sucking, dick-nosed, thug wannabe, motherfucker." he spewed to no one.

"Jesus, Miles." A voice said from his blindside at the corner of the building. "If Gary catches you talking like that, he's going to have an aneurysm."

Miles turned to find his best friend, Dennis Montgomery at the corner of the building. Dennis: six and a half feet of lean, brown skin wrapped in black jeans and a threadbare, Bauhaus band T-shirt topped with a bleached high and tight haircut. He was never without a smile, but the devilish grin was a little less vibrant today.

"Oh, hey. I didn't see you." Miles stopped. "When did you get here?"

"I just pulled up. Pearl is in the car." He thumbed towards the powder blue Cutlass a few feet to his rear.

Behind the glare of the windshield, Dennis's plump, pale as a ghost grandmother gave a smile and an enthusiastic fluttery wave.

"Hey, darlin!" she said.

"Listen, she wants me to ask if you'd help us look for Mary," Dennis said.

"Mary? You lose your sister faster than JoJo loses points on his driver's license. I thought you were taking her to the preacher for that exorcism thing today."

"Yeah, about that." Dennis let out a half snicker. "We got her to hold still long enough to get her bathed and get a confirmation dress on her before going to the church. Pearl slipped two of her pills to her peanut butter sandwich so she wouldn't be on edge when we got there."

"And?"

"And Preacher David and Deacon Joe had a whole table full of anti-Satan stuff set up. He said he'd even blessed the dunking tank behind the pulpit. Anyway, we took her in through the front door as she acted pretty calm about the whole thing. She let them do all their speaking in tongues and mumbo jumbo up until it came time to try and use that dunking tank."

"Oh shit. Mary thought she was getting another bath, didn't she?"

"Yeah, as soon as he acted like he was going to pull her into the baptismal pool with him, she went completely batshit. She spit out of the pills we thought we'd made her swallow and hit the preacher in the eye, began yelling,

9

kicking, bit Deacon Joe on the arm, and then called the preacher a 'shit-ass.' I wasn't able to catch her in time before she dove out the window next to the choir stand and started tearing across the field, heading back this way."

"She's headed this way, huh? I'll tell everyone to keep an eye open for a girl in a communion dress."

"That's another thing." Dennis winced.

"What's another thing?"

"She was out of that dress and buck naked before she hit the tall grass past the church van. Her pale ass just vanished in into the tree line like a specter. The little nudist is going to be covered in mud, burrs, and poison ivy by the time we find her. At least we know she likes to come here, so that helps narrow things down a little bit."

"The last few times I've found her she was playing on those rusted out semi cabs on the back end of the lot," Miles said, already glancing around for the naked girl. "I'll keep an eye out for her."

"Can you come with us now?" Dennis asked.

"I can't, sorry. Gary is pissed at me, and I have to get these potholes filled before I can do anything. Shit, the sun is already getting high in the sky, so it looks like I'm not going to be done until close to quitting time."

"Why in the world is Gary pissed at you? What did you do?"

"It's not me. JoJo showed up and got under his skin. Are you and the others still up for hanging out later?"

"Yeah, definitely. Pearl is letting me take the car as long as I top off the tank before I bring it back. Oh, I've also got a surprise for you."

"What is it?"

"If I told you, it wouldn't be a surprise." A blast from the horn of the Cutlass made them both jump as Pearl's head leaned out the window.

"Honey," Pearl said. "Get my scratch-off lottery tickets so we can get going. My little angel is running around in her birthday suit, and I don't want her getting snatched up by some pederast!"

"Ok, I'll be back later." Dennis gave him a punch in the arm before heading inside. "Get back to patching, pothole boy." The lake of gravel beckoned to be smoothed of all its ripples. Miles looked down at the faded image of the woman's face on his shirt.

"C'mon Siouxsie, we've got work to do," Miles said to her. He headed toward the closest cluster of holes, the headset of his walkman tape player slipping over his ears to drown out the sound of the trucks. His heartbeat quickened, and he wiped his brow. The shovel felt a little lighter. The first notes of "Hong Kong Garden" began to play and the parking lot, the pumps, the building, the whole truck stop itself seemed to fade away behind the melody. An hour or two of uninterrupted hole filling followed. Mindless and repetitive. If not for the sweet voice in his ear he'd have become fit to be tied. The diesel fumes coming off the gas pumps made the building itself appear like a mirage in a desert. Everything seemed dreamy and out of focus. A deafening horn rang out. Miles's consciousness slammed back to the reality that he was staring down at the grill of the Peterbilt semi-truck that brought the daily fuel supply.

"Kid? Are you high?" the man barked while waving an arm to shoo him off. "Get the hell out of the way, so I don't run you over!"

Miles backed to the edge of the gravel as the truck lurched into first gear and huffed away. He blinked twice, regaining his senses.

Three abandoned semi cabs stared back at him from their resting place in the tall grass. Their round, bulging eyes and crooked teeth grills glared with silent displeasure. The rusting Mack trucks seemed out of place in Gary's clean operation, consumed by weeds and blanketed in the dirt no rain could wash clean. A hint of movement caught his eye.

"What the hell?" There it was, behind the grimy glass of the sleeper section—not his imagination going wild.

Miles strode forward. Handprints—too small to belong to an adult—had wiped away grime from the door handle. He drew the door open and a swath of white skin and natural long brown hair ducked away into the back of the cab. While being actual siblings, Dennis and Mary each had a different father, hence his dark skin and Mary being as pale as a sheet like Pearl. Dennis once mentioned he had no idea who their sperm donors were. The location of their mother had become just as big a mystery.

"Mary!" Miles climbed up on the gas tank. "Mary, I saw you! Get out here! Pearl and Dennis are looking for you." The cabin sweltered like a sweat lodge, and Mary didn't have the sense to roll down the window. If she wasn't careful, she'd end up like the babies and pets he'd heard about dying of heat from being left in a hot car. He yanked on the curtain separating the sections of the cab to expose her, but she retreated further around the corner. Another tug broke the curtain free and it came off in his hand.

Unable to hide any longer, Mary, soaked with sweat and what looked like mud, flopped down on the old, bare mattress hanging on the back wall. The entire cabin reeked of rank body funk and another smell. Mary, in all of her naivety, had been playing with her menstrual blood, even going as far as to finger paint smeared pictures on the walls and ceiling with her own bodily fluids and God knows what else. The blood, the heat, Jesus, it was like a sauna in a slaughterhouse. He pulled the neck of his shirt over his mouth to keep from gagging.

"Honey, what are you doing in here? Pearl is looking for you. You need to go home."

Mary ignored him, continuing to play with her vagina with her legs spread. Her hair hung down over her face and couldn't tell if she was looking at him. She seemed almost fascinated with the texture of the fresh blood and the colors it made when she coated a new finger and wiped it on the once grey lining of the sleeper. Miles shuddered but tried to stay calm. The universe had to be fucking with him.

"Mary, stop, please stop, that's not clean." He said, looking away to anywhere in the cab but at her. "Come on, let's go inside and get you cleaned up." She stopped for a moment and began to get up. Thinking she'd listened, he held his hand out. Mary reached up with both of her hands sandwiching his and slathered a fresh coat of shed uterine lining across his wrists and knuckles.

"God….dammit," Miles swore, trying not to shout as he shook the hand away in disgust. "Mary, Pearl is worried sick about you, and you can't stay in here. If you come with me now, I'll get you cleaned up and I'm pretty sure there are still a few good chicken legs left on the food bar."

"Chicken?" she said without looking up.

"That's right, chicken." He leaned out to offer his hand a second time. "Wipe your hands on that mattress and let's go."

"Okay, Mills," she said to his surprise. Mary began flopping her hands about on the cushions like little fish out of water, and a bit of the blood came off. As she stood up, he pulled his Siouxsie and the Banshees shirt over his head and put it on her. It fit like a dress. He helped her down out of the truck. When they started out across the gravel, Mary whimpered "Ow, hot."

Miles tried to scoop her up to carry her, but it was too late. She was off again and running. Mary darted across the main road and bounded fast down the hill into the woods beyond. Thank god no cars hit her.

"Mary! Mary come back! Ah, shit." Not thinking twice, he picked up a jogging pace and set out after her. Across the blacktop and through the tall grass he ran, stopping only for a moment at the tree line to survey the wide downhill slope. He paused to listen. The din of the cicadas and wind moving through the trees waned just enough for his ears to catch the echo of her childish laugh. East. He bounded himself, galloping two steps at a time to get down the hill fast without falling. Near the water at the bottom, he scanned ahead to see her vanishing over the next rise. How did she move so fast?

"This isn't a game, Mary!" Miles shouted. Except for her, it was. A game of Tag and Miles was it. He took off after her at a full sprint, the underbrush and trees slipping past in a green blur. He gave chase, but for every crest and hollow crossed, Mary somehow stayed ahead of him. Every time he thought he was almost upon her she ducked out of sight and reappeared further away. Fences and fallen logs didn't seem to slow her down. At one point she eluded him completely. There were no signs or sounds of which way she'd gone. A gust of wind moved through the trees to tussle his hair. As it slipped around him, he thought he heard a voice speak in a voice neither Mary's or his own.

"*Find me*," it whispered.

"What?" Miles replied, glancing around wildly. There was no one there. "Who said that?" Just then, a full head of dark hair bounced into view over a far ridge. "Hey, wait up! Mary!"

It wasn't until they approached the ruins of the old Booth distillery that Miles managed to get closer and call out to her.

"Mary! Stay away from there! It's not safe!" The old ruins were a broken arm or leg just waiting to happen. Gary once paddled his ass for playing near them ten years ago. Built on the side of a hill near the creek, the distillery had burned down in the 1890s, leaving the gutted basement and rick house footprint as a potential danger. Most of it burned down, anyway.

The whole distillery had been built into the side of a steep hill, so the remaining footprint of the rickhouse resembled a thirty-foot deep, Olympic-sized swimming pool made of stone in the downslope.

He approached from the high side, hoping to get a better view. Looking down, Mary was nowhere to be found in the basement, only mounds of debris and dirt here and there to layer the bottom. But to his left, Miles found her standing out on the remnants of the freestanding third floor. Most wood would have deteriorated after all that time of being abandoned, but the thickness of the support must've been easily as big around as a tree when it was constructed. Seated atop a single post, the platform looked like the crow's nest of a pirate ship. The shoddy contraption actually shifted an inch or two as Mary walked around on it.

"Mary! Come to me, it's not safe out there." She didn't make eye contact but instead chose to continue skipping in circles, humming and singing to herself. The platform shifted a little more every time she jumped and brought her weight down.

Miles moved as close as he dared to the edge of the higher retaining wall without stepping out on the rickety single beam connected to the platform.

"Come on," He reached his hand out to coax her towards him. "Get off that thing. That's not wood, Mary. That's just termites holding hands."

She paid him no mind and continued to dance. Miles took it all in to size up the situation. The structure hadn't fallen yet, but it wouldn't hold much longer with her jumping about on it. He didn't want to do what came next. Against his better judgment, he squatted atop the retaining wall and pressed on the beam to check how sturdy it might be. Unlike the platform, it didn't seem to budge. It appeared just wide enough to crawl across without falling in.

"Mary, I don't want to come out there. Please come back over." She began to sing about peanut butter and swing her arms. If he couldn't stop her from ending up in the hospital from falling, Dennis would never forgive him. "Damn it, girl."

He got up and stepped away from the edge to gauge what it would take to get a running start and tiptoe across the span when a rustling of leaves from behind startled him. Standing four feet to his right next to a tree, an adult deer had been camouflaged in plain sight. Miles almost jumped out of his skin when the animal raced past him in a frightened state, rushing straight for the lip of the retaining wall. It all seemed too surreal to watch the buck leap headlong over the thirty-foot ledge, emitting a desperate cry as its hind hooves dipped below the surface.

No sooner had it fallen, the pillar supporting the platform Mary shifted violently. Miles hurried to the edge to see the deer, now with a broken front leg, kicking and crying as it tried to get to its feet. The animal bucked and kicked, striking the pillar time and again. Mary teetered as the platform rocked back and forth, the wood beneath her groaning as it began to fail.

"Oh shit, Mary!"

Without thinking twice, Miles bolted across the remaining planks and snatched Mary by the arm. She squealed and pulled away, running back across the plank to safety. The platform shuddered and cracked beneath Miles. He tried to get to his feet to dash back, but his weight was too much for the ancient wood. The entire support pillar began to crack and split. There was no more time. Miles cried out to Mary who stared back him with nothing behind her eyes but confusion. "It's gonna fall! Get help! Mary! Do you understand me? Get Dennis or Pearl! Bring them here! Get help! Bring-"

The beam snapped, and the whole thing crashed down around him. His stomach turned as there was no longer anything holding him three stories above the basement floor.

For a few seconds, Miles Burkich tumbled weightless through the air. There were no thoughts of regret or anger for Mary or anyone else, and there wasn't enough time for his life to flash in front of his eyes. It was only gravity doing its job and the impact at the bottom that made the world vanish.

CHAPTER TWO

Nightfall.

Miles sucked in his first conscious breath as though he'd been submerged. He found himself on his back, pushing kicking away boards and debris like a baby kicking off blankets.

Every motion pained him, the muscles and bones of his limbs crying their condemnation. High above, a giant full moon illuminated everything. Full moon? How long had he been out? The night became a pale twilight with the singing of the cicadas around the ruins where he lay. A blanket of nocturnal air chilled him to the core, and everything ached or throbbed, everything but the numbness in his left shoulder. A stick of wood rested diagonally against his left temple. He tried to shove it away like the others, but when he pushed against it, nothing. A stickiness covered it and he pulled his hand away expecting common sap. Instead of the usual residue, his hand came back covered in blood.

When the same hand traced the path of the wood from the tip down to the base where it emerged, he found the source of the numbness in his left shoulder. The fall had caused him to become impaled on an upended wooden spike.

Panicking, Miles struggled to be free of the thing holding him in place. Animal whimpers and keening filled the basement. The piece resembled a huge toothpick. He tore and pulled at the foreign object, but the more he pulled, the more pain he inflicted upon himself. The initial shock was wearing away fast, and the burning pain of being impaled made him more desperate. He found leverage by arching his back to twist against it.

He pressed and turned, the pain becoming white-hot, like electric current burning its way from the inside out.

"It's just wood," he said, panting. "I can break it off."

Summoning all the strength he could muster; Miles found the will to even reach up with the left hand and hook his trembling hand about the shard. *No going back now.* The arching of the back was only the first part. Followed by his heels digging in to push him back further. What started as a low groan, grew in intensity and volume to surpass a cry and evolve into a full primal scream. The sound scattered night birds from their roosts as Miles pulled his right leg further up under his ass and kicked to twist violently to the left. The wood relented with a sharp crack.

It broke off where it entered his shoulder from the back. Miles fell free and slid down the mound. Past his feet, the injured deer tried to get away from him. But with one of its front legs bent at an awkward angle, it pushed itself just out of reach before going still again. In the bright moonlight, Miles could see its heaving chest.

He'd managed to break free from being impaled, but he was still in danger of being slashed by antlers if the animal went batshit. The only way out of the caved-in basement was blocked by the deer. Choosing a club-sized piece of lumber from the pile, he clumsily swung it in an arc towards the buck.

"Out!" Miles shouted, swinging it again. "Get out of here!" The animal didn't budge. It didn't even make a sound. But Miles heard something…a sound came from beneath the pile of debris he was sitting on. He'd once heard the roar of a mountain lion on a television show. It sounded like that. Something feral, not human.

Afraid he'd somehow disturbed a den of wildcats, he scooted and backpedaled to the only shadowed spot spaced between the wounded deer and the wall too steep to climb. When he put his back against the wall, the wood protruding from his shoulder twisted in the flesh. It took every ounce of control he had left not to scream for fear of attracting whatever was emerging from the debris. The sound grew in size, far too loud to be a wildcat, and the far side of the mound began to shift by force beneath.

Oh shit, I woke up a bear.

The pile of stone and wood moved like oatmeal being pushed around a breakfast bowl. The deer stirred again. The more the pile moved, the more it tried to stand, but the bone of its broken leg pushed through the skin. Miles pulled his knees close in an attempt to make himself appear smaller and not provoke the animal.

The mysterious entity's growl transformed into a shrill howl. Planks flew across the basement. In a terror-fueled attempt to escape, the deer bolted. It didn't make it out as some kind of bipedal thing stepped from the shadows, into the moonlight and attacked the deer, tackling it in one fluid motion. The two fell as one and rolled to land at Miles feet.

Terrified, Miles scooted and kicked to get away only hit his injured shoulder on the wall a second time. The two

21

animals kicked and tore at the other. Miles was too enraptured by the spectacle to look away. The longer he watched, the more the second one looked like a person. On its back, the deer flailed and brayed as the person-thing tore and swung its arms. The battle might've lasted longer, but in the middle of the fight, the person snatched the swinging broken leg mid-air, tore it free from the animal and jammed the bare bone like a knife into the deer's neck. The buck's body contorted, becoming rigid before relaxing and falling into the person's grip. Its death rattle echoed in the air.

For a moment, things grew quiet. The only sound to be heard came in the form of sucking and smacking noises from the entity's face buried in the deer's neck. While it was distracted, Miles slowly shifted his weight from his one good arm to his butt to his feet to put some distance between him and whatever was eating the deer. When he reached the archway the deer had blocked, he found it mostly choked by rubble. He'd need both hands to move the large objects hindering his exit. For now, it was impassable. Unless there was another exit somewhere on the other side of the mound, he could be trapped and killed by whatever animal it was that could tackle and pin a full-grown deer in three seconds. He continued scooting as quietly as he could manage until he was sure he wouldn't be watched. The thing continued to eat, and Miles pushed himself to his feet. As bad as the throbbing in his shoulder was, standing was worse. He felt dizziness profound enough to cause his stomach to turn in protest. He knew if he was going to get out of here, it had to be now.

Carefully, Miles climbed to the top of the mound, where he had a better vantage point. From there the

22

moonlight showed him potential escape routes. There wasn't another doorway along the bottom, but enough of the foundation had crumbled in certain spots that scaling a different part of the wall was possible. As he stepped over the place he'd landed and started down the other side, the newly felled lumber shifted. His right ankle buckled, and he couldn't catch himself.

Miles twisted in place, tripping on his own feet. He tumbled down, landing on his stomach in such a way that the shard of wood protruding from the front of his body wrenched against his collarbone. He couldn't stop from crying out as his body convulsed and shook. Wails expelled from him until his throat burned and grew horse. He lay sprawled and panting, the moon and sky above him, the mound past his shoes.

In a fleeting moment of clarity, he thought of Gary. If only he would appear at the top of the retaining wall and gather him up, take him home. But that wasn't going to happen. There's no way he would know to look for him here. Something moved in his peripheral vision, and when he looked past his shoes, the being had appeared. Standing atop the mound, a thin girl with blonde hair.

She, whoever she was, stepped slowly toward Miles, her hair flowing on a breeze that didn't exist.

Miles's brain snapped awake, and he found the strength to shuffle backward and get to his feet. The wall was closer than he remembered, and with the adrenaline coursing faster now, the footholds didn't seem so daunting. He lumbered towards the first hole in the wall and planted one foot in it as he grasped a handhold before planting the other foot. Instinct took hold and Miles methodically scaled the basement wall as though he'd practiced a hundred times before. Higher he climbed, stealing a glance every five feet to see that the girl wasn't climbing after him, but standing below, waiting for him to lose his grip and fall. The moonlit wall became a blur of hurried steps and weight shifting until Miles found himself just nine feet away from the top. The adrenaline was fading fast. He felt winded and tired. There were no more footholds or handholds to help him climb and even if he had two fully functioning arms, it would be impossible to leave.

"Please don't leave me," a familiar voice said aloud. It was a girl's voice, the same one in his head that said "Find me" before.

Shocked, he turned and looked down at the girl staring up at him. Long flowing blond hair and a pale face, a thin body wearing what looked like a filthy communion dress or sleep shirt.

"Please don't leave." She repeated. "I won't hurt you." His options limited; Miles stopped to hear her. "Don't run away. You came to set me free."

"I didn't know that you or anyone else was here." He looked away for a moment in hopes that the lip of the wall had somehow lowered an inch or five since he tried to reach it last. Standing on his toes, Miles reached his arm as high as the muscles would allow. It was just too high. Every part of his body ached.

"Why are you leaving?" she asked.

"Because I just saw you tear open a deer."

"I was hungry."

"What are you doing down here? Are your parents keeping you in this place?"

"My parents..." she said. The moonlight was stark enough that Miles could see her face wrinkle with sadness. She closed her eyes and when she took a slow, deep inhalation, and held it. All sounds of the night ceased as though the ruins had become as a vacuum. He could hear his heartbeat in his ears. It sounded as though the trees, no, the whole forest, were holding the same long breath. To his astonishment, the blood that covered three quarters of her clothes, body, and face began to disappear. Slowly at first and faster until the patches of dark red were no more. When the last drop of blood was gone, she exhaled. With that release, the vacuum dissipated, and a stiff evening breeze flowing through everything. She opened her eyes and the expression lessened. With no provocation, she took a seat, pulled her knees to her chest and continued looking up at him.

"Won't you please come down?" she asked.

"And if I don't?"

"You can't stand on a ledge the whole night. Do you really want to stay up there?"

"If it's safer than being down there."

"It's not. If I wanted to, I could reach the top before you." A wave of nausea found Miles, and he felt weak again. His head swam, and he couldn't feel his limbs.

"I don't believe you."

"Don't you?" The girl's voice came from above his head. Miles's head whipped around to find the girl's twin seated atop the retaining wall, her bare feet swinging playfully in the moonlight. When he looked back, the other girl was gone. Startled, his left foot slipped on the crumbling masonry and he fell off the wall. He twisted counterclockwise and might've had a chance to catch himself if not for his injured arm being so useless. The floor was coming so fast, and if the first fall didn't break his back then this one would cripple him for life. He crushed his eyes shut and waited for the impact a second time. Flashes of light appeared like starbursts behind his eyes before the blackness enveloped the rest.

The last thing he remembered was a girl with blonde hair kneeling over him. He thought she said, *"Here, let me help."*

But that might have been a dream. Disjointed pictures and mottled noise came and went through the fog. Somewhere in the confusion of all of it, the smell of gasoline filled his nose. Strange voices he didn't recognize lingered out of reach as phantasmal hands found him and pulled at his clothes. A thumb wrapped in latex pulled his eyelids up and the brilliance of a flashlight shot through his cornea to rouse him.

When Miles opened his eyes, the passing ceiling of a hospital hallway paraded past his line of sight. To his left and right, a doctor and nurse shouted unintelligible nonsense. Beyond them, Gary following close behind. Gary's hand clutched Miles's leg. After that, a sterile room with brighter lights and a pair of scissors cutting away at his clothes. A flashlight appeared in front to his eyes and a man with a surgical mask tried to ask him questions. More hands lifted and turned him poking at his back and shoulder until he couldn't feel anything at all. For all his effort he couldn't focus his attention on a single person or stationary object no matter how hard he tried. A pinch in the crook of the arm preceded the intravenous needle slipping under the skin. Somehow a waft of bourbon found his nose, and the voice from before, the girl's voice, found him again.

"Maybe it's best that you not remember all of this."

CHAPTER THREE

Miles awoke in a hospital bed surrounded by familiar faces. Gary was closest on the left, his face brightening when Miles met his eyes. Gary rolled his chair next to the bed and took Miles by the hand. Miles looked past Gary and saw Miss Pearl in a chair with Mary in her lap. Dennis was next to her. He stood and came to the hospital bed. Miles heard voices, glanced at the door and saw a man in surgical scrubs talking with the sheriff, and two other men in uniform. Deputies maybe.

"Hey, he's awake!" Dennis exclaimed. Hearing this, Mary Jumped from Pearl's lap and tried to climb into the bed before Dennis wrapped his arms around her torso to reign her in.

"Mills!" She blurted.

"Girl take it easy," Pearl said. "Don't go jumping on the bed, you'll hurt him worse. Come over here, I've got a sweet for you." Hearing that, Mary lost interest in trying to get towards the bed.

"How are you feeling, boy?" Gary asked him.

"Everything hurts."

"What the hell happened to you?"

All eyes in the room were on him as he searched for the answer. Miles recounted what happened to him from the time he left work to chase Mary to when he woke up in the hospital, leaving out the part about the girl for some reason. He wasn't ready to talk about her yet.

"I fell through the rotten floor. I don't remember much after that, but I guess I climbed out."

"That makes sense." The sheriff nodded. "Mr. Talley from the hardware store says he was driving back from doing some fishing later in the evening and found you lying on the side of the road across the street from your house, blood all over you."

"This is just terrible," Pearl added. "You all excuse me, but I don't have the stomach to hear any more of this. Miles, we'll come back and visit later. Dennis, get Mary away from those machines before she breaks something expensive."

"Thank you for coming," Miles replied. Dennis scooped up Mary and walked her out of the room. At the last moment, he turned, waved, and made the telephone gesture with his hand. Miles smiled and nodded to the affirmative.

"Gentleman, I think that's enough for now," Gary said to the sheriff and his deputies. He nodded towards the door. "Miles has been through a lot and needs his rest. If you need a statement, I'm sure we can find time to come down and give you one after he's recovered."

"That'd be fine, Gary," Sheriff Wallace said. "I'm going to send some men over to the old Booth property and look things over." The men left, and Gary closed the door to the hospital room. When he returned, he took a seat in the same chair next to the bed.

"How are you feeling?"

"You already asked that."

"Yeah, well." Gary leaned forward and scratched the back of his head like he always did when he was stressed out and didn't want to show it. "You scared the shit out of me. This whole thing is god awful, and I don't know what I'd do if something happened to you. You mean too damn much."

"I'm going to be fine," Miles tried to reassure him.

"Yeah? That's another thing that's strange. When they brought you in, you were covered in blood. The doctor said when they cut your clothes off, they couldn't find a single cut or gash. But said you needed two pints of blood."

Miles pulled at the wide neck of his hospital gown to see his left shoulder, noticing for the first time that the wood impaling him was gone. When the flesh was revealed, no traces of the wood shard or ruined flesh could be found. He prodded and kneaded the skin. It was tender and bruised but as for scars or stitches, not a one. Confused, Miles lay back trying to imagine how he'd come away without a scratch.

"I could've sworn…" he said, unable to finish the rest.

"Hell of a thing, huh?" Gary said, as he crossed his arms. "Nurse said they did an x-ray. You may have a slight concussion from the fall, so they want to keep you for another day or so for observation.

"This is too weird," Miles managed to say.

"Yes, it is. Can I get you anything?"

"Um, water? I'm really thirsty." Gary searched the room and found a small cup before filling it in the sink of the adjacent bathroom. He returned and handed it over. The cool fluid quenched Miles's parched throat, and he downed it all in one pull.

"Thanks."

"Sure thing. I don't entirely understand what happened, but I'm glad you're not hurt. That's what's important. Those distillery ruins are a hazard, and somebody needs to bulldoze that old mess. Do you need anything else?"

"No, I'm good." He yawned. "I'm just tired."

"I'll leave you alone. Listen, I'm going into work for a while, but I'll be back later. Get some sleep." Gary walked out and closed the door gently behind him the exact same way he used to do it when was small enough to need to be tucked in at night. When the door clicked, Miles pulled the neckline of his gown aside to inspect the skin of his shoulder again. It was the same as the first time he looked, bruised but no sign of a puncture where he thought it would be. His head hurt. Had the "slight concussion" caused by his fall made him imagine the rest? Did he dream it all in a daze as he stumbled or crawled back to the road? The pain and fear felt so real. Had there been a deer and phantasmal girl in the ruins of the distillery with him? What about what Gary said?

"You were brought in, covered in blood... no cuts or wounds...needed two pints of blood." Thinking about it made his head throb more than it already was. The only way to get any answers would be to return to the distillery.

Fatigue set in. Miles lay his head back and shut his eyelids, which had grown far too heavy to keep open. Sleep came, but nothing peaceful. Jumbled images from the day before intermixed with one another, his mind splicing a visual compilation of confusion and trauma: The sound of a wounded deer, the stickiness of blood on his hands, the snapping of the wood. As the noise built to a fevered climax, he found a vision of the girl from before, a small frame in a nightgown and blonde hair that flowed without the wind blowing upon it. He saw everything as he imagined it before, the open ruins, bathed in moonlight. She stood with her back to him and when he reached out to grab her shoulder, she slowly turned to face him, her eyes still closed. Her lips moved but no words came out.

"Who are you?" he asked. "Say that again?" She did but he couldn't place what she was saying. "I can't hear you." She spoke and her voice still sounded muffled. "I can't hear you! Who are you? Speak up!"

To his horror, she opened her eyes, piercing red glowing pupils looking right through him and into his heart. Her voice becoming as clear as any voice he'd heard before.

She placed her index finger over his heart. "Wake up, Miles."

Miles came out of his sleep like a shot, his body leaping from the mattress. The noise from his throat was a scream in reverse. It filled the dark room so violently that the nurse walking past the open door recoiled and dropped the tray of instruments he was carrying. Sterilized metal became unusable as they skipped across the floor. The bearded man gathered his equipment and stepped inside the room, turning on a small, foot-long fluorescent bulb attached to the wall.

"You all right in here?" Miles grabbed the plastic water cup at his bedside and chugged the contents.

"I had..." He paused to catch his breath. "I had a bad dream." The nurse took the tray and left the room. Miles closed his eyes and considered resting but felt too anxious. Maybe a short walk around the floor would help him clear his head. It took extra effort to shift his feet over the side of the bed and open the plastic packet nearby marked "footwear." Inside, a pair of flimsy purple, foam slippers. They felt like wet cardboard and made about as much noise as dry cardboard as he shuffled out of the room. His IV bag of saline solution hung from a prong on a tall metal pole with four wheels on the bottom. One of the wheels refused to roll correctly and walking too fast made the wheel wag back and forth like a spastic grocery cart. Down to the end of the hallway and back, he went. The sign above the elevator read: THIRD FLOOR. After two laps of the hallway, he noticed that there wasn't another person to be found. It was so quiet on the hall he could hear the faint but high-pitched tone starting to come from the room on the very end. Closer he walked to investigate, peeking in each room as he passed, hoping for an orderly, or nurse to explain the sound. It hadn't been going off a minute ago. What was happening in that room?

It felt like it took forever to travel the length of the hallway. Every cold waft coming from the air vents in the ceiling overhead defied the laws of nature found its way down or through the thin fabric of his gown. At last, he reached the end. A pungent smell; a piercing stench both sour and sterile at the same. Shit and disinfectant, like a miasma of death.

The constant "eeeeeeeee" of the machine grew louder, shriller. When he rounded the corner of the room, Miles stopped fast. A lone light shining down from over the headboard revealed the pale and wrinkled head of an old woman. The sparse white hair lay matted on the brow above a slack-jawed face. Her eyes were as tightly closed as her fists about the blankets pulled to her chin. Miles reached over and grabbed her foot over the covers, shaking it a little as he tried to rouse her. She was stiff as a board.

He placed the back of his hand against her forehead and found it cold before yanking his hand away. Around the foot of the bed, Miles stepped to study the face of the heartbeat monitor. A green line should have been bouncing to show her heartbeat. Nothing, just a repeating loud flatline, a heart symbol with two zeroes' next to it and the text "ALERT" flashing in red at the top. The tone began to hurt his ears, and he looked for a way to silence the machine. At his touch, it became silent but continued to mutely flash and blink its warnings.

He looked up at the sound footsteps in the hallway, but no one was there. When he looked back to the bed, the woman's eyes were wide open where they'd been shut before.

Then the eyes blinked.

Miles recoiled as the head rotated to look him in the eyes.

"Hello," the corpse said.

"Jesus Christ." Miles almost broke the machine as he backpedaled.

"Don't be frightened." Her voice had an ethereal tone to it; sounding in his ears before her mouth opened and fading after the mouth had shut. "Are you well? Has your shoulder healed?" the body asked. Was the cadaver really talking to him? Miles shook his head to cut loose the dreamy strands around his mind. "This body is so cold."

"That's because you're dead." Everything seemed too surreal.

"Dead." The head turned back to its original position and the eyes looked away to the ceiling. "Deceased. That might have something to do with it. It doesn't feel the same when there's no blood pumping."

"I should go," Miles said, backing away. The head turned towards him again.

"But we've hardly talked." The face looked more animated now. "I'd like to know more about you."

"I-I don't." He stammered, looking around the room before seeing the dry erase board with the name 'Ellie Jean Stamper, Age 92' scrawled across it.

"I don't know what to tell you, Mrs. Stamper."

"That's not my name, Miles," she said. "Do you think you're talking to the one who used to wear this face?" Miles's stiffened, and his brow creased.

"You're not Elle Jean Stamper?"

"No," the voice said. "Who did you think you were talking to?"

"I-I thought that…" The words died on his lips.

"Do you always talk to corpses in hospitals?"

"You spoke to me first. What do you want?"

"To talk to you, but not like this," she said.

"Then how…are we supposed to talk?"

"You'll have to come to me."

"Yeah," he scooted away from the bed a little more. "I don't think that's a good idea."

"But what if I can help you get something you want?"

"How could you know what I want?"

"You're trapped, just like me. I can see it in your eyes. You want your freedom, the power to get away whenever you want to go wherever you want. I think you and I could make a deal in which we both get what we want."

"And you're going to climb out of that bed and give me that?"

"Of course, not This vessel has already begun to rot. You'll have to come to me," she said again.

"Who are you?"

"Who do you think I am?"

"You could be a million things. You could be the devil or just a figment of my imagination."

"Come meet me face to face, and I'll tell you. We could help each other."

"Where?"

"Come to the ruins of the Booth distillery after the sun has set." The head turned to look at him again. "And come alone."

"People would think I'm crazy if I told them I was talking to a dead body."

"But you're not talking to a dead body."

"Of course, I am. I'm looking right at you."

"No, you're sound asleep in your bed on the third floor and you should really think about waking up."

"Why?" he asked. For the first time, the face began to show something besides slack-jawed droopiness as the corners of the mouth curled back to reveal black gums and a sinister rictus grin.

"Because you've just stopped breathing."

CHAPTER FOUR

After a brief and astonishing visit from the doctor on call, Miles was found to be in perfect health and discharged in the morning. He and Gary took the elevator down to the lobby.

"You sure you're all right?" Gary asked.

"I just want to go home," Miles said.

"I understand that. Hospitals give me the damn creeps. Other than the arrival of babies, nothing good ever happens here. Even then it depends on the baby." The doors opened, and they walked through the sparse lobby before automatic doors let them outside. Gary's brown suburban waited just outside with a familiar face sitting in the passenger seat.

"Hey, loser! Get in!" Dennis yelled with a smile and a wave. Miles climbed into the rear seat and sprawled his limbs in every direction while Gary walked around the front and got behind the wheel. The drive down highway 460 back to White Wreath only took about fifteen minutes, but Dennis made it seem like less than that with his animated recounting of their friend's reactions when they learned about Miles's brush with death. "Everyone's talking about it, man. You're going to be a celebrity by the time school starts."

Gary hushed Dennis with a look that could kill. "Miles almost died. That's not funny. Do you think that's cool? There's nothing cool about that."

"Sorry," Dennis mouthed to Miles.

"I have got to get my own wheels," Miles replied. Dennis pivoted about in his seat to face Miles.

"You've been saying 'I have got to get my own wheels' for over two years now, but you never go out and actually look for a car. Do you have any money saved?"

"Yeah, a few grand."

"Good. Then we'll go looking together. It would be nice for someone besides me to play 'taxi' once in a while. Do you know what you want?"

"No," Miles said, "but I'll know it when I see it." Soon enough, they arrived at the house and Pearl's powder blue Oldsmobile sat parked in the side yard. When Miles got out, he immediately found himself gazing at the gate across the street toward the distillery ruins.

"You're home." Dennis patted him on the back. "What do you want to do first?"

"I think I'd like to get a shower and then lie down."

"You didn't get enough sleep in the hospital?" Dennis asked.

"No, just bad dreams." Miles rubbed his eyes.

"Do you need anything?" Gary asked in an almost maternal fashion. "Can I get you anything?"

"No, I'm good."

"In that case, I have to get back to the station. I gotta arrange somebody to come and do repairs after some crazy drunk driver decided to play chicken with my gas pumps." Gary wrapped his arms around Miles and squeezed hard.

"But I'm glad you're safe, boy. I don't know what I'd have done if something had happened to you." Miles squeezed back.

"I'm going to rest some, and I'll see you when you get home later."

"All right," He finally let go. "I'll talk to you boys later." With a jingle of his key ring and a pat on his back pocket to make sure he had his wallet, Gary was gone. Past the door, the basement welcomed Miles home with twinkling lights. The security in his own meticulously curated space away from the world made him feel safe again. Safer, anyway.

Miles found some shorts to sleep in and turned on the shower. Dennis helped himself to the turntable and put on a David Bowie record to kill the silence. The hot water felt fantastic. As he bathed, Miles pinched and prodded the skin around his left shoulder. He felt as though his own senses had betrayed him and formulated a calculated lie to protect him from what had happened.

But for all his doubt, no small amount of evidence emerged to substantiate the assumption. After cleaning himself, Miles appeared in the shorts to find Dennis kicked back in his desk chair with the heels of his boots propped up on the edge of the desk.

"Why don't you tell me about what happened," Dennis said. Miles recounted what he remembered from when Dennis asked him to help find Mary to when he fell into the ruins.

"After that, I woke up in the hospital."

"Is that everything? You sure?"

"Why wouldn't I tell you everything?"

"Because I'm your best friend and I know you keep things to yourself. In fact, I KNOW, you haven't told me everything."

"What makes you think I wouldn't?"

"Playing dumb, huh? That's fine." Dennis let his feet down and stood up, taking a step or two towards the stairs. "If that's what you think of our friendship, then I don't need to hear any more."

"Wait," Miles said. "I can tell you more, but you're going to think I'm crazy."

"We're best friends *because* I think you're crazy."

"Fine, sit down." Dennis did and Miles pulled up an unused plastic milk crate. It took about ten minutes to fill him in about the strange voice he'd heard and the bloody shirt with a hole but no wound beneath it. Dennis's eyes grew large when he told him about the talking corpse. After that, Miles brought the story to a close. Save for the part about meeting the mystery girl, he divulged it all.

"Well, what do you think?" Miles asked.

"If what you're saying about the shirt is right, then there should be some blood where you landed. You said the deer had a broken leg with the bone sticking out. That probably put blood everywhere."

"And the talking corpse?"

"It means you had a bad dream, dude. This isn't some George Romero, *Night of the Living Dead* shit. You need to drink water, take some vitamins, get some sleep... But what you really need is a party!"

"A party?

"Hell yes, a party! You just survived almost dying! You're my best friend and we're going to celebrate your brush with the grim reaper in fucking style! I've managed to organize music, booze, weed, and even some girls together. After that, we're going to have such a head-splittingly awesome time that you're might even shuffle lose that virginity you've been clinging to!"

"And when is all of this supposed to happen?"

"Tonight, mufungo! It's all in readiness! I'm going to pick you and the others up later tonight and we're going to party at the Booth crypt."

"I've been out of the hospital for less than an hour. Do you think it's a good idea to imbibe to excess after all I've been through?"

"Weren't you listening? That's the best reason to do it!" Dennis got up and started for the stairs. "So, get your beauty sleep or a disco nap or whatever you need to do because this is happening. Later, diesel boy." Sleep sounded like a good idea. He lay down in bed and closed his eyes for what felt like a second before Dennis was upon him again, shaking him awake.

"Wake up, it's time to party!"

"What? What's going on? You didn't leave?" Miles said in confusion which in turn made Dennis look confused.

"No, sleeping beauty!" His friend yanked off the sheets and comforter which sent a crashing wave of cold air up Miles's body. "I've already worked my shift. Man! You must've been sleeping like the dead! Get up! Get dressed! Move!"

"Fine! I'm up!" Miles dragged himself to his feet, palms and fingers running across his face to try and get fully awake.

"No offense," Dennis said, "but you look like the dead."

"I lost two pints of blood."

"Sit. I'll fix your face." Miles sat, down and Dennis opened his miniature tackle box of makeup, selected the stick of kohl, and positioned Mile's face towards the light. Steady hands went to work, applying the smudges and brushing the strokes with his bare finger.

"Sweeney says he scored some tabs of X when his parents took him to Florida last month and Lucifer said she can contribute at least a fifth of Makers," Dennis said.

"Sounds like a good time. Can I chip in?"

"Stop moving and close your eyes." Dennis grabbed his jaw and held it rigid, tilting it upward. "Pearl's car needs gas if you can help with that."

"Sure, I can do that." Dennis let go of his face and Miles opened his eyes.

"How does it look?"

"Like your skinny ass needs to be in New York walking a runway, bitch. Go look in the mirror." Miles jumped up and rushed to the bathroom mirror. Black, smoky rings framed his eyes with enough touches of red on the eyelids and edges to give an irritated, burnt look.

"It's perfect," Miles said.

"But is it worth a kiss?" Dennis asked.

"Fuck yes, it is!" Miles crossed the room, put one arm around Dennis's lower back and pulled him close before cupping his other hand over Dennis's mouth and kissing the back of his own hand. "MMMRRRMMWAAAH!" Having given what he promised, Miles let go and began dressing. A pair of black stockings with the crotch cut out and more holes than material slipped over his head and became a low-necked pair of long sleeves. The black sleeveless shirt with the bold white text "MINISTRY" across the chest covered the rest of his upper torso.

"You're a fucking tease you know that?" Dennis said, crossing his arms and tapping a foot with faux impatience.

"I think being a tease implies I don't want to put out."

"I'm ready when you are."

"You know I like girls. So, unless you're like one of those frogs from Jurassic Park that can just up and swap sexes because you felt like it, I don't know what we're going to do. Also, it would be weird. You're the closest thing I have to a brother."

"Well, we're in the south, man. Incest isn't just okay here. It's encouraged."

"Fuck you."

"That's what I'm talking about." Miles pitched the soccer shorts and plucked another ruined pair of black nylons from the floor and pulled them up his legs and over his hips. The ruined stockings with their runs, tears, and holes resembled distorted spiderwebs before he pulled a black, knee-length, pleated skirt up to his waist and over them. A black belt with a fat wad of chrome for a buckle cinched on one side and hung from his right hip like a cowboy's pistol holster. The "broken-in" leather army boots from the salvation army thrift store felt like heavenly slippers. To top it off, he snapped a spiked collar around his neck and grabbed his own leather jacket before herding Dennis up the stairs. He half expected to find Gary unwinding in front of the TV like he always did, but he wasn't there.

"Gary?" He peeked into the kitchen. "Gary!" he said loud enough to have his voice heard in every room in the house. "We're leaving!"

"I'm out here," a voice said from the front porch. The two pushed open the screen door to find him standing next to the wooden railing with a beer bottle in his hand and staring off into the night air.

"We're leaving," Miles repeated, but Gary didn't answer. "What is it?" Miles stared off in the same direction, trying to see what Gary saw.

"Do you hear it?" Gary asked without turning his head. Both boys perked their ears and paused to listen but neither seemed able to find the source of Gary's preoccupation.

"I don't hear anything," Miles said.

"Me either," Dennis agreed.

"Exactly. Listen to that." Gary looked back and forth between the trees. "It's dead quiet. No crickets, no birds, nothing. That's damn eerie. The cicadas have been buzzing non-stop for over a week."

"Yeah. That is weird," Dennis added. "But…we gotta go." Gary turned and finally looked at them. Both eyebrows crawled up his forehead.

"You and your friends are all gonna do the space vampire look thing tonight too, huh?" Gary asked.

"Hell, yes," Dennis said. "Everyday is Halloween." The boys climbed into the Oldsmobile. It wasn't until they were down the road that Miles considered who else might be at the party.

"Is Lucifer going to be there?" he asked.

"Funny you should ask that," Dennis said, lowering the radio. "She's asked three times this week if you're coming to Booth's tonight, so you know she's interested. She also said she's invited the triplets, so we're picking them up too."

"Cool."

The "triplets" were a trio of eleventh graders who'd moved to White Wreath late last year. There was Nora who always keeps her black hair in pigtails. The other two were both 6'5" and looked like bookends although one was a boy, Christian, and the other was a girl, Kate. Christian was lean, chiseled and shy, and exactly Dennis's type.

"Both Lucifer and Nora seem to like you," Dennis said, "So who knows? Maybe if you're lucky and play your cards right, you could be on your way to a three-way deflowering." Miles had heard worse ideas. Dennis lowered his voice to sound like a creepy old pervert. "Just say yes and shed the skin of purity, my delicious one. Offer us your pink parts."

"Pump your brakes, Satan," Miles said. "I'm a virgin, not a leper."

"Maybe not a virgin for much longer," Dennis sang.

CHAPTER FIVE

Everybody in the county knew the story of the once prominent Bourbon tycoon, John Booth. He was the only person to ever make a name for themselves in White Wreath. The size of his grave reflected the wealth he'd once accumulated in life. The two-story crypt was domed and circular in shape, like a half of a bubble resting atop another half-bubble. A beautiful place to be buried. An even better place to party.

Hefting a thick coil of extension cords from the trunk of the car, Miles crossed the long, headstone-filled tract of land, tiptoeing between the moldy markers and statues of angels. At the end of the row, he found what he was looking for—the caretakers shed. The twenty-foot by ten-foot cinderblock shanty had but a single window on the wall facing him and a garage door on the opposite side. The tiny unlocked window on the back wall was just the right height to reach in and connect the cord to an unused power outlet atop the workbench. The others looked impatient when he returned.

"I hope you brought bolt cutters," Nora said, pulling on the padlock sealing the gate of the crypt.

"Bolt cutters? How crude," Dennis said. Miles reached into his inner jacket pocket and began fishing out a strand of knotted twine with a key on the end of it. Once produced, the brass lock clicked open and they yanked away the chains.

"Everyone in!" Dennis said. One by one the children of the night entered. "Sweeney" went in first. Todd was his real name but after landing the lead role as the maniac barber in their middle school play, the nickname stuck. He had greasy jaw-length black hair, an homage to Trent Reznor if ever there was one. The triplets, Nora, Christian and Kate followed. It was funny to call them triplets since they were born at the same time, but Nora was shorter than the other two. She wore a baby doll dress and a pair of chunky platforms while her two taller siblings were dressed identically in black with Doc Martens up to their knees and neon pink and green "Chelsea" haircuts. Lucy West, "Lucifer" as she preferred to be called, followed in a skin-tight black midriff shirt and miniskirt with striped stockings and a black deathrocker mohawk. Her backpack clanked and rattled with the sound of glass bottles.

Miles brought up the rear, pulling the last of the extension cord inside before shutting the doors behind them. The doors themselves were oxidized iron with large rectangular panes of glass in the center. Just inside to the left, he dropped the cord with the multiplug on it and picked up a handful of magnets and fifty-gallon trash bags. Dennis took his flashlight and Miles used the trash bags and magnets to create "blackout blinds" over the doors' windows. Once the tomb was sealed and shrouded, Miles inserted the two plugs hanging down from the wall into the surge protector and flicked the switch. Two industrial-sized halogen lamps with makeshift red and blue covers lit the stone crypt in conflicting shadows like a pair of supersized 3-D movie glasses.

"This is too cool," Nora said as she spun about to see that fifteen feet over their heads, the windows of the dome had been blacked out as well. The others craned their necks to take in the statues of angels perched upon a lip at the base of the dome above.

"How did you find this place?"

"Miles found it a few years ago," Dennis said. "He came up here to check out the family plot one day and found the door open. We keep it swept clean on the inside and polish the brass markers for the family. We're the caretakers for a house of the dead."

"Sweeney? How's the music coming?" Nora asked. Bathed in red light next to the wall, Sweeney squatted over the ghetto blaster. The sound of a plastic cassette tape being inserted echoed louder than it should.

"I want to hear some rock before we take the tabs," Sweeney said.

The press of a button filled the tomb with a woman's musical snarl over fast, crunchy guitars. Sweeney stood in the center of the room. From within his denim jacket, he produced a small orange prescription drug vial and proudly displayed it for all to see. He cleared his throat in faux dramatization and addressed us as a snake oil salesman beckons to passersby:

"Ladies and gentlemen," Sweeney began. "If you'll step right this way and peruse my wares I think you'll find something spectacular you could all use in your lives! Step right up, children, step right up, don't be shy, for I hold in my hand a miracle cure for what ails you. Gather around, please." Everyone pulled in close. "You, young man," He pointed a long finger at Miles. "Do you find yourself restless as you toil throughout your day wishing for some kind of release?" Miles nodded. "And you, young lady." He leered at Lucifer. "Do you continually find yourself conducting your daily business listless, counting the endless and laborious minutes in an existence you wish was just a little more exciting?"

"You bet your ass I do!" She offered an uncharacteristic laugh.

"Then, by all means, step forward and witness the miracle drug of our time!" He popped the cap with his thumb and shook out a single gelcap. "MDMA." He held it aloft. "Methylenedioxymethamphetamine. Effects include euphoria, increased heart rate, dilated pupils, an altered sense of time, relaxation, mild hallucinations, enhanced sensations of perception and reality, a sense of general well-being and happiness, and ultimately one hell of a good time! Now, having said that, can I interest one or all of any of you fine upstanding people but one of my wares to assist you in surrendering your eternal souls to the void?" Everyone stuck their hands out like the children in the Willy Wonka movie, reaching for their Everlasting Gobstoppers. Sweeney looked to Lucifer. "Young lady, would you happen to have some of your local spirits to help wash down this miracle drug?"

Lucifer, already holding something behind her back, produced a bottle of bourbon topped in red wax. She peeled away the sealing strip, and when Sweeney placed a tab in her palm, she popped the pill in her mouth and turned the bottle up. Everyone hooted and cheered her as she proceeded to swallow a good three or four shots before passing it on. Around the group they went, each one washing down the drug with a pull from the bottle with the amber fluid that burned all the way down. Miles attempted to copy Lucifer's vertical guzzle but ended up choking on the alcoholic burn. He managed to pass the bottle back to Dennis before doubling over to grab his knees and hack away the fumes that stole the air from his lungs. Dennis raised his arm high to slap him across the back.

"Ha! What were you trying to do, knock it back like Lucifer? You know you can't handle booze like that!" Sweeney drank last, grimacing and shaking his head.

"Huggabuggah! Damn, Lucifer! That's strong shit!"

"Then you don't know what strong is." She brushed errant particles from her miniskirt and took the bottle back. "If we party here on Halloween, then I'll be sure to bring a bottle of high-end shit." Eyeing the remainder of dark fluid swirling in the bottom, she turned it up and finished it off without so much as a twitch before licking her lips. "Ahhh." Sweeney looked longingly at the empty bottle as she handed it back. "Don't worry," she smiled. "There's more."

"By the way, how do always have all that extra alcohol? Doesn't your dad suspect something when the inventory comes up short?"

"Nope." Nora balanced the bottle upside down on her palm. "I work at the store and when he's outside or in the bathroom, I ring up the bottles on the register and pay for them out of my own money. That way the inventory never comes up short. I don't steal from my parents. I'm not an asshole. If I want to get tore up on a weekend when I'm free of all my responsibilities, then it's nobody's fucking business what I do."

"A very conscientious young lady," Sweeney said. "Hey, Dennis! Where's the rest of the lights?"

"Almost ready," Dennis said as he filled the last two spots on the power strip. Attached to walls above the halogen lights, one small black box began projecting simple but morphing multicolored layers on the backdrop of the crypt while the other, a simple strobe, pulsed its flashes in time to the beat. The triplets clapped their approval. "There," he said with satisfaction. "Now it's a party."

Sweeney chose the tracks, and the alcohol broke the ice enough for everyone to get up and dance. Punk, rock, metal, alternative, electronic, whatever. To Miles, the bizarre events of the past two days evaporated and became as nothing. Like the others, he swayed, bounced and stomped to the sounds. To make things better, it only took 45 minutes before the invisible tentacles of the hallucinogen began creeping their way up the collective spines and brain stems. Rolling bass rhythms made the walls breathe. When the flood of sensations arrived to lift them higher, the anthems of rebellion and escape made the surrender all too irresistible.

"It's time to know!" The lyrics shouted over rolling synth lines. "It's time to live!"

With all the flesh in motion, the temperature of the tomb steadily rose with the volume. 'If it makes you nod our head or shake your ass, it's good music.' Sweeney always said. He turned the volume up as high as it would go, and the acoustics of the solid marble and granite tomb amplified it all to a fever pitch.

Somewhere in between the second and third hour later, clothes began to become a liability. The punk girl, Kate, was the first to shed her top. The threadbare Dead Kennedy's shirt slid away to reveal a pair of pale b-cups in a mesh bra with electrical tape in the shape of X's over the nipples. All the boys shed their jackets. Twenty pounds of metal-spiked, band logo patched, spray-painted leather hit the floor. And as the clothes dwindled, so did the inhibitions. Partners were selected as the music commanded them all to form circles and tribes of whimsey. A new harmony bound them together as they pulled and pushed slammed against one another to keep the blood pumping. At one point, Christian tripped over his own feet and jostled the Boombox. It might've brought the mood down if the CD hadn't skipped just enough times to perfectly align at the start of the chorus.

The kids went berserk.

Sweeney kept the music flowing and the bodies moved in time. By the end of the fourth hour of dancing, even young flesh, no matter how willing, yields to fatigue. The music took a slower, more mellow tempo tone. Dennis thought the strobe was too intense and unplugged it. Stacks of green, wool, army blankets were unfolded from their place in the corner and overlapped to create a place for everyone to lounge while the drug hit its hardest. Canteens of water passed back and forth as a calming atmosphere saturated the tomb. They situated themselves in a comfortable pile, each participant content to lay motionless and silent, soaking in the moving tapestries of color from the projector above. This went on until an unknown perpetrator ripped a fart that echoed off the stone walls, sending everyone roaring with laughter.

For a little while, Miles was content to use his jacket as a pillow, Lucifer lying on his arm. She was close but didn't seem to pay him any special attention even when he asked about her jewelry or clothes. She seemed more interested in nursing the remainder of the second bottle of bourbon than speaking.

Miles's bladder gave a prodding twinge, so he worked his arm free, pushing himself vertical and put on his jacket. Gravity felt strange and his knees wobbled, threatening to topple him onto the carpet of bodies below. Looking around the room, everyone looked satisfied to cling to their partners.

Christian and Dennis had taken it upon themselves to be nominated for the party's "public display of affection" award. Through a chemical filter, their light and dark kissing faces blurred for a moment to appear as a yin-yang symbol before righting themselves. Miles smiled and hoped the attention his best friend was getting wouldn't be limited to the opening and closing times of the "White Wreath Cemetery End of Summer Orgy."

"Where are you going?" Sweeney asked from the floor with Nora and Kate each half-naked and nuzzling his neck. Next to them,

"I gotta whiz," Miles grunted, trying not to step on anyone. "Back in a minute."

Upon approaching the door, he opened it just enough to squeeze through and pulled it shut behind him. The night air felt cool, and he gladly breathed in the smells of the newly cut grass and the trees. He walked out far enough and found the biggest tree to lean against as he experienced the best piss of his whole life. "Ohmigod," he groaned. His entire body felt like a jar of fluid being tipped over and spilled.

When it was done running its course, he lowered the black pleated skirt and stared off across the landscape. Near to the tree, an onyx headstone in the shape of a bench invited him to sit. He stepped around the headstone of Grace Freeley 1908-1986 and sat upon it. To his surprise, the surface of the bench still held a remainder of the warmth from catch the sun's light all day. The effects of the drugs made his senses acute, finding nuances in his surroundings he might've missed in a lesser state of consciousness. The first thing that he noticed was the air. The smells of autumn hadn't quite arrived, the dry scents of the dying leaves that would herald the eventual heavy snows. But autumn or not, the air always smelled sweeter in White Wreath. He noticed it as a child whenever he visited festivals in other towns or when Gary drove them up to Lexington to get supplies for the Imperial. It didn't smell bad or sour in those places, but it didn't have the same subtle aroma. Even cut grass smelled differently here.

To live in White Wreath was to experience the tree line of the county opening and closing the scenes of life as you travel its roads. Shutters of an unseen camera revealed panoramas of a movie no one knew the name of. Above, the stars twinkled and drifted back and forth in hypnotic patterns. It took an act of conscious will to look away. Halos rippled around the corners of his eyes, and he crushed them shut to push them away. When he opened them, he looked out amongst the trees to find a familiar sight. There, far in the distance, a white electric glow pierced the darkness. The cemetery sat at a high enough elevation that the halogen bulbs on the front pumps of the Imperial could be seen over a mile away. In the moment of lucid thought, Miles couldn't shake the memory of the dark place he'd fallen into, and what he'd seen there.

It perplexed him that during a full omnipotent view of the real and intangible that anything could be hidden, and so close to his home. It was all too much, just too damn much to think about right now. An unexpected touch on his shoulder from behind caused him to leap from the bench with a yelp. It was instinct that spun Miles about with both fists balled for a fight. He turned to find Dennis with his own hands in the air.

"Jesus!" Dennis exclaimed. "Easy!" Miles relaxed and sat down with slumped shoulders.

"Sorry," he said. Dennis's long legs stepped over the bench and he sat, pulling Miles close.

"Where have you been? We were missing you in there."

"I told you I was coming out to take a piss."

"Yeah, that was close to an hour ago!"

"Really?" Miles ran his hands down his face to try and sober up just a little." Has it really been that long?"

"I checked my watch before you stepped out and it's been close to a full hour. What have you been doing out here?"

"Nothing, I thought. I came out, took a leak, sat down, looked at the light coming off the Imperial, looked at the sky and then you appeared."

"You must be rolling balls like I am because I bet you've been staring at the sky for forty-five minutes. Come back inside, Lucifer has been getting handsy with everyone. Sweeney's definitely not going to stop talking about this for a long time."

"What about you? How are you and 'giraffe boy' in there getting along? Any potential boyfriend material?"

"Christian is ok to make out with, but I'm not sure about the rest. I mean, we just met, and I already have a boyfriend. What about you and Lucifer? You've been opposite from each other all night."

"She's ok. She doesn't act like she's interested in me, so I'm not going to push it. She's standoffish."

"Yeah, maybe." Dennis stood up and offered a hand to help Miles off the bench. "Come on, I told everyone I'd bring you back in so you could tell them about the Booths."

"Do they really want to hear that?"

"Of course! We've been partying in their house all night might as well let them know about our host." Miles took his hand and stood upright. The two wrapped their arms around one another and squeezed.

"You're my best friend," Miles told him.

"And you're my best friend. Come on, its cozier in the tomb."

"That's got to be gothest thing I've ever heard."

Inside, the animal exchanges continued for close to an hour. Hungry tongues forced their way into panting mouths. Hands found their way across flesh to liberate restrictive clothing. Miles lay down in an unclaimed section of the makeshift bedding, occasionally watching the others writhe in their enthusiastic cloud of naked abandon. He closed his eyes and rolled his neck to massage the muscles. Before he knew what had happened, Lucifer had crossed the distance between them, straddled him, and plopped down on his lap with yet another bottle of bourbon in her hand. Her shirt was gone leaving only a black mesh bra with a silver bat necklace hovering over her ample cleavage. It would be a lie to say he wasn't aroused as she set to grinding her sex against his.

"Well, look who's awake." She purred, taking a pull from the bottle and making one long, slow gyration of her hips. "How's it going down there, Miles? Don't you have a birthday coming up *shoon*?" It might've been the perfect invitation if Lucifer hadn't slurred the last word. They were all high and had all partaken of the booze she'd brought, but hearing the alcohol speak for her, something didn't feel right. A moment of clarity found its way through the chemical haze. The nuances of her drunken sway became impossible to ignore.

"October 30th."

"Devil's night, huh?" She leaned forward, close enough that he could feel her breath n his neck. "Would you like to have my gift to you early?" Miles began to panic. He'd fantasized about losing his virginity to Lucifer here in the Booth tomb all summer, he wanted it so much he ached. But now, with the moment of truth staring him down and with the goth girl blitzed out of her head, it didn't seem right at all.

Abort, fucking abort.

Just as the fingers of Lucifer's free hand traced their way into his pants, an unnatural guttural, sound echoed behind her. Somewhere between the MDMA, and a mouthful of Kate's crotch, and way too much bourbon, Sweeney's stomach took a turn for the worse. Poor Nora and Kate barely had time to scramble backward out of the way before he sprayed a high-pressure stream of vomit where they'd been lying. The liquid expulsion must've come too close to Lucifer because she leaped off Miles in a blink to yell at him.

"WHAT ARE YOU DOING?!" she shrieked, kicking him in the hip. Sweeney responded by puking a second time. Whatever teenage horniness that might've been lingering in the air, evaporated as everyone near him scrambled to pull their clothes to a safe distance.

Sweeney groaned, trying in vain to scoop the mess together with his hands repeating, "Oh god, I'm sorry guys. I can fix this. Oh god. Oh my god, I'm so sorry."

"Mother…fucker!" Lucifer stomped again. "AUUUGGGHH! Goddamn it, Sweeney, couldn't you wait another five minutes?" The others giggled and snerked at her frustration. Seeing their reaction, she rolled her eyes. "Whatever." She threw her clothes on fast as possible. "I'm fucking done. Dennis, take me home, now. Everybody get your shit together; I'll be waiting in the car."

Lucifer gathered her backpack and stomped out the door before slamming it behind her.

"Well, shit." Miles sighed, plopping back down. "I guess the party's over. Hey Dennis, what time is it?"

"Almost 5 am."

"Really? It can't be! We haven't been here that long."

"I'm afraid so. We've been up all night and the sun will be up before we know it. Don't you have to work today?" A revelation struck Miles between the eyes and gravity of having to be something other than useless for the next twenty-four hours hit him like a ton of bricks.

"Yeah, and I'm still high."

"We all are."

"Are you ok to drive?"

"I can manage. We'll come back and clean up all this later." He pointed an accusatory finger. "Especially you, Sweeney."

"I'm really sorry guys," he said, panting.

Dennis clapped his hands as loud as he could manage and the echoes from the mausoleum walls compounded it ten times louder to make everyone wince. "Let's move, people!"

The cords were collected and stashed inside the tomb and chain threaded through the handles as before. When locked, the group started the trek back to the car. No one spoke. On the horizon, the sky was becoming lighter. Beyond their sight on the limbs and trees, the cicadas began to stir. And like creatures from a silent movie shrinking from the coming dawn, the black-clad misfits vanished behind the tomb to head back to where the car was hidden. Lucifer insisted on being dropped off first and upon arriving at her home she stormed away from the car without a word or a glance backward. The others were dropped off in quick order before Miles was dropped off.

"You know what?" Miles said. "To hell with it. I'm taking a day off from work and sleeping in for once. The trash and potholes can survive without me for a day."

"I wish I could do the same," said Dennis. "But I need money for new school clothes, and I've got a shift at the grocery today." They each leaned into the middle of the car and gave one another a big hug, which with the lingering chemicals in their bodies, felt amazing on its own. "You'd better get in there before Gary wakes up or you'll get a lecture. Try and catch some sleep if you can and I'll check on you later in the p.m."

"Cool. See you later."

"Later."

Miles unlocked the front door as quietly as his key would allow and slipped inside. The sounds of rushing water told him that Gary was in the upstairs bathroom shaving. Quick, light, steps got him down the hall and into his own room without one of the squeaky floorboards under the carpet giving him away. The basement stairs didn't betray him either. Miles's clothes smelled of dried sweat and he peeled the garments off one by one. He threw them in the "dirty" pile, which looked identical to the "clean" pile to anyone else. Booted footsteps sounded aloud at the top of the stairs and Miles bolted, practically leaping into bed. The covers fell int place just as Gary opened the door at the top of the stairs.

"Kiddo, you getting up?"

"No…" He feigned a croak in his voice. "I think I'm going to sleep in today and get my strength up."

"You didn't stay out late last night, did you?"

"I came home at an early hour." *It's not a lie if most people think 5 a.m is an early hour.*

"Ok, kiddo. You catch up on your sleep. I'm going to work. You call me if you need anything."

"I will." The door clicked shut. Lying there, his mind still spun from the drug coursing through his system. He felt tired and wired at the same time. Eyes fluttered and danced to keep track of the perpetually exploding symmetrical patterns expanding like licking flames across the ceiling. In the distance, the sounds of screaming, as if people far away writhed in agony. For a moment it became too much, and he closed his eyes. The fiery visions followed and slipped underneath his eyelids to dance on in his brain, twisting and replicating in numbers too big to count. Miles felt weightless, carried on a disembodied slipstream of nightmarish wails. In his minds' eye, he burning tails spun faster and faster in a psychedelic cyclone until they spiraled away, dissipating into nothingness, drowning him in the same.

Then the door at the top of the stairs opened.

His eyes snapped wide, the room crisp and clear as Dennis came galloping down the stairs. Strangely, he was wearing a different shirt than he was five minutes ago.

"What are you doing here?" he asked.

"I came to see how you're doing," Dennis said, jumping with both feet down to the concrete floor with a "whomp".

"Don't you need to get to get home and shower so you can go to work?"

"What are you babbling on about? I already did my shift. What time do you think it is?"

"Almost six?"

"You'd better look again," Dennis said, pointing to the alarm clock on the nightstand. Miles looked; the red digital numbers read 6:45……PM.

"Is it really six at night?" he asked. Dennis looked amazed.

"Holy shit, did you just sleep all day? You're starting to make that a habit, you know?"

"There were…flames, screams."

"Ok, I have no idea what that means." Miles looked around the room, his eyes darting between the ceiling and Dennis. "Wow. You must've been blitzed out of your gourd. I promised a good time, which I delivered. Think about it. No one is naïve enough to think that partaking in heroic amounts of bourbon and recreational hallucinogenic pharmaceuticals which were not prescribed or administered by a licensed medical physician while standing in a mausoleum in the middle of the night is an experience that 'just happens.' That's the kind of shit you have to go looking for and you had the time of your life doing it. As for the screams and all, well, you had a very realistic nightmare on the tail-end of taking MDMA and getting almost falling to your death. It's just tracers, man."

"Yeah," Miles said, rubbing his eyes before collapsing into his swamp of blankets. "Tracers."

"Listen, I have my own consequences from the party."

"Really?" Miles opened one eye to peer over the top of his comforters. "What?"

"Christian called me."

"Nora's brother?"

"Yeah. He got my number from Nora and called me after I got off work, says he wants to go out on a date."

"That's great."

"I know, right? He's handsome, his parents already know he's out and he's really a good kisser."

"That's fucking awesome, man." Miles sat up and gave Dennis a hug. "Hey, I think I'm going to go back to sleep."

"You just slept for twelve hours!"

"I might've been asleep, but I don't feel rested."

"That's fine. I'll let myself out. Oh! By the way, before I forget, I think I heard there's going to be a string of yard sales coming up soon, so you and I can do our thing and find clothes before school starts."

"That sounds good. Talk to you later."

"Later." Dennis' boots pounded their way up the stairs followed by muffled footsteps tracing their way across the house and out the front door. His bed had never felt so welcoming. He didn't want to think about anything at all, but a nagging thought kept him from relaxing enough to sleep. Sundown would be around seven o clock.

"Damn it."

The closest arm lunged out into the darkness and found the alarm clock on the nightstand. Without looking at the device, muscle memory and his hands changed the usual alarm to nine p.m. before replacing it in its spot.

A few hours later, he woke without the aid of the alarm. Rolling over, he gazed upon the clock in time to witness the piercing red digital numbers blink from 8:58 to 8:59. The voice of game show host Alex Trebek echoed through the ductwork above his head informing him that Gary was home. Other than Jeopardy! the man refused to watch anything else and religiously taped the trivia show on the VCR so he could watch it after dinner. The ritual included yelling answers at the screen.

"What is parricide?!" Gary's voice rang out. Miles turned off the alarm and pushed his feet over the side. To his surprise, the disorientation he expected to feel wasn't there. Thinking he was still half asleep, he rotated his arms, legs, and neck through their range of motion without so much as a twinge. He stood before the light of the bathroom mirror, inspecting his body. The ugly blotches of blue, black and green where he'd been penetrated in the accident were nowhere to be found. Pinching and prodding produced nothing abnormal.

What the hell?

His reflection in the mirror confirmed there were no additional marks on his back, so he gave up trying to understand to it. A pair of jeans and a black Bauhaus band shirt waited in a pile on the back of the toilet and he grabbed them up. Paint splattered Chuck Taylor shoes finished the ensemble. Upstairs, Gary was yelling at one of the contestants on the screen who didn't know the answer to the final jeopardy question was 'the social security administration.'

"That's it." He hopped up and turned off the television as Miles appeared in the hallway.

"That's enough of the idiot box for tonight."

"You don't have to stop because I'm here," Miles said.

"Nope, nope, I'm done." He shook his head. "Stupid show has me worked up again."

"You could watch the news to see if they say anything to say."

"That's what newspapers are for. What do I say about television?"

"That every show is trying to sell you something," Miles answered, rolling his eyes a little. "Especially the news."

"That's right, every show but Jeopardy. You can actually learn things from watching Jeopardy. What are you doing out of bed? Shouldn't you be sleeping?"

"I've slept all day and I'm hungry. What's for dinner?"

"I've got some stuff for salads, sandwiches, a couple cans of soup. If that doesn't suit you, I can always make a run into town. Do you want anything else?"

"No, soup sounds good. Besides," he pointed to the beer in Gary's hand. "You don't need to be drinking and driving."

"Now you know I drink one beer every day after work. One, uno."

"I'm just giving you shit." He offered Gary half of a smile. "Drink your beer, I'm getting soup and a sandwich."

"Ok, if that's what you want. What are your plans for the rest of the evening?"

"I'm going to eat and then maybe read a little."

"Why do you have shoes on?" Gary said, looking at his feet. "You're not going out, are you?"

"No, my feet were cold." He lied.

"All right. If you don't need anything, I'm going to turn in early. I've got a big day tomorrow trying to find a contractor or repairman to come out and start fixing those damaged pumps." Gary then emptied out the rest of his beer in the sink and pitched the bottle in the trash.

"G'night, Gary. Love you."

"G'night, kiddo." Miles's ears traced the sound of footsteps as they made their way down the hallway and into the bedroom. The door clicked shut behind Gary and a moment later the sound the shower nozzle spraying could be heard. As fast as he could manage, Miles pulled a can of soup from the cupboard and threw a sliced turkey sandwich together while pouring a glass of milk. Ravenous, the sandwich was gone in the time it took to put away the meat and twist the tie around the bread. He was too eager to wait for soup, so he put the can back in the cupboard and polished off the glass before turning out all the lights. Listening down the hallway, the sound of the shower continued. Perfect.

The emergency flashlight he was looking for was waiting on the shelf in the kitchen. Two clicks of the button its side ensured that it had batteries and worked. With the same noise discipline he'd used when returning from the party in the tomb, he snuck to the front door. Delicately he pulled it open, simultaneously pushing on the outer screen door and pulling the inner door shut behind him.

The flimsy screen door swung shut and the cool night air welcoming him back. With a small breeze blowing and a symphony of cicadas playing to his emergence, he set out across the yard. No headlights of cars lit the countryside. After being cooked by the sun all day, the asphalt of the Kentucky road radiated a halo of warmth of its own. When Miles held his hands horizontal with the ground, the variance of a degree or two could be felt in his fingertips and palms.

At this distance, the light from the front porch began to dwindle. The flashlight came to life, throwing a wide beam across the field. High step over high step, he tromped through the knee-high wild grass. On the far side, the foliage in the tree line at the top of the hill parted like a curtain.

The clusters of trees were thicker than he remembered, so thick he couldn't see far at all. Branches and undergrowth crunched unnaturally loud beneath his shoes as the beam of his flashlight revealed the distillery ruins at the bottom.

Finally, he reached the bottom and stood at the base of the foundation. Something seemed eerie. He waved the flashlight to illuminate the darkness in every direction to discover what it was. Then it hit him. The cicadas. Somewhere between entering the property and crossing through the barn, the insect symphony had all stopped playing. He stood motionless waiting for the sounds to resume. But for his patience, nothing. No nightingales, no owls, no crickets, just silence.

"You're here!" A girls' voice said from somewhere behind him. Miles wheeled about, his light erratically waving back and forth past the trees and back. "Higher, up here."

Miles shined the beam higher in the air. Twenty feet in the air above him, a barefoot girl of about fifteen years, dressed in a white sleeping gown with buttons and lace-ribbon adornments sat upon one of the lower tree limbs. Her blonde hair was exactly as he remembered it, long locks of blonde appearing to flow in slow motion on a breeze that didn't exist.

"Why are you up there?" he asked.

"I like climbing trees, so I climbed this one." Miles flashed the light over the tree and the ones around it.

"Okay," said skeptically.

"Something wrong?" she asked.

"Where's the other person?"

"What other person? It's just me."

"The person that helped you up in that tree."

"No one helped me up."

"Why are you lying to me?"

"What makes you think I'm lying?"

"Because there's no way you could get up there. You're nowhere close to six feet tall, you're not wearing climbing equipment, there's no rope, you're not wearing shoes, and your feet aren't dirty. So, unless you have the nails and strength of a bear or just magically appeared up on that branch then someone helped you."

"Oooh!" She clapped her hands with glee. "You're a smart one, I like you."

"You said you have something for me?" he asked.

"Maybe," she said, kicking her feet back and forth like a child sitting on a swing. "That depends."

"Depends on…?

"On whether you're going to continue shining that light in my eyes." Miles lowered the beam to the base of the tree.

"That's better." A voice said from just behind him. Startled by the presence of another person he'd hadn't seen, Miles almost jumped out of his skin as he turned to face them. The girl's twin, standing a few feet away, covered her eyes when he shone the light upon her.

"See?" he shouted over his shoulder. "I knew you had help."

"Who are you talking to?" the twin asked. Miles shone the light back up to the tree limb, which now was empty.

"Very cute." He aid pointing the light back to the twin who had vanished as well. Miles spun left and right, the light spanning every direction, both girls were gone.

"Down here!" the voice said again, this time coming from the basement of the ruined rickhouse. Cautiously, he approached the edge, placing only one foot before putting the light over the lip. The girl stood where he'd seen her before he woke up in the hospital. In her hand, a fistful of jewelry. "Isn't this what you came for?" She waved them.

"What is that?"

"Diamonds and gold. Enough to put you closer to whatever it is you want. Come down and get them." She smiled, waving them again.

"Why don't you bring them up here?"

"That's not how this works," she said. "Stop shining that light in my eyes and come down. I'd like to talk."

"How do I know you don't want to hurt me?"

"If I wanted to hurt you, I wouldn't have gone through all the trouble of bringing you here. Your house is across the road." The girl made sense.

"Hold on." Miles walked to the right, following the retaining wall until the slope of the hill gave way to a place to safely step down. He approached the blocked doorway from before and kicked is way through the branches until they bent out of his way. Even with the moon not shining as bright, the ruins looked as he remembered them the other night. To his left, a smattering of blood where the deer had been. Up the mound, he climbed. At the top, a broken board greeted him with dried blood on it, his.

It wasn't a dream.

"No, it's not." the girl said, sitting where she'd been standing before.

"No, it's not what?"

"It's not a dream. When you thought you were speaking to the dead person before? That was a dream." Her words made his head hurt.

"Who are you?" Miles asked.

"Who do you want me to be? Because as it stands at this moment, you and I aren't anything to one another."

"What are my options?"

"We could be friends, which I would like for you and me very much to become. Or…?"

"Or what?" he asked.

"The other option isn't very good for either of us, especially you," she said. Miles reached down and picked up the diamonds and jewelry.

"If you always try to start friendships with threats, then I can't imagine you have a lot of them." The girls' expression became somber, and she looked at her feet.

"I don't have any friends," she said. "I was hoping you'd be my first."

"I think we've gotten ahead of ourselves. I don't even know your name."

"You're right." She perked up some. "Where are my manners? Proper introductions are in order." He offered his hand for her to shake.

"I'm Miles Burkich." By grabbing the sides of her nightgown and taking a step to the rear, she made a well-practiced courtesy that seemed more sincere than showy.

"It's a pleasure to meet your acquaintance, Miles." She stood to her full height and shook his hand in a cold iron grip. "I'm Annabelle May Booth."

"Right, and I'm Jack Daniel." He dropped her hand.

"You're not old enough to be Mr. Daniel, and you don't have a mustache." The two eyed each other suspiciously Miles scowling a little with disappointment.

"So, you're not going to tell me your name, huh? I thought we were being honest with one another."

"I told you my name, Annabelle Booth."

"Annabelle Booth? Like the bourbon distillers' daughter?"

"Annabelle May Booth, after my mother. And I am a bourbon distillers' daughter."

"What's your dad's name? Anyone I might've heard of?"

"Anybody who's put Kentucky whiskey to their lips knows the name of Jonathan James Booth," she boasted.

"Then you know that everybody for two states Jonathan James Booth and his whole family died before the 1900s, so unless you're over a hundred years old, then you're a liar and wasting my time." The girl hung her head. Whatever phantasmal breeze was blowing hair stopped blowing and the long blonde locks fell over her face. Beneath the hair, the girl began to weep.

Great, I'm in the company of a crazy person who thinks they're a vampire.

She continued to sob and sniffle. Miles looked at the ground in front of Annabelle's feet. He hadn't noticed it before, but in the moonlight, it looked like someone had dripped black paint on the ground. A flick of the switch on the flashlight illuminated the ground. The paint wasn't black but red, and it was still dripping, from her face.

"Hey!" He reached out to grab Annabelle by the shoulder and pull her upright. "Do you have a nosebleed?" When she stood upright and the locks fell away, the blood wasn't coming from her nose but from the inner corners of her eyes. "Holy shit!" He jumped, pulling his hand back. "You're bleeding! Hold on, hold on." Without skipping a breath, he set the flashlight down between them and pulled his black t-shirt up over his head. He folded it over twice before using his shirt covered hand to start trying to wipe away the tears from her face. But as fast as he wiped it away, the vermillion continued to flow as she cried. "Calm down. It's going to be all right."

He tried to console her. He wiped and wiped, the shirt saturating in every quadrant he used to absorb the blood. This continued for minutes on end as she cried. Even all his consolation and encouraging words to get her to stop, the blood continued.

"Annabelle, please stop crying." He begged her as her breathing approached the feverish rate of hyperventilation. "You're breaking my heart, here." When he said that, the "bloodworks" began to ebb a little.

"You d-do care." She sniffled, her chin quivering.

"Please stop." He said. "At this point, the shirt isn't soaking up the blood, it's just smearing it."

"I'm trying," she said. "But I can't go home now."

"Where is your home?"

"Weren't you listening? This used to be my home, and now it's gone."

"You lived here in the distillery?"

"Our home was built into the side of the main building, over there." She pointed back the way he'd come. Considering the immenseness of the footprint of the building, it was all feasible. The shirt reached maximum saturation. And now all he was doing was getting blood on his hands and smudging her face in places that weren't dirty before. If poor Bela Lugosi was dead, there was enough blood in the t-shirt to bring the count back to life. Just pathetic.

"Annabelle, you are by far the worst vampire I've ever met."

"What's a vampire?" She asked, the last of the sniveling dying as she caught her breath.

"Isn't that what you are? You drink blood and can only come out at night?" Hearing his words, her facial expression became one of amazement.

"Yes! That!" She grabbed his wrists so painfully that it felt like he'd been slapped with handcuffs. "What you just said. With the blood and the daylight. Say it again."

"You're... hurting me." He recoiled. "Let go of my wrists."

"Tell me first." Her grasp eased a little, but she didn't let go. "Blood and daylight. You know what's happened to me. Tell me why the sunlight burns my skin."

"Because you're a vampire?"

"You've said that twice now. If I'm a vampire, how did I get this way? I wasn't always like this. How do I get rid of it?"

"I don't know how to get rid of it. I think once you become one there's no way to undo it."

"Are you sure? How do you know? How many other vampires do you know?"

"You're the first one I've ever met. Didn't someone you make you this way?"

Annabelle gave him the strangest look of confusion and released his wrists. Set free, he wrung the stinging appendages in his hands. "Ow. Your grip is like iron."

"Tell me everything you know about vampires."

"Do you want me to make you a list?"

"I need to know, Miles. This is a serious matter. I have this affliction and I can't come out while the sun is up."

"Ok. I'll tell you what I know but not all of it may be true because vampires supposedly don't exist. The first thing you've figured out for yourself; you can't be exposed to sunlight for a long time or you'll die." She nodded in agreement.

"That much is true. It's painful to be in anything other than darkness."

"You have to feed on the blood of the living to stay alive." Annabelle pressed a finger against her cheek, and it came away red like Miles's hands. As he remembered before, she closed her eyes and took a long, slow, deep inhalation of air. The area around them became as silent as a vacuum and the blood on her skin began to seep inside like a sponge soaking up water. By the time she exhaled, her skin was as pale and perfect as it was before.

"There." She licked her lips. "That's right, go on."

"What about super strength? How strong are you?"

"I'm not sure."

"I mean I saw you tackle a deer, but the deer had already fallen and broken a leg. See this big wooden beam?" He kicked an old support post the size of a telephone pole with the heel of his shoe, then pressed his heel against it and put his whole weight behind it. It didn't budge an inch. It had to weigh four or five hundred pounds. "Do you think you can move it?"

Annabelle walked past him, bent over and reached down to grab the post with both hands. The whole thing shifted and raised vertically like she was carrying a wooden broom.

"Good gracious," Annabelle exclaimed. "I can lift it."

"Ok, showoff. Put it down before somebody gets hurt." With an effortless toss, the post flew through the air to smash against the retaining wall at a diagonal angle, creating a narrow bridge out of the basement.

"This is so strange." Annabelle looked at her hands. "What else can I do?"

"The rest of it is kind of open to interpretation."

"Whose interpretation?"

"Stories in books, movies, plays, comic books, poems, look, it really doesn't matter unless I know where you came from. If you're Annabelle Booth, the real Annabelle Booth," he paused to count the years. "Then you're about a hundred and twenty years old. So, if you've been alive all those years, then how do you not know what you are? Where have you've been all this time?"

"I've been here." She waved her arm towards the mound of dilapidated masonry. "I was trapped under here until you came and set me free." Miles sat down across from her and the jewelry. He turned the flashlight on and

79

placed it on its butt, the beam shining up into the night air, the bulb giving off just enough light for the two to see each other. She sat with her legs crossed on the ground across from him. Curious, she held her hands over the top of the light and managed a half-smile. "It's so warm. Can I hold onto it?"

"If you want."

Annabelle shone the light up and down her legs as if it gave her satisfaction to do so. She moved all over her body before she pressed it against her chest and held it there. "That's nice." With the lamp flush against her, the remaining light appeared as a red and white and red halo emanating from her chest.

"Why did you sleep for so long?" Miles asked as she continued to play with the light.

"I didn't have a choice."

"Everyone has a choice. And with the power you have, I can't imagine that any person could be strong enough to make you do anything you didn't want to do." Annabelle's expression soured again. She removed the flashlight from her chest and set it on its end between them so that the beam shot straight up into the sky.

"There is one, but it's a long story."

"We've got all night." She looked sad for a moment but then began speaking.

"The last day I remember seeing the sun was the day of the big festival. Our Independence Day celebration."

CHAPTER SIX

July 4th, 1890:

Annabelle knelt on her haunches next to the water, hands cupped and inching closer to scooping up a small frog just below the clear surface. The amphibian twitched this way and that against the lapping of the water against dry land. With the toes of her shoes dug into the dirt on the edge of the water and the excess folds of her dress accordioned into her lap, she prepared to strike. Almost. Almost. The eye and hands worked as one. There was a large splash, and her hands returned, the squirming frog in their clutches. She was careful not to crush it but cautious enough to keep it from wriggling away as much as it tried.

Annabelle held it close to her face, inspecting the bright green skin with brown spots. "Hello, Rana pipiens," she said. "Or should I call you by your common name, Northern Leopard frog?" The frog blinked twice but didn't move, allowing her to inspect and admire the golden rings within those eyes. The rings darted a little but stared back to view the pink-skinned face now mammoth and overshadowing it. Annabelle shifted it over to hold it in her left hand while her right hand disappeared from view. When it returned, the thumb and finger had a small cricket pinched between them. The cricket was held in front of the face, and the frog studied it, unmoving.

"What?" she asked. "Did you think I was going to croak you or put you in a jar? Take the food. The cricket is the unlucky one today, not you. Take it."

The frog complied, lurching forward in her grip to gobble up the insect in three bites. When the cricket was in its belly, she lowered her hands back on to the water and the frog leaped away. The last thing she saw of it was its long rear legs slipping away under a grassy overhang downstream.

"Annabelle!" A voice called through the woods.

"Here, Mother!" Annabelle gathered her assortment of small mason jars and shoved them into a tanned leather satchel and buttoned the flap to keep it closed. Rising at the water's edge, she hurried up the hill to the distillery. Annabelle Booth's steps back could've been retraced with her eyes shut. By sensation and smell alone, she recognized every rock and root along the edges of the dirt trail. Here and there, birds in trees scattered at her arrival. The closer she got to the building, the more abundant the smells of the mash and sounds of industry. Whiskey in the air and whiskey in the barrels bearing her family name. Her mother waited for her at the path's end, next to the south door. She stood as regal as any statue, hands crossed at the waist and long blonde hair tied like hers in a blue ribbon. "Here I am, mother." She panted from ascending the incline so fast. "I was at the water's edge."

"You're always there with your creatures," she said, smiling. "Anything good today?"

"A pair of common toads, one Narrowmouth, and a Northern Leopard with gold rings in its eyes."

"Aren't you a little old to be playing with toads, and Narrowmouths and Northern Leopards? Perhaps it's time to grow up a little?"

"I suppose I'd not want to grow up if I couldn't collect toads and Narrowmouths and Northern Leopards and Fowlers and Spadefoots and Pickerels and Barkers. If there's more to be found, I'd want to find them and document them in my catalog. I want to know what they do and what they eat, how and where they lay their eggs to reproduce."

"And for what purpose would learn all of this?"

"I once heard someone say that if you find a new species of animal, they name it after you."

"Is that what you want?" mother asked her, a curious look upon her face. "You want a frog named after you?"

"It doesn't have to be a frog. It could be a bird, or a fish, or a tree, or an insect or a bee. It could be anything. I want to have my name on something. I want people to know I've done something. If I were to go to university up in Lexington, I could learn more.

"Darling," Her mother opened her arms. "Come here."

When Annabelle did, her mother hugged her and ushered her to the bottling room. Inside, the sights and smells of the distillery came alive. At her beckoning, a grey-haired man working nearby handed her a dark, amber-colored bottle of the freshly matured whiskey.

"See here." She pointed to the part of the embossed glass that read: BOOTH. "There's your name right there."

"But it's father's whiskey."

"It's our whiskey. You see, we make bourbon, and that's something special. All bourbons are whiskey, but not all whiskeys can be bourbons. You know why that is?" Annabelle perked up and began to recite the knowledge her father had bestowed upon her over her sixteen years.

"Because we use Kentucky water. Kentucky water is the best because the state naturally has limestone running through it that filters the water and makes it taste better. You could make bourbon in New York, but no one would buy it. Bourbons made in New York would still be just plain old' whiskey that tastes like fancy horse piss."

"Annabelle!" Mother shouted.

"But that's what papa always says. He says they got shit water in New York."

"Mind your mouth! Those are not the words a young lady uses!"

"She's not wrong." A man's voice said from behind. Both turned to see Jonathan Booth. "They do use shit water in New York, and you can't make bourbon without clean water. But that's for me to say. It's that's not appropriate language for a young lady to be using. I raised you better than that. And if I hear any more words like that, you're going to spend the whole Independence Day celebration with me at the sales stand." Annabelle became rigid at the idea of not being able to walk freely around Pikeville during the festival

"Sorry, papa. Sorry, mama." Annabelle looked at her shoes.

"John, do you think it's right taking her to Pikeville? Some of the McCoys moved up there, and I don't want either of you two to be anywhere near their kind. They carry guns wherever they go."

"The sheriff and his men will be out and about to make sure nobody starts any funny business. I'll take the shotgun along and have Annabelle sit behind me with it sitting in her lap. That should be enough to keep anyone from thinking about filching a bottle from the stand as well." Mother's hands shook.

"Johnathan Booth, I'll not have our daughter perched on a barrel of whiskey with a scattergun in her hands. People will think we're not raising her right. They'll think she hangs around card games and doesn't go to church."

"Well, that's not the truth, and I'll have words with any man or woman who says anything to the contrary. Annabelle reads better than I do and she's honorary master distiller to the family business, so I don't think any of those accusations will hold water." Annabelle beamed with pride.

"But what about the news about the two girls who went missing," her mother said. "Haven't you heard? One from Paintsville and one from Prestonsburg. Both of those towns are just north of here. Each of them was about Annabelle's age."

"I've heard the news, and I know that both of those girls are the right age to get married and I'd bet even money they eloped with smooth-talking young gentlemen that their fathers' didn't care too much for. It happens every day. That's how I stole you away." He said, kissing her on the cheek.

"Jonathan, I'm serious."

"So am I. No one is going to take Annabelle away from us. I'll have her right next to me most of the time at the stand. Father looked to Annabelle. "You run along to the tasting room and tell Mr. Lincoln I'll be there in a minute."

"Ok, papa!" Annabelle hurried away, almost knocking over a man carrying a wooden crate before exiting to the far part of the distillery.

Morning came soon enough. Before the sun rose, Jonathan Booth and Annabelle set out for Pikeville on a horse-drawn cart stacked with crates of bourbon. Mr. Lincoln left just before them with a second cart that would be used as a makeshift sales stand. Mr. Booth held the reins as Annabelle sat beside him on the long wooden seat. Mother waved goodbye from the front door of the main building.

"Be careful!" she called after them. "Sell the lot!" Both Jonathan and Annabelle waved back and continued down the southeastern pass. Father occasionally glanced over his shoulder. When the road had twisted and turned enough to be out of sight of the distillery, he slowed the cart to a stop, stuck one arm beneath the seat and produced a double-barrel shotgun before handing it to Annabelle.

"What's this for?" she asked.

"You're old enough to make bourbon, so you're old enough to hold a gun. If you're going to ride 'shotgun,' you should be holding a shotgun."

"Do you think we're going to need it?"

"Not really. But you never know. Thieves and pickpockets don't walk around carrying signs to tell people who they are. Having a shotgun visible just reminds dishonest people to think twice about wanting to take what's yours. Works every time on cowards."

"And what if they're not cowards?"

"That's what the triggers are for. I also had Mr. Adams cut off half the length of the barrels, so it's not so heavy." Annabelle ran her fingers along the metal and wood, feeling the intricacies of the rounded surfaces. When pulled to the rear, the twin hammers jutting straight off the top the gun sat vertical, resembling a pair of rabbit ears, hence the name, 'rabbit-eared shotgun.' A worn leather strap hung along the bottom to allow it to be slung over the shoulder if one were so inclined.

"Does mama know you're letting me carry it?"

"Maybe." He let a sly grin slip. "I may have forgotten to tell her. Maybe we'll have to keep it a secret between you and me, so she doesn't worry."

Annabelle smiled and clutched the gun against her chest. With that, father gave the reins a snap and the two horses pulled on their restraints to start moving again. When they exited town and head north, they joined the slow caravan of buggies and carts all headed the same way. Horses and their riders emerged from all the hollers and smaller trails to head to Pikeville. What more significant occasion for everyone to come out and celebrate than the fourth of July? The White Wreath fall harvest festival was fun but always paled in comparison to the sights, sounds, and smells of the crowds. There would be games of course, not that she had any interest in joining children's games. Salesmen came from far and wide selling everything from work boots, to tools, medicine, and even Colt "Peacemaker" pistols.

All these things she hoped to see for herself, but in resting the barrel of the shotgun across the crook of her left arm, her thoughts went to that of watching the whiskey stand with father. It was a nice slow trip, no need to even get the horses up to a gallop. About the time that the sun approached the top of the trees, father handed Annabelle the reins. He opened the napkins covering the top of their food basket and doled out the contents. Once he'd finished eating, he made himself comfortable and closed his eyes to relax. Annabelle didn't mind a bit. The rhythmic stomping of the two horses lulled her into a peaceful sway that made the miles seem like nothing at all. She kept the cart in line with the others and was halfway through eating her chicken breast and cheese when William McCreedy rode up alongside her on a freshly groomed Rocky Mountain mare. Its long silver mane and spotted silver dapple coat made its whole body appear to shimmer.

"Good morning, Annabelle." He tipped his hat to her.

"Morning, Mr. McCreedy." She returned a small nod. Hearing the voices, father came alive and sat up in his seat.

"Howdy, Will!"

"That's smart thinking letting Annabelle keep that shotgun at the ready."

"She's protecting the shipment. There'll be no whiskey thievery while 'Annabelle Oakley' stands guard."

"I meant having her armed after the disappearance of those two girls up in Prestonsburg. The whole town is in an uproar. I hope those two lambs show up all right."

"Will, you sound just like Mrs. Booth. I have no intentions of letting Annabelle fall victim to abduction. Any man with deviant thoughts on his mind will get a gut full of buckshot. If he survives that, he'll get a noose from a judge."

"All right, all right," Mr. McCreedy said. "Let's talk about more pleasant things, shall we? I'll have a fair amount of business to conduct today, but would you do me the pleasure of holding a bottle in reserve at your stand until I can return for it?"

"I'd be happy to set aside a special bottle just for you!" Annabelle offered. Mr. McCreedy was all smiles.

"I do appreciate it, Ms. Booth!" He tipped his cap again and kicked his horse to quicken its pace. "Fine saleswoman you have there, Jonathan!" He called back as he galloped away. "Let her do the talking and you'll sell the whole lot before noon!" Father beamed with pride as he patted her on the back and took back the reins.

Soon enough, the town of Pikeville came into full view. And the people…so many people gathered and walking in all directions. As they rode down the main street, two men atop the courthouse unfurled the biggest American flag Annabelle had ever seen from the second-story balcony. The courthouse dwarfed any other building in town. Annabelle craned her neck to see the top as they drew nearer. To the right of the building, in the shade of an oak tree, Mr. Lincoln called out to them and waved them closer. Even in a large crowd this size, it's hard to miss a man the size of a bear.

Father brought the cart to a stop next to the other one. To Annabelle's delight, Mr. Lincoln had erected the full stand and hung the specially made sign with the family name on it. He'd even gone so far as to pry the bung from a barrel and offer small samples to those that inquired. Leave it to James Lincoln to heft a full barrel of whiskey without batting an eye. Father looked it all over, and pleased by the work, the two set to unloading the second cart's cases of whiskey. It didn't take long for the two of them to move it all. When the last case was stacked into place, her father handed her some money.

"Annabelle, take the horses over to the livery." He pointed behind her. "Find the stable boy, tell him who you are, and they'll take care of the horses. Come straight back when you're done."

"Yes, Papa." Annabelle looped the leather sling of the shotgun over her head and left shoulder before taking hold of the bridles around the heads of the horses to lead them. They came along easily enough, and she pushed her way across the busy street and down the alley. A handsome young man a few years younger than her in a grey cap met her at the opening of the elongated stable barn.

"Morning!" he said, wiping off his hands.

"Morning. I'm Annabelle Booth. My father reserved a stable for these two."

"Booth? Sure. It's forty cents for the stable and fifty cents if you want them fed and watered. You don't em shoed or nothin?"

"No thank you. Just a place to put them with hay and water." Annabelle fished the money from her dress pocket and counted out the coins.

"You're lucky your papa reserved a spot. We've got so many people in town today I've had to send horses over to the Adam's farm because he's the only other person with a corral big enough." He took the coins, counted them again, and put them in his own pocket before pointing a thumb towards the back of the barn. "Thank you, Miss. You want to leave those with me?"

"I'll do it."

"You'll do it?"

"Yes, I will."

"All right. You gotta go all the way down and you've got the last stall on the left. Put your cart with the others past the far door and an unhitch 'em. Just lead them into the stall and close the gate and I'll be there in a bit to tend to 'em."

"All right." As she pulled the horses towards the back of the building, a terrible odor leaped into her nose. It wasn't the usual smell of horse shit but instead, a reek of death strong enough to turn her stomach and water the eyes. *Lord, that stench.* Somebody must've put down a lame animal nearby. If a horse threw a shoe and broke a leg that'd be reason enough to put it out of its misery. She found the stall and exited the barn to circle and park the

91

cart. Outside, the smell got even worse. She covered her nose and mouth with her sleeve to keep from gagging. A shadow crossed overhead and she looked skyward to see buzzards circling. Annabelle glanced about, but there was no dead horse or animal to be found.

Not wanting to linger, she hurried to untie the horses which seemed restless and almost pulled her to the ground when she released them. They were in the stall soon enough. She stepped outdoors again to see what or who was making that god-awful reek. The long-winged scavengers spun about in lazy circles in the air, their shadows making symmetric patterns on the dirt as they glided. Annabelle spotted a funeral coach parked away from the stable in the backfield. She had only seen such a vehicle once before when the last mayor died. Had somebody important passed away?

Curious, Annabelle walked closer, breathing through gritted teeth. The ornately carved wood of the black frame seemed to absorb the sunlight. A shadow without an owner. What should have been long panes of glass to allow an onlooker to peer inside were blacked out with pitch or black curtains. Someone had even gone as far as to drape dark burlap across the length of the coach like a tablecloth, which seemed queer in itself.

"You!" a voice said from behind. She turned to see the stable boy beckoning her from just inside the barn door. "Get away from that, it don't belong to you!" Annabelle retreated to meet him. "Don't you go near that funeral cart."

"It smells like fresh hell, who'd want to?"

"Sure, it smells god awful, but the owner gave me two whole silver dollars to keep people from getting near it."

"Paid you two dollars?" The boy reached into his back pocket and produced two polished coins.

"That's right." He smiled big. "Two whole dollars, and another two if nobody bothers it. I want that money so don't you go pokin' your nose where it doesn't belong. Ain't yours anyway."

"Who's cart is it?" she asked.

"Mister William Earl Lalande, from the city of New Orleans. He paid me to keep people from touching his coach so that's what I'm going to do. I thank you for *your* business of course. Now if you like, I'll walk you out."

"Of course," Annabelle said, looking back at it. "By the way, what does Mr. Lalande look like?"

"A tall man, real lean like Abraham Lincoln but without the beard. Clean-shaven, had a really long face. He came in late last night, pale as all hell like a damn ghost he was."

"And where is he now?"

"You sure ask an awful lot of questions. Hell, I don't know, probably at the saloon or hotel I imagine. Can you walk a little faster? Being back here by that smell is putting me off my breakfast, and I have to shoe a horse. You wouldn't happen to have an extra bottle of whiskey on that cart, would ya?"

"I'm afraid not. My father keeps all the bottles under a watchful eye."

"Shucks, I was wanting to get myself a bottle."

"You're too young to be drinking."

"I am fourteen and a half years old, that's more than old enough to get myself a bottle of whiskey and enjoy it. I bet I could drink half the bottle in one pull."

"You'd make yourself sick and look like a fool for doing it. Why even a big man like James Lincoln knows better than to drink half a bottle on his own, and he's four times your size."

"I'll bet you a dollar I could drink half a bottle in one pull. I'll bet you right here and now. I've got the money."

"I don't doubt you could."

"I bet you're scared to lose a dollar."

"You must think I'm simple to fall for a trick like that. I don't have a spare dollar, and I'm not giving you any whiskey. If you want a bottle so badly, you march yourself over to my father's stand across the road there and *you* buy a bottle."

"Your daddy isn't going to sell me a bottle of whiskey."

"Well, then I guess you're shit outta luck."

The stable boy curled his lip with disappointment when he realized he wasn't going to get any booze.

"Are you going to get to see any of the festivities, or are you stuck here all day?" she asked.

"Papa says I can go out later after my chores are done, but I don't know how long it's going to be. He says they got an actual real genuine chinaman over at the hotel who does a show where he can twist his body like a piece of rope, spin a plate on a stick that he holds in his mouth, and breathe fire."

"A man that can breathe fire?"

"That's what he says. He says they also got women who beat drums and make all kinds of racket banging stuff together while he dances and spins around. I can't miss something like that."

"That does sound exciting."

"The show starts after dark in front of the hotel."

"Maybe I'll see you there. Goodbye."

"Goodbye, Ms. Booth. You enjoy your day."

Annabelle rejoined her father and Mr. Lincoln at the stand where business was already in full swing. The two men were discussing mash bills but couldn't finish a complete thought without someone interrupting to inquire about the distillery or purchasing a bottle. As usual, they graciously made the customer a priority, making small talk about the special events happening throughout the day. Annabelle sat upon an upended empty crate and laid the shotgun across her lap. Sitting quiet, she watched the manner in which father talked to the people; pleasant and asking the names of the customer and then using their name as they departed. The customers smiled and thanked them, already sure in their mind that their money was well spent. Mr. Lincoln's size could make him seem intimidating to someone who hardly knew him, but with his broad smile and full beard, it didn't take long for strangers and passersby to warm up to him. His frequent laugh was loud enough and infectious enough to attract attention on its own. So much that several women with no interest in alcohol made conversation long enough so that it didn't seem forward when they asked if there was a "Mrs.Lincoln," to which he professed being married to his work. It was then, during a break in the stream of customers that father asked him about his plans for a family.

"I've got responsibilities, John," he said, restacking crates that didn't need restacking. Father gave him a half-hearted punch on the bicep.

"You can't put your life aside to just make whiskey, James. You're a good man, you need a good woman. Think about it; you don't drink other than the batch tastings, you don't play cards or disrespect women, and you're always sitting next to me at church on Sunday." James lowered his voice and turned slightly away, attempting to keep Annabelle from hearing.

"I appreciate it, John, but I don't know if you've noticed it or not but women around these parts are thin as twigs. The good lord made me bigger than most, so I'm going need something a little healthier to work with if I'm going to think about children."

"In that case, I'll talk to May. She's bound to know a few ladies who'd be lucky enough to be 'Mrs. Lincoln'." James smiled and returned the awkward punch, not taking into account his own strength, almost knocked John from his feet. But as soon as father was off-balance, both big hands shot out and steadied him by the shoulders. "Sorry."

"Don't give it another thought. C'mon. These people walking up to the stand look like they could use a drink." The two went back to selling bottles which was a surprising amount considering it was still so early in the morning. As the hours passed, more and more people flooded into the town. Annabelle had never seen so many. She sat still, slowing her breath to be as quiet as possible and soak in the sights and sounds. Carts and carriages flooded through the streets, intermingling seamlessly with the crowd. A bustling song with no words. The "clip-clop" of hooves and the laughter of children intermixed in an intoxicating fashion, distilling in itself the sound of Kentucky from the mash bill of the people and animals that inhabited it. Sitting there, her eyelids felt heavy, and she leaned back against the courthouse foundation to rest her eyes. Annabelle hadn't rested long when she felt a tap on the shoulder. She opened her eyes to find a handsome boy about her age with large ears and a pleasant smile looking down at her.

"Excuse me, miss," he said.

"Yes?"

"I don't mean to tell you your business but that man in the grey coat over there," He pointed to a man walking away with one hand rooted inside his suit jacket. "He just stole a bottle of your whiskey while those two men at the stand were distracted with another customer." The whites of her eyes doubled in size.

"That man? Are you sure?" she asked

"Sure as I'm standing here."

"You're not shittin' me?"

"No, ma'am! Do you think we-" Before he could finish the sentence Annabelle was already on her feet, her thumb cocking the rabbit ear hammer of the shotgun. She aimed the barrels skyward and pulled the right trigger causing an explosion to fill the air. Everyone within eyeshot cowered to look at the source of the noise, including her own father, Mr. Lincoln, and the thief.

"Annabelle! What in the name of-" Her dad exclaimed, covering his ears. With a clean line of sight, Annabelle leveled the gun on the whiskey filcher and called out to him.

"Mister, don't you move an inch!"

"Annabelle! Put that gun down!" Father yelled.

"That man took a bottle, papa." Everyone looked to the man who hadn't removed his right hand from the inside of his jacket but had the other one held up in a surrender pose.

"Hey, you! Did you take a bottle from my stand?" Mr. Booth called out to him. The man didn't say anything, but his head swiveled to look at the gap between two buildings as if he were thinking about making a break for cover. Annabelle didn't think twice to pull the second hammer back and raise the gun to her eye. With everyone in the crowded street holding their breath, the metal click sounded as clear as a church bell. The southern twang Annabelle Booth normally kept restrained began to squeeze every word crossing her lips.

"Mister, that's my bourbon you got in your pocket, and if you don't put that bottle down right this second, you're about to have a lot more holes than what the good lord gave ya!"

"Annabelle!" Father yelled. "Language!"

"Sorry, papa." The man's hand emerged from the coat, and sure enough, as the boy said, a bottle of Booth whiskey was in it. He slowly set the bottle upright on the ground and backed away with both hands still in the air. "Now, git." She said. The man turned and ran down the alley like the devil was after him. Good thing too because the sheriff materialized out of the crowd with two deputies behind him. Mr. Booth described the man and pointed to the alley the deputies followed. With the barrel pointed skyward, Annabelle pulled the trigger just enough to lower the hammer without firing the shell and retrieved the bottle from the street. Unexpectedly, a few of the people in the crowd who'd witnessed the exchange began to clap their hands.

More joined in, and within seconds the whole crowd was applauding her. Some men even threw their hats in the air. She didn't know what to do next, so she waved, walked back, handed the bottle to her father, and took her place on the empty crate again with the gun across her lap. The sheriff, a silver-haired man with a matching silver mustache wearing a black vest, a Colt Peacemaker on his hip, and a stern look on his face rounded the stand. Having the lawman stare her down, Annabelle felt as small as a mouse.

"Young lady, was it you that fired that shotgun?"

"Yes, Sir," she said, placing the gun against the courthouse and standing up. "That man was trying to steal a bottle of whiskey."

"Do you know you're not allowed to fire a weapon within the town limits of Pikeville?"

"I do now, Sir. I wouldn't have done if I wasn't being robbed and the law should protect my right to defend myself and my property from thieves."

"The law does allow you to reserve that right. But you know a gun is a deadly thing not to be played with, correct?"

"Yes Sir, uh, Sheriff. It's for hunting and self-defense only."

"What's your name, young lady?"

"Annabelle Booth, Sheriff. My family makes whiskey in White Wreath."

"You're John Booth's daughter." He looked to father who confirmed it with a nod.

"Your father's a respected man." She saw the sheriff look to father with a small wink. "I'd hate to see his good name ruined by having a girl running around thinking she's Annie Oakley."

"No, Sir. Guns are just for hunting and defending yourself."

About that time, everyone turned to see the two deputies return from the alley with the man in the grey jacket between them fighting to get loose. They didn't stop but instead carried on in the direction of the jail across the square.

"All right then." He relaxed. "You did the right thing, Miss Annabelle. And seeing as how you did the right thing. I'm going to make you an honorary deputy for the rest of the day."

"You mean it?" she asked. The man reached into his vest pocket and produced a small tin pin shaped like sheriff's star. He squatted down a bit, pulled off the backing, and pinned it to the front of the chest pocket of her dress.

"There you go, for the rest of the day, you have all the rights and privileges of a Pikeville deputy...provided of course, you don't go firing that scattergun again."

"I promise." She smiled.

"Very well. Now that that's been settled," He pulled money from his pocket. "I'd be delighted if you'd sell me your finest bottle of bourbon."

"That would be any bottle at the stand, Sheriff." She gave a wide smile before handing him the bottle the thief was attempting to get away with. "We only sell the finest." Father beamed with pride. The sheriff took the bottle and turned it over in one hand as the other retrieved cash from a vest pocket.

"That's what it says right here on the label. Hell of a saleswoman you got here, Mr. Booth. You all take care, I have a thief to tend to."

"Have a good day, Sheriff."

"I intend to." As the Sheriff walked away, the majority of the crowd collapsed upon the stand to get a better look at Annabelle and ask her father and Mr. Lincoln about a bottle of their spirits. Several people shook Annabelle's hand and congratulated her for standing up to the man.

"I'll handle this," Father said, tucking two dollars into her dress pocket. "Here, why don't you go and have yourself a time. If you can handle that man, you should be ok. James and I can watch the stand. Come back by noon, and we'll get some lunch."

"Ok, papa." Annabelle grinned as she looked to the boy who'd woken her. "What do you say? Want to walk with me and see the town?"

"I'd be delighted, Miss Booth. I can follow you as far as the square, but then I have some errands I need to run. That's where I was on my way to when I saw that thief." he replied as the two walked away from the stand. Annabelle didn't realize she'd casually slung the shotgun over her shoulder as she walked. "You should be fine to be out on your own. You got a scattergun and you're an honorary deputy," said the boy with the big ears and pleasant smile. "I don't think there's a person in town who'd cross you."

"Thank you for telling me that man was stealing. I do appreciate it. What's your name by the way?"

"Pardon my manners," He offered his hand and she shook it. "My name's Julian."

"Julian what?"

"Julian Van Winkle."

"I've never seen you around here before, Julian. Where ya from?"

"Up in Danville."

"Danville is a few days ride away from here. What brings you to Pikeville?"

"I'm learning about whiskey. I know a good deal about making whiskey, but you can always learn more. I imagine that if I keep gathering more facts about what all goes into making it, I'd eventually know enough to be a salesman or even begin making my own batch. I think clean water and a good mash bill are the most important things in making a quality whiskey."

"I couldn't agree more."

The two walked for a little while each pointing out the sights to the other, enjoying one another's company. There was a man from Paintsville who could juggle three small hatchets at once, and also a young negro man tapdancing in the square upon a wide metal tile that might have been a sign at one time. He had a hat placed on the ground in front of him and as people stopped to watch they threw pennies into it.

The two moved along to see the sights, one after the next. Stands lined each side of the street, wild preserves here, some home-sewn dolls there. Julian mentioned whiskey and the two talked about mash bills, corn, rye, even wheat as they walked. Hours passed, and Annabelle found herself so comfortable with hearing Julian talk that she forgot about visiting the shops as she'd intended. He even took her arm. She followed his lead around town to stop at a few shops to pick up provisions. He told her of his own horse he'd left tied up at the stable across from the stand.

"I think they must've shot one of those horses," he told her. "When I was in the stable, it smelled something God awful. Something had definitely died."

"There's a funeral cart out back. The smell is coming from it. A dozen buzzards were circling it."

"A funeral cart with a body still in it? That doesn't sound right."

"Stable boy said the person riding the cart was from New Orleans."

"With a body still in it? I don't think there's enough gold in the world to bribe me to deal with that smell for a whole day let alone a ride from New Orleans."

"Me either."

Annabelle and Julian talked away the hours. Banners hung from every building. The smells of pies, popcorn, firework smoke, and the fresh smell of the breeze slipping through the trees above permeated everything. When they got hungry Annabelle bought lunch with the money father had given her. Before she knew it, time got away from Annabelle Booth. It wasn't until the sun began to set far over the trees that the two realized they'd walked all the way to the far end of town, lost in pleasant conversation.

"Look how late it is!" Annabelle panicked. "My father is going to tan my backside if I've made him worry. Julian, I'm sorry, I have to run."

"I'll come with you," he said. Julian pulled her along, and with shotgun in hand, the two ran as fast as their legs would carry them. Through the streets and up the main thoroughfare they sprinted. A crowd big enough to block the whole street had gathered in front of the hotel blocking the way to the courthouse. They slowed long enough for Julian to take the lead and spearhead a path straight through. Through the mass of people they shoved and pushed, apologizing all the time. Annabelle keeping the sling of her shotgun tight to stop the barrel from waving about and striking anyone. It was getting dark fast and they emerged on the other side. Julian looked back for only a moment to check on Annabelle when he ran headlong into a wall he didn't remember passing. The sudden stop caused Annabelle to smack into the back of Julian before the two fell on their behinds. Both looked up to see a wall named James Lincoln.

"There you are!" The man bellowed, reaching down to assist him with his mammoth hands. He pulled them vertical so fast that their feet floated second before striking the ground. "Your father and I hadn't seen you all day." He lowered his brow to scowl at Julian a little. "We were getting worried that a smooth-talking young suitor might've run off with you."

"Mr. Lincoln, you be nice." Annabelle brushed herself off. "Mr. Van Winkle has been nothing short of a gentleman all day, and you'll be disappointed to know that he and I are not eloping."

"We sold everything but the stand!" he said excitedly. "Your daddy wanted me to come and find you so and tell you he wants you to get your cart from the livery."

105

"That's where I was headed," Julian offered.

"It's getting dark fast, Annabelle," Mr. Lincoln said. "Go and get the cart and don't fiddlefart around. Your daddy wants to head home soon."

"I'll go get it right this moment. Come on, Julian." The two sidestepped the big man and carried on, this time with Annabelle leading the way. Around the courthouse and down the side alley they hurried until they stopped at the open barn doors.

"Hello?" she called into the barn. "Hello?" Again, there was no reply. "Now where could that stable boy have taken off to? You know what? I bet he went to go see the fire breathing chinaman at the Hotel."

"That explains the crowd we passed. Do you really need him?" Julian asked.

"I suppose not. I've already paid him." They started walking through the barn on their own. Halfway through Annabelle asked Julian. "Where's your horse?"

"Right here." He raised a hand and a white horse stuck its head over the gate to allow him to pet it along the bottom of its head. "This is Pappy."

"You named your horse Pappy?"

"Sure. Why not? It's as good of a name as any. I think he likes it." He ran his hands between the horse's eyes before offering an apple he'd purchased earlier. The animal didn't take the apple but instead stomped about and turned in its pen. One of its rear feet shot out to strike the gate, startling the two.

"What's gotten into your horse?" she asked

"I don't know. He'd do anything for an apple. Something's got him spooked. Where're your horses?"

"My two are in the last stall on the left and my cart is just outside the door by that smelly old funeral cart."

"There's no light out there. I saw an extra lamp by the front door. Let me go back and get it and I'll meet you outside. It'll be easier to hitch the horses."

"Okay."

"Easy boy." He tried to soothe the horse before turning away. "Easy, I'll be right back." Annabelle moved on but didn't get a few more steps before something caught her eye. To her right, just a few stalls down from Pappy's, a terrible sound, unlike anything she'd ever heard before filled the stable. It was worse than any hog being slaughtered, or shrill cry of a rabbit caught in a trap. The sound filled everything and every horse within the livery began to thrash in an attempt to break free of their pens.

She froze to the spot as a large horse in one of the shadowy stalls toppled and fell out of view in the shadows. No sooner had it disappeared than blood began to spray out of the stall in every direction. The horse cried out as whatever was in the shadows with it was tearing it apart.

Annabelle took a step back, repulsed but mesmerized by the sight of it all. Her feet froze to the spot. Splashes of red found her dress and face as fast as being caught in a flash rainstorm. From the horror within the stall, something in the shape of a man emerged, too tall and almost too lean to be a man. Pale skin the color bleached ivory wrapped taut around bone thin limbs. Piercing eyes like the coyotes and wolves that stared back from the tree line at night. Annabelle began to scream. Her jaw opened wide and primal wail poured out of her at such a velocity that she thought her head might split in twain.

The creature's elongated arms and legs bent and distorted at unnatural angles to allow it to twist horizontally through the boards in the gate without stopping to open it. Its eyes burned with the fires of hell itself. Annabelle wanted to run, but her feet wouldn't obey. A stream of urine poured down the inside of her legs and past shaking knees to soak her socks and shoes.

Its eyes…Its eyes…

Julian came running back with the lantern in his hand as one of the thing's arms left its side and raised toward her face.

"Holy shit!" Julian yelled. "You! Get away from her! Annabelle, run!"

Even with his words in her ears, Annabelle couldn't move. The long, spindly fingers inched closer, widening to take her in its grasp. Julian heaved the lantern back and hurled it through the air. The lantern struck the slender thing upon the bicep, the glass shattering and spraying oil to create a burst of fire about its shoulders and head. It screeched and writhed in pain, trying to bat the flames away.

She remained entranced. Julian snatched her by the hand and attempted to pull her away when the burning creature flailed between them and clubbed Julian across the chest and face. The boy's feet left the ground as he flew ten through the air and hit a bale of hay. Seeing him collapse into a pile on the ground became enough to shake Annabelle from her trance. She lifted the sling of the shotgun hanging over her head and shoulder. The stock and barrel gravitated into her hands, her thumbs cocking the rabbit-ear hammers. The creature collided with a pair of water buckets stacked atop a haystack next to it, extinguishing the flames. No longer alight, its angry scowl turned upon her. Long hands shot out at her faster than her eyes could follow, one clutching her by the waist as the other drew her legs together to hold her to the spot.

"Let go of me!"

Its head drew closer, the mouth spreading wider and even wider at the corners to reveal a maw of sharp teeth and fangs. Annabelle retained enough courage to level the shotgun under its chin and pull the first trigger.

CLICK

Both she and the creature looked shocked at the weapon's lack of report before the thing ducked its head to knock the barrel aside. In her hurry to fire the weapon, she'd forgotten that she's spent the first round to frighten the bourbon thief earlier that day. It buried its face into the left side of her neck, the protruding two fangs entering the skin just below the jawline. Annabelle's body went rigid as two syringes as cold as icicles penetrated her jugular and suckled. Hungry and feral, the creature gripped her legs and torso so tightly she wondered if she'd snap. He turned her upside down to drink from her as from a whiskey bottle.

"Papa…" The word lingered on her lips…

Below, still clutched in her hand, the shotgun hung midair. The leather sling swung back and forth. Past that, Julian still lay on the floor, unmoving. Far in the distance, the sound of shouting and dozens of feet began to grow louder. The glow of lanterns appeared beyond the barn door. Papa had heard her scream. Papa was coming. The creature continued to hold her upside down, draining her, the fangs still cold as ever. The bottle was almost empty. Her eyes fell back to the shotgun still dangling in her hand. Every muscle in her arm cried out in protest for her to let go. She couldn't feel her hand anymore, but it never let go. The second hammer was already cocked and the gun was ready to fire. She needed only to raise it once more.

"Annabelle!" A familiar voice called from far away. He wouldn't be able to make it in time.

"Papa… help." she gasped.

Be it by will or fear, she found the strength to pull the gun higher, higher. The arm bent at the elbow, black steel cylinders rising and wavering towards her own face, then towards the beast holding her.

"Papa, I'm sorry." Annabelle lined up the barrel at the thing's head and began squeezing the trigger. It didn't go off at first and she began to believe that somehow it might not fire at all. She felt cold and wondered if her hand would respond at all. Her sight fell away from the gun and to the cross beams of the barn. Annabelle's vision doubled and turned white around the edges. Maybe it was all an illusion. Maybe she'd dropped the gun and didn't know it. She believed she was squeezing as hard as she could. And then, an explosion filled the air, as violent as a strike of lightning. The waves of that sound called upon the shadows of the world to combine and swallow her whole. It echoed like the last note of a hymn as poor Annabelle Booth tumbled end over end into a bottomless black.

CHAPTER SEVEN

Annabelle awoke with a start. To her surprise, she found herself in familiar surroundings. A pair of oil lamps on her dresser and nightstand were turned down. Even in the low light, she recognized the voices of her parents talking to a man at the foot of her bed. Her vision doubled whenever she looked at the light, so she squinted to stem the dizziness it caused. She felt too weak to move, her throat parched. The man spoke in low whispers.

"In the twenty years I've been a doctor, I've never seen anything like this. It's been twenty-six hours since she was attacked. She's slept almost the whole time. The gashes on her throat are all but gone with no signs of infection of any sort and that's the damnedest thing I've ever seen. But still, there's the matter of the anemia."

"What can be done?" Father asked. "I let you take more blood if you need it."

"Mr. Booth, it would be a danger to your health to take any more than I already have. As a practitioner of medicine, I cannot in good conscience draw another drop. You mentioned Mr. Lincoln expressed an interest in donating some blood?"

"He does, he does, and he'd freely give it if it helps our Annabelle."

"Then, by all means, bring him directly. Your daughter requires every drop, although it is beyond me where the blood is being depleted at such a rate. It's astonishing, really."

"May." Mr. Booth said to his wife. "Stay with her, and I'll get James."

"Please hurry," she said. He kissed her on the cheek and exited the room.

"M-Mama," Annabelle managed to say. Mrs. Booth rushed to her side where a stool waited. She sat down upon it and took Annabelle's hand.

"What is it, dear?"

"Mama, I'm thirsty." She whispered.

"Of course, dear." She poured water from a nearby vase into a tin cup then helped her daughter to sit up. Annabelle tipped the cup to her lips and tried to drink. She didn't get the first gulp down before choking. She spit up the contents on her mother's blouse before coughing and gagging to find her breath again. Mother grabbed a nearby towel, patting herself down. When Annabelle calmed a little, she attempted a second time only to come to the same result. Thankfully, May Booth had the towel at the ready to keep from getting drenched.

Mother looked to the doctor. "What can be done?" she asked. "She asks for water, but every time she tries to drink, she can't keep it down."

"I'm afraid I have no answers at the moment, Mrs. Booth. This anemia has the most peculiar symptoms." Annabelle overheard them talking about giving her another blood transfusion. She'd taken a pint of her daddy's blood and now Mr. Lincoln was giving his. She was thirsty for more water but whenever she tried to drink it, she choked. "There was some kind of large wild animal in the livery that attacked you and that boy from Danville."

"Julian?" She perked a little. "Is Julian all right?"

"He's a little beaten up, some bruises on his chest, head and back, but he's going to be fine."

"What's happening to me?"

"The thing that bit you caused an infection that's making you sick. We called for a doctor and he's going to help you get better."

"What was it?" she asked.

"We don't know. They all heard you scream and came running as fast as we could. Some people say it was a man, others say it was some kind of tall animal standing on its hind legs. Whatever it was, you took a chunk out of it when you shot it with your scattergun."

"Did I?" she said, unsure of herself.

"You did. That thing made a noise something fierce, dropped you in the middle of the stable and bolted out into the night. The sheriff formed a posse of men he knows to be hunters and trackers to follow its prints. Don't you worry, they'll find it wherever it is and put it out of its misery."

"I'm so tired."

"Then sleep. We'll get you home soon."

A dreamless sleep found Annabelle. She awoke long before dawn in a room with no light in it. Despite the lack of illumination, she could see into every corner. Shadows retreated from anywhere she looked. She rubbed her eyes in case they were playing tricks on her. Outside the window, the night seemed as clear as day. She blinked and then blinked again to shake the mirage she knew not to be true. Try as she might, it wouldn't go away. Her head had stopped throbbing. She threw her covers aside and put her feet on the floor. The floorboards didn't creak like they normally did. *How odd.*

Annabelle crossed the room. Stealing a glance at the basin mirror, her reflection remained absent as she passed by. The door to her room opened without a sound as well, and she wondered if her ears were stopped up from being ill.

To her surprise, she could hear every sound in the distillery save for the ones she created—from the wind blowing outside in the summer night to the tiny mouse scurrying its way across the rafters ten feet above her head. Further on, she poked her head into her father's office to find him sleeping across his desk. He'd fallen asleep with his face on a stack of invoices. In his hand, a small framed picture of her. She didn't wake him but instead retrieved a quilt from her bed and draped it across him before moving on.

Everything in the dark distillery seemed as twilight to her. Shadows scattered before her wherever she roamed. She walked through one room after another until the building gave way to the massive rick room. Stacked thirty feet into the air, hundreds upon hundreds of oak barrels sat nestled in their shelves. Some had been maturing for only a few days while others had been sitting since her fourteenth birthday.

Annabelle ran her fingers across the end of the closest one, her name displayed on the barrel head. Each of her senses reached out in heightened awareness. The smell of the wood and aging alcohol was almost as intoxicating as the whiskey itself. Annabelle unlatched the door on the end of the building and stepped outside. The night came alive all around her. Nocturnal creatures climbed, crawled, slithered and flew about in every direction. High in the trees, the hoot of an owl seemed as loud and clear as the horn of a locomotive. The side to side motions of a black snake in the undergrowth sounded like a bag of corn dragging across the ground.

She turned this way and that to catch one fascinating sight after the next. A pair of rabbits nibbled leafy things behind a tree. It was unnatural the way they remained absolutely still as she approached. The bigger of the two didn't twitch so much as an ear as she reached out and snatched it up. The other hopped a few feet away but didn't scamper far. She felt its coat of fur and found it to be soooo soft. It didn't fight her at all. Holding on to it tight, she turned it about until she could look it in the face. Upon doing so, the fidgety animal relaxed in her grip and a strong smell entered Annabelle's nose.

Blood.

Its' heart fluttered as fast as a hummingbird's wings. The blood smelled so sweet and the rabbit went limp as though offering itself to her. She thought there was something wrong with her instincts until she felt a dull ache in her mouth near her front teeth. She felt her teeth with a finger to find that her canines had elongated into pointed feral instruments. An urge built inside her and Annabelle pulled the rabbit closer before pulling the ears tight and sinking her teeth into the neck. The animal twitched and kicked in her grip as she began to drain its essence. She closed her eyes and drank deep. Not long after, the hummingbird heart began to slow. Slower and slower it beat until it fluttered no more. Annabelle pulled the rabbit away from her lips, licking the last drops away. The coppery sweetness felt like heaven on her tongue. Ashamed but undeterred, she set the body down carefully and crawled on her hands and knees towards the other rabbit.

"C'mere, bunny," she whispered. The second rabbit faced her but didn't flee. When it looked her in the eye, not only did it relax, but it moved closer to her. Annabelle tucked her feet below her and sat upright, the bunny moving closer and closer, hopping right into her lap. She studied it, stroking the long ears, watching the nose wiggle back and forth, its heartbeat just as fast and a minute later, its body lay unmoving in the weeds next to the other.

Annabelle didn't feel sick any longer. In fact, she felt so good she decided on a walk down to the creek. The influx of the second animal's blood satisfied Annabelle's hunger to the point that she felt inebriated like the men when they'd had too much of her father's whiskey. Down the winding path, she wandered until she reached the water's edge. She settled down on a flat rock near the water's edge and pulled her knees to her chest. It all seemed so beautiful. Frogs croaked here and there before jumping from the edges into the water. Crickets, owls, nightingales, animals big and small, each a part of an orchestra of the evening playing symphony just for her. Content, she rested her cheek upon her knee and looked out upon the rippling surface of the water. For hours she stayed there, clinging to something familiar to outweigh the horror that had befallen her.

She looked back over her shoulder in the direction of the dead rabbits and felt conflicted. Upon wiping at her mouth, her fingers came away with dark crimson smudges. Confusion welled up inside, fast as the rush from the blood. She wiped time and again with her hands across her mouth only to have more blood. At the water's edge, handfuls of water washed away all the traces of red from her face and fingers. She tried to look at her reflection in the water, but there was nothing to see. Annabelle Booth simply wasn't there. The confusion morphed to worry, which then evolved to panic. She pulled her knees to her chest again and rocked back and forth. Visions of the dead rabbits swam throughout her head.

Annabelle began to cry. The tears came quick, tracing their way down her face. She attempted to wipe the first ones away with the back of her left hand. Just as she pulled the hand back, she saw that a large smear of blood had marked her skin. Dabbing the other cheek with the other hand produced the same result.

Her tears had turned to blood.

She tried to keep from panicking. The sudden change of the song in the air didn't help. Her head twisted about trying to figure out what it was, looking this way and that.

The songs in her ears were no longer of owls and nightingales, but morning birds. Out across the water to the east, the sky began to brighten at an accelerated rate. The incoming sunrise burnt Annabelle's eyes until finally she had to look away. Almost like the feeling of goosebumps, her exposed skin took on a prickly heat sensation. She turned away which made it feel better, but the side of her body still facing it began to burn instead.

"I have to get away from the light."

Up the winding path of the hill she ran. Her legs carried her faster than she thought she could move and covered the distance in a matter of seconds. The trees and undergrowth blurred and unblurred to deliver her to the distillery door she'd exited. Once inside, she latched it behind her. Past the ricks and men rolling barrels she hurried. Each worker gawked at the girl with blood on her face and tried to stop her to ask her what was wrong, but she batted them aside. One after another she pitched burly men out of her path to get back to the residence. Bursting through the door frightened her parents, but her appearance with blood streaming off her face horrified them.

"Annabelle!" Mother yelled as the two ran to her side.

"Jesus, Annabelle!" Father grabbed a small towel out of a pile of laundry and tried to wipe away the blood. "Good god, what's happened to you?" The more he tried to remove the blood from around her eyes and nose, the more that came streaming out. "Are you crying blood?"

"I'm trying to stop!" she cried, sniffling. It was then that they saw the redness of her skin.

"What's happened here?" Mother asked. "Did you burn yourself in a fire?"

"The sunrise." Annabelle took the towel from her father's hand and blotted off the rest of the new streams. By this point, her whole face was slathered in crimson. "The sunlight burnt me, and I killed some rabbits. Daddy, what's happening to me?"

"You killed some rabbits?" Mother asked. "Why were you killing rabbits?"

"I needed…" She paused. "I needed their…."

"You needed their what?" Mrs. Booth asked her. Annabelle's lips curled up in a pout. She didn't want to say. She didn't want to admit to what she'd done. Father knelt and grabbed her by the biceps to get hold of her.

"Annabelle, answer your mother this instant."

"I needed their blood because I was hungry." Mr. and Mrs. Booth looked flabbergasted. No words could be spoken to answer what had come from their own child's admission.

"I'm sorry I did it." She sobbed again, a fresh pair of crimson drops tracing their way down each side of her nose. "I didn't want to do it. I couldn't help myself."

Her parents looked at one another and Papa wrapped his arms around her to where she could rest her head on his shoulder.

"It'll be all right, dear. It'll be all right." More light crept in through the window and Annabelle tilted her head away from it. As the light increased, Annabelle whimpered. "Honey, what's the matter?" Mother asked her.

"The light. It's coming in."

"The light?" Father looked around. "Okay. Okay. Just a moment."

He hurried into Annabelle's room and returned with the biggest quilt and wrapped it around her. She grasped it and followed behind her parents as they led her to her room. Once inside, she shied away from the open window. Father moved quickly to pull the curtains. Seeing it wasn't enough to stop the coming sunrise, he left the room and returned with a roll of canvas, blankets, hammer, and nails. Mother pulled Annabelle into the furthest corner and spoke soothing words, holding her as Mr. Booth set to the task of covering the windows from top to bottom with the materials until no light came through it. Once he was finished, when all traces of light were blocked out, Annabelle shut the door and removed the quilt.

"How long will this last?" she asked him.

"I don't know, dear." He stroked her hair and kissed the top of her head. "I just don't know."

For the rest of the day, Annabelle stayed in her room. She cleaned herself in the basin but needed her mother's help getting the last few spots since she couldn't see her own reflection. She could tell her mother was frightened, but she held her close and sang to her just the same. After that, she slept unmoving under the surface of a shifting swamp of blankets and quilts. No dreams, only darkness. She didn't know how it happened, but the moment the sun slipped beneath the far hills, her eyes opened. Carefully she made her way to the door and peeked under it to see the light was gone. Convinced it was all dark, she turned the doorknob.

When she opened it, her parents sat waiting in chairs facing her. Behind them, Mr. Lincoln sat in a chair next to the far wall. Each of them sat up straight as she entered the room. A lantern glowed in the corner next to him, its wick recessed to allow the least amount of light needed for them to see. Annabelle emerged wearing a fresh white nightgown, to the shock of her parents and Mr. Lincoln, her skin was now as pale as the sleep shirt she wore.

"Hello mother," she said, rubbing the last of the sleep from her eyes.

"Annabelle?" Mother asked. "How do you feel?"

"Rested."

"Are you hungry?" Mr. Lincoln asked with a nervous tone in his voice.

"No, I don't think so." Again, her eyesight pushed every shadow aside to allow her to see everything in the room. A strange glint behind Mr. Lincoln's far leg caught her attention. The shimmer of a polished axe head. Her sense of smell heightened, as well. She could smell sweat seeping through Mr. Lincoln's brow. It smelled strangely good, almost like the hearty tang of a fried chicken dinner.

"Why are you sitting all the way over there, Mr. Lincoln?" she asked. Her father interjected before he could answer.

"I'm glad you feel well enough to be out of bed because the doctor is coming by any time now to check up on you."

"But why is Mr. Lincoln-?"

"We don't know if what you have is contagious, so he's keeping his distance."

"But you're not."

"We're your parents. If we get sick, then that's our responsibility. If we do, then Mr. Lincoln needs to be able to handle the needs of the distillery."

"How is having an axe going to keep him from getting infected?" She walked past them to stand before the big man. He remained seated in a wooden chair creaking under duress to hold his weight.

His hands never left their places on his knees but more than once, his eyes darted to the handle of the axe. Other than the sweat on his brow and palms, she could smell the freshly ground metal of the axe blade. By smell alone, she could sense the fresh grooves in the metal left by the sharpening stone. His sweat had dripped and mixed with the water giving the blade a scent of its own.

"Why, Mr. Lincoln, I'm disappointed. You don't need that." She reached out to take the axe from him. His hand shot out to grab the handle but came away with nothing. Annabelle had moved faster than his eyes could follow, and the wooden handle was already in her hand. The whites of his eyes grew to the size of dinner plates as she held it out for him to see.

"I'd never do anything to hurt you." She held the axe by the head and offered it back to him by the handle. He slowly took it from her before setting it down next to his leg again.

"What's happened to you, Annabelle?" he asked her.

"I don't know what to call it." She closed her eyes and rolled her neck and shoulders about. Her expression was one of satisfaction before she opened them again and looked directly at the front door. "The doctor is here."

No sooner had the knocks resonated Annabelle vanished from her place at the far side of the room and appeared at the door to twist the knob.

The door opened and the doctor stood on the other side looking surprised to be greeted by her. She stepped out of the way and held her arm out to invite him in.

"Well hello, Annabelle!" He tipped his hat. "I see someone is out of bed. Are you feeling better!"

"Yes, I am, doctor. Won't you come in?"

He entered and set his medicine bag on a nearby chair. She took his coat and hat from him and hung them upon the nearby hat rack. "Thank you, young lady. That's very nice of you. Why is it so dark in here?"

Upon him saying this, Annabelle crushed her eyes tight and imagined the room being brighter. To her delight, all oil lamps spaced about the room sparked and blossomed to life. Everyone's eyes but Annabelle's darted about the room as every shadow evaporated before the warm light.

"Annabelle, did you do that?" Mother asked.

"I don't think so." She smiled at her.

"This is most peculiar," the doctor added, adjusting the glasses on the end of his nose to get a better look at her. "My dear, your skin is as pale as ivory." He took her hand and grasped it and her arm in several places, inspecting it. "And you're ice cold! How do you feel?"

"I feel well, doctor. How do you feel?" The man smiled a bit at being asked.

"I'm fine as well. Have a seat in this chair, my dear."

She did as she was told and sat with her hands in her lap as the doctor opened his bag and produced a long thin object like a candlestick but made of wood. At each end, the item flared out like the end of a trumpet or bugle. One of the ends was larger than the other. He unlaced her nightshirt down to the sternum and placed the larger end against her chest and while holding it stationary then knelt to put his ear to the other end. For a moment, he didn't move but then moved both the device and his head around. The Booths looked on. James Lincoln's curiosity got the better of him, and he crossed the room, leaving the axe in its place.

"Is something wrong?" Father asked. The doctor looked at his device strangely, even lining it up with the flame of one of the lamps to look through it.

"Perhaps. Mr. Lincoln? Would you do me a favor and unbutton your shirt, just to the chest, please?" Mr. Lincoln did as he was asked, and the doctor put the item to him in the same manner. He listened intently for a minute. "Yes, yes, that sounds right." He then returned to Annabelle and repeated the process. Looking concerned, he asked Mr. Booth to do the same which produced the identical result as Mr. Lincoln. "That's fine. Gentlemen, you can button your shirts again, you as well, Annabelle." The doctor then took a long inhalation of breath, put his hands on his hips and stared at the floor in the strangest fashion.

"What is it, doctor?" Annabelle asked. "What does the device do?"

"This is a stethoscope. A medical device that amplifies my ability to hear what goes on in the human body. Could you blow on my hand? Take a deep breath and blow as hard as you can on the back of my hand." Annabelle thought it strange but did as she was told. " Most peculiar."

"Tell us what it is." Mrs. Booth said.

"This stethoscope allows me or anyone who uses it to hear the beating of the heart or inhalation or exhalation of air into the lungs as someone breathes. Now I've used on both of the gentlemen here to test a theory but for the life of me, I cannot find a trace of breath or heartbeat from Annabelle. It's doubly strange in that I can't detect any trace that she is breathing but she was able to blow air across my hand. I've never seen anything like it. With no pulse or heartbeat, she should be dead."

"That's not possible," James Lincoln said. "If her heart stopped beating, how is she alive? She is alive. Look at her." The doctor looked confused. Annabelle offered her his seat and sat down, wiping his brow with a handkerchief.

"You are a mystery, Annabelle," he said, dabbing a little more. "I've never seen anything the likes of this. I tell you the truth I've not wasted a single minute in trying to discover a cause or explanation to your condition. For all my years of practicing medicine, I cannot account for the anemia or this." As soon as he said that, Annabelle stood straight and looked at the front door, staring at it for seconds on end.

"Annabelle, what is it dear?" father asked.

"Someone is here." She sniffed the air. "Four men. Three of them have guns."

"How do you know that?"

"I can smell them." She backed away from the door to stand next to Mr. Lincoln at the far side of the room. "They're coming." The clomp-clomping of boots upon the wooden front porch raised everyone's awareness and a loud rapping came at the door. Before he knew it, Annabelle was pressing the handle of the axe into Mr. Lincoln's hand before standing behind him to hide. Mr. Booth opened the door to find not only the sheriff from Pikeville but two deputies and Father Graves standing behind them.

"Evenin' Sherriff." Mr. Booth greeted them.

"Evening, John." The sheriff took off his hat. "Wondering if I might have a word with you outside."

"We can talk right here." Mr. Booth said. "What's all this about?"

"It's about that thing that attacked your daughter."

"You tracked it?"

"No, Sir. Whoever it was got away clean with two men I know to be expert trackers on its trail. One of them is a

Cherokee man who took a special interest in helping find the attacker and even he says the person we're after left no trace. He said the person; *'became as air and slipped away in the trees.'*"

"That's unfortunate to hear."

"That's not all. There's also the matter of a black funeral cart that was behind the livery stable. Stable hand says it arrived on the night of the third and that the man driving it paid him the sum of four dollars to keep people away from his cart which he and others can confirm as smelling like something died in it."

"Yes, Annabelle says she saw and smelled the same one. What about it?"

"The cart and driver have gone missing as well. The trackers couldn't find it anywhere. I sent word through my deputies to every town in every direction and no one has seen hide nor hair of it. What they have found was the dead bodies of the two girls that vanished from Paintsville and Prestonsburg."

"That's god awful." Mr. Booth shook his head.

"Poor things were about Annabelle's age and each one had been torn to bits by whatever got it claws into them. It wasn't no man with a knife or razor that made those wounds. They were sliced open like spring lambs." Mr. Booth grimaced, and one of the deputies spit in disgust.

"What brings you out here in the middle of the night then?"

"Came to check up on Annabelle, of course. Wanted to ask her some questions about what she saw and if she remembered anything distinctive about the cart or the one that bit her." Mr. Booth looked about and saw the two deputies but couldn't quite make out the face of a man standing back behind the cart they'd arrived upon.

"Who's that hiding back in the shadows there?"

"Pastor Grant," the sheriff told him. "He saw us when we were passing the church and asked to accompany us to your home." Although they spoke in low whispers, Annabelle heard this whole conversation from inside the house.

"Papa," she whispered. Her father turned around in looked in the door. Annabelle shook her head. "Don't let him in. Pastor Grant. Please?" Her father nodded and faced the sheriff again.

"You're welcome inside, but you'll pardon me if I don't invite Pastor Grant inside. I don't want to scare Annabelle with too many men around her."

"I see." The sheriff scratched his chin. "Well, I guess I ought to talk to her and let her get her rest then."

"Just you and your men. Father Grant can wait outside."

"I find that agreeable." He looked to his men and nodded before taking off his hat. "Lead the way." Mr. Booth let them in and closed the door tightly behind. Inside, the sheriff said hello to everyone and invited Annabelle to come out from behind Mr. Lincoln. "Come on out young lady." He beckoned. "You remember me from the other day, don't you?"

"Yes, Sir," she said and emerged. When she did, the three men gawked at her paleness.

"Are you sure you're feeling all right? Child, you're as white as a ghost," the sheriff said. His two men nodded in agreement.

"I'm feeling better. The doctor says I have anemia."

"Well then, I'll try not to keep you too long so that you can get back to bed and the doctor can do his medicine." He interrogated her for close to ten minutes. She recounted everything she could remember about the funeral cart and the man or thing that killed the horse. Satisfied, the sheriff and his men relaxed some. Annabelle felt his eyes on her the whole time. Pastor Grant was at the closest window peering in.

"Tell me something, Doctor," the sheriff said. "Pastor Grant is awful spooked about Annabelle. Can you think of a reason he might have reason to be such upheaval?" The doctor was still sweating profusely and stammered his words.

"It's a rare case to be sure. There's no change in her respiration, heart rate, pulse."

"I don't know too much about the details of anemia, doc. I've seen a man go pale and weak after taking a bullet because he lost blood. This the same thing?"

"Not exactly." It was then that the sheriff noticed that Mr. Lincoln had been holding an axe next to his leg the whole time. He too looked uneasy.

"Mr. Lincoln, that's your name, isn't it?"

"Y-yes, sheriff." The big man managed.

"Any particular reason you've got an axe by your side?

"No, Sheriff. I was sharpening it earlier for…"

"For what?"

"Chopping wood." The sheriff raised the palm of his hand and set on the heel of his pistol.

"Well if it's only for chopping wood, would you mind terribly to set it over there in the corner?"

"W-why?"

"Because I asked you nicely. It would put me at ease. Set the axe down and have a seat." Mr. Lincoln hesitated and looked to Mr. Booth who nodded to the affirmative. Mr. Lincoln crossed the room to the far corner. He set the axe where the sheriff said before returning and plunking down in the chair where he was before. The sheriff stretched his arms wide and put them in his lap.

"Now, then." The sheriff paused before pulling the pistol from its leather holster and laying it across his leg. It wasn't pointed at anyone. It wasn't put away either. "I came out on a routine visit to ask some questions, but something isn't right here."

"What are you saying?" Mrs. Booth asked.

"Something's going on that you're not telling me. Now, I've got a spooked preacher outside who's acting nuttier than squirrel turds and screaming about the devil, a doctor who's sweating more than a ditch digger, a man with an axe in the house after dark, and a girl who's as pale as a sheet who doesn't blink." Annabelle gasped.

"What do you mean she doesn't blink?" her mother asked.

"I've been watching her the whole time, Mrs. Booth. Annabelle hasn't blinked since I stepped in. The blacks of her eyes didn't shrink and grow when I stretched and raised my arm between her face and the light from the lamp. Now I'm not stupid, so why doesn't everyone just cut it with the horseshit and tell me what's going on. If you're on the right side of the law and I can help you then I will."

"We're just concerned for Annabelle' health. That's all."

"I think you're telling the truth, Mr. Booth. What would you like to tell me, doctor?" By this point, the doctor's hands were shaking so much he dropped his glasses. He appeared to be weeping. "Doctor? You all right?" The two deputies grasped their guns around the hammer and trigger but didn't draw them. The sheriff raised a hand to ease them back but took the same grip on his own revolver. "Doc? If you've got something to tell me, you need to tell me now."

"I'm sorry," the doctor sobbed, looking to Mr. Booth. "I don't know what to do."

"Doc?" The sheriff asked again.

"It's Annabelle. She doesn't have a…a pulse. The child doesn't have a pulse." The sheriff looked confused.

"What do you mean she ain't got a pulse. Of course, she does."

Annabelle flinched as the sheriff pressed his fingers into her neck. When that failed, he placed the back of his hand against her chest but found no heartbeat. He almost fell out of his chair to back away from Annabelle. The pistol was in both hands and pointing at the floor between himself and Annabelle. "What the devil is going on here?"

"Calm down, sheriff. That's what we've been trying to tell you," Mr. Booth said, getting up from his seat. The gun moved in John Booth's direction. Annabelle stepped in front of it.

"Annabelle, get behind me right now," her father ordered. She swiftly obeyed.

"Everybody, calm down." Mrs. Booth said. "Put your damn guns down! You're all getting worked up over nothing. Annabelle is sick and we're trying to get her well!"

"Mrs. Booth, there's something very wrong with your daughter, and I'm not sure the doctor here can fix whatever that is," the sheriff said. "Now I want everyone to sit down."

"What are you going to do, Sheriff?" James Lincoln asked.

"Whatever bit Annabelle in the livery stable has infected her. I think it's in everyone's best interests if

Annabelle comes with the deputies and me to the jail in Pikeville until we can figure out what's wrong with her." Annabelle looked at her parents.

"Papa, I don't wanna go." she said.

"Don't worry, Annabelle," Father said, trying to calm her. "You're not going anywhere. I'll be damned if anyone is going to take you anywhere, let alone to a damn jail."

"She doesn't have a pulse," the sheriff said again. "That girl is the walking dead, and I'd be a fool to leave her here where she can't be watched." He held his hand out for her to take. "C'mon girl, it's time to go." Annabelle refused to budge. Her father stepped closer, almost between them

"Annabelle, go to your room and lock the door. Sheriff, you're not taking my daughter."

"Little girl, stay here. John, I got two murdered girls on my hands, and Annabelle might be the only lead to finding the one that attacked her and killed the others."

"Annabelle!" Father yelled. "Go to your room!" The sheriff raised his pistol and leveled it at the hip to point at Mr. Booth.

"I know what she means to you, but I can't have you obstructing justice." In her mind's eye, Annabelle pictured the axe in the corner. She thought about walking over there and picking it up, hiding it behind her and returning to where she was standing. Just as fast as she could imagine it, she found herself grasping the hardwood handle with the axehead resting between her shoulder blades. The sheriff took another half step towards her, his hand attempting to grab her. She easily stepped out of reach.

"I'm not going anywhere," she told him. "And if anyone puts a hand on me or my daddy, you're not going to get it back."

"Annabelle, go to bed," her father said as he snatched the axe from her hand. She walked to her room, looking back at papa once before shutting the door behind her. He was afraid. Afraid of the sheriff, and afraid of her.

CHAPTER EIGHT

When sunrise arrived, Annabelle was soundly asleep in her room. As terrible as things had been and despite all the changes she'd gone through, she fell asleep comforted that Papa would do everything in his power for the family and distillery. The room was pitch black until the door opened. Annabelle recoiled from the light by pulling the covers over her head. Even under the sheets, the smells of a man fresh from the stables found her nose. The hands reached up under the end of the covers and found her foot. Even since she was little, he'd always tickled her feet to make her laugh.

"Hello, Papa." She giggled.

Something metal clamped about her leg. Alarmed, Annabelle threw the sheets aside in time to see that it wasn't her father, but one of the deputies that had attached one of the handcuffs to her ankle, and the other cuff was threaded through a thick rope.

"What are you doing? Get that off me! Papa! Help!"

"Now!" the man shouted. Another man she hadn't noticed by the far wall grasped two fistfuls of the canvas and yanked them away to flood the room in sunlight. Annabelle shrieked and pulled the covers tighter before the man yelled again. "Now, Earl!"

The air filled with the sound of the cracking of a whip and the whinny of horses. Before she could react, the slack in the rope attached to Annabelle's ankle went taught, yanking her from beneath the covers and into the sunlight. Off the bed and through the door she flew, dragged by a pair of workhorses. Everything moved too fast. She flailed this way and that to get hold of the door jam or wall, couldn't get a handle on anything stationary. Her world exploded into blinding light and flames as her skin began to scorch. Annabelle screamed in agony as she was pulled from her room to the next. All the windows and doors had been opened, leaving no place in the home for shadows to hide.

In the flash of the moment, she caught a glimpse of her parents and Mr. Lincoln being held in the living room with guns upon them, helpless to act. Tables and chairs fell away as she became a battering ram through the house. Annabelle's skin blackened and smoked. She wailed from the pain as she was pulled helplessly along. Between the rope dragging and being burned alive, Annabelle couldn't grab the cuff about her ankle to break it free. Through another doorway and into the large distilling room she slid, the skin on her face and hands beginning to catch fire. Once she was in the middle of the next room, Earl Smith, a large deputy who was almost as big as Mr. Lincoln used an axe to sever the rope from her leg. She skidded to a stop next to the only thing resembling cover to get away from the shining force burning her alive.

Through squinted eyes a lone barrel sat upright in the middle of the room, inviting her into its shadow. But even in this moment of absolute torture, when her skin was peeling off in gruesome chunks, she saw the barrel for the trap that it was. She hesitated before the hulking deputy closed the distance between them and swung his axe again

137

at her head. The blunt blade side of the instrument found the crown, spraying blood across her, the ground and the far wall. She went down. The blow wasn't enough to kill her, but the added injury pushed her close to the quickly approaching edge of the abyss.

"Get in the barrel, you!" he shouted at her, kicking her closer with his boot "Get in there!"

The sun continued cooking her, flames leaping from her fingertips. And a long pathetic wail of pain pushed past her lips. More footsteps approached from behind. They were almost upon her, and Annabelle could hear the inhalation of the man's lungs as he raised his axe behind her. His heartbeat as fast as that of a rabbit.

When the axe fell, she moved the one arm she'd propped herself upon and went flat to dodge the swing. Next to her, another barrel beckoned. With the remaining strength she had left, she grasped the barrel by the top and bottom, the fire from her hands already setting it alight and flung it blindly to keep them away.

The vessel struck one of the two vertical support posts of the tall ceiling room, shattering, sending an entire barrel of high proof alcohol all over the room. And with the fire from her own hands igniting it, the room, and the people in it exploded like a firebomb. Blossoms ten feet wide flared in every direction. Screams not her own filled the air.

She watched helplessly as her parents and the men who'd followed along at gunpoint cried and flailed to get the burning clothes from their bodies. Deputy Earl Smith struck her with his boot a second time. His fist clenched her nightshirt and slung her like a doll into the same post as the barrel. The combined stress became enough to break it. In her mind, feral instincts pushed the human parts of her deep down to obey a solitary thought.

Slaughter.

Annabelle's attack caught Earl Smith by surprise as she flew across the room like a shot, her hands catching him by the face. Her palms to his temples, she dug her thumbs deep into his eyes, the nails piercing the orbs like old grapes. The sun at her back continued to scald away every remnant of Annabelle Booth's humanity. It left a wild thing behind to blind a man.

Her parents, Mr. Lincoln, and the distillery they'd built burned around them. The more wooden barrels of high proof alcohol it found, the bigger the inferno. The more the deputy's hands pummeled and thrashed her, the more her thumbs sank further inside his face. But it wasn't enough to just drive the digits deep. She pushed downward until the webbing between her thumbs and index fingers found the outsides of his eye sockets and could go no further. Her grip obstructed, she began to yank the embedded thumbs away from one another. The separation of the sections of the man's skull sounded like the muffled breaking of wood inside his head. He jerked one last time and went limp before Annabelle's hands pulled the two halves of the skull free of the body in motion that created a long, wet, "squuuikkk."

An ominous crack filled the air overhead. Looking over her shoulder, the main support post for the room failed at last. Heavy timber fell at awkward angles, smashing the floor around her. Gathering flames forced her to move from the corner just as the support beam collapsed to take the floor out from under her. Blinded by the fire, Annabelle couldn't find a hand or foothold and fell into the rickhouse storage room beneath. Above her, more of the ceiling gave way and the fire spread faster under the open winds surrounding the distillery. The charred bodies of her family toppled to land in a pile next to what was left of the eyeless deputy. Falling debris smashed more barrels, spraying their flammable contents. The fire became as large as a dragon her father had once described in a bedtime story. No knight would save her from this beast of flame. The fire climbed and spread faster than the eye could follow, eating its way up the walls, and into the other ricks of aging whiskey. Given another minute, the whole building would be engulfed. To leave the building now and run out into the sunlight was certain death.

Annabelle held her hands up to see the charred flesh. The cooked skin peeling back at awkward angles to reveal the pink and aching muscle tissue beneath. A noise not unlike a cough in a quiet room burst from a barrel on the far side of the room. More alcohol igniting. The rest of the building began to collapse down on top of her.

Along the back wall, away from the bodies and barrels, a larger barrel glistened with a clear liquid. She leaped over fallen debris to stick her hand in it. Unlike the other barrels, this one was an ordinary water barrel. Fire belched from one barrel to the next, lighting everything ablaze. Above, more supports groaned and began to fall, exerting so much force that chunks of masonry tumbled in on top of her. The whole thing was coming down. She picked up the lid lying next to the barrel and stole one final glance back at the nearly unrecognizable human remains before climbing into the barrel. Water spilled out around the lip. Annabelle took one final breath and pulled the lid into place.

1994:

"And that's the last thing I remember," Annabelle said, pulling her knees to her chest and wrapping her arms around them.

"That's...that's so sad. I can't believe they tried to kill you," Miles said in disbelief.

"They were frightened of me. They didn't understand, and they tried to protect themselves. I wish none of it had happened."

"What do you think happened to the vampire that attacked you in the barn?" Annabelle's face lit up with shock

"I have no idea. Where do you think he would go?" she asked.

"Don't ask me," Miles said. "Until I met you, I thought vampires were just in books and movies."

"What are movies?" she asked. The question threw him for a loop.

"Holy shit, you are from 1890," Miles said with his hands on his hips. "It's like, um, it's like seeing a play only it's all done with moving pictures."

"I've never seen pictures move."

"Well, they do. I can show one if you want." Annabelle paused, twiddling her fingers

"Miles? Why aren't you afraid of me?"

"What makes you think I'm not afraid of you?"

"I can hear your heart. It's at an easy rhythm."

"If you wanted to kill me you wouldn't have bothered to leave me on the road the other day. I could have bled to death down here. It would've taken less effort to do nothing. "

"And you're curious," she added.

"Of course, I'm curious. Who wouldn't be? As far as the world knows, you're not supposed to exist."

"But I do," she said. "Here I am. Now what? What do I do?"

"Anything you want, I guess," Miles said. "Wish I could."

"If you had the means, what would you do?"

"I'd buy a car. A carriage," he said. "Horseless carriage. We call them cars."

"Why that?"

"I could go anywhere I wanted whenever I wanted."

"You want your freedom." She smiled. "What anyone wants. And if you bought your carriage, and could go anywhere, what then? Would you still come and talk to me?"

"Is that what you want?" he asked.

"It is. It's what I always wanted."

"One thing that's better now than when you were, um…alive. Girls can go to any university they want."

"Is that true?"

"Yeah, of course, it's true. Although most classes are during the day."

"But still…" She nodded. "I propose that you and I make a trade, Miles Burkich."

"What kind of trade?"

"I'll give you my mother's jewelry to help pay for your horseless carriage, and in exchange, you'll help me acclimate to your world so that I can find my own freedom. Do you find that arrangement to be agreeable?"

"I do."

"Then let's shake on it." Without hesitating, she spat on her right hand and shook his.

"Then it's done. What do you think you'll want to do first? "Miles asked her.

"I'm not sure, so much time has passed, and there's so much I don't know. I didn't know about movies or cars until you told me. The southern states didn't try and secede from the union again, did they?"

"No." He grinned. "But we did put a man on the moon." Annabelle looked high over her shoulder to look at the moon.

"You mean you figured out a way for a man to fly? And then he flew high enough to land on the moon?"

"That's right."

"And I might've lived long enough to see it happen. I'd have been a little old lady. Did you see it happen?"

"No, I wasn't born yet. But I've seen the footage."

"Footage? What's that? Is that like the moving picture movies?"

"Exactly like that. You're a fast learner."

"I always did well with my lessons when I was in school. Miles? Could I ask you for a favor?"

"That depends on how big the favor is."

"Nothing too big, I don't think. Do you think you could find me some new clothes to wear? I hate to ask you for something, but my nightgown has become a pile of rags."

"I think I may have some older clothes that will fit you until we can find something your size."

"I'd appreciate it. The nights get cold around here."

"Are you sleeping here in the ruins?"

"I did last night, but now that you know where I am, I don't feel safe sleeping here."

"You don't trust me?"

"The last day I spent in the sun involved my own neighbors trying to kill me. It may take a while or even forever. I like you, Miles. I may learn to trust you in time, but for now, I have to look out for myself."

"I can see that." He glanced at his watch. "It's 4:04. We've been talking all night. Let me run home and get you some things. I've got some clothes and a sleeping bag you can use. That should keep you warm."

"I'd like that. Please hurry. When the sun gets closer, I'll have to leave."

"If I hurry, I can be back in about twenty minutes."

"I'll be right here." Miles left the ruins. He jogged home thinking; *I must be out of my mind. Talking to vampires.* He crossed the road and managed to sneak into the house easily enough. It took some next level tiptoeing to get past Gary's bedroom and into the basement without rousing him, but he managed. Once there, he rummaged through stacks of clothes to find something that would fit her. To his delight, he found the most vital component of a wardrobe first; shoes. Years ago, Dennis once left his pair of candy apple red Doc Martin's under his bed after he'd stayed over one night five years ago.

He said his feet were growing too fast and that they pinched his toes too much to wear them anymore. They looked to be just about the right size. After that, he found a pair of black stockings without too many holes and runs in them, a few black t-shirts, a pair of army camouflage cutoffs with a belt to cinch the waist, and lastly, a crimson hoodie with his high school's name on it.

With the obstacle of finding clothes out of the way, he pulled out the green army surplus sleeping bag from under his bed and brushed the dust bunnies from it. On the far wall, he selected a half dozen, fifty-gallon trash bags, a full roll of silver duct tape, and a single edge razor blade. That was everything. He stuffed everything but the sleeping bag into an old backpack and started back. It was closing in on 4:30 and Gary would be up before long. He'd have to hurry. The last thing Miles needed was a lecture for being out of the house when he was supposed to be recuperating. Miles jogged back to the ruins but didn't find Annabelle where he'd left her.

"Over here."

Miles shone the light behind and was startled to find her standing within an arm's distance. Where she'd been shorter before, she was now the same height. He looked down to see how'd she'd grown; she hadn't. She was floating, her toes pointing down with six inches of air between her and the grass. Startled, he took a step back at the unnatural gesture.

"Jesus! You can float too?"

"Oh! I'm sorry. I didn't mean to, I was thinking about birds flying," She giggled. "And it just happened."

"Well, could you not do it right now? You're weirding me out. Here, I brought you some clothes and a sleeping bag."

Annabelle sank and landed on her feet while laid out the items on the retaining wall for her to see.

"Here are some clothes I think might do you for now. Until I know what fits, you'll have to wait to get something the right size." Annabelle's eyes bulged at the sight of the boots as they emerged.

"These are the greatest boots I've ever seen! Maroon is my favorite color." She grinned with innocence and Miles forgot for a minute that she'd once gouged a grown man's eyes out.

"Then you're going to love this," he said, pulling the hoodie from the backpack. The folds of crimson unfolded for Annabelle like a thing from a dream.

"It's...so beautiful." She took it with both hands and buried her face in it, rubbing back and forth across her cheeks. "It's so soft. Pikeville High? What does that mean?"

"Pikeville High, it's the local school. All the other students from White Wreath and the surrounding area go to Pikeville High School."

"Boys and girls?"

"Yeah, of course."

"I love it. I always wanted to attend school. College, I mean. And with boys, like Kentucky University in Lexington? How exciting."

"If you like it that much, it's yours."

"You mean it? Thank you. I want to put it on right now."

"Sure. Try it all on." He turned his back and she began putting the clothes on.

"Well, how do I look?" Miles turned around to find a different girl standing before him. With the oversized sweatshirt, matching boots and black hosiery connecting the two, she looked as modern as any girl from White Wreath.

"Well?"

"I'd say you're the best-dressed vampire I've ever met," Miles said.

"Do you think I could pass as a normal person?"

"I'd stop it with the floating bit or people might suspect something." Annabelle looked down to see that her toes weren't touching again, which she immediately corrected.

"Sorry."

"It's okay. Oh, I almost forgot." Miles knelt down and showed Annabelle the black trash bags and tape, demonstrating how to use the razor to slit the bags longways to create a sun-proof liner to wrap around the sleeping bag. "I can bring you extra material if you need it. But that should keep the rain away so that you and your clothes don't wet. If you double the layers, it might block daylight altogether."

"Thank you very much."

"It's fine." He blinked twice before rubbing his eyes.

"What's the matter?"

"I'm just tired and I need to get home before Gary wakes up."

"Who's Gary?"

"He's my dad, well, actually, he's my adopted dad. I never knew who my real parents were, but Gary adopted me and he's the only family I have."

"Where are your real parents?"

"I don't know. They gave me up because they didn't want me, but Gary did."

"Is he good to you?"

"Yeah. He's hard on me sometimes, but it's because he wants me to be strong."

"Then it means he cares." She let a small grin slip. Annabelle handed him a diamond ring and some gold necklaces, emerald earrings, too. "Here, take this with you before you go."

"Jesus, where did you get all this?" he asked, staring at the large diamond glinting in the moonlight on his palm.

"It was my mother's wedding ring," she said, her eyes far away and sad. "I found all her jewelry in the ruins. Papa used a metal box hidden inside a bourbon barrel as a safe. It was all buried in the fire and I dug it out of the mess. It was supposed to be mine when I grew up. But I guess I'll never grow up, will I?" She held out her hands and looked at them, the same size they'd been a hundred years ago. Miles felt for her but didn't know what to say.

"I'll come back tonight," he said. "How will I find you next time?"

"I'll be around. But if you want, we can meet here at sundown," she said, beginning to levitate off the ground a few inches.

"You're going to keep doing the floating thing, huh?"

"I can't help it."

"So, meet you here after sundown tomorrow? See you then." Miles was about to turn away when he turned the fistful of jewelry over in his hands eyeing the ashy diamonds and jewels. As desperately as he wanted the extra funds to acquire a car, it didn't seem right to take the few possessions she had left from her family. "You know what? Keep your jewelry." He pushed the handful back upon her so that she'd have to take them to keep from dropping them. "You might need them in the future for something important."

"And you'll still help me?" she asked, looking at the jewelry. "But your freedom...."

"I said I'd help you. I'll find my freedom and help you find yours."

CHAPTER NINE

Gary was awake by the time Miles got back to the house. Fortunately for him, the paper had already been delivered and he plucked it from the ground as he walked up to the house. Boom. Instant alibi for being out of the house. The front door opened noisily as he expected, and he played it straight to walk into the kitchen and have a seat at the dinner table.

"What are you doing up?" Gary asked.

"I woke up early for some reason." Miles lied. "I thought I'd get the paper."

Gary finished his breakfast as Miles read through the thin, local paper, The Mountaintop Observer. There was however a bumper crop of listings for yard sales and garage sales like Dennis had said before. Most of the notices read about the same, baby clothes, bikes, antiques, limited edition NASCAR memorabilia, etc. There was one that caught his eye. maybe it was the excessive use of exclamation points.

EVERYTHING MUST GO!!!! ESTATE-GARAGE-
YARD SALE!!!!!

I DON'T HAVE TIME TO BARGAIN!!!!!!!!

Jewelry, dishes, linens, tools, furniture, beds, dressers, art, silverware, rugs, clocks, tons of clothes, old toys, baseball cards, records, knick-knacks, coins, push and riding lawn mowers, chairs and tables!!!!! Everything must go!!!!! Show up with cash in hand and leave with a carload!!! Bring a trailer!!!! I'm not looking to get rich; I just need to empty the whole house by the end of the week!!! No reasonable offers will be refused!!! My loss is your gain! Show up early and get a jump on the rest of the crowd!!! Cheap cheap cheap!!!!!! 442 Duell Drive, White Wreath, KY.

Miles looked at the date. *Holy shit, that starts today...better call Dennis.* His interest must've been pronounced enough for Gary to notice.

"You see something? He asked.

"Yeah, big estate sale over on Duell Drive. I thought I might be able to get some back to school clothes shopping in."

"Duell Drive? There's nothing but old people living on Duell Drive. You're not going find anything your speed over there. It's going to be a bunch of disco-hand-me-downs and Lawrence Welk albums."

"Now I <u>know</u> I'm going."

"Do you still have the money I gave you for school clothes?"

"Yes." He pointed over his shoulder to where a strong magnet had pinned the cash to the face of the fridge next to an intentionally misspelled note scrawled in childish letters reading "SKOOL CLOTHS."

"Skool Cloths?" he said, reading it aloud. "You're a real smartass sometimes."

"It beats being a dumb ass."

"Ok, smartass. Don't go spending all your school clothes money on Duell Drive. I need to make a supply run up in Lexington soon. I'll take you to the mall. You can get new jeans and some more black shirts. Since you've got a driver's license, I'll let you do some driving on the way."

"Sounds good." Miles replied. Gary looked up at the clock on the wall. And almost jumped from his chair.

"Sonofabitch, look at the time. Here I am gabbing when I should be getting my ass out the door. You staying home today?"

"Yeah. I haven't been sleeping right."

"After what you've been through, I can understand that."

"I thought I'd have Dennis take me to the yard sale just to see if there's anything and then come home."

"All right then, take it easy. How's the wound on your shoulder coming along?" Miles pulled his shirt down to reveal the perfect pink skin beneath. "Well, I'll be dipped. Doesn't look like anything happened at all."

"Weird, huh?"

"Hell, I've had bigger scars from papercuts. I don't understand it, but it beats the alternative, I guess. Tell you what kiddo, we'll talk later, but right now I got to get to work.' He patted his pockets for wallet and keys before making a beeline for the door. "You be good!" He yelled before pulling the door flush behind him.

One phone call, a shower and 40 minutes later, the two friends pulled up in front of the house having the sale. The

153

regular roving caravan of "yard sailors" as Pearl called them was already on the scene picking through boxes and trying to lowball the middle-aged man sitting behind a folding table. He sat with his legs crossed, paper folded across his lap. Anytime someone asked for a lower price on an item, he'd reply "I will, if you'll give me cash right now," to which most found agreeable and fished money from pockets before he changed his mind or someone else saw the item. Compared to the rest of the crowd there, Miles and Dennis looked like aliens and the others regarded them as such. Dressed from head to toe in black, spiked collars, band shirts, spiked leather jackets, and calf-high boots, they might as well have been from another planet. Some would make eye contact for a moment but then look away. Others glared until one or both glared back. The two aliens gravitated towards a sagging cardboard box on a table with vinyl records poking out the top. Per their own private ritual, Miles began thumbing through the 33's while Dennis scooped up the 45's, each reading off the artists that the other might want.

"What you got?" Miles asked first. Dennis' face contorted with skepticism as he shuffled through the stack.

"Lessee, I got—Mama's and the Papa's, Elvis Presley, Elvis, Elvis, *More* Elvis, even more Elvis, Otis Redding, aaaaand 'It's Beginning to look a lot like Christmas' by Bing Crosby. What you got?"

"I got Captain and Tennille, Elvis, Hawaiian Elvis, Big Band Favorites, Best of Frank Sinatra, The Beach Boys,"

"Which Beach Boys?"

"Pet Sounds."

"That's mine," Dennis said, snatching the record from his hand. "Anything else in there worth a damn?"

"No, just some Lawrence Welk shit and four copies of 'Whipped Cream and Other Delights' by Herb Alpert and the Tijuana Brass. At least you got one out of the stack, and it isn't warped."

"It'll do." Dennis nodded. "I wasn't holding my breath for Nitzer Ebb."

"Come on, let's see what's on the other tables."

Around the other people, they walked, searching and rummaging. In the end, the rest of the sale was a complete bust. They walked over to the folding table and the middle-aged fellow with a Chicago Cubs baseball hat man gave a big smile.

"You two look like you know where the fun is!" he said a little too loud. "Is that a Nine Inch Nails shirt you're wearing?" Miles looked down to realize he, in fact, was wearing a shirt with the band logo on it.

"Uh, yeah. Trent Reznor is the best."

"Yeah, he's got crazy talent. I saw him in 1991 when he was on the first Lollapalooza tour. That was a hell of a show. I'm from Chicago by the way." He pointed to his baseball cap.

"What are you doing here in White Wreath?" Dennis asked

"Oh, I grew up in this house. I moved to Chicago after college and never left. The only reason I'm here is my dad passed last week, and I'm trying to settle things here, so I can sell the house and get back home."

"Sorry for your loss," Miles said, Dennis nodding in agreement.

"Well, that's awfully nice of you." He let out a bigger smile. "You know, that's one thing I miss about this place is everybody's so nice all the time. You want that Beach Boys record?"

"Yes, please."

"That'll be a quarter. Wait, you know what? Just take it. I've already made a killing this morning. That record was my dad's. I've already taken out what I wanted, but I never cared too much for the Beach Boys. If you'll give it a good home, you can have it for free."

"It's a deal!" Dennis said, taking a step away. "Come on, Miles, let's get going. Nice to meet you, Mister!"

"Nothing for you, Trent Reznor?" the man asked Miles.

"I'm good," Miles said, turning away.

"Nothing?"

"Not unless you've got an extra car in a box somewhere," Miles said to which the man tilted his head slightly to the left and made a peculiar face. "What? What did I say?"

"Are you seriously looking for a car?" The man asked.

"I am."

"You got any money for a car?" he asked.

"Yeah, I've got some money for a car." Dennis was still backpedaling to imply they should leave when Miles told him he'd meet him at the car.

"Meet me around back." Said the man. "I might have something you'd be interested in." Detached from the house at the end of the driveway, a white garage sat alone, twenty feet off the back porch. Newspaper had been taped over the windows of the automatic garage door. The man emerged from the back door of the house, the jingle jangle of keys in his right hand. "Wait here," he said as he walked past Miles. "Give me just as second to get the door open."

Miles hung back as the side door lock popped and he vanished inside. Muffled sounds of intermittent footsteps only made him more anxious before the abrupt hum of machinery began to raise the popping and groaning door. Curiosity moved him closer as the creaking door climbed inch over inch up the track. The first thing that came into view was a set of tires too far apart to be a compact car. After that, a chrome bumper wider than his bedframe winked back from out of the shadows. Higher it moved, revealing bulbous headlights and a flawless black paint job that reflected every ounce of light that found its beautiful shape. The shape of the machine was curvier and more seductive than any of the girls he'd seen and the symbol in the middle of the hood left no mistake about what it was.

They don't make visions like these anymore.

When the whole car was in view, the starter turned over easy, and the engine roared to life. It was so big it took up the entire garage.

"What do you think?" the man said, getting out. "It's a monster, isn't it? 1976 Cadillac Brougham. Dad bought it new but rarely drove it. He said he didn't want to put any undo miles on it. He only let me drive it once, and he rode in the car with me while I did. He washed and waxed it when he took it out on the weekend but drove his pickup the rest of the time. The car runs fine. Everything works. It doesn't leak oil, there's no rust on the frame, and it's been garaged its whole life. You could drive this car to California tomorrow with no problems. There's a full-sized spare in the trunk, and the trunk itself is big enough to hold four of your friends if you wanted to sneak them into a drive-in movie. Dad even kept a heater plugged in here, so it never got too cold. Well? What do you think?"

Miles approached the car and ran his fingers across the vibrating polished paint. It was a black mirror, a breathing shadow.

"It's...it's beautiful."

"Sure is! Well, go on and have a seat. See what you think."

Miles slipped inside and smelled the vintage leather. Everything gleamed like the day it was made. Somebody loved this car. The engine hummed a lullaby to Miles as he ran his hands over the steering wheel. A small black silhouette of a fox hung from the keyring with the name Mary etched into the body. When he tapped the gas pedal, the whole thing shifted from the engine's torque. "Well?"

"You're selling it?" Miles managed to say.

"I hate to, but I live in the city and there's nowhere I can put it. I got a kid in college, so if I can get some decent money out of it I'd rather put it towards that. Do you like it enough to want to buy it?"

"I can give you four thousand dollars in cash today," Miles said without hesitation.

"Really?" The man looked surprised. "You got four thousand?"

"Cash." Miles repeated

"Well, that's a bit less than what I was thinking."

"But you want to settle the estate as fast as possible, so you can get home," Miles parroted hims words.

"Right but the market value is probably-"

"I would love this car as your dad loved it. It's beautiful." Miles said.

The man paused to sigh and look at the ground. Miles gripped the wheel of the car in hopes that it would be enough to keep the black beauty from slipping through his grasp. He wanted something significant to show for the money he'd earned from the countless hours of hauling trash, clipping weeds and filling potholes. Miles' eyes burned holes through the man's head trying to control his mind. *Say yes. Say yes. Don't think about it. Just take the money. This is what I want. This is what I want. This is what I want. Please God, say yes.* The man stomped his foot.

"You know what? If you love it and you can get me the full four thousand today, then it's yours."

"Yes!" Miles exclaimed with glee before shutting the car off and handing the keys back and shaking the man's hand. "I'll take it." Miles walked back to Dennis, waiting by his car.

"What took you so long, and why do you look so happy?" Dennis asked.

"I was talking to the guy running the yard sale. Can you run me on a few errands? I need to go by the house and over to the Imperial."

"Sure man, but what's up with that crazy smile?"

"It's good news. I'll tell you on the way, drive."

"Sure thing," Dennis said, putting the car into gear. "I have some good news myself."

"What's that?"

"Christian's been calling me non-stop at the house."

"Aww, that's cute. Everyone deserves to have a stalker."

"No, nothing like that. He calls, and we talk on the phone for hours at a time."

"That's super cool. So, you're going to date?"

"Looks like it. Anyway, what's going on with you? What did you and the guy at the yard sale talk about that's got you so amped? You're practically bouncing in your seat."

The two traveled back to the Burkich house where Miles collected the stash of money that represented years of hard work. From there, it was onto the Imperial truck stop.

Dennis wandered off towards the snack aisle while Miles went looking for Gary. He found him in his usual place, huddled over an invoice strewn desk and telling somebody on the phone to pay their overdue bill.

To his dismay, he found JoJo had situated in the other chair. He looked even more emaciated than the day his crew was trying to heist Coronas. Whatever he was taking on the regular sure as hell wasn't vitamin supplements. His 'wifebeater' shirt was practically hanging off his bones. Just straight up 'speed-freak-junkie thin.' Miles got an uneasy feeling when his adopted cousin began to eyeball the stacks of cash in his hands.

"Yo, let me borrow some of that money," he said, making a half-sincere attempt to grab the stack. Without unclamping his hands, Miles pushed the rolling chair back with his boot, causing JoJo to whack his elbow on a filing cabinet. This made him jump from the chair to stand over Miles. To his relief, Gary finished his call at the same time, and he turned to see Miles standing there.

"What are you doing here?" he asked Miles. "JoJo quit standing over him and have a seat." JoJo continued to invade his personal space, staring him down. Miles looked into his eyes; the irises didn't look right. The brain was making the eyes move, but there was nothing behind them. He was probably on pills again, his breath reeked of the low-end weed he and his boys always smoked. "JoJo, sit your ass down. Miles? What do you want? I've got tons of shit I need to do." Miles stepped past him and laid the cash in front of Gary on his desk.

"What's all this for, Mr. Moneybags? How much is this?"

"More than four grand. Four thousand for the cost of a car plus extra for tax and tags. I found a car I want, and the owner isn't going to be in town long."

"You want to buy a car? Whose car do you want to buy?"

"An old man on Duell Drive passed away and his son is in town to settle things. Look, he's not going to hold that car long and I told him I could get a bank check and sign it over today. Hey," He leaned close to Gary to make eye contact. "I wouldn't bother you at work if it wasn't mega important. Here's the guy's number." Miles forced a piece of paper into his hand

"Well, shit. If it's mega' important, I guess it can't wait." He stroked his mustache as he thought aloud. "Old man on Duell drive...old man on Duell drive."

"Gary, we have to go now! I need you to deposit my money and get a bank check for the car and cover the tax and tags!"

"All right, all right, hold your horses, let's go get you a car." Gary pushed himself out of the chair and scooped up the money looking like he didn't know what to do with it before opening the burnt old grey safe, throwing the cash inside and slamming it shut again.

"You're buying him a car?" JoJo whined.

"No," Miles glared back at him. "I'm buying *me* a car."

"But what about me, Uncle Gary?" he whined again. "Don't I get something?"

"That's right," Gary said. Without skipping a beat, opened his wallet and pull out two fifty-dollar bills and shoved the money in JoJo's hand. "See that your mother gets groceries out of that." The motion of the hand to the wallet was automatic like Gary wasn't even thinking about it. Miles's cheeks flushed with agitation. Not a dime of that cash was going to reach a grocery store. The only thing it was going find was fresh green smoke or pills. He wanted to say something, but again he told himself to let it go. If he started an argument now it would take longer to get the car and that was not fucking happening, not today. Miles hurried out front and explained to Dennis that Gary was going to take him to the bank.

"I'll call you as soon as everything is finished," Miles told him. Just then, JoJo walked out the front door. waving the cash in the air to his crew of goons in the lowered Ford Explorer. The knuckleheads hooted and cheered. Seeing the two standing there, JoJo spit on the ground between Dennis and Miles. "Later, homersessuals!" he said, giving them the middle finger. Miles said nothing, but Dennis was already chambering a retort and letting it fly.

"It's homo-SEXUAL, Joseph. And I'd be offended if I thought you could spell it."

"Whatever, fags," he said, climbing into his wagon of idiots.

"Ignore him." Miles tried to console Dennis.

"It's ok, it's not your fault he's got dogshit for a soul. How is it that Gary is as awesome as he is, but JoJo is....whatever that is?"

"Gary isn't a cracker junkie."

"Miles!" Gary stuck his head out the door. "What are you doing? You want to go to the bank or not?"

"Yeah, I'm coming."

"You better pick me up and take me for a ride," Dennis said.

"You'll be the first, man. I promise. Talk to you later." Gary drove him downtown and had the bank manager print him a check for four grand like it was no big deal. It made sense considering the amount of money that Gary moved through the Imperial. When the manager asked Gary which of his personal accounts he wanted the funds taken from, Gary just looked at his shoes.

"I don't care, just pick one of the checking accounts." The manager bypassed the young fellow at the teller window to handle the transaction personally. He moved like a fire was under his ass. The check printed quickly enough, and he walked around the counter to deliver it by hand.

"Will there be anything else, Mr. Burkich?"

"I'd appreciate it if you'd be kind enough to let me use your phone." The manager almost fell over himself to open the door to this office and give him access. Gary didn't talk about money much, and he never flaunted it. To see a man who likely knew exactly how much Gary Burkich was worth making a fool of himself was something in itself. Miles waited in the lobby as Gary called Mr. Fox about the car. Each minute he wasn't sitting behind the wheel of that beautiful machine seemed like agony having to wait. For some reason, a line from Shakespeare's Romeo and Juliet wouldn't go away: 'I have purchased the house of love but have yet to possess it.' He snatched a few free lollipops from atop the counter and put them inside his jacket pocket as the tellers glared at all six feet of black spiked leather and calf-high boots. The two men finally shook hands again, and they left. On the way out of the bank. Gary grumbled under his voice.

"Jesus, what a kiss ass. He's happy to lend me money, but I never see him buying gas from me. Remember this, Miles—always watch how people treat you when you don't have anything to offer them. They smiled to my face, but I imagine no one said a peep to you, am I right?"

"Right."

"Then again, it might have something to do with you dressing like a damn space vampire all the time. White Wreath is full of good people but havin' the younger generation running around wearing dog collars and spiked hair and wearing makeup to look like a gaggle of dead French whores makes the old people a little nervous."

"Oh, like your generation wasn't burning their draft cards, dropping LSD and having mud orgies at Grateful Dead concerts."

"Maybe so, but they never dressed like dead whores. It's punk rock. I get it. That's what people your age are into. Hell, I can't imagine what the future will be like when

165

you're my age. You mark my words, if things keep going like the way they are, kids will be a bunch of maniacs in twenty-five years. They'll be running around dressed up like cartoon characters trying to cornhole one another and fighting each other for internets!"

"That sounds a little extreme."

"I guess we'll have to wait and see." Gary smacked him on the leg with the back of his hand. "This is exciting, isn't it? Going to get your first car." Miles hadn't seen him this animated in forever.

"I'm psyched."

"You should be, kiddo. You never forget your first set of wheels. Tell you what. The guy who does my insurance has an office right next to the courthouse. As soon as we sign the car over, we'll stop and get your insurance. Tell you what, you've got a birthday coming up, you're not too old for birthday cake, are you?"

"Hell, no."

"Good. I don't think you ever get too old to have a birthday cake. Here's the courthouse. Look at that, there's your car." Miles peered across the street to see five thousand pounds of 'sex on wheels' slide into a parking spot. "Look at that," he said again. "You know I tried to buy that car from Harold Fox ten years ago, and he wouldn't sell it to me?"

"You did?"

"Sure did. I think I offered him twelve thousand and he wouldn't take it. Shit, Miles. Four thousand in cash? You stole that car." They parked and met with Mr. Fox before going in. He and Gary strolled slowly, shooting the breeze as the county clerks processed the paperwork. In a bigger town, it might've taken longer for the transaction to take place. With Mr. Fox having all the paperwork for the will and title ready and everybody in the building knowing each other, it didn't take twenty minutes to complete the deal. Gary paid the cost of the tax and tags. They might've gotten out faster if every other single woman in the place hadn't either flirted with Gary or stopped to remark how big Miles had grown.

In the end, Gary handed him the check, and Mr. Fox handed Miles the keys. The enameled Cadillac symbol on the keychain resembled a holy icon. Like meeting an undead girl who'd slept for a hundred years, it didn't feel real at all. His thoughts drifted away from him as he imagined her being alone and sleeping somewhere in a ditch or a cave. The images of her floating and her hair waving on invisible wind mesmerized him enough to lose track of the conversation in front of him.

"Miles," Gary said, leaning over to look him in the eyes. "Mr. Fox is talking to you."

"Huh?" he said, looked up at the man, confused. "What?"

"I said, I hope you'll take care of the car. It meant a lot to my father."

"It already means everything to me," Miles said, meaning every word.

Within five minutes, Miles was walking towards the car with had the keys, title, and insurance card in his hand. Gary fired up the Suburban and sped away. Across the street people on the sidewalk were already stopping to admire the car, cupping their hands next to their eyes and pressing their faces against the windows to get a better look. The vehicle looked ominous, like a slumbering beast ready to be awakened. Every car needs a name. What was it that Mr. Fox said when he first showed him the car?

"What do you think? It's a monster, Isn't it?"

"Monster. Yeah, that's it."

The last of the morning coolness evaporated as the sun got higher in the sky. The leather jacket got to be too stuffy. And as though he'd done it a thousand times, he peeled it off and threw it through the open driver's side window to have it land perfectly folded across the top of the front seat. The engine came alive and a passing child holding onto their parent's hand on the sidewalk changed their path to get away from the growl. Miles checked his mirrors and pulled away at a brisk pace. With a full tank of gas and nowhere to be, the steel beast offered to take him anywhere he desired. For the life of him, he couldn't have cared less as long as the air slipping through the open windows didn't stop blowing. His boot pressed the gas pedal to the floor and Monster lurched from a gallop to a sprint, carrying Miles away from his cares on a symphony of mechanical music.

CHAPTER TEN

Miles picked up Dennis, Sweeney, Lucifer and the triplets to go for a ride. With bigger seats than Pearls' Oldsmobile, everyone easily fit inside. All afternoon they drove along the backroads, talking about all the places they could go; parties in other counties, the myriad of stores along the college campuses of Lexington, concerts in other states. Of all the ones riding, Lucifer seemed to like the car the most and made a point during their numerous stops to work her way into the front seat to sit close to Miles. When the others were busy talking amongst themselves, she asked Miles when he thought he'd be taking her on a date. More than once she made suggestive comments about the less than puritanical activities that can happen in a large parked car at night when there's a guarantee of lack of parental supervision. He almost steered the car off the road, killing them all when she whispered into his ear that she wasn't wearing any panties.

Sunset arrived, and the others had places to be. Even though it was summer, most still had to meet curfews. Dennis had to be home in enough time for dinner but was given the added duty of bathing Mary because she'd had an absolute ball laying down in a mud puddle before rolling in a bed of pine needles.

Dusk found Miles guiding Monster in the Imperial with only fumes left in the gas tank. The numbers on the pump ticked for what seemed like forever as fuel refilled the huge tank. It cost a damn arm and a leg to top it off, but that wasn't anything he hadn't counted on. Once finished, he headed home. The car eased into the driveway as slick as you please. To his surprise, Gary had parked hadn't parked in his usual spot. He'd Pulled the Suburban into the side yard and turned it around to leave room for the new car. Nice. The windows rolled up and the doors locked before he went inside. The smell of dinner filled the air when he opened the front door. Fresh burgers.

"Hey, Kiddo!" Gary said from his chair as he watched his Jeopardy! show. "I grilled us some dinner. Yours is in the fridge."

"Thanks."

"Were you out showing off your car to your friends?"

"Yeah, they liked it."

"That Lucifer girl with half her head shaved must've liked it. She's called twice already asking for you."

"Lovely," Miles groaned. He prepped the burger and wolfed it down as he wanted to meet with Annabelle as soon as possible. He almost choked between mouthfuls when Gary cursed at the game show contestants.

"Oh God Damn, how do all three of you not know that? What is Nosferatu?!" When Miles opened the front door to go outside, Gary looked up from his chair.

"Are you going back out with your friends?" he asked.

"No, just going for a walk. I won't be gone long."

"You shouldn't be staying out all hours of the night with school starting soon and all. I don't want you too tired to study."

"When do I not get good grades?"

"Good point. Get some fresh air. I might be in bed when you get back, so don't forget to lock the door when you come back in."

Miles grabbed the flashlight and shut the door behind him. Outside, the cicadas were out in full force. Their raspy song grew and fell as he strolled off the front porch, over the road, and through the field. Miles watched the trees. The insects were so numerous that the trees themselves seemed to move without wind. He figured Annabelle would be waiting in the ruins. As he walked through the old dilapidated barn on the way, a familiar voice stopped him.

"Hello, Miles." He turned this way and that, the beam of the flashlight searching into all the corners of the wooden structure.

"Annabelle?"

"I'm here." She spoke again, her words coming from every direction at the same time. The light whipped about with no sign of the girl.

"I can't see you."

"Up here." He flipped the light skyward. Annabelle was directly overhead. She hung upside down from the ceiling like a child on playground equipment.

"Annabelle, this barn is ancient. I wouldn't hang from those old rafters if I were you."

"I'm not hanging from the rafters," she said. Miles looked closer and watched in amazement as she began to walk across the ceiling of the barn, her boots making the

171

planks creak with every step. She reached the edge of the roof where it met the top of the wall, took a big step to put one foot on the wall, and kept walking. She didn't seem concerned at all. A girl without gravity. Down the wall and to the ground Annabelle traveled, one foot in front of the other. She drew closer and he shone the light at the ground as not to hurt her eyes.

"How was your day?" she asked.

"I had the best day of my life."

"Really? What happened?"

"I got a car!"

"That's wonderful!" she said. "What's a car again?"

"Horseless carriage? Remember?"

"Oh, yes, of course. You found one?"

"I think it found me," Miles said.

"Will you show it to me?"

"Do you want to go for a ride?"

"Would you do that?"

"If you want me to. Do you want to go right now? We could take a ride up to Pikeville."

"You'll have to wait a moment," Annabelle said, looking towards the tree line. "I'd have to get my things."

"What for? We won't be gone long."

"I was just there, Miles. It takes two hours to travel each way. That's four hours. If we lose track of time, I don't want to be stuck in a place where I can't protect myself from the sun."

"Annabelle, it takes twenty minutes to get to Pikeville in a car. We could drive there, walk around for twenty minutes and be back in an hour."

"It moves that fast? Then I wanna do it, Miles. Let's go."

"All right then," He thought for a moment. "Have you…eaten?"

"I did," she said, sucking at her teeth. "Two foxes. I got a little fur in my teeth. Do you people still use toothpicks?"

"Yeah," he laughed. "I'll get you some. Wait, I told Gary I wasn't going out for long. I'll have to sneak the car out of the driveway."

"I don't want you to get in trouble."

"It'll be fine. Wait here. I'll be back in a few minutes." Miles ran back across the field, pulled Mr. McCreedy's gate all the way open and checked in each direction for cars. He unlocked the driver side door and slid inside. The car slipped into neutral and the downward slope of the driveway provided everything needed for him to roll the Caddy across the road, through the open gate and into the field beyond. Annabelle waited at the barn door until he called her over. The look on her face mirrored the one he'd had when the car was revealed to him.

"Miles, it's so beautiful." She ran both of her hands across the paint and chrome as if it might vanish any second. "It's the prettiest thing I've ever seen!"

"You said that about the boots I gave you."

"They are! I mean, boots are one thing, but this is something else. I don't know what words to use."

"That's the same way I felt when I saw it. I guess that means you appreciate nice things, Miss Booth. Come on, get in." He opened the passenger side door for her. She sat down and pulled her feet in. The door shut behind her and Miles walked around to the driver's side. When he closed his door, he sat and watched Annabelle as she ran her hands across the leather seat cushions and dashboard.

"This is so fancy." She giggled. "All this for a machine?"

"Now you know why I was so excited."

"Make it move, let's go somewhere."

"Let's do it." He turned the ignition and the car thrummed. Annabelle looked both shocked and overjoyed. He let off the brake and rolled across the grass, giving as little gas needed to keep it rolling. The last thing he wanted to do was rev the engine in front of the house. No one was coming from either direction on the road, so he pulled out. Once pointed away from the house the headlights clicked on and lit their path. Annabelle squirmed. She didn't stop moving to look around the car. Everything appeared to be enthralling.

"The roads are so smooth!" She exclaimed.

"Roll down the windows." He showed her how and when the glass slid out of the way Annabelle stuck her head out the window. Her hair whipped on the wind, and she pressed her face against the slipstream.

"It's a wonderful machine!" she said aloud before retaking her seat. Onward the traveled. When they got closer to town, more and more lights appeared. From front porches to streetlamps, more brilliance came and went.

"The night lights," she said. "How do they burn so bright?"

"Electricity. It's like man-made lightning we can control. It creates light, powers other machines, it runs our world and makes it easier."

"What happens if it goes out?"

"Then it goes out for a while, but people from the power company show up and make it work again."

"It's all so much to take in. I want to know all of it," she said, looking out the window at a billboard sitting in a field. "If I'm going to be living in this world then I need to know more about it. I need to know everything that's happened between 1890 and...what year is it?"

"It's 1994."

"Really 1994? Who's the president of the United States?"

"Bill Clinton."

"Where's he from?"

"Arkansas."

"Arkansas. That's something familiar."

"Who was president in your time?"

"Benjamin Harrison!" she said excitedly. "Wait. Shouldn't you know that?"

"I'm not the best history student."

"I see. How many states are there?"

"Fifty."

"Last I remember They were about to make a new state called Idaho."

"Idaho. That's way out west."

"How long would it take for your car to get there?"

"Depends on how much you want to drive during the day. I'd say you could get out there in two or three days." Annabelle swooned and collapsed in her comfy seat

"Wow. This is all too much. I'm so behind on what is going on. Is there a place where I could read about American history? Do you know where I can find a library?"

"There are libraries in almost every town."

"Can we go there now?"

"No. The library usually closes around five and six."

"If it closes before sundown, there's no way I can go in."

"I could go to the library and check out some history books for you."

"That's nice, but it's not the same. Being a vampire is less fun if you can't go into a library. How long do vampires live?"

"Vampires are immortal as far as I know. You'll live forever as long as you don't get caught out in sunlight or get staked in the heart."

"My parents didn't live to see fifty years," she said sadly as she continued staring out the window. "They were burned alive and buried in a ruined distillery."

"No, they're buried in the Booth family Mausoleum in the cemetery." Annabelle shot up from her seat.

"They're what?"

"They're buried in White Wreath Cemetery in the Booth Mausoleum."

"Take me there, I want to see it!"

"You don't want to go to Pikeville?"

"To hell with a bunch of Pikeville, I want to see my parents!"

"Okay, okay. Calm down. Cemetery it is. We're heading that way." Monster split the night like a black bullet. It didn't take long before Miles was parking the car in the vacant lot across the street from the tall iron gates. Annabelle leaped from the vehicle and ran across the street to stand at the edge of the high stone wall surrounding the cemetery.

"Miles! Come on! Hurry!" He picked up his pace and crossed the street, looking left and right.

"I'm coming, I'm coming." He looked both ways to make sure they were alone, but there wasn't another soul in sight. Miles took a running start, leaped, planted a foot on the wall and grasped the top of the masonry. With a grunt and a heave, he pushed himself up to sit upon the top. Once he landed, he looked back to the lip of the wall. "Ok, Come on."

"I'm waiting on you," she said from behind, causing him to jump in place.

"Jesus, don't do that. You scared the shit out of me. I thought it was someone else. "How do you move that fast? Did you float over or just move through the wall?"

"I jumped over the same as you did."

"If you don't want to climb, then don't, but don't sneak up on me."

"Do I frighten you? You shouldn't be scared of me. I wouldn't do anything to hurt you unless you did something to try and hurt me. You wouldn't do that, would you?"

"No. I'm trying to help you. Look who's climbing over cemetery walls after dark."

"That's true, I suppose. Which way now?"

"Up," he said, pointing to the top of the hill. "Remember, we have to be careful. There's a caretaker, and if I get spotted here, I'll be in deep shit. Let's keep to the shadows just to be safe."

"Okay. You lead the way." Miles led her from tree to tree up the long hill. It was two hundred yards to the top. It would've been easier to take Monster up the back road

178

behind the cemetery at the top, but if there was a chance that limbs and branches could scratch the sides of the car then he didn't want to risk it. Past rows and rows of headstones they walked. "This is all so strange," Annabelle said passing the graves. "Look at the dates carved into the stones. They were born fifty years after I was, they lived until they died of old age, and I'm stepping over their graves."

"I'm not sure what to tell you. I'm sorry I don't have an answer."

"But you know so much about vampires."

"Everything I know about vampires came out of books and movies. As far as the world knows, you're a fictional character."

"But here I am. Do you think there are others?"

"There's the one that bit you. How many there are after that or if that one is still alive is beyond me."

"I have to find out if there are others like me."

"What if they're not good people?" Miles asked.

"Why would you say that?"

"You seem like a decent person to me, but then again, for all I know, you spent your days pushing children into mud puddles and laughing at them."

"Miles, that's a terrible thing to suggest."

"Calm down, I'm just pointing out that you're making an effort to not kill people. That doesn't mean that the others, if they exist, are doing the same. For all we know, the one that made you still wanders the country biting young girls."

"We can't allow that to happen!"

"Keep your voice down. We're getting close to the caretaker's shack and sometimes he closes up late. He lives at the bottom of the hill, so I'm not trying to attract any attention."

"Sorry," she said. "I just don't want anyone else to go through this."

"That says a lot about you. I don't actually think you pushed children into mud puddles."

"That's not entirely true." She looked solemnly at the ground. "One day, when I was walking home from the schoolhouse, Georgie Smith pulled on my hair. It made me so mad I may have tripped him on purpose to land on a certain place on the ground."

"A mudpuddle?"

"A big ol' pile of horse shit," she grimaced. "He landed in the biggest pile in the road."

"Ha!" Miles laughed out loud. "I bet he didn't pull on your hair again, did he?"

"No, but his mama got so angry about his clothes that she marched him over to our house while he was still covered in shit to tell my daddy what I'd done."

"What did your daddy say?"

"He said if Georgie hadn't pulled on my hair, he wouldn't be covered in horseshit. I still got in trouble though. I had to do extra chores in the distillery, and I didn't get dessert for two weeks."

"That's rough," he told her as he stopped in front of the mausoleum. "Here we are." Miles took one last look around the cemetery before briefly shining the beam of his flashlight over the threshold. Annabelle saw with her own eyes her family name carved into stone.

"How did this come to be? Who built this?"

"The people of White Wreath banded together and made this for your family. Building a distillery here gave a lot of people jobs who needed them. I'd imagine whatever money was owed to your father for outstanding shipments and any money they might've had in the bank paid for all this. It's the biggest, most ornate mausoleum in White Wreath."

"So, it's true." She laid a hand upon the door. "This is where they're laid." Miles fished the key hanging about his neck out of his shirt and began unlocking the door. "Miles? What are you doing?"

"Don't you want to go inside?"

"Why would I go inside, and why do you have a key to my parent's tomb?!"

"Keep your voice down!" he hissed. She lowered the volume, but the inflection of displeasure remained.

"Answer me. Why do you have a key to the door of my family tomb around your neck?"

"I come up here when I want to be alone."

181

"You surround yourself with dead people when you want to be alone? That sounds too strange, Miles."

"The dead don't make a lot of noise, and sometimes the living sometimes make life unbearable." The lock popped open, and he pulled the chain free of the handles.

"Those sound like the words of a very sad person."

"Yeah, well sometimes life can be a sad thing. It helps to have friends who feel the same way. And when we all feel like that we climb into a car and we come here."

"You must have very unusual friends."

"They're my friends *because* they're unusual."

"I've never heard of a social circle that congregates where people are buried."

"Stick around, and maybe I'll introduce you."

"Do you think they'd be afraid of me?"

"You couldn't tell them you're the undead. I know I can keep a secret, but you'd be pushing your luck with the rest." With a yank, the door opened just enough for a person to squeeze through. "Are you coming inside or staying out here?" Annabelle took a deep breath to prepare herself but didn't move. "Come on."

"Don't hurry me, this isn't easy," she said but didn't move. "I wasn't expecting to go in."

"Don't be scared." He held his hand out for her to take. "You came all this way you might as well see their plots."

"Damn it all to hell." She stomped her boot before taking his hand. When she was past the door, he pulled it shut and activated the flashlight to illuminate the inside. Annabelle immediately began to smell the air. "Why do I smell whiskey?"

"My friend Sweeney spilled some here."

"You were drinking in my parents' tomb?"

"It's a beautiful place to drink." He waved the flashlight. "Look around."

"Don't shine the light at the windows, someone might see."

"Not to worry, I blacked out the windows with magnets and the same kind of trash bags I gave you to wrap around your sleeping bag. Light doesn't get in or out."

"There." She pointed at the far wall. Miles aimed the beam to reveal the aged brass plates with the names on them. Annabelle approached them. Like when she sat inside the Cadillac, she quickly took to putting her hands upon them. The first one she gravitated to was that of her father. She lingered for a moment, fingering each letter in his aged brass name plate before going to the next. Then she did the same with her mother's name. Miles watched her reaction. It seemed as natural as any... until she looked and saw the third plate. She balked at first. Who wouldn't? It's not every day you see a tomb with your name and death date on it. She touched it as well. Her fingers clamped around the edge of the plate and with a sharp "PANG!" she pulled it off.

"Annabelle! What are you doing?"

"I'm not dead, so this doesn't belong here." She crumpled the brass plate in her hands like it was tinfoil and flung it into the corner with disgust.

"How do you feel?" he asked.

"How do I feel? How do you think I feel?" Miles had the flashlight pointed in her direction but away from her face. Even still, he could see the teardrops that should've been clear, tracing a pair of twin crimson paths down her cheeks.

"I didn't want to believe that any of this was real, I was furious with them for what they did to me." She kicked the section of the wall with her father's marker hard enough to crack it. Traces of red streamed passed her mouth and met underneath her chin. "They left me behind to come here. I don't want to be here! I want to go home!"

"There's no going back, Annabelle. Time only works forward. You can't go back."

"I'd trade places with them if I could." She wiped her nose with the back of her hand, smearing the blood across her face. "They should have to be out here dealing with you, and I should be in the grave."

"Annabelle, please. Don't say that. There's nothing you can do for them now. Maybe you can-"

"Maybe I can what, Miles? Maybe I can sneak around the dark like some kind of monster?" She kicked the wall in the same spot and the granite began to crack more. This time her foot left an indentation. "What am I supposed to do? Where am I supposed to live? I don't want to live in a sleeping duffel wrapped in trash bags forever!"

"Look, I was trying to help. I didn't want you sleeping in the ruins of the distillery." Annabelle kicked the wall a third time and with a thunderous crack, the stone panel caved revealing a casket within.

"Do you hear me, father?" she yelled. Annabelle ducked down, grabbed the casket with both hands, and yanked the whole thing out of the hole and into the room. Miles wanted to intervene but didn't dare step between her and the burial vessel. "Do you know what they did to me? Do you know what I am?!"

Before he could stop her, she grasped the handles locking the lid in place and began to twist them open. The top came free, and she flung it aside, almost hitting him. He looked back to the casket, which was empty save for some charred bones halfway arranged in the shape of a person. In the low light, the skull was the only part he could identify for sure. The shock of seeing the remains must've been enough to break Annabelle. She collapsed next to the casket, bawling, and moaning as she stared upon the remains.

"It's not supposed to be this way," she sobbed over and over. Miles remained silent and kept the flashlight upright enough to keep the room from being dark. Annabelle tried wiping the blood away but like before it just smeared. When she consoled herself a little, she took a long deep breath and the blood-soaked back through her skin like a sponge. She looked directly at the source of the light.

"What am I gonna do, Miles? Where am I gonna go? I'm not an animal, I'm a person. I was going to do things with my life. I wanted to attend university to learn about animals. Papa was going to have me run the distillery one day."

"You can still do anything you want. You've got all the time in the world."

"As long as it's not done while the sun is up."

"Life isn't perfect. At least you knew your parents. Look at me, I never knew who mine were. They gave me up after I was born."

"But you have Gary."

"I do, and I can't help but wonder who they might've been or if I have brothers and sisters who are out there somewhere."

"You have more than I have. I've lost everything. I've even lost my way."

"Then it's time to find a new one. You can't go back to the world you came from, so you'll have to find your way in this one. If I can help you, I will."

"You'd do that?"

"Everyone needs help every now and then. Busting up monuments isn't going to fix things." Annabelle sighed. She stood up, brushed herself off and walked past him to retrieve the coffin lid. She hefted it from the floor with one hand like it was made of cardboard. For a moment she paused over the remains. Unexpectedly she knelt down on both knees and whispered something before kissing the skull above the eye sockets and replacing the lid. Miles set the flashlight down facing them and helped her lift the coffin back into the hole. There wasn't anything to do about the opening, so he gathered the chunks of granite and put them in a pile in the corner. Fortunately, the damage was inside the tomb; otherwise, the caretaker might notice.

"Thank you," she finally said. "I think you're right. There's no use in sitting here being sad. That's not going to change anything. I need to accept what's happened and move on. That's the right thing to do, huh?" Miles laughed to himself as he recalled one of the lessons in his psychology class about grief. He recalled how for people who've suffered a significant trauma they need to progress through the five stages of grief; denial, anger, bargaining, depression, and acceptance. The process can take days, weeks, years, sometimes a lifetime to come to terms with something terrible, but here it was Annabelle had hurdled all five, in that order, in a matter of ten minutes.

"What's so funny? Are you laughing at me?"

"I didn't laugh."

"Not out loud, you were thinking about me being upset, and you laughed in your head."

"I wasn't laughing at you, I was laughing at the situation."

"What could possibly be funny about any of this?"

"I'm standing in a tomb in the middle of the night with a vampire who's been asleep for a hundred years. It's something I never thought I'd do. That's what I find funny. I feel bad about what's happened to you."

"I don't need someone to feel sorry for me."

"I'm not throwing you a pity party. I'm offering my help until you get yourself squared away."

"I suppose that's for the best. Do you think you could give me your assistance now?"

"What can I do?"

"Let me have your key to the tomb."

"You want the key?"

"I do." She held her palm out. "I'd like to come here now and then again to sleep during the day. Sunlight doesn't get in, correct?"

"Right. I blacked out the windows."

"Then let me have the key. It's the only home I have left." Miles hesitated but then reluctantly began to fish the key out again. He pulled it over his head and gave it to her. She looped it around her head and stuffed it down her shirt. He wasn't sure what he was going to tell the others, but he'd cross that bridge when he got to it. "I need something else," she said.

"What's that?"

"A map. I need to know where things are so I can get around on my own."

"Ok. I'm pretty sure there's a local map in the library."

"Then I'll go to the library. There are history archives there, right?"

"Yes, but the library isn't open after dark."

"Then I'll open it."

"Don't go breaking anything. I'll get you inside."

"You'd go with me to the library?" she asked.

"Sure, between the two of us we should be slick enough to slip in and out without being noticed."

"Thank you, that means a lot to me. I can't sit around White Wreath like a bump on a log. I need to educate myself."

"That's where I'd start." Annabelle looked at her surroundings and gave a long sigh.

"Look, I hate to hurry you along, but I need to get home." Said Miles. "School will be starting soon, and Gary wants me in bed earlier so that I get a good night's sleep. You just woke up, I, however, need to get to bed."

"Would you mind if I asked you to leave me here, tonight?"

"You want to stay here? Don't you want to get your things?"

"Could you bring them to me tomorrow night? The sleeping bag and other things are in the southeast corner of the barn across from your house. I think I'd like to stay here for a while."

"If that's what you want. After I leave you can take the lock and chain and lock the doors from the inside so no one else gets in." He turned and walked towards the doors, pulling one open. "Oh, and there's some books and blankets over in the far corner if you want them. There's also some extra batteries for the flashlight."

"Thank you. Oh, and Miles?"

"Yes?"

"I'm grateful for you helping me in my time of…change. I think it's strange and unusual that you've been so eager to help someone like me when it's my new nature to feed on living things, even humans." Miles smiled at her as the perfect response came to mind.

"That's okay, Annabelle, I myself am…strange and unusual."

"You look like a normal boy to me."

"I don't know. Maybe I thought you needed a friend. I gotta go. See you tomorrow. Goodnight, Annabelle Booth."

"Goodnight." Miles stepped outside and shut the door flush with a "thunk." Almost immediately, he heard the chain being threaded through the handles on the inside and the lock clicking into place. The night air smelled just as sweet as the last time he was here. His eyelids drooped a little. Time for bed. With a cautious look at his surroundings, Miles slipped into the shadows and started the trek back down the hill to the car.

As he walked past the tombstones, he considered what Annabelle had gone through and thought of his own path in life. Looking at the names and dates on the headstones he wondered how many of the people buried beneath his feet here were born and never saw beyond the hollers of White Wreath.

The world is so big. I can't just sit around and die here. There's too many places to go, too many people to meet. I have to see New Orleans.

New Orleans, the fantastic city he'd read about in novels, travel brochures and encyclopedias in the library. Somewhere a thousand miles Southwest of White Wreath was a bustling city of liquor and depravity he'd only witnessed on the printed page. How many books had he collected over the years to fill his bookshelves? All the sights of the "Big Easy" would welcome him with open arms as one of their decadent own. Jackson Square, the garden district, the Quarter. He wanted all of it; the churches, the cemeteries that looked like cities of the dead, the people, the sights, the sounds, the smells, all of it. No death before New Orleans.

Inside the tomb, Annabelle shone the light to the tall ceiling above to take in her surroundings. The light exposed one of the magnets that had slipped to allow the trash bags to sag away around the edge. Deadly sunlight could slip in that way. The heels of her boots lifted from the ground followed by the toes. Upward she rose—five feet, ten, fifteen. She pulled the magnet free and reattached it with the black film pinched beneath. The domed ceiling was within reach. Annabelle's personal gravity reversed. She somersaulted to land boots first upon the ceiling, the hood of her sweatshirt and shoelaces dangling back and forth. The sensation felt no different than being right-side up. She balanced one step in front of the other until she reached the back wall. Upon placing the first foot upon it, her gravity shifted again and the back of the tomb becoming another flat surface to walk upon. Down, down, down, she paced, reaching the floor once more. She didn't really need the flashlight to see. Annabelle had learned quickly that a bonus of her transformation had been the ability to see in the absence of natural light. However, the minuscule uptick in temperature from the bulb in the flashlight felt welcome indeed. Next to the wall, just as Miles had said, a pile of coarse green wool blankets sat folded in the corner.

Beside them, a small stack of books. Curious about what they might be about, she thumbed through them reading the strange titles: Frankenstein, Thus Spake Zarathustra, The Metamorphosis, Naked Lunch, Principia Discordia, The Church of the Subgenius, a few others, and lastly, a black book entitled with a word she'd never heard before. Sinister bright red letters dared her to say the title aloud.

"Dracula"

CHAPTER ELEVEN

Miles awoke the next morning to the sound of the blaring alarm clock. Shit, shower, rise, and shine. Gary was finishing the last few bites of his breakfast when he entered the kitchen.

"Morning," he said to the top of Gary's head.

"Morning. You ready for work?"

"Let me grab a breakfast bar and some juice in a cup and we can leave."

"Take your time, there isn't a lot to do today. In fact, I was planning on making a run up to Lexington to get a few things. Nothing big. I was thinking…if you wanted to, we could take your new car. I'll even top off your tank off when we get back."

"Works for me. Other than the trash barrels and swapping out a load of towels for the showers, it should be a slow day. You forgot to order something for the Imperial? That's one of the signs of the apocalypse, isn't it? The end times?"

"Now don't you start with that shit," Gary said, pushing his chair back before washing his dish out in the sink. "Get your juice and let's get on the road. It'll take all day. If we hurry and don't fuck around too much, we can get lunch and be back by around noon. I've got a fuel shipment coming in later."

"Transylvania University is in Lexington, right?" Miles asked, already knowing the answer to the question.

"Yeah, it's near downtown on the north end. You thinking about going to school there?"

"I want to get something while we're in Lexington."

"Ok, as long as you don't take all day. Let's go."

"Here." Miles tossed him the keys. "You can drive Monster."

"Is that what you named it? You and your spooky zombie shit, I swear." Outside, Gary got behind the driver's seat. Feeling the cushy leather seats caused a huge smile to spread across his face. "Oh, that's nice."

Monster rolled out of the driveway, down the road, past the Imperial, and towards Prestonsburg beyond. They glided down the highway like the asphalt was made of glass. The broken white lines vanished a dozen at a time for the black machine. Gary couldn't find a channel he wanted to listen to on the radio so he clicked it off.

To be honest, the two didn't mind enjoying the silence of each other's company. The opportunity to 'just shut up and be' as Gary would sometimes say. One of them would speak every now and then to point out a change in the scenery, a collapsed barn or new house being built. It wasn't until they were approaching Lexington that Gary finally said something.

"I made plans to have the front fuel island fixed," Gary said. "I've meant to find the right time to buy new pumps and pull the tanks. We got lucky though. I called some people, and it turns out some contractors just finished a job down in Harlan, so they have the machines, equipment, and personnel needed to do such an operation in an incredibly short amount of time."

"That's great. When will all this go down?"

"November first, right after your 18th birthday. I'll keep the station open on Halloween and close it all down early that night."

"What about Mr. Jenkins and the others? They're gonna lose a week's pay."

"Nobody's losing anything. Everyone's going to get a paid vacation, even you."

"Oh, that's ok, I guess."

"I didn't think anybody would put up too much of a fuss for a paid vacation. Anyway, the Imperial will be closed for about a week. They're going to reconfigure everything so the whole station is going to be down. I asked if we could shut down half but they're going to have to cut the power. I'll need your help."

"Anything," Miles said. Soon enough they arrived in Lexington and the large supply store Gary had talked about. It was built into a two-story warehouse in the industrial district surrounded by shotgun houses, car repair garages, and a recycling center. Gary spoke with the person at the counter, the metal mesh basket he needed for the fryer was already waiting for him. To his surprise, the person at the desk informed Gary that they sold receipt tape as well. That would save having to make a trip to another store. He opened a box to inspect the dimensions of the paper before buying that box and another. Miles helped him pack the things out to the car.

The trunk was so large that they could've purchased ten times what they'd gotten and still had enough room to comfortably fit an adult inside. Miles took the keys and Gary navigated them towards a series of buildings a few miles down the road. It didn't take long to find Transylvania University. Neither was sure where the university store was until a pedestrian pointed them in the right direction. Five minutes later the two were standing in a cramped little store, pushing past customers and racks of merchandise with the university name on it. It reeked of textbooks, the dusty musk of knowledge. Tucked in a corner he found a crimson sweatshirt. It came off the hook easily enough, the soft material velvety to the touch.

Fresh pressed white vinyl letters spelled out TRANSYLVANIA in arched letters across the chest. It was just the right size for Annabelle, so he tucked it under his arm and waited in line to check out. The smell combined with seeing the other people his age choosing their course books and classes caused Miles to feel a small twist in his gut. For all the time he thought about who he was, he never really thought about the future, other than New Orleans. What would he do after his senior year?

Dennis had talked nonstop about getting a job outside of White Wreath so he could make enough to take care of Mary. He had a knack for makeup and fashion, so it would make sense for him to go somewhere that had something more than hunting camouflage as a template. Even Sweeney had a plan to work for his aunt's oil company somewhere in Oklahoma. The world is bigger than White

Wreath. But what about Gary? What about the Imperial? Who would run it when Gary got too old to run it? Would someone want to buy it from him? Would it still be running in thirty years? What if they weren't mining coal in 2020? Without the regular flow of trucks, the Imperial would likely wither and die.

"Sir?" A woman's voice behind the counter pulled him out of deep thought. Miles paid cash for the sweatshirt. Again, he threw the keys to Gary who gladly put himself behind the wheel. It wasn't until he pitched the bag in the backseat that Gary asked him why he'd purchased it.

"It's for a friend. She talked about going to school up here."

"It's not that Lucifer girl is it?"

"No. It's someone else, and she's just a friend."

"It's nowhere near Christmas. She must be more than a friend for you to go and spend money on her. Tell me what she's like." Miles smiled without realizing it. "What's that funny grin for? Go on, what does she look like?" Miles thought for a second, choosing his words carefully.

"She's sixteen, blonde, and um, she lives near the cemetery."

"What do her parents do?"

"Her parents died in an accident a long time ago."

"I'm sorry to hear that. Does this mystery girl have a name?"

"Annabelle."

"That's a pretty name. Annabelle, what?"

"Annabelle Booth."

"Booth, huh? I wasn't aware there were any more Booths in the area. The last ones I've ever heard of were the ones who built the distillery across the road a hundred years ago. It wiped out the whole family when it burned down. If her parents are dead and she's sixteen who does she live with?"

"She's emancipated. She lives alone."

"Really? At sixteen? And she's planning to go to Transy? That's a girl who sounds like she has her act together. She doesn't have half of her head shaved and a bunch of metal shit in her face, does she?"

"No."

"Then you should invite her over for dinner or something."

"We're not dating."

"Then quit messing around with that Lucifer girl and ask her out."

"I don't think we're compatible," Miles said, leaning on the door to watch the buildings of the city go by.

"Why the hell not?

"We're too different."

"Not so different you didn't think to buy her a twenty-five-dollar sweatshirt."

"She's going to pay me back."

"Ok, well, forget I asked. I was curious about whose company you keep these days." Gary paused. Then said, "We've never talked about it, but do you want to go to college? Transy is a private school. It costs a bit more to go there than a public school. What do you want to do after high school?"

"I want to travel some, get out of White Wreath."

"I can understand that. That's why I'm asking now. You're not dumb, so you need to take the SATs, ACTs, other stuff for college. Shit, you could even take the ASVAB and join the military for four years. They're giving away college money, and they'll let you travel all over the world.

"I'm not trying to get shot for college money."

"You don't have to be an infantryman like I was. Or you could join the Air Force or choose an Army job that isn't combat-related. Look, you don't have to do any of those things, but you need to do something."

"What about the Imperial?"

"What about the Imperial?"

"I could work at the Imperial. Eventually, you'll retire, and I can run the place."

"I'm not going to retire for a long-ass time. Do you still want to be working for me when you're in your forties? I get the feeling that'll wear thin. We live all right, but I can tell you there's not enough in the Imperial's monthly income to compensate a second manager. You'd be making a little more than what you make now, and you'll want to keep your own hours, so that means you'll need to get your own place. That means you'll need to make enough for rent, utilities, car insurance, gas for this car which won't be cheap, and none of that can be spent on having fun which I know you're going to want to do. I think you need to make plans that don't concern the Imperial. What about music? You've got more records than any person on the planet. That's got to be worth something. You could be a disc jockey. How about that?"

"I don't know," Miles said, still looking out the window.

"Then do what you need to do so that you can know. Because I'll tell you something. Tomorrow always comes and if you don't have a plan to meet it, things can suck major ass."

"Fine, I'll make a plan."

"Don't do it for me. Do it for yourself. There's plenty of people out there who don't have a good home or a good head on their shoulders. You have a lick of sense so don't waste it doing nothing."

"I said I'd do it."

"Then I won't say another word about it. And don't go 'knocking up' that Lucifer chick either."

LATER...

As dusk settled over White Wreath, Miles sat in his car in the vacant lot across the street from the cemetery. To his delight he watched the caretakers' pickup appear near the

200

gates at the top of the hour. The man locked the gates, climbed into his truck and sped away, a Johnny Cash tune lingering on the wind. Miles scaled the stone wall of the cemetery and climbed the long slope to get to the Booth Mausoleum. The cicadas made a bigger racket than usual, their wings beating, their membranes thrashing up another angry cacophony. When he arrived at the door he gave three knocks. There was no answer. He waited for a minute then knocked again.

"It's open!" he heard Annabelle say. Miles pushed the door open and stepped inside.

"I can't see anything," he said.

"The flashlight is two steps to your left on the ground." Her voice echoed off the stones. Miles bent at the waist and felt about until his fingers clumsily found the cylinder-shaped item. The bulb clicked on, and he shone it about the room, revealing the same bare walls and the hole that Annabelle had kicked in yesterday. The beam waved left and right before climbing the wall where Annabelle sat cross-legged upside down in the middle of the ceiling. No sooner had the light found her overhead when a book fluttered into view and hit him between the eyes.

"Ow, shit!" Being a small paperback book, it didn't hurt as much as it scared him. He rubbed his forehead and plucked it from the ground. Dracula.

"Why didn't you warn me about that book? It gave me nightmares!"

"It scared you?"

"It's terrifying. They stabbed the count with knives, and he died!"

"He's the villain, he's supposed to die."

"Being a vampire, I can't say that I'm happy with you for leaving it for me to read."

"I'm sorry it scared you. Maybe it wasn't the best example of a vampire story to show you, but it's the most well known."

"Do you have any books where the vampire doesn't die?"

"Sure, I have some others. If you're going to be a vampire, then you need to know how to stay hidden and blend in with the rest of us. Otherwise, you're going to get staked, and I don't want that to happen to you. You don't want to end up as a pile of ash, do you?"

"No, no, I don't."

"Then you need to get up to speed on how the world works, and I've already taken the first step on getting you educated. Will you come down? I have some things for you." Annabelle stood up from where she was seated and began to walk about as she'd done before; across the ceiling, down the far wall, and eventually the floor. Miles held the items behind his back.

"I smell paper, cloth, and something metal."

"You're right," he said. "I brought you this, he held out the thin black item for her to see.

"What is that?"

"Hold out your wrist and I'll show you." She did as she was told, and he wrapped the black band around her wrist and fastened it. She looked at it with a confused expression trying to figure out the foreign device's purpose.

"What, what does it do?" He pressed the button on the side and the face emitted a cool blue glow with square numbers that moved. "It's a clock?"

"Sort of, it's a wristwatch. It'll tell you how long you have until dawn is coming so you don't get caught out in the open," Miles explained.

"Was it expensive?"

"No, it's an older one I already had. I put a new battery in it so it should run for several years."

"Won't I have to wind it?"

"Not once," he said. Annabelle pressed the button a few more times to get the face to light up. She was like a kid with a new toy. "I also have a map for you." He pulled out a piece of folded paper and handed it to her. She opened it to reveal a map of White Wreath. "I've marked where different landmarks are around town." He pointed to different spots marked and named with ink. "Here's the library, here's the Imperial, this is where I live, here's the distillery, and down here is the cemetery."

"Thank you very much," she said, taking it and folding it up. "This will help."

"And lastly, I have this." He held the plastic bag out for her to take. She canted her head to the side to read the name of the campus shop upon it.

"What is it?" she said excitedly before thrusting both hands inside and grabbing the garment within.

"I don't know. What do you think it is?" Annabelle practically bounced in place as she read the sweaters lettering.

"It's a sweater! Why does it say Transylvania?"

"It's another school near Kentucky University. Funny, right?" He said. But she wasn't listening. She peeled off her hoodie and as fast as her fingers could manipulate the material, she pulled the new crimson garment over herself.

"It's beautiful, look at it." She marveled, running her hands over the letters. "It's just my size. It's perfect!" She threw her arms around him, squeezing almost hard enough to bruise. "It's the best gift ever. Thank you."

"Glad you like it. Gary and I were in Lexington, so I made sure—"

"Tell me about Lexington." She let go of him. "I bet it's huge and full of people."

"That's pretty much it. Lots of people. Tens of thousands more than White Wreath." She continued to smooth her hands across the sweatshirt's material as though it might vanish at any moment.

"Look, Annabelle," Miles said. "Gary doesn't want me staying out too late anymore, so I have to go home and get used to going to bed earlier so I won't be tired when the school year starts. This may mean I visit less often. I can't do it tonight, but I'll still take you to the library tomorrow night if you want to go. I'll sneak out of the house after

Gary goes to sleep come back. I'll be waiting for you in my car across the street from the front gate."

"I'd like that very much, and it's probably a good idea for you to leave now, anyway."

"Why do you say that?"

"I haven't fed yet." Miles flinched a little and the warmth of their conversation dissipated.

"I'm sorry I have to ask you to leave," Annabelle said, "but blood is blood and I'd rather not take it from you."

"Say no more," he said backing away.

"Please don't be offended." She offered as he opened the door to the tomb and stepped outside. "This sweatshirt is now my most prized possession. I promise to take care of it."

"One last thing," he said. "Interview with a Vampire."

"What does that mean?"

"It's one of the books in the pile in there. Interview with a Vampire by Anne Rice."

"Does it have Dracula in it?"

"Sort of."

"Does the Dracula die in it?" she asked. Miles mulled the question over for a minute.

"No, Dracula lives. I'll see you across the road as soon as I can get here."

CHAPTER TWELVE

The door to the tomb pulled shut and Annabelle took a few more moments to enjoy the gift before removing it. She carefully folded the garment and placed it down before approaching the back wall and yanking her father's coffin from the hole. One good tug exposed the vessel enough to open it. She pulled the lid away as she'd done before to reveal the empty interior covered in a green blanket. As much as she disliked sleeping in a coffin, she had to admit it provided an oddly comforting space in which to sleep. Father's remains now rested intermixed in her mother's in the second coffin. It didn't take much to open her crypt.

It was fitting the two should be together, and the idea of sleeping in her own tomb seemed a little too creepy, so she slept in her father's. Annabelle removed the rest of her clothes, including the boots and placed them next to it. She didn't want to be naked when she fed but without extra clothes and washing supplies, she needed to keep her clothes as clean, and blood-free, as possible.

To her delight, she no longer perspired, and the donated clothes didn't smell of body odor after being worn more than once. She'd removed everything but the watch. The coffin closed, and she tiptoed naked across the stone floor, enjoying the cold temperature on her toes before opening the door. She trembled with the excitement of visiting the library, but she felt her energy starting to fade. *Food first.*

Outside, the coast was clear. Smelling the wind, there were no signs of others, so she wrapped the chain about the handle, applied the padlock, and stowed the key out of sight. All around her, the noisy cicadas filled the night. It was so grating and constant that she wished it would stop.

Perhaps they would if she asked nicely. Annabelle raised a single finger to her lips. "Be quiet," she whispered. "Go to sleep." At her command, the racket waned and stopped. Near at first, then in growing circles of space until the entire evening air lacked a single beating of wings. The hoots of owls and the chirp of the crickets remained the same, but the din of the burrowing insects had ebbed all together.

Into the tree line and undergrowth, she moved. It didn't take a more than a few steps under the canopy of the trees filtering the moonlight for Annabelle to fall in love with the night again. The songs of night birds filled the air, painting an enormous canvas of sound while the nearly inaudible swooping of owls on the hunt framed the rest. Her pale skin seemed to reflect any beams of light that slipped past the swaying filter overhead. Down a sharp slope she slid until the ground became divided by a brook. She had no interest in it until a familiar croak leaped into her ears.

"Rana pipiens!" she exclaimed before squatting in the water and snatching a frog from beneath a swatch of grass. Annabelle held the frog an inch from her face. "How many?" she asked with a smile, looking deep into those same beautiful gold rings she remembered. "How many generations have passed since I saw you last?" The frog squirmed and kicked a little but didn't reply. "Things are different now. We have to be careful. You look hungry like me. Would you like something to eat?" Again, no reply. The rings shifted to one side then the other. "C'mon. I think I see a place."

Annabelle carried the frog over to what was left of a large tree that had fallen some time ago. With one hand she felt under the lip of the trunk and lifted. The wood groaned and cracked in twain to reveal a plethora of bugs and creepy crawlies scurrying to find a place to hide. "Dinner time."

She set the frog down in the middle of the squirming mass and took a seat upon the other half of the log to watch. The frog went to work snapping up as many as it could before they were out of reach; pill bugs, larvae, termites, grubs, spiders, millipedes and little red things the size of a pinhead she couldn't name. For minutes on end, it fed. The tongue snapped in every direction. When the selection got scarce, she prodded the ground next to the log and more bugs appeared. A tiny pair of black eyes peered at her from the shadows beneath.

"Hello, copperhead. Snug in your spot?" She stood up and closed the distance between herself and the snake. "Come out," she said. "Come on." At any other time in her life, Annabelle Booth might've been scared of such a creature, let alone a venomous one. But tonight, in a place like this, in a life like this, it seemed as natural as making whiskey from corn. The snake didn't move. "Oh, don't be a chicken shit." She extended her arms and picked it up with both hands, holding it's head an inch from her nose. "Look how pretty you are." She smiled. "Come with me. Maybe we can find something for you to eat as well."

As casually as one might put on a shirt, Annabelle lifted all four feet of its wriggling body and draped it over neck and shoulders. It dangled a moment before coiling itself around her arms and resting its head in her right hand as she walked. The air smelled as fresh and fragrant; the smell of pine trees and sap framing it all. Upon the passing breeze, she caught a whiff of musk. Deer. A buck. A big one. She sniffed again. Not far away to the east.

Annabelle made no audible noise as she walked. Her feet touched the ground, but no sound came from her steps. Fingertips traced the leaves of bushes lining a well-tread deer path. Her new eyes saw past the shadows and the whole forest was presented for her to explore. Another scent entered her nose. Musk again, but different. It seemed awfully strong. Sixty yards, thirty. At twenty-five yards the biggest buck she'd ever seen stepped into view from behind a cluster of sycamore trees.

The size of the beast was already impressive enough before she managed to count the fourteen points on its full antlers. In all her years she'd never seen anything like it. She wished she could tell her father of such beauty. The deer lowered its head, nibbling on something and paying her no mind. She continued to walk directly for it. The strange smell from before got stronger—rank deer piss and shucked corn.

Annabelle purposefully stepped upon some undergrowth to make noise, and the buck looked up from its spot to look directly at her. A few feet in front of her on the ground a mound of corn lay piled. Thinking the buck might like some, she knelt and scooped up a handful. Like courting the copperhead, she held her open hand out for it to come to her. "Come here. Come to me." The buck hesitated, looking about the area and to the trees before beginning to take steps towards her. Halfway there, it stopped and smelled the air again before coming close. "It's all right."

The magnificent creature grew in size with every step, its horns perfectly symmetrical like in a drawing she once saw in a book. One might think it would stay away because of the copperhead draped about her. But like the snake, it seemed eager to obey. When the buck was a few feet away, the snake perked up. "You be nice."

The deer stood close, smelled her hand, and began to nibble the corn. When it ate everything in her palm, it lowered its head and began to munch at the pile on the ground. She ran her fingers through the fur along its neck and traced it all the way up to its antlers.

They were rigid and smooth to the touch. The animal was mesmerizing, the way that it shifted and moved. For something so beautiful, she felt sorry she'd have to cut its life short to extend her own. Annabelle stepped close enough to feel the fur against her, her canine fangs already growing in size from hunger. When the wind changed the reek of deer piss shifted. It was then that Annabelle realized the smell didn't belong to this buck at all. The hairs on her neck stood on end as a metallic click sounded in the distance. A frightening "BANG!" sounded from high in a tree to her right. The deer twisted as it reared, colliding with Annabelle and knocking her to the ground before scampering away down the closest hill. To her credit, she'd managed to catch herself in such a way that that snake around her shoulders wasn't crushed by her weight. She hadn't injured, but her entire torso was now painted with a splatter of deer blood.

"Holy shit, Dale!" A voice came from the trees in the same direction as the shot. "There's a kid down there!" Annabelle leaned back to see two men climbing down from a platform high in a tree. Each one was covered head to toe in clothes made to look like trees and bushes. Hunters. "Hurry up, get out of my way. Oh shit, oh shit, we're fucked but good if you shot a damn kid!"

"I'm movin', you dumb son of a bitch. Stop trying to step on my hands." The two climbed down a makeshift ladder and rushed over to Annabelle, flashlights already cutting a swath through the darkness. They rounded the tree, blinding her with the beams to the face. She held the luminescence away with her palm.

"What….in…the actual fuck?" one hunter asked the other. "Clay, you seeing this? Honey, are you hurt?"

"I'm fine, it's the deer's blood," Annabelle said. "Get your lights outta my face." They lowered their lights a little but didn't take their eyes off her.

"What the hell are you doing running around naked in the woods at night for?" the other hunter, the one called Dale asked.

"I was hunting," she said. "I almost had that deer before you shot it."

"Hunting, huh?" said Clay. "You run around hunting deer naked with no bow or gun?"

"Usually."

"Hey Dale, ain't this Pearl's granddaughter? The one that runs around naked and don't know her ass from a hole in the ground? What's her name? Honey, is Pearl your grandmother? Yeah, that's you. Dale, you dipshit." He punched the other man in the arm. "You almost shot Pearl's girl."

"I don't know anyone named Pearl," Annabelle said. As she spoke the snake began to move again.

"Is that a copperhead?" Dale said, shining the light on it as he backed away. "You keep that thing away from me."

"It's my copperhead, and I wasn't planning on sharing," she said, annoyed by the men making fun of her.

"Girl, you are nuttier than squirrel turds. Come on, Clay. Let's leave shit for brains here alone."

"Don't call me names." She growled at them.

"Whatever. Tell ya what, let me give you a nickel's worth of free advice; if you keep running around in the dark where people are hunting somebody is eventually going to shoot you." Both men turned their backs and started walking away, laughing. "Get your gun and we'll track the buck. I'm getting that rack."

"That's my deer," she said loud enough to interrupt their chortles. "Don't you go near it."

"What was that?" Dale asked, shining his light back at her face again.

"You heard me." Her eyes narrowed. "That buck was mine, and you went and shot it. You're not going to lay a hand on it, and you're sure as hell not cutting its head off."

"Look, you little fruitcake..." Dale took a few steps back in her direction. "You need to run your pale little ass on home because you almost got it blown off just now by fucking around in the woods. Now run on home."

"Mister, I'll forgive you for almost shooting me. But that buck is mine. If it's dead by the time I track it down, I'm going to be pissed about it. If that's the case, you might not want to be anywhere near here."

"What are you gonna do with a dead deer? You don't have a knife or a saw, and I know a guy who will pay me three hundred dollars for a mounted head that big. If you've got three hundred dollars, then hand it over, and it's yours. Between you and me I don't see any clothes with pockets. Unless you've got a bundle of cash in your cooch, then I'm taken what's mine." Annabelle held her hand out with the snakes' head still resting upon it, and the man almost tripped over himself staying out of striking distance.

"That's it," she said, her head canted to one side. "You're afraid of snakes." She took a step towards him and both men backed away. "Now if I threw my friend here on you, you might be able to fight it off without getting bitten. Maybe. But you might be in a real pickle if there were a bunch of snakes, like the ones on your legs and arms." She pointed towards Dale's foot. Dale aimed his flashlight down at his leg to find a thick copperhead coiled about his ankle. He immediately began to dance and scream to get the snake off. Clay shone his own light upon the man.

"What the hell is wrong with you? There isn't anything on you!" Dale continued to scream and flail.

"Get it off! Get it off!" The man tore at his clothes and jacket so frantically that he tripped on his own feet and went tumbling into the underbrush. The only snake to be seen was the one wrapped around the naked girl covered in blood. Clay aimed his light at Annabelle.

"What the hell did you do to him?"

"Nothing he didn't deserve," she said. "What about you?" She offered the snake towards him. "Are you afraid of a snake?"

"N-not really," he said.

"You don't sound so sure. How about a dozen snakes? They're everywhere out here." She pointed at her feet. Clay shone the light at her feet to see a slithering carpet of copperheads advancing past her feet towards him at a fast pace. He backed away fast enough to stay out of striking distance before a snake fell from the tree, landing about his shoulders. The man squalled. He retreated up the hill thrashing and yelling as he fought at nothingness, leaving his possessions and hunting companion far behind. Turning to track the wounded deer, Annabelle listened to the men's screams. As she walked, she remembered a line from the book she'd just read. It all felt so personal to her now.

"Our ways are not your ways, and there shall be to you many strange things. Listen to them — children of the night. What music they make."

Traces of blood littered the branches hanging in her path. She followed the drops and smears, running her fingers across them and licking the coppery deliciousness. The more she tasted, the more she wanted. Its aroma grew more and more heavy as she approached a clearing. There, lying down beneath a break in the canopy of the dense forest, the deer's legs had given out. Its eye was upon her as she approached it. A puddle of its blood began to accumulate next to the body, and its breathing was shallow, frightened, near death.

"Hello," she said, one hand outstretched. The animal spooked, jumping halfway to its feet before losing its balance and falling again. "Oh, please, don't run." She cooed in a soothing voice. "The end is near, but you shouldn't be afraid. I wish you hadn't been shot by those men. It shouldn't be this way. You're too beautiful." The deer flinched when she placed her hand over the wound but didn't fight anymore. Annabelle got to her knees and soothed the deer by running her hands along its neck and face. "I'm a friend, I promise. Be still."

The buck relaxed, and she showed her fangs before plunging them deep into the flesh of the throat. The animal didn't resist and gave itself over to her. Annabelle drank deep, the beating of the animals' heart already slowing. There was so much blood. She took every drop until the heartbeat arrived at its last quivering pulse. And when it was done, so was the meal. She pulled her face away, blood slicking its way down her lips, chin, and legs. The thought of leaving came straight away, but instead she lingered a moment longer to soak in the coming rush.

Her pupils dilated as the ecstasy took hold, her cheeks flushing with fresh crimson. Knees went wobbly. The view of the buck's slumbering body seemed iconic in the way it lay. Angles of the antlers atop one another seemed to multiply in fractals to create strange symbols of things she couldn't understand. Annabelle's mind swam in a sea of sensations, raw and pure. The moonlight slipping through the trees became a blinding light show on their own, each beam kaleidoscoping into prisms and exploding into rainbow starbursts in every direction. Miniature constellations of stars appeared and disappeared like lightning bugs all around her. Round and round she spun, trying to count the multiplying branches of the trees in the moonlight as they swarmed. Dizzy from all of it, Annabelle collapsed to the ground in a cloud of bliss. Sometime in the hours before dawn, the copperhead uncoiled itself from the girl's neck and disappeared into the underbrush as her laughter echoed amongst the trees.

CHAPTER THIRTEEN

Morning came soon enough, and Annabelle climbed into her coffin. Her veins were full, and the windows of the tomb remained covered, but after the night she'd endured, she felt drained. Lying there, she reached a hand outside the coffin and grabbed the flashlight as well as the first book on the pile next to it. The light clicked on and she closed the lid. She wasn't sure what the eerie picture on the cover or the title Frankenstein meant, but she hoped to find out. The pages flowed quickly one to the next, the story of the creature enrapturing her. To be honest, she identified more with the creature as was likely the writer's intent.

After finishing four chapters in as many minutes, Annabelle realized she'd developed the ability to read faster. She'd retained every nuance and detail of the story and absorbed it all in a tenth of the time. The process was almost as fascinating as the story itself. Almost. The pages turned faster and faster until the last ones arrived to tell how the creature drifted away on the ice flow. She tried not to cry because it would stain her face and blankets, so she choked back all but one stubborn droplet before turning off the flashlight and closing her eyes.

Sundown approached to find Annabelle sleeping soundly. Whether it was by temperature, or sound, or the rotation of the Earth, something inside her stirred to rouse her when it was time to wake. As the last rays of light no longer touched the Booth mausoleum, her eyes snapped open. The coffin lid slid away, and she sat up to give a long, lazy stretch like a cat. She wasn't hungry so tonight she wouldn't have to walk about naked. Given that she wanted to venture into town and visit the library, any townspeople still out after dark might take notice of someone walking around in their birthday suit like a crazy person.

It didn't take long to get dressed. The tights, camouflage shorts, shirt with the letters "Pretty Hate Machine" across the top and the candy apple Doc Martin's slipped on as easy as you please. Summer or not, it would take an army of stable-hiding vampires to stop her from wearing her new sweatshirt. Seeing the name 'Transylvania' across the chest reminded her of Count Dracula. That's why Miles laughed when he gave it to her. That was enough to get her to laugh for the first time since she could remember.

The padlock fell away, and she opened the door. She considered locking it back but decided against it. Miles was the only person who ever visited. The chain was left hanging from the handle with the padlock dangling from the end. She started down the hill, her boots occasionally forgetting to touch the ground every few steps.

"Vampires." Annabelle giggled to herself as she pulled the hood over her head. "That's just silly talk."

At the bottom of the hill, she glanced through the cemetery gates to see no one around but Miles standing against the black car. He waved her across the street and opened the door for her. The machine came to life and rolled as smooth as creek water into town. The night air slipping in through the lowered windows tickled her hair and neck as she took in every sight along the way.

Miles parked the car in a darkened alley not far away from the stone building marked "LIBRARY" in black letters over the front doors. A few people were still out, walking this way and that as they traveled the final block. Two lovers entwined passed her by, whispering sweet words and giggles between themselves. When no one was around, Miles led her underneath the second story window he'd mentioned on the drive over. She stood behind him and grasped her hands around his chest before lifting him off the ground, levitating him high enough to reach the window and climb inside. When he'd squeezed through, she followed and closed the window behind her.

Miles led her down a hallway to stand at the top of a wide flight of stairs. Beyond those steps, the largest congregation of books she'd seen in her whole life sprawled in every direction. The whites of her eyes grew as shelves covered every wall and filled the room with entire aisles of eight-foot-tall stacks.

"Miles," she whispered. "This is amazing, there are so many books. Am I dreaming?"

"Not a dream. This is actually a small library compared to ones in bigger cities."

Anabelle's feet couldn't move fast enough to get her down the stairs and to the nearest rack, hands pawing at the spines to tilt them as she read the names. Much of it seemed self-explanatory, minus new words she didn't understand. When she found something she didn't understand, Miles explained it to her. It was far more than she could have hoped for.

The first thing she got her hands on was the local paper. It said so much. There were sections marked business, lifestyle, and even a sports section. A sense of relief found her when she discovered that Americans still played baseball. The Reds were no longer in Boston, they were in Cincinnati. And what was this "basketball" that was so popular now?

The area marked REFERENCE in huge letters along the back wall got her attention, but the shelf marked "encyclopedias" sparked her curiosity. Annabelle plopped herself down in front of it, pulled the first book into her lap and reclined against the shelf just behind. She preferred to use a flashlight to see, but with the drinking of blood came the ability to see in low light. And in that spot within the span of eight thick books, the hundred years she'd slept through unfolded in a parade of pictures and words. Famous inventors, new machines, terrible wars on the other side of the world, and even a trip to the moon were found within the volumes.

It was a lot to take in. Too much. Humans had figured out how to fix polio and smallpox, but some reason still gave colored folks a hard time after they'd been set free. Poor President John Kennedy, some crazy person shot him like they did Abraham Lincoln. She hadn't noticed that hours had passed until Miles got her attention.

"Annabelle?" Miles said from the stairs. "Can you let me down from the window? It's almost three in the morning. I need to get home."

"I sure can." She set the book in her hands down.

"You remember how to find your way back to the cemetery?"

"I know the way. I still have the map you gave me."

She'd crossed the lobby and almost made it to the bottom of the stairs when a familiar word across the room caught her eye.

BOOTH.

Her path diverted to the waist-high, twelve-foot-wide rectangular glass display case by the eastern door. Curious to what had gotten her interest, Miles followed her over. A title overhead the exhibit read: *The Booths of White Wreath: Distillers and Disaster*. The small display began at the left and read to the right and Annabelle began to read it all. It started with the story of her dad, and Mr. Lincoln then talked about mama and the distillery. Pictures on old yellow paper revealed the distillery, her home, just as she remembered it. There was even a picture of her as a young girl standing with her parents. She remembered when the man with the camera came to visit and take their picture. Father had been so handsome, and mother just as lovely. Next to the image, an article from the Pikeville paper. The headline said it all; *Calamity in White Wreath! Distillery and Booth family perish in distillery fire!*

The article went on to read like an outsider might've imagined. No one knew how the fire had started. Thousands of gallons of aging whiskey burned for days and might've burned down the woods if not for the efforts of the people of White Wreath pulling water to fight the blaze.

Unidentifiable bodies had been found beside her parents and Mr. Lincoln. She went on to read how family members identified the remains of the doctor, sheriff, and deputies by their personal effects. There was speculation about them having gone missing but didn't account for why they would all be gathered at the distillery. It was a miracle that she'd somehow survived. Annabelle pressed her nose against the glass to read every word.

"The loss of the distillery has left many people without jobs. There's a small amount of saving grace in that the money remaining from the last shipments of Booth Bourbon will be enough to cover the cost of the burial of John, Mae, and Annabelle Booth in the White Wreath cemetery. The distillery fire is suspicious as it occurred right after the incident at the fourth of July festival in Pikeville where John Booth's daughter was attacked by an unknown wild animal."

"Wild animal," she said with a snort. "That wild animal is probably still walking around."

The final picture at the end of the display was from the paper sometime later to show the Booth-family mausoleum. *"Local Booth family finally laid to rest in the newly erected tomb. The picture was taken by Jim Donothan, September 1890."* The expression on her face soured.

"It wasn't supposed to be this way," she said.

"I know," Miles agreed.

Annabelle pushed herself back and almost left before she noticed the tall glass case next to the one she'd been studying. The three-foot by three-foot display case caught her eye. What lay inside would've stopped her heart if it hadn't stopped beating on its own over a hundred years ago. In disbelief, she took a few steps closer to put her hands upon the case. Another picture of her sat upright on a stand on the bottom while the dress she once wore at home hung on a hanger. The faded bloodstain on the left side was created by the one that made her as she was. More important than these two things, the last item inside made her drop her books.

"Hoooolllly…shit." Annabelle gawked.

Staring back at her from its glass prison, the twin barrels of her scattergun called out to her as it leaned in the back corner. Its leather strap hung limp and lifeless without its owner to cradle it. A small card next to the stock read:

Left behind in Pikeville after the attack on Annabelle's life, this dress and shotgun are the only remaining possessions of the Booth family lost in the Distillery fire of 1890. Both belonged to the daughter, Annabelle May Booth.

"My shotgun." She excitedly tapped on the glass. "That's the shotgun my daddy gave me," she said, looking the case over. "Miles? How do I get it out?"

"Get it out?"

"Yes, get it out! That's my property! I want it!"

"Annabelle, no. It's locked up. It's a part of the exhibit now."

"The hell it is! Those things belong to me!"

"They might have a long time ago, but you have to let it go. Look, if you break that glass, the alarms in this place will go off, the police will come, and I'll go to jail. Do you want me to go to jail?"

"No, of course not," she said, wiping away tiny spots of blood welling up in the outer corners of her eyes. Seeing this, Miles stepped to her and wrapped his long arms around her.

"Don't cry. It'll be all right."

"Easy for you to say." She rested her cheek against his chest. "Your home hasn't been burned to the ground, and your only possessions put on display."

"You're still alive." He said, trying to comfort her. "Be patient. We'll figure something out."

"It all seems too big to handle."

"Then take it a little at a time." Annabelle backed away and dabbed at her eye, nodding that she'd heard him.

"Come on," she waved. "I'll take you outside." Once upstairs, Miles peered out the window. First to the parking lot, then to the gas station across the street. He paused.

"What's the matter?" she asked.

"Two cops are camped out at the gas station drinking coffee. We'll have to be quick, so they don't see us."

Annabelle climbed out of the window and stood not on the edge of the sill, but with her feet on the vertical stone face, defying gravity. Miles climbed out, and she took both of his hands before grabbing him by the wrists. Like an unnatural elevator, she walked down the face of the building, holding him the whole way. Once low enough, Miles let go and landed without a sound. "I'm sorry I have to leave you," he told her "When you're done here, push the window shut behind you so nobody knows we've been here."

"I will. Goodnight, Miles."

"Goodnight." With that, Miles stole another glance at the gas station before walking back to the alley where the car was parked.

Annabelle pulled the window shut and returned downstairs. The library seemed so magnificent. There were too many books to count. All through the early morning hours, she read. She'd become so enraptured in the twentieth century and the ones before it that she never left the reference section to explore the rest of the library. There was so much to learn. From Thesaurus to Atlas, she soaked in every word and picture. It wasn't just American culture she wanted to learn. The world was so big that she spent an entire hour learning the history of China alone. Whole countries and civilizations she never could have imagined came pouring out of the volumes; pharaohs and dynasties, tsars and samurai, south pole explorers, geishas, the Taj Mahal, and a space race. There were even pictures of Earth from the moon. Annabelle loved it all but too soon, the night gave way to early morning. At five A.M. sharp her wristwatch beeped.

"Ah, dammit," she said, tucking an encyclopedia and another brightly colored book entitled: *Frogs and Amphibians of Kentucky* under her arm before starting up the stairs. She made it halfway to the top before a glimmer of the glass on the Booth exhibit caught her eye again. Annabelle paused. The idea of leaving her belongings behind ate at her, made her skin itch. It didn't feel right to see her shotgun on display. It reminded her of the time she managed to catch a butterfly in a mason jar to keep on the windowsill of her room. She didn't have it long before her mother saw the jar and made her set it free. "Only food belongs in glass containers." Mother said.

Annabelle didn't think twice. As fast as she could manage, she ran down the stairs, crossed the room and put her boot through the glass. The pane shattered, shards collapsing and collecting in the bottom. No sooner had the case broken that a terrible grating alarm noise sounded overhead. Frightened by the racket, Annabelle hurried to gather the items.

When grabbing the shotgun, however, she found a small, threaded silver cable holding it fast to the display's metal base. Two tugs weren't enough to pull it free but planting one foot on the base and yanking as hard as she dared resulted in the case dislodging from the floor.

Annabelle yelped as the whole display tipped and came crashing down upon her. Glass exploded everywhere, hundreds of little razors cutting at the skin of her arms and face. She brushed them away and regripped the stock to pull again with a foot on each side of the hole where the cable vanished into the bottom. A shrug of the shoulders. The cable's moorings groaned loud enough to be heard over the alarm before finally snapping and coming away in her hands. If not for the thickness of her sweater, the broken glass would have cut her to pieces.

The alarm sounded louder now, and Annabelle pulled herself out of the mess. Strange red and blue lights flashed from somewhere outside, frightening her. She had no idea where they'd come from, but she wasted no time in gathering the books, dress, and shotgun to escape. Upstairs, she peered out the window before climbing out and floating up another twenty feet to the roof. No sooner had her feet touched the gutter when light from below caught her climbing over the edge.

"I see you!" a man shouted on the ground. "Ed, I'm over on the North side. There's somebody on the roof!"

"Understood." A strange little voice sounded in the same spot. "I've got both the exits and the fire escape covered on this side. No one's going anywhere. Move up to the second floor, there's access to the roof at the top of the stairs."

"Copy that. Coming your way now."

The deputies from across the street are coming up. Annabelle thought in a panic. She climbed across the roof with the bundle of books held tight against her chest.

While she may have climbed in on the second floor, the high arches of the libraries ceiling made the building four stories in total. Annabelle had never been atop a building and the view was disorienting, to say the least. The lights came from the west side of the building and she scooted closer to peek over the edge. From the higher vantage point, she could see the scene unfolding below. Two identical cars with winking and blinking lights upon them blocked the street, a man stood between them. She looked closer to find a badge on his chest.

Deputies. She thought. *That means guns and hand-irons. I need to get out of here.* A loud bang sounded as a trap door opened not far from her. A young man with short cut brown hair saw her immediately.

"Stop, you!" he yelled out. Annabelle made a run across the roof for the south edge. In the panic of the moment, she forgot how she was going to get down. There was a sycamore tree close enough to climb onto. She pitched the books and dress off the edge to land at the base of the tree.

"What's going on up there?" The device on the man's shoulder spoke.

"I got a teenage girl up here in a red shirt, and she's armed with a sawed-off shotgun!"

"Keep your distance," said the device.

"Put the gun down!" the man commanded. She turned about with the weapon in her hands. When she saw him again, he had a pistol already drawn and pointed at her. The heels of her boots were almost over the lip. "Get away from the edge!" He yelled. "You could fall off!"

Annabelle looked over the edge and back to the lawman.

"You're right," she said with a smile. "I could." With that, Annabelle tipped backward on her heels and went over.

The officer holstered his weapon and rushed to the end of the building. Upon approaching it and peering to the ground below…there was no sign of the girl. Only a gingham dress splayed on the ground with some books strewn about.

"What's going on?" said the other voice on the radio.

"She went over the edge of the south side!"

"Is she dead?"

"No, she's gone!"

"All right, I'm coming around." The man looked down as the other officer appeared around the corner with his flashlight and gun drawn. The swath of light shined upon the empty dress before pointing upwards at him. "I thought you said she fell over here! Where is she?" He shouted.

"I don't know! She went over the edge! She should be lying right in front of you!" The man looked about some more.

"There's nobody here! Are you sure she jumped?"

"Yes, I'm sure! It was a skinny little pale bitch in a maroon Transylvania Sweatshirt with a damn shotgun!"

"Well, there's nobody down here! Do you think you saw a ghost or something?

"You know what? Fuck you, Ed! I'm getting the hell off this roof." Not far away, in the tree line, Annabelle watched the two men talking. Overhead, the sky was growing lighter. Morning birds began to sing. She hated herself for not listening to Miles and leaving the display alone. The mausoleum was still so far away. It was then that she remembered the map Miles had given her.

Her hand reached to her back pocket and pulled it out. The map of White Wreath showed her everything she needed to know. The topography resembled an upturned horseshoe with the gas station and cemetery far at the bottom and the library on the upper left-hand point. It was a long way back there, but the distillery ruins and Miles's house, by what would be the top right-hand point, was a shorter trip by far. She'd be racing the oncoming sun. If she couldn't find shelter in time, she'd be a pile of ashes for sure. She pulled the hood of the sweatshirt up to hide her head and pulled the sleeves out to cover her hands.

As fast as Annabelle could manage, she headed east into the woods, through the underbrush, and over the hills. Birds flushed from their perches. Ground animals scurried back to their burrows. Across open fields, she sprinted, hurdling the sporadic fences and single lane roads to return to the canopy of the lush woods. The night sky began to peel away a little at a time, causing her skin to itch. Faster she ran until at last, she happened upon the Burkich homestead from the side yard.

As soon as she arrived, a small man with a full mustache emerge from the house. He got into his vehicle, backed it out of the yard and traveled out of sight. She breathed a sigh of relief that Miles's "Caddylak" was still there.

The sun was getting dangerously close to rising. Even with the thick garment covering most of her torso, Annabelle's skin began to burn. It felt like it did on her last conscious day in the nineteenth century. With no more time to waste, she pulled the drawstrings of her hoodie to closing it around her face. Annabelle broke from the shade of the canopy of the trees and ran blindly towards the house. She rounded the corner of the house to the front porch where she ran headlong into Miles. They collided, and he fell backward across Gary's porch chair. He tried to catch himself from falling, and his left hand stopped on the small tempered glass table before the pane broke and his hand went through.

"Gah!" he cried out.

"Miles, you have to help me," Annabelle said. He struggled to get his hand out of the shards but it wasn't easy with her pawing at his chest.

"Annabelle? Get off me, my hand."

"Please, I have to get indoors," she pleaded as she pulled at his t-shirt.

"Annabelle, move," he said again. She didn't hear him as she was frantically trying to say something about the library. The shards cut deeper into his palm.

"Some deputies came to the library, but that was after I broke a case and I tried to get away on the roof!"

"Annabelle, get off me!" With a hard lurch he pitched her off and she fell backward on her ass. He looked to the sky. The sun was coming. Miles leaned to the non-blood covered hand and pushed himself to his feet, tucking the injured hand against the stomach of his shirt. The screen door flew open and the inner door swung inward to reveal the living room. "Come on." He nodded with his head. "Get in." Annabelle jumped to her feet and rushed over to the doorway. Upon reaching the threshold, however, she stopped cold. "What are you waiting for?" he asked. "Get in." She said nothing but looked up and down at the door frame. Blood slipped between his fingers and fell onto the deck in a perfect circular droplet. "Annabelle, I'm bleeding all over the place here! Go!"

"I can't," she said in a voice barely louder than a whisper. The sun grew brighter by the second. Miles used his clean hand to try and nudge her in.

"Get…in…there…" He pushed against her, but she didn't move. "What's the matter?"

"I can't. Something's wrong."

"Don't be afraid, just get inside."

"I'm not afraid. I can't enter your house. Help me."

"Wait." he exclaimed. "I forgot, vampire rules." He slipped past her and stood in front of her. When he crossed the threshold, he turned around to face her.

"Would you like to come inside my home?" he asked. Before an audible reply could be heard, Annabelle was pushing past him. She kept running, hugging the wall furthest from the front windows to stand in the hallway where the shadows were thickest.

Miles shut the door before going to the kitchen. In there, he found the small towel hanging from the cabinet handle below the sink he was looking for. The stream of cold water stung the pale flesh as it washed the red swirls of blood away. "Aw, horse piss." He cursed as he looked at the wounds in the heel and fingers. The slices weren't big enough to need stitches, but band-aids weren't going to cut it either. Gary wanted him to replace a broken nozzle on one of the diesel pumps this morning, and diesel fuel in any cut burns like the devil. Even worse, he'd have to make up some kind of story about what happened to the table which Gary would be less than thrilled about.

"I can't fix the table," Annabelle said from just outside the kitchen.

"Who said anything about you fixing the table?"

"No one, but you were thinking it."

"I wish you wouldn't do that, look in my mind that is."

"I can't help it. There's no one else around and you were thinking really hard about what to do. It's like not hearing what someone is saying when they're standing in front of you."

"The table isn't a big loss. Gary will be a little pissed but it's just a small table, I'll get him another one. My day, however, is going to suck. Even if I can find a rubber glove to go over my hand, it's going to sting and fill with blood or just burn for the next few days."

"I can fix your hand," she said.

"Really? Then get in here and do it because it hurts like the devil."

"There's too much light in there. It burns. Is there room with no windows?"

"Sure. Let me get this washed off and we'll go to my room." He held the hand still and blotted at the cuts with a paper towel to stem the flow. Past Annabelle and down the hall he walked. The door opened and he flicked the light switch. Annabelle paused. When he didn't hear her footsteps, Miles looked back to see her apprehensive expression. "Come on." He waved at her. "It's artificial light. It shouldn't hurt you."

"Shouldn't or won't?"

"It won't. Should I ask you why you have the shotgun from the library slung over your shoulder?" She started down the stairs, pulling the hood from her head and lifting the gun from her back.

"The shotgun belongs to me, so I took it back."

"I thought you said you weren't going to take it."

"You said I shouldn't. I never agreed with you. I had to break the case to get it. Then a terrible sound filled the air and the deputies came with their red and blue lights. One of them chased me off the roof!"

"What were you doing on the roof?"

"I don't know, I was scared, and I was trying to get away. I had books, but I dropped them."

"The cops are going to shit themselves about the stolen gun, but the last place they're going to look for it is a locked tomb in the cemetery. That thing isn't loaded is it?"

"No, I checked. There's no shells." She laid the gun down next to the stereo.

"You said you could do something for these cuts?" he asked

"Give it here," she said, leading him to the chair at his desk. He sat, and she knelt before him, her hands unfolding the dish towel. None of the cuts were too big on their own, there was just a lot of them. Annabelle bared her fangs and bit into the meat below her right thumb before holding it over his hand. Crimson flow poured from her cut into his, causing a tingling in his fingertips. More than that it created a soothing sensation that calmed him.

"How do you know how to do this?" he asked.

"I'm not sure," she said. "It seems natural somehow but it's nothing I've ever learned. I did this to your shoulder the night we met in the distillery. I can't explain why I thought to do it."

"I'm glad that you did." He smiled down at her.

"I'm glad you freed me. If you hadn't fallen into the ruins, I'd still be sleeping. Who knows how long I could've stayed that way. Wouldn't that be terrible? What if you hadn't been there and I kept right on sleeping? Why, I might've slept for another hundred years and you would've been born, lived to old age and died before I opened an eye. The world is strange enough now. You got cars, airplanes, rocket ships that go to the moon, moving picture shows, trimmed trees with ropes between them that talk to each other..."

"Talking trees?"

"Yeah, like the ones outside. They're all over the place and scary as shit. I try and stay away from them. If you stand really quiet, you can hear them talking to each other the same way you and I are talking now."

"Trees can't talk."

"The hell they can't, Miles. You've got one outside your house. And I can hear it from here."

Miles mulled over her words. "Trimmed trees with ropes tied between them." Did she mean telephone poles? His hand felt better despite now being covered in blood again. Annabelle held her own hand up to the light of the desk lamp as the wound mended itself before their eyes. Little by little, the edges of the bitten flesh pulled themselves back together until there was no more.

"There," she said. "Try washing your hand off."

He stepped into the bathroom and did as she asked. Sure enough, as the water from the sink ran over his palm, the blood washed away to leave undamaged skin underneath. How it worked didn't matter as much as the fact that it <u>did</u> work. He dried his hands and returned to show her the results. When he stepped out, he found her slumped over in the chair.

"Annabelle?" he asked. She jumped with a start and looked up at him with surprise." Are you all right?"

"I'm tired." She rubbed one eye. "The sun is probably way up in the sky by now. I'm not going to be able to get home."

"Then you should sleep here."

"Do you mean it?"

"Sure. You can sleep here. I have to go to work, but I'll be home later. When the sun goes down I'll drive you back to the cemetery."

"You will?"

"Why wouldn't I?"

"That's very kind of you."

"Annabelle? Can I ask you a question?"

"What would you like to know?"

"You don't have to answer immediately, but what are you going to do now? You don't want to spend all of eternity sleeping in a tomb in White Wreath, do you?"

"Where would I go? What would I do?"

"See the world, I guess. Maybe seek out others like yourself."

"If they're anything like the one that bit me then I don't want anything to do with them."

"It bit you, and you didn't turn out like a monster. There could be others who've gone through what you have but didn't sleep for a hundred years." Annabelle's gaze lowered to her lap.

"Are you saying you don't want me around?" she asked. Miles stepped closer, took a knee and put his hands atop hers.

"That's not it at all." He lowered his head to look her in the eye. "But I'm not always going to be around, and I want to help you find others who can be with you after I'm old and dead. Shit, I plan on leaving White Wreath myself."

"Where are you going?"

"Anywhere else. College probably, maybe even the army, I don't know, maybe New Orleans. Either way, I'm leaving town after I graduate next year at the latest. Annabelle, I don't want anything to happen to you, but I can't care for you forever."

"Why not?" she asked. "If you'd let me bite you, then you could be like me, and we could do whatever we wanted."

"I don't know if being a vampire is right for me."

"I didn't know either." She pouted. "But I didn't get a choice." Miles reached up and put a hand on her cheek. The skin was pale and cold.

"Don't be sad, listen. I have to go now. You stay and sleep. You'll be safe, and Gary rarely ever comes down here. Sleep in my bed if you want," he said as he started up the stairs.

"Miles?" she asked.

"Yes?"

"Why are you nice to me?" Miles paused for a moment to think about that.

"I know that if what happened to you happened to me then I'd want at least one person to understand. You said it yourself, you didn't have a choice to be where you are now. I guess I want to help so you don't have to be alone while you figure things out."

Annabelle hung her head. "I-I never wanted any of this."

"Yeah..." he said, starting up the stairs again. "I know."

Miles left Annabelle to sleep and drove towards the Imperial. Monster glided away the miles, the reflections of trees and telephone wires shifting past the windshield in intermittent waves.

Far too soon Monster rolled into the truck stop already bustling with semi-trucks. It would be foolish to park the car in an area where trailers constantly bumped into things, so he guided the car into the shady area just off the gravel lot. It would keep the vehicle from turning into an oven and protect the paint as well. As soon as he killed the large engine the sound of rattling windows and musically rhymed expletives sounded in the distance and getting closer. Miles rolled his eyes so hard he thought they might fall out of his head entirely.

JoJo's Ford Explorer careened into view, its "too tiny not to be on a go-kart" tires squelching off the asphalt and across the gravel. The large Samoan scowled at him from the passenger seat, flipping him a lazy middle finger as they passed.

Great, just great.

Although, after the incident with Annabelle, it didn't surprise him that the "yo dawg cracker wagon" had found a way to tap dance its way into his morning as well. The SUV almost sideswiped a pickup as it swerved and skidded into a handicapped parking spot. In most cases, he'd mention something to someone using the spot that Pearl used to park her car. Today he'd keep his mouth shut. After all, the spot was being used by the mentally impaired. JoJo hopped out first, peering around the lot before finding Miles.

"Yo, where's my uncle?" he yelled across the lot as he always did.

"Probably working a job like you should be," he said under his breath as he pointed in the general direction of the office.

"What?"

"I said, he's probably in the back office!" He pointed again.

"Thanks, dipshit! How about you let me and my boys borrow that car of yours?" He yelled again. "I'll bring it back with a full tank of gas!" JoJo said to the merriment of his thugs.

"How about you eat me?" Miles replied. The faces of JoJo's crew lit up with excitement at the possibility of some drama.

"Oh shit!" said the one with the '606' tattoo on his neck. "Jo, you gonna let that faggot talk to you like that?" At their prompting, JoJo was already two steps off the curb and headed straight for Miles.

"Get him, Jo!" said the other one in the back seat. It took to the count of "four-Mississippi" for him to stand toe to toe with Miles. The closer he got, the more the hard lines in his face began to show. If it were possible, he looked thinner than last time. The hollows of his cheeks began to show.

"You got shit to say to me?" Miles took the obligatory step back but JoJo's fist was already in motion. It was a good punch though, a small twist of the hips followed by a rotation of the body moving its way up through the shoulders. The final result is a whiplash effect that delivers a punch, if timed and aimed directly, is as powerful as it is fast. The shot caught Miles square between the left temple and eye. A white flash filled his head followed by his shoulder blades striking the gravel of the lot. He lay stunned, trying to make words, but none came. JoJo stood over him, kicking him in the hip. "Got something else to say? Is that it? Huh? Say something." He kicked him again. "Yeah, that's what I thought, ya little faggot." How embarrassing, getting your ass beat for being a "faggot" the without the pleasure of getting the sex needed to be considered one.

"WHAT THE HELL IS GOING ON OUT HERE?!" A voice bellowed out over the roar of the trucks. Miles stopped guarding his head long enough to look up with his remaining good eye and find Gary already next to JoJo pushing him away from him. "The shit's gotten into you two fighting in front of the station? JoJo get out of here. Miles? Where have you been for the past twenty minutes? The trash is already overflowing on pump two and I got four people asking me where the clean towels are. JOJO I SAID 'GIT'!"

"But Uncle Gary, I wanted to get-"

"I don't want to hear it!"

"But Uncle Gary…"

"GODDAMMIT, I SAID GET OUT OF MY SIGHT!" Gary yelled louder than Miles had heard him yell before. JoJo cussed something under his breath and backed away a few steps before turning and heading back to his vehicle.

His boys looked on without a word from the inside. Whatever their expectations were for JoJo to score money and buy them booze or a bag of smoke deflated fast as he walked back empty-handed and got inside the Explorer. Gary and Miles watched as the sport utility vehicle, comically small wheels and all, tore out of the parking lot and sped out of sight. A helpful hand reached down to lift Miles from the ground. He accepted and staggered to his feet.

"Ah, shit," Gary whispered as he saw Miles's face up close. "Looks like he dotted your eye something good. What the hell were you two arguing about?"

"Nothing," Miles grumbled. "He's just an asshole, and I didn't feel like sidestepping him today."

"Yeah? Well, JoJo's bigger than you and you need to learn and pick your battles."

"I shouldn't get hit because he's a piece of shit. He hit me, Gary. That's assault. If we go inside and call the sheriff and file a report, he'll put a warrant out for JoJo."

"Did he just walk up and hit you for no reason or did you mouth off to him beforehand?"

Miles said nothing. "Well? I'm listening. Did you say something to piss him off?"

"He wanted to use my car, and I may have told him to eat me."

"I thought that might be the case. You can't run around shooting off at the mouth to whomever you want or stuff like this is going to happen."

"Did you just say whomever?"

"Isn't that the right word?" Gary asked.

"Yes, actually."

"Then don't give me no shit about it. You've got a small cut there. Come on inside and let's get some iodine on it. I think you're going to end up with a black eye."

"Okay," Miles said, holding his palm over the throbbing socket as he followed. "It's assault, Gary. He's twenty-three and I'm not eighteen. He struck a minor."

"I'll call my sister in a bit and let her know what's going on. She'll swat his ass."

"Aunt Karen is ninety-eight pounds and fighting cancer. She's not going to swat anything."

"Then I'll have a talk with him too. Would that make you feel better?"

"Not really. He's just an animal that's all."

"Don't go calling names. Everybody's got their faults."

"Why do you always defend him?" Miles asked, his voice more agitated now. "I've got a black eye and he's driven off to do god knows what. You're lenient with him because he's your blood." Gary grabbed him by the bicep to stop in in his tracks and gave him a light slap across the cheek. It wasn't meant to hurt as much as it was to get his attention but with the throbbing eye, it hurt a lot more than it was supposed to. His grip tightened more.

"You listen, Miles. You're smart. You've got a brain between your ears. JoJo's got jack shit between his. Get on inside and let me get you patched up. I'll make things right."

"All right." Miles nodded. He stepped indoors and into view of all the people within. Everyone, including Darla behind the register, couldn't help but stare at the already spreading bruise. The pair navigated through the aisles of food and the truckers waiting with their toiletries for the showers.

Inside the office, Miles plunked down in a chair while Gary retrieved the dusty first aid kit from atop a filing cabinet. He actually brushed off the top and blew on it the same way a wizard does in a fantasy story when he's about to reveal an ancient artifact that's been put away for a long time. As he opened it, Miles half expected the room to darken and for the contents of the box to emit light of its own while heavenly melodies revealed the contents within. The plastic lid flopped over to reveal three wrinkled band-aids, an empty tube of Neosporin with no cap and half of a loose cigarette.

"What the shit, Gary?"

"That can't be right." Gary sighed. "Hold on." He left the room to which Miles mentally followed him through the store, listening to the moving of people and sounds that seemed so familiar. The murmur of his voice near the front counter followed by the electronic song of the register. Booted footsteps got louder until he returned with an armload of medical supplies. He tossed them in a pile on his desk and pulled up his office chair to sit across from Miles before opening the first box marked antibiotic cream.

"Hold still and I'll square you away," he said. "By the way, did you hear what happened last night?"

"No, what?"

"My friend Ed Powers, you know Deputy Ed, he was patrolling past the library last night when the alarm went off and the dispatcher called in the alarm. He and Henry Garrett went in and found a girl had broken in and stole the old shotgun out of the Booth Distillery exhibit they have there."

"Why would a girl steal an antique shotgun?" Miles feigned surprise.

"I dunno, probably out of her head on pills or something. But something he said made me take notice."

"What's that?"

"Ed said that Henry described the girl as about sixteen years old with light blonde hair."

"What does having blonde hair mean?"

"I wasn't finished. He also mentioned she was wearing a large Transylvania University sweatshirt."

"Okay."

Gary looked Miles in his one good eye. "Now I'm not the smartest person in the world, but I'm not stupid either. All your clothes are black. You haven't worn anything but black clothes since you were eight and stayed up watching those crazy-ass late night 'Dr. Wolfenstein creature feature movies' on the TV. So, tell me this; how is it you and I just happened to pick up a brand-new maroon, Transy sweatshirt, and not a week later a girl your age is seen wearing one? Tell me the truth, boy. Do you know who broke into the library and took that gun? Don't you lie to me. You've never been one to lie." His eyes did waver a bit as he stared Miles down.

"What if I said a girl asked me to get her one? But I had no idea what she was going to break into the library."

"Then I'd say that's something Deputy Ed needs to hear. What's the girl's name, and how do we find her?"

"I don't know where she lives." Total lie. "She said her name was Annabelle."

"Annabelle what?"

"Anabelle Booth."

"You see that right there? That should have tipped you off that the girl was up to no good. Do you know who Annabelle Booth was?"

"No." *Suuuuper lie.*

"Hell, Miles, this is why you need to study history. You know the old ruined distillery across the road from our house? The one you nearly died in. That once belonged to the Booths. Annabelle Booth was the name of the daughter that died in the fire. The pill head girl that pulled the prank at the library was probably so jacked out of her head on god-knows-what that she probably thinks she *is* Annabelle Booth. I'll tell you something else—the other night Dale Wrigley, the rough fellow who comes into the Imperial all the time? Well, he and his friend Clay were out hunting recently and said they came across a girl that fits that Annabelle girl's description. They said she was out walking

246

through the woods buck ass naked with a snake draped over her and almost shot her by accident. What kind of person not on pills wanders around in the dark with a damn copperhead draped over them like a bathrobe?"

"Beats me."

"Beats me either. Oh well, if you say you don't know her, then I guess there's no reason to call Ed. Whoever that girl is, you keep your distance. The cops don't think stealing firearms is a laughing matter, and they'll be on the look-out for her. I don't know about you but if I was a cop and I missed catching a girl from ten feet away I sure as hell wouldn't tell anybody. Anyway, I still don't know how she got it out of the case either unless she had a pair of bolt cutters or something. Last time I stopped to look at that old gun, I'm pretty sure they had the whole thing mounted and tethered so that somebody couldn't take it. Don't go messing with pills. They'll turn you into the living dead, or worse, a thieving-ass junkie."

"Like JoJo?"

"Now I just told you to knock that shit off." He pointed a finger. "I'm telling you for the last time, leave him alone."

"Fine."

"That eye isn't looking good at all. How does it feel?"

"It's killing me. I hit the back of my head on the gravel. There's no blood, but it's going to leave a lump."

"You know what? I think you should go back home."

247

"I can't miss work. I just got here. Besides, I've missed enough lately as it is."

"I know you've always been a good worker, but it's not going to do you any good to be walking around here with one eye shut. I'll sign off on your timecard so that you don't miss any of your pay. You go on home, now."

"Are you sure?"

"Sure, I'm sure. You look miserable. Are you okay to drive with one eye?"

"Yeah, I'm good. See you at home."

"Oh, and when you get home use an ice pack to help with the swelling. There's some small bags of frozen vegetables in the freezer if you want to put one of them on your eye."

"Ok, I'll do that, bye."

"See you at home." Miles walked out of the office and through the aisles towards the front door. There wasn't one person that didn't make a wild expression at his injury as he passed. It took ten times longer than it should have to reach the car and get on the road again.

CHAPTER FOURTEEN

Miles arrived at home to find Annabelle still awake and sitting cross-legged in her sweatshirt in front of his stereo. Speakers resonated the subtle notes of the somber track throughout the room. He descended with little noise, pausing to watch her sway to the dwindling toes. When it ended, she rocked forward to her knees, reached up and placed the needle at the beginning of the song before moving back to the same spot.

"You like that song huh?" he asked

"I do," she replied without opening her eyes. "What's the man's name who sings this?"

"Ian Curtis. The band is called Joy Division."

"It sounds so sad, but it's beautiful. Where does Ian Curtis live?"

"In a cemetery in England. He hung himself not long after I was born." Annabelle's eyes widened in surprise when she looked at him.

"That's terrible. Why would someone—holy sweet Jesus!" She jumped to her feet and rushed over to him. "Miles, what happened to your eye?"

"It's nothing."

"Nothing?" It looks like you got in a fight!" Annabelle pressed her fingers around the skin and made him wince enough to push her away.

"A fight would imply that two people are throwing punches."

"Someone hit you?" she asked. "Who hit you? Who did this?"

"Some crankhead. But now that I think about it, I provoked him."

"What's a crankhead?" Miles considered his next words. *Were people junkies in 1890s?*

"It's um, someone who uses a medicine in the wrong way so they can get wasted."

"Oh, like laudanum users. Miss Vice at the general store has a husband who'd drink a bunch of poppy extract and lay around for days at a time."

"Who's Miss Vice?" Miles asked her. Realizing what she'd said, Annabelle corrected herself.

"Oh," she said with a touch of melancholy as she remembered Miss Vice and even her kids could be dead by now. "There used to be a woman named Miss Vice, who owned the general store in town. Her husband used too much laudanum. She had to hold him up by the arm just to get him to church on Sunday. Papa said he was sleeping his life away. Is he like that?"

"Kind of. Only instead of sleepy, he's really aggressive."

"He sounds like a drunk bully. Why didn't you hit him back? Is he bigger than you?"

"It's not that simple, he's Gary's nephew."

"He sounds like he's good for nothing. You should have punched him back."

"I probably could, but he always has two or three friends with him in case of a fight."

"Cowards always run with gangs. They move in groups because they're yellow little chickenshits who don't have the guts to stand up for themselves."

"That describes JoJo and his crew perfectly." He winced again. "Ok, my head is really throbbing."

"What can I do?"

"Let me get something from the medicine cabinet." Annabelle stepped aside and Miles retrieved the small white plastic pill bottle from the bathroom. He popped the cap, emptied two pills into his hand and swallowed them with a drink of water he got from the sink.

"I can help you with the pain if you want."

"What can you do?"

"My blood." She tried to touch the eye again before he pulled away. "It healed your shoulder and your hand. It could heal your eye."

"You don't mind? Doesn't it hurt when you bite yourself?"

"It always hurts, but if it eases the pain, then it's worth it. The wound heals fast."

"If you don't mind, then sure."

"If I do it for you would you help me with something?"

"What do you need my help with?"

"My shotgun." She walked over to the bed where it was leaning against the frame and held it out for him to take. "I don't have any shells for it. I can smell that you have some gunpowder upstairs, but I didn't want to take something that didn't belong to me. I was hoping we could work out a trade. I'll fix your eye in exchange for a handful of shells."

"What do you need shells for?" he asked.

"What good is having a gun with no shells?"

"That's true. I have to ask though, you're not intending to use that gun on anyone, are you? Because I'm not going to enable you to go out and shoot someone."

"I don't want to shoot anyone. It would be for personal defense only. I'm not a bank robber or a cattle rustler."

"No." Miles laughed. "I didn't think you were. If you can heal my eye, then I'll see what I can do about getting you some shells."

"Deal." She stuck her hand out for him to shake.

"Deal." He agreed, sealing the pact. "What do you want me to do?"

"Just lay down on the floor." Miles did as she asked and reclined in front of the stereo. The song on the record ended again and she moved the needle back to the beginning. *Atmosphere*. The slow minimalist droning of the opening notes relaxed him as he lay staring up at the imperfections of the ceiling. Annabelle knelt next to his shoulder and smiled down at him, her canine fangs already elongating. With the tiniest effort, she pressed her right thumb upwards into her mouth impaling the fingerprint upon the porcelain spike, letting slip the smallest of whimpers. A crimson droplet welled from the flesh. She held his head still with one hand while she brushed her thumb atop and below his eye. It tingled the same way the makeup did when Dennis had applied it.

Oh shit. He realized. *Dennis. I've been neglecting my best friend.*

"What's his name?" Annabelle asked.

"Who?"

"The person you were thinking about just now."

"Can you seriously read minds?" he asked.

"I get little flashes in my head. Quick visions. You felt happy when you thought of them. It's more of a feeling. You thought you haven't seen them for some time."

"You're right, I was. Everything has been a whirlwind lately. Dennis is my best friend in the world, and I haven't spent any time with him."

"A lot has been happening," she said.

"That's true," he said with an expression of discomfort.

"Is your eye still hurting?"

"Not as much as before. It feels like it's subsiding some. Stay here, I'm going to get some things from the tool shed." Miles went upstairs and returned a few minutes later with heaping armloads of things she didn't recognize. The items landed in a pile on the desk with a "thunk."

"What's all that for?" she asked

"You said you wanted shells. I'm going to make you some," he replied, blinking the bruised eye a little more before pulling a seat up to the desk.

"Make some? What's wrong with giving me some of those there?"

"Oh, no. You don't want to do that. Your shotgun was made to fire black powder shells. If you put new shells like these in it, the whole gun would blow up in your face."

"Oh." She frowned. "No, I wouldn't like that. I didn't mean to interrupt. Do what you were going to do." His hand clicked on the articulated lamp overhead and swung it over the middle of the desk. White light washed over everything as he gathered the items needed: shotgun shells, a metal scalpel, long pliers, half a bottle of black powder he'd picked up at a yard sale, small bottle of glue, a dirty rag, a pen, scissors, a plastic bottle cap, and lastly, a black candle with a lighter.

Annabelle didn't stand over him as much as she began to float. As naturally as one sits on the floor, she reached up to the wall at the back of the desk and laid her hand upon it. With no effort, she turned herself over in a slow-motion somersault to sit upon the back wall over the desk with her legs crossed.

"You're going to ignore gravity again?"

"You don't have a second chair, and I didn't want to look over your shoulder. I don't mind if you don't."

"Whatever you want." Miles spaced all the items around the desk. Before he began, he wheeled about in his swiveling chair, changed the record on the player, laid the needle and spun back to where he was before. Simple guitar melodies filled the air and pleasant voices began to sing over the music. His hands went to work with the crude tools, prying open the ends of the shells and prying out the contents with the scalpel. He dumped the shot pellets, wad and powder into separate piles until only the casings with the firing primers remained. The lid of the black powder can fell away and the plastic bottle cap scooped out a little at the time. Using a rolled piece of paper as a crude funnel held over the empty shells, he scooped small amounts of powder into each before cutting small squares of the rag and stuffing them inside. The small handles of the pliers made excellent tamping dowels. Upon looking up at Annabelle, Miles noticed her swaying along with the music.

"This is good too," she commented. "Who is this?"

"The Beatles."

"The Beatles? This sounds happier. He says he wants to hold a girl's hand. That's nice."

"Yeah, they're the best."

"Is their singer still alive?"

"Unfortunately, no.

"Oh, my goodness. He didn't hang himself too, did he?"

"No," Miles grumbled as he gathered the buckshot and poured it next. "Some crazy asshole named Mark David Chapman shot him in New York the early 1980s. The other three members are still alive."

"Why did he do it?"

"Because he was a hateful piece of shit with nothing better to do but bring misery on others."

"Like the 'JoJo' person that hit you in the eye?" she asked

"Sort of. JoJo has always been a piece of shit. He'll never change. He'll be a piece of shit till the day he dies."

"That's kind of sad that he doesn't know any better."

"Yeah, well..." Miles tamped down the contents of each shell with the plier handles again and then proceeded to use the lighter to drip black candle wax, sealing the shells. Trimming the excess shell length with a scalpel made the ends look clean for a homemade job with no proper equipment. "There you go, Annie Oakley." He handed two of them out for her to take. As she was about to pluck it, he pulled it back into his palm. "But first I want your word that you're not going to go shooting someone with these."

"I promise not to shoot a person out of anything other than self-defense." She held her hand closer to his. "I've never wanted to kill anyone in my life."

"Promise?" he asked. "I could get in big shit for making shells for a stolen gun."

"It's not stolen." She smiled. "It's always been mine, and I still promise."

"Fine." He opened his hand, and she took them. No sooner had she taken them that the sound of the shotgun opening sounded to his right. When he turned his head, Annabelle already stood across the room inserting the shells into the barrels. They slid in as easy as you please before the barrels locked into place with a metallic "Ca-chak"

"That's better," she said, feeling the weight of the weapon in her hands.

"Why even need a gun at all, Annabelle? You moved across the room faster than any bullet. You could do more damage with a pocketknife or bare hands."

"I don't need it." Her hands ran up and down the wood and steel. "But everything I knew of my life before is gone except for this. I can't help that I want to cling to something familiar when everything else has changed so much."

"It would be in your best interests to keep the gun hidden in the tomb, preferably out of reach of where some 'daywalker' types could get their hands on it." As soon as Miles used the word 'daywalker' Annabelle began to yawn again. "You look tired. Why don't you sleep? I have some thread to mend the cuts where the glass cut your hoodie."

"You sew, you make shotgun shells, is there anything you don't know how to do?"

"Dodge a punch, apparently." He laughed as he felt his eye. The bruised skin had become less tender to the touch, but the pain medicine hadn't quite taken hold for a headache.

"You don't have to fix the holes," she said. "They're small and I think it gives it character."

"Whatever you want." He snatched a small green canvas pouch with a strap hanging next to the stereo and dumped the rest of her shotgun shells inside. Once gathered with the rest of the items, he put all her things, including the shotgun, under the stairs. Annabelle crawled into his bed before pulling the covers up to her chin. A few seconds later the last of her garments emerged from beneath the sheets and fell to the floor.

"When sundown comes, I'll take you home." One of her eyes popped open to follow his path across the room.

"You're good to me, Miles. Who takes care of you?"

"I take care of myself," he said as a finger traced the tender skin around his eye. "Most of the time."

Annabelle fell asleep and Miles cleaned off his desk, dumping all the contents into an old shoebox and stuffing it far up under his desk where it wouldn't be seen. He turned the stereo off and turned on the television in its place. Stacks of VHS tapes beckoned from their sleeves; titles like Fright Night, Near Dark, Nosferatu, The Hunger, The Lost Boys, The Last Man on Earth. For all of these being his favorites, the arrival of Annabelle left him unable to bear another vampire story.

In the end, he selected *Blade Runner*. He laid down in his usual spot on the floor and used a bundle of dirty clothes as a makeshift pillow. The old television blinked and crackled as the tracking feature fixed the out of focus screen. His favorite story unfolded; Replicants. More human than human. Miles's eyes drooped, and the scenes skipped unnaturally from one to another in a blur of rain and neon until he drifted into a deep sleep. He remained sprawled on the floor dozing all day until he finally heard an echo of Gary's voice at the top of the stairs. The words were still fuzzy, but he managed a half-coherent response when he was told he had a visitor. It would be Dennis of course. The door at the top of the stairs closed and boot steps followed. Drowsy, Miles lay in place until someone stood over him. "Hey, how's it going?" he managed to speak. The excess sleep kept his eyes unfocused and stayed blurry until the person dropped down right on top of him. The eyes opened wide to find not Dennis…but Lucifer.

"Hey there, sleepyhead, have I caught you at a bad time?"

"No, no." He rubbed his eyes. "I was just…um, just."

"You were lying here all alone hoping that I would magically appear, and look at that, here I am." She purred. Lucifer wore the same low cut, death rocker shirt she always sported. Her boots climbed from her ankles to her to the knees with thigh high stockings leaving a flash of white flash skin before reaching the bottom of her black miniskirt. All that bisected by a garter strap. The belt with the bondage rings spaced around it hung lopsided below the midriff 'Christian Death' band t-shirt methodically torn to shit and safety-pinned back together with spider-webbed black stockings covering her arms. "So, now that I'm here and you don't have to wait anymore, what do you think we should do?" She'd straddled him and traced an index finger from his pants up to his shirt and navel. "Because I don't have to be anywhere for a while, and I thought you and I might get to know each other a little better. Would you like that? Gary said he was stopping in to get the mail and would be leaving directly." The finger moved a little higher, taking his shirt with it. "That means he's going to be gone for hoouurrss. Doesn't that sound nice?" Her enticing words dripped over him like honey. "I thought things were getting pretty hot last time we were together, don't you agree?"

"I do." Miles quivered as Lucifer lowered herself down to where her lips hovered an inch over his. *Jesus Christ, she smells amazing.* The electricity between them became strong enough that his brain began to sizzle. One hand balanced her in place over him, but like before, the other hand was already working the buttons to his pants loose.

"Then I think right now be a great time for you and I do something really hot. Something animal. Because I've got something for you…" Lucifer's hand shot down the front of his pants. "And I know you've got something for me."

As Lucifer began to kiss her way across his chest, she whispered something about the two being alone. A lightning bolt of fear hit Miles as he remembered Annabelle sleeping in his bed across the room. *Holy fuck! How could I have forgotten?* He craned his head back to look towards the bed but didn't see any sign of movement.

260

"Shit, Lucifer," he panted. "We have to be quiet."

"I can do that." She smiled as a long, wet, lick found his hipbone. Her face angled downward, and Lucifer swallowed him whole, her hands and tongue working with a skill borne of practice and abandon. The sly eyes of Jareth the Goblin King spied with jealousy from the Labyrinth movie poster on the ceiling above him as black polished fingernails raked their way down his ribs.

After ten minutes, Lucifer raised her head and gasped for air. Swallowing more oxygen than flesh for the first time. Miles reached down to touch the black dyed hair of her crown and she looked back with guile-filled eyes. Her thick black mascara had watered and been sent down the outer corners of her eyes and past her cheeks. She paused only for a moment before her face disappeared again. Miles' cheeks flushed, and he felt something twist inside of him; teenage hormone boiling to a flashpoint in his brain, the pressure racing it down his spine. Every hair on his body stood on end and his back began to arch on its own. Lucifer quickened her pace. Lucifer, no wonder they called her that, her technique of pistoning velvet perfection was so evil that it had to have been of the devil's own design. Fingers clawed at the old rug beneath him as his nerve endings sang in unison. He tried to resist, but it was too much. All sensations became a molten flow of ecstasy pouring out of him at the speed of sound. He dared not open his eyes, resigning himself to a blind void fed by raw input and the images they created as they burned their way across his brain.

As dark as it was in the dimly lit room, a shadow still fell over him. He tried to ignore it, but the out of place blackness on his face caused him to open his eyes. Miles found not the eyes the Goblin King staring back but the vacant stare of a naked blonde girl standing over him.

"Miles?" Annabelle asked. "What are you doing?"

Upon hearing the second voice, Lucifer's face emerged from Miles's lap with a short, startled scream right behind it.

"What the fuck!" Lucifer retreated backward so fast that she hit the shelves behind her; piles of cassette tapes, books, movies, and records to fall in a cascade around her. Miles scrambled to pull his pants up, almost catching his erection in the zipper as he stood.

"Annabelle! What are you doing awake? I thought you were sleeping!"

"I heard noises," Annabelle said with a straight face.

"Annabelle?!" Lucifer yelled as she pushed random objects off her and slapped Miles across the face. "Miles, who is this and why is she naked in your room?"

"I could smell both of you in my sleep," Annabelle said.

"You could *smell* us?" Lucifer wrinkled her nose.

"Calm down, she's a friend, Lucifer," he stammered. "Annabelle, go back to bed."

"Were you watching us from the other side of the room?" Lucifer yelled. "Did you know she was watching us, Miles? Huh? Did you?"

"Lucifer, just calm down."

"Calm down? You know what?" Lucifer said, straightening her clothes with one hand while grabbing her purse with the other. "To hell with this, I'm out of here."

"Lucifer, don't! Let me explain." Miles called after her.

"Get fucked, gas station boy," the goth girl said, giving both Annabelle and Miles the middle finger as she stomped up the wooden stairs. "You smell like fucking diesel fuel anyway." The steps continued to the top of the stairs, out the door, down the hall, and out the front, slamming the screen door. Miles's face was frozen in a pained grimace until all the sounds were gone.

"Did I do something wrong?" Annabelle asked.

"You just..." He paused to find the words before giving in to a long sigh. "No, Annabelle, you didn't do anything wrong."

"What was she doing to you?"

"She was... she was...nothing. She wasn't doing anything."

"Really? Because it looked like she had her mouth on your dinger. Is she a whore? She dresses like a Jezebel." The absurdity became too much, and Miles was too disappointed to cry so he did the only sensible thing to do; he burst into roaring laughter. Annabelle looked confused. "What's so funny? Miles? Why are you laughing?" It took a minute for the gut laughing to die down enough for him to answer but when he did, he spoke loud and clear.

"She's not a whore, Annabelle... she's just... easy."

"Well, what does that say about you if you're with her? Shame on you, Miles! Inviting easy girls over for sinful, naked acts."

"Says the girl standing naked in front of me. You know, the gentlemen callers aren't going to buy the cow if you give away the milk for free, Jezebel." Annabelle froze as she looked at her own body and realized she'd been naked the whole time. She blushed and positioned her hands over her private areas.

"Miles! Avert your eyes!"

"Fine," he said, turning in place. Before the count of three, she was already dressed and stepping around him into view. "Lucifer won't be upset long. She'll have another boyfriend by tomorrow."

"I'm not a Jezebel," Annabelle said in a serious tone.

"I never thought you were."

"Don't tease me. What happens now?"

"It'll be sundown in a few hours. You relax, I'm getting a shower."

"Do you need one? You didn't spend long at work so you shouldn't be sweaty."

"That's not what it's for." Miles huffed as he grabbed a towel from atop the clothes bin. "I'll be out soon."

Sundown came, and Gary returned from work. He made himself dinner and sat in his favorite chair to watch *Jeopardy!*. Miles emerged from the basement first to make sure the coast was clear while Annabelle waited at the bottom of the stairs.

"How's the eye?" Gary asked. Miles stepped closer to let him see the unblemished flesh. "Well, I'll be damned." The man peered closer. "You must be healthy as an ox because it looks like the swelling and everything has up and vanished. Did you put the bag of frozen vegetables on that like I told you?"

"I sure did." Miles lied.

"I thought that might be the case. My mother showed me that trick years ago. Are you going out?"

"For a short drive. I won't be gone long."

"You be safe. I'm going to sit here and watch my show." Miles was about to go down the hall to tell Annabelle to wait, but when he looked up, he noticed that she was already standing behind Gary's chair with the shotgun over her shoulder. Annabelle put a finger to her lips for him to stay silent. "Go on and get your drive out of the way. When you get home, take the trash to the curb and do the dishes. I did them last time."

"Okay," Miles said with an unnatural casualness. "I'll do that." He ushered Annabelle outdoors and out to the car, looking back at the house every few steps. No one spoke until the doors shut. "We need to talk about something. Gary already spoke to me about you."

"About me? How does he know about me?"

"No, your Transylvania sweatshirt. He was with me the day I bought it in Lexington. He's also friends with the police officers you had the run-in with at the library. He asked me if I knew who you were because he wants to turn you over to the cops for trespassing in the library and stealing that shotgun."

"What did you tell him?"

"I lied to him, Annabelle." Miles fired up the engine and put the car into gear. Monster slipped out of the driveway onto the evening road. "I've never had to lie to him about anything before, but I lied to him for you."

"I'm sorry." She hung her head a little as she cradled her shotgun. "You shouldn't have to lie for me."

"I can't keep doing it, so you're going to have to be more careful from here on out. People are on the lookout for that gun and your maroon sweatshirt."

"I promise to be more careful. I don't want you to get in trouble."

"Don't do it for me, do it for yourself. You haven't been in this century for a week, and you're already drawing attention to yourself. But to be fair, it's not all your fault. Whoever it was that bit you and bailed left you in a difficult spot. They abandoned you without knowing anything about being a vampire and how to survive. I don't want you to end up as a pile of ashes."

"I don't want to be a pile of ashes either. I'm grateful for everything you've done for me. I know you have a life and problems of your own."

"I know you're grateful. Just be more careful. Please?"

"I will." The ride went faster than Miles expected and the two found themselves sitting in the small lot across the cemetery in no time. As soon as they arrived, the caretaker's small pickup appeared through the gates and the man took his sweet time in getting out of the truck to lock the gate. Miles looked over at Annabelle who stared unblinkingly at the dashboard.

"Are you okay?"

"I'm hungry," she said without moving

"It won't be long now. He's almost done. Then you can go hunting."

"I'm getting tired of deer," she said.

"What does that mean?"

"Nothing. It just means I'm tired of drinking from deer."

"Does that mean you're going to start feeding on people?"

"I don't want to feed on people," she said. Across the street, the pickup truck pulled away and faded into the distance.

"I didn't ask if that's what you wanted to do, I asked if that's what you're going to do."

"I haven't decided."

"You haven't decided on *if* or *when*?"

"It means I don't want to feed on people, but I just might, Miles." Annabelle's voice deepened. "I've never wanted to be a burden to you, but I have urges, urges you wouldn't understand. You, Gary, the girl from before, you all smell like the most succulent things in existence. Deer blood will do but being around humans is like sitting down for Christmas dinner and not being able to eat what's being served." Miles shifted uncomfortably in his seat. Annabelle's eyes moved just enough to look in his direction. "And now you're afraid of me," she sighed.

"I'm not afraid of you," he said.

"Don't say that. I can see it in your mind. I can feel it when your heart beats faster. I can feel it when your fingertips graze the handle of the car door," she said. Miles gazed down and realized he'd subconsciously reached for the metal lever.

"You're afraid," Annabelle continued. "You've always been afraid, just a tiny bit. But despite that fear, you go out of your way to help me anyway. That means we can be friends, and I wouldn't want to kill a friend. However, I don't know how much further our friendship can go. Like you said, we're different. Our lives won't run parallel forever. I need to sit down and plan for what comes after tomorrow, and if we're honest with one another, I don't think I should stay in White Wreath."

"Where will you go?"

"If there are others like me, I'll have to leave this town to find them, I have so many questions."

"What would you ask?

"I'd ask if we really are what the stories in books make us out to be or if we're something else. I'd ask why we're like this. Most importantly, I want to find the one who bit me."

"What would you do if you found them?"

"I don't know..." Annabelle said. "I'd probably just kill them for what they've put me through." She got out of the car and walked around to the driver's side. "I'm sorry I haven't been the most cheerful company, Miles," she said, slinging the weapon over one shoulder. "I know there isn't a lot you can do to fix what's happened to me, but it helps that you listen when I want to talk."

"Everyone wants someone to listen to them when they have something to say that's worth saying."

"I think you're wiser than you let on."

"If I had a lick of sense, I wouldn't get in half the trouble I do."

"A little trouble never hurt anyone," she said as some headlights appeared far away in the darkness. "Someone is coming, I have to go." With that, she turned and ran across the street. Miles watched her as she moved, her boots hardly touching the ground. Upon reaching the stone wall, Annabelle leaped up, planted one hand on top of the wall and vaulted over it into the night.

CHAPTER FIFTEEN

Once over the wall, Annabelle hurried up the hill. Halfway to the top, she looked back to watch the long sleek Cadillac carry on out of sight. The cool night breeze felt like heaven on her skin. Nothing seemed out of the ordinary in the cemetery as she climbed past the headstones; until she saw the door to the Booth mausoleum. The chain she'd used to seal the door hung limply from the left door handle. Thinking someone might be near, she unslung the shotgun and approached with caution. The severed lock lay in the grass before her. She plucked it from the ground and eyed the mangled metal. It was cut. Someone had purposefully entered her home. Annabelle instantly remembered how she'd promised not to kill anyone with the new shells but cocked the rabbit ears on the weapon anyway. Giving an intruder a flesh wound could still be an effective way of giving someone a warning to stay away. She lifted her nose and smelled the air laced with pheromone; something sweet and familiar.

No sounds came from within the tomb, so she pressed the door wide with the barrels and slipped inside. Moonlight followed her in. The tomb was empty. The rabbit ears eased forward. Here and there, clues of the intruders made themselves known; a broken bourbon bottle here, a cigarette butt or two there. To her dismay, she discovered the books Miles had loaned to her scattered across the floor. One was torn in half, the others flung against the far wall. In her urgency to take stock of what remained, there was one book that hadn't been accounted for. While looking for it she noticed her father's coffin had been moved from where she left it last.

One hand pulled it free of the hole and another sour smell crept from the edges of the container. The lid opened to reveal all the pages of Miles's copy of Dracula had been ripped free and scattered like leaves within the coffin. Crude letters spelled out in black sprayed paint on the inside of the lid spelled out the phrase "Miles Burkich is a goth poser faggot." The final insult came in her identification of the foul stench she'd caught a whiff of when she entered the tomb. Her meager bedding, extra clothes, the pages of the book, the entire inside of her father's final resting place...all soaked in piss.

Someone had pissed in her bed.

What started as a burning stare escalated into an involuntary shiver of anger. Annabelle began to shake, her body trembling more violently as her face twisted in a grimace of rage. She bit into her bottom lip so hard that it drew blood she couldn't spare to lose. But in her anger, her senses became heightened, especially her sense of smell. Another scent besides the alcohol, tobacco, cannabis, and urine remained; the sickly stink of perfume. It wasn't just any perfume; it was the smell of the girl who'd been at Miles' house earlier in the day. No mistake. Fortunately for her, the smell was toxic enough to follow anywhere.

For Annabelle's nose, the subtle musk of a buck or doe is easy to find a few miles away, but Lucifer's artificial rose smelling rank was so offensive that it might as well have been a skunk the size of Pikeville. Words her mother once said came to mind:

"Annabelle. The world needs ladies in it. I've raised you to be a proper lady, but don't be anybody's fool. Be a lady until people won't let you be a lady."

"Forgive me, Mama." She whispered as her grip tightened about the handle of the shotgun so firmly that the wood stock began to emit a low groan. "I'm about to not act like a lady."

With that, she exited the mausoleum, shut the doors, and threaded the chain through the handles once more. She didn't have a lock, so she grasped the last link of the chain with both hands and pulled it apart before fitting it through the loose ends and sealing the link again. Lucifer's scent and that of the others who'd been with her drifted in on the wind from the North West. That's where she'd find them. There were also some deer less than a quarter of a mile away, but Annabelle didn't want to feed yet. She wanted to be hungry when he found who she was looking for.

She took off through the tree line and into the woods at a furious pace, boots pounding the soil and underbrush as she followed the scent of the perfume. When the topography changed, and she found herself face to face with a gap or ravine, she glided across the span weightlessly, effortlessly, before touching down again. It didn't take long. Even at the hurried pace of a human in peak physical condition, it would've taken less than an hour to reach the destination buried deep in the woods.

What once might have been a quaint one-story farmhouse had become a disheveled shack; age, rot, and mold eating it up a day at a time. The barn on the property hadn't been used for a long time. A tree had recently toppled, striking the barn. The rotten wood appeared to have given little resistance as the branches and trunk divided the stables in half. A rickety silo towered over the property like a ruler of rust watching its decaying kingdom. The smell was stronger now. Lucifer was here. But as Annabelle lifted her nose to the air again, a second, more potent scent presented itself, foul and noxious. It bothered her nose to breathe in the noxious cloud, so she snorted it away and continued breathing in only through her mouth. Loud voices and rhythmic noise came from the house with more cars parked in front of it. To her left, ten paces from the house, another structure showed signs of life. It looked like a long metal house made of tin cans with windows and a door like an ordinary house but sat atop a few sets of wheels like a wagon. *How strange.*

No one was outside, but she heard two voices coming from within. Annabelle crept closer. The closer she got the more the cloud of foul-smelling awfulness stung her eyes. She levitated just enough to boost herself up and peek through the closest window of the odd house on wheels. Inside, two men covered in strange masks moved back and forth between makeshift tables with vats of boiling chemicals on it. Clear tubes snaked this way and that over the whole thing. It wasn't easy to hear what they were saying as they talked, but a little slipped through.

"No, don't do that," said the taller one of the two. "Watch what the hell you're doing. That shit's flammable man so be careful with it, or the whole batch will go up in flames and take this trailer with it."

"Sorry, man," said the other.

"I don't care if you're sorry, I ain't trying to end up like some kinda crispy critter. By the way, how much does JoJo think he can get for the whole batch?"

"I don't know, I didn't ask him."

"Well, why don't you go ask him? I got shit locked down here. Oh yeah, take this sample in there for him to try, should be good shit."

JoJo, eh? Annabelle thought as she remembered the name of the person who gave Miles a black eye. *Yes, why don't you go have a talk with him?*

The shorter one walked out and shut the door behind him. When he got a dozen paces from the trailer took his mask off to reveal the face skinny young man with a tattoo of the numbers "606" tattooed on his neck. Annabelle followed behind him in the shadows, her footsteps making no sound to alert him of her presence. The young man walked through the yard, stopping off where several motorized cars were parked to smoke a cigarette as he eyed the small transparent bag with the white crystals inside. He even took the time to pick his nose and wipe the same fingers on his pants before digging a little more.

Ew. You're about a vile one, aren't you? The fellow finished his smoke and headed towards the front door of the house. Easily half a dozen more voices could be heard inside. It sounded like a party. She followed behind until he reached for the door, ducking out of the light emerging from within. Annabelle moved to the closest window and found a space between the curtains to see what was happening.

She instantly spotted Lucifer standing on a short table in the center of the room. She gyrated to the beat of the music, seductively running her hands across her full pale breasts, and down her ass and legs. Where her shirt had run off to, God only knew, but the missing garment allowed Annabelle to see the web tattoos around Lucifer's breasts, the piercing in each nipple, and a small silver chain suspended between them. The more she shimmied, the more the others seated around the room hooted and cheered. It was then that the nose picker wandered into view. He side-stepped past Lucifer to deliver the tiny baggie to another man sitting in the middle of the couch. *JoJo.*

He looked like a rough character. He couldn't have been too old, but the lines in his face and gaunt features pointed to unhealthy living. Two strange-looking rifles and a pair of shotguns leaned against the wall just within reach with a revolver on the table to his right. Whatever was in that bag was the likely reason for his hard looks and the guns.

No sooner did JoJo have the bag in his hand that he pulled out a small glass pipe from underneath the table. Annabelle and everyone else in the room watched intently as he inserted a little of what was in the baggie and used a small red device put a steady flame under the bowl-shaped end. JoJo sucked deep and long before expelling a plume of smoke large enough to fill the room. He handed the pipe to the person next to him before standing up and pounding his fists against his chest. The others cheered more as he howled like a wolf and shook his head with his tongue out like a crazy person. They refilled the bowl and passed it around, each one sucking from the glass pipe. Each of them twitched and jumped around, grabbing each other and wrestling like boys shed seen who'd had too much of her father's "liquid courage." The strange powder in that baggie was the reason they were all the way out here with all those guns.

Annabelle laughed a little to herself. She'd vanished for a hundred years and returned to find that people still got inebriated on their own stills. But whatever crazy substance they were making in the home on wheels made them act like crazy people. Was it peyote like what the Indians smoked? Either way, she bet that whatever it was the sheriff would probably want to know about it. She could leave a note for the sheriff to get them in trouble, but that wasn't going to be enough to make up for someone pissing in her coffin. The smells of the people in the party matched the scent from the Booth mausoleum; a trespass she would not let stand.

These people needed to be taught a lesson.

But what lesson to teach them? The incident with the hunters came to mind, and the idea of making them see terrible things seemed appropriate. What was it the preacher always used to say? An eye for an eye? There were two eyes to pay for tonight; the first was Miles's black eye. The second? A disrespectful trespass. But how to teach that lesson? There were so many people in the house. Then she remembered the one person in the mobile home and her lips parted in a devilish smile.

Inside the house, JoJo and the others were still partying when the other man in his protective suit entered the house.

"Hey man!" He yelled at JoJo over the blaring music coming from a stereo. "Come outside!" Entranced by Lucifer's seductive dancing, JoJo didn't want to leave. It wasn't until the guy insisted that JoJo jumped up from the couch and followed him out the front door and into the fresh night air. He shut the door behind him and trotted out to meet the other man in the middle of the yard.

"What's so important? This spooky bitch is taking her clothes off in there." The man stood motionless, his arms hanging as limp as the expression on his face. Even in the low light, his eyes looked glazed. "Well? The fuck do you want?" The man said nothing before collapsing to his knees and keeling over onto his face. When he toppled over, Annabelle, who'd been standing behind him, revealed herself.

"It's not what *he* wants, JoJo. It's what I want," she said

"Who the fuck are you?"

"I'm Annabelle. Annabelle Booth."

"What did you do to him?"

"Nothing yet. He's just sleeping."

"Yo, you best get the fuck off my property before I beat your little ass."

"This isn't your property anymore. This is my property, and you're all trespassing."

"Look, whatever chick. You're cute and all but if you don't get your ass out of here, Imma go back in this house, get my gun, come back out here and put a bullet in that head of yours."

"That's going to be difficult since the door is locked. Your friend here twisted the knob so you'd have to yell for one of your friends to open the door for you." JoJo looked at the door and back at her.

"Who the fuck are you, bitch?"

"Like I said, I'm Annabelle Booth, and I wouldn't go calling names if I were you. You said you have guns in the house. Do you have a shotgun?"

"Yeah, I got two of 'em."

"Do either of them look anything like this?" Until now, Annabelle had been standing with her hands behind her back. She revealed them at the same time to show him her own weapon and leveled it at his legs.

"That shit probably ain't even loaded."

"Oh, it's loaded all right. Two rounds of heavy buckshot. And from this distance, two rounds would be more than enough to give you a limp for life...

"Yo, what do you want?"

"I want to give you a black eye."

"That ain't happening. I'll beat your little ass before I let you give me a black eye."

"Oh, I'm not going to do it," The devilish grin appeared again. "You are. You see, I can talk to animals and other creatures. If they're dumb enough, I can even tell them what to do."

"Bitch, you're high. There's no way I'm- URK!" JoJo was interrupted when his left hand made a fist, and he clocked himself in his left eye. His head flew backward from the blow, and he staggered before falling on his ass and striking his head on the porch. It wasn't enough to put him out, but it was enough to ring his bell. He looked frightened and confused as he tried to gain his footing. He didn't understand what was happening. Annabelle had moved so fast to grab his hand, buckle it and force it into his face that he didn't see her move at all.

"What the hell was that?" he said, looking shaken up

"It looks like you've had an accident." The look of fright becoming more pronounced on his face as he struggled to grasp what had happened. It was a hard punch that left him as a woozy, wobbly, white trash marionette. "You sure took a wallop to the eye, JoJo, but it doesn't look black quite yet. Give yourself another shot and make it a good one. Really put some effort into it." JoJo cringed as his fist rose again, knuckles catching him just below the eyebrow. He yelped and fell over again, his back making a dull thud as he collided with the ground "There you go, that's a good one!"

"Why are you doing this?" he asked as he sputtered to spit out some grass. "What the fuck do you want from me?"

"I want you to stop being terrible to people."

"Fuck you, you dumb bitch."

"You see that right there? You and I are meeting for the first time, and you're not treating me like a man should treat a lady. I'd use the word gentleman, but you and I know that sure as hell ain't the case. My daddy used to say, 'no matter how far a jackass walks, it never comes back a horse.' I never understood what that meant until now. You've brought this pain on yourself."

"You're hitting me!"

"No, you're hitting yourself." She cocked her head to one side and looked at his face. "You know what? That eye doesn't look angry enough. Why don't you give yourself another good swing? Really let yourself have it."

"Otha! Otha! Fuckin' wake up, man!" JoJo called out. His arm straightened with a fist on the end of it before it launched back. A meaty "thwack" filled the air and JoJo expelled a squeal of anguish. At this point, the eye was puffy and bleeding. "Stop! Just Stop! I'll do whatever you want!"

"Anything I want?" Annabelle asked,

"Anything!" He flailed. "But stop hitting me!"

"I'm not hitting you; you're hitting yourself." Annabelle moved a little slower this time and grabbed him by the neck of his dirty tee shirt. "And I'd be tempted to let you go, but I got a feeling you'd be back to your old tricks and causing trouble for people." Annabelle raised the end of the shotgun nice and close to his face so he could see the barrels. His one good eye, the one covered in blood opened nice and wide.

"I won't! I won't cause trouble for anyone!"

"You promise?"

"I promise!" he said in a panic. Annabelle raised the gun closer and pressed the barrels against JoJo's temple.

"You better swear and swear good that you won't go picking any more fights with people, because if I find out you haven't stopped, and you've hit more people like Miles Burkich, I'm going to lose my religion." Annabelle moved close enough that JoJo could feel her cool breath on his face. She cocked the rabbit ears of the gun and pressed the barrels further so that his neck bent to the side at a painful angle. "And if that happens, I'm going to find you and when I'm done with you, you're gonna beg for the devil to take you if it gets you away from me."

"I swear I won't hit nobody!"

"That'll have to do, I guess. By the way, which of you sonsobitches pissed in the Booth Mausoleum?"

"It wasn't me!" JoJo pleaded. "Danny did it! It wasn't me!"

"Do any of these cars belong to Danny?" she asked.

"The grey one. That's his grey Monte Carlo."

"The grey one you say? All right." She let go of him. "Give yourself one more shot, and I think we're done. Make it a good one."

"Wait! Don't!" JoJo yelled as he slugged himself in the eye again, knocking him out cold. He fell flat with another thud. Not only was his eye beaten to a bloody pulp, but his nose looked broken as well. The other fellow, Otha, continued to lay face down like a bump on a log. "Mister Otha? You should get up now. I could use your help." The big man slowly began to move like the summoned golem he was. Once vertical, he made no sound and stood with sagging shoulders. His clothes and special suit reeked something terrible. "What are you doing in that square house on wheels over there?" she asked.

"Making methamphetamine," he replied.

"What is that?

"It's a kind of drug," Otha mumbled

"Can you burn it?"

"Yes, it's very flammable, explosive."

"Whose house is this?"

"No one. Danny found the house was abandoned and figured out a way to steal power to turn the lights on."

"Could you set those drugs on fire and not hurt yourself?"

"There's a cloud of fumes. I could prop the door open, stand back a way, and throw a road flare at it."

"Would that burn it up?"

"The fumes are volatile. The whole thing would go off like a bomb, probably set the other house on fire too."

"That sounds like a good idea. You're so nice, Mr. Otha. Would you please be a dear and go prop open the door and come back over here with that fire thing. I'm going to go find some rocks."

"Yes, Miss Annabelle." The man lumbered away to do as he was told, as Annabelle gathered half a dozen rocks, each as big as her fist. Otha threw opened the door, releasing a foul-smelling, toxic cloud and wedged the door open with a large stone. Without a mask over his face, he coughed and gagged. He returned to stand at her side with a brightly colored red stick in his hand that looked like dynamite.

"Ready?" she asked.

"Uh huh."

"Good. Let's get started." Annabelle closed her eyes and took in a long deep inhalation of breath and held it. Her mind reached out for miles in every direction, putting her in touch with a hidden wavelength as electric as any man-made radio. In that spanning transmission, she found the connection she sought. The reply?

"We are coming."

She exhaled, opened her eyes and gathered the rocks in one arm before proceeding to hurl them one after another through the windows of the old house. Pane after pane she smashed one to the next with precision until the last went sailing into the living room where all the others were partying. The music stopped. Excited shouts sounded within before faces began peeping out from around the edges of pulled curtains. Annabelle nodded to Otha who in turn sparked the road flare and hold it over his head bathing the entire front yard in a brilliant red light.

"Oh shit, look at that! JoJo got knocked out!" said one person.

"Yo, Danny! There's some girl with a shotgun standing on the hood of your car!" said another.

"Why is Otha out there holding a road flare?" said yet another. The front door opened, and four skinny, young, white, country boys stepped out of the house with firearms in their hands. Each one brandished their weapon in an aggressive manner and spread out shoulder to shoulder. One knelt and tried to wake JoJo who was still unconscious.

"You're trespassing in the wrong place, girl!" one said. Lucifer appeared in the doorway behind them, trying to get her shirt back on.

"Hi, Lucifer!" Annabelle waved from atop the primer-painted Chevrolet. Everyone's head swiveled to look at the girl covering herself.

"Lucifer! You know this crazy chick?" someone asked.

"No, I don't know who the fuck she is."

"She seems to know who you are."

"Girl, you better get your Goldilocks-looking ass of my car before I beat it down!" Danny yelled.

"Are you the ornery son of a bitch Danny who pissed in a coffin today?" Annabelle asked.

"Maybe. Who the fuck wants to know?"

"You should apologize for what you did to Johnathan Booth's tomb." She raised the gun towards the windshield. "Or your car is going to have an extra window in it." Danny raised his rifle at Annabelle.

"Yeah whatever, go ahead and pull the trigger on that gun and see what hap-" Annabelle squeezed off a round and the rest of Danny's words evaporated in a 12-gauge thunderclap. Glass blossomed a violent eruption, blowing shards in every direction. What used to be a leather driver's seat now resembled tattered rags. The crowd collectively held their breath in shock and looked to the car's owner. Danny's face twisted with anger before he raised the rifle and popped off a shot. Everyone stared in disbelief as she remained standing. Danny had missed.

"You can't shoot for shit." Annabelle taunted him. Danny leveled the gun and emptied the magazine, twelve rounds in all, hitting nothing.

"What are you waiting for?" Danny shouted. "Shoot her!" The others began firing dozens of rounds, only to find the same result...all misses. When the echoes from the reports faded, confused looks came across all their faces. Annabelle changed hands and waved the gun towards the front of the car. During her time in the reference section of the library, she'd absorbed the schematic of "the modern automobile's combustion engine and its parts" and remembered the description of the part marked "radiator." She'd promised Miles that she wouldn't use the gun on people.

Property isn't people.

The gun went off a second time, puncturing the metal hood, quickly followed by the sound of the radiator's contents dripping to the ground in puddles. Danny hopped in place from rage.

"Stop...shooting...my...car!" He yelled as Annabelle broke her gun down and replaced the spent shells with new ones.

"Oh, I'm done with your car, but I'm not done with the rest of you." She waved the gun across the crowd. "You people have some bad habits. Those drugs you're making can't be good for you. So, let's fix that. Go ahead, Otha," she said. Upon hearing her command, Otha O'Reilly turned towards the trailer and flung the still sparking flare towards the makeshift lab. It landed inside the door and wasn't there for a split second before an ear-ripping explosion filled everything, sending burning pieces of trailer sailing far into the night in every direction. Everyone present, save for Annabelle and her corn-fed golem, leaped to the ground.

The explosion tore off the main house's far wall and part of the roof as well. Burning pieces of the trailer littered the property fifty yards away, even blowing out a few windows of the other people's vehicles. Some people got up, calling out to the others and pointing to the fires burning. Others clung to one another in fear of the blonde figure standing in the middle of the chaos. If the roar of the fires weren't enough, another sound began to swell around them.

Scared out of her wits, Lucifer retreated inside and slammed the door shut. That's when Annabelle's voice rang aloud.

"Lucifer!" Annabelle called her out by name. "I wouldn't stay in there if I were you!" The low droning buzz that emerged from behind the nearly audible licks of the flames grew and grew to a larger and larger cacophony. The moonlight became blotted out by the countless wings of a swarm.

Cicadas. All of them by the sound of it.

They dove down from the sky by the tens of thousands. A modern plague for modern sinners. By Annabelle's unspoken commands, they formed long flowing chains and found their way through all the broken windows on the house at once. Anyone who might've been indoors, including Lucifer, came screaming out of the residence as they filled the structure from floor to ceiling with a deafening insectoid bleat not seen since the fall of pharaohs.

The winged minions clung to hair and clothes, frightening their victims and scattering them to the tree lines until none were left. When everyone was gone, Annabelle jumped down from the car hood and surveyed the aftermath. The only ones to remain were the golem and JoJo, still laying on the ground.

With all her mischief tended to, Annabelle tapped Otha on the shoulder and spoke: "You did a good job. Why don't you go lay down in that field over there until morning comes?"

"Okay." Otha nodded. He followed where she pointed and lumbered off in his sleepwalking fashion out of sight. The cicadas had done their job but were still making a terrible racket. She closed her eyes again and found their wavelength, the place where the insect clicks met her thoughts.

Just as fast as they'd appeared, the swarm took to the air and departed in all directions back to their trees and resting spots. Minus the crackling of burning wood, an eerie silence fell over the farm. Out of the corner of her eye, she noticed the fire began to spread to more of the house. If the whole house went up in flames, it might spread to where JoJo lay and there was no guarantee the others were coming back to get him. She sighed and grabbed JoJo by the leg, dragging him to a safe distance. She couldn't let him burn to death. That just wouldn't be right.

CHAPTER SIXTEEN

Early the next morning, things were already hopping at the Imperial when Gary and Miles arrived. Two fire trucks, an ambulance, and three police cars fueled up at the same time. Emergency crews milled about, their clothes and equipment dirty from a long night's work. The mud on the tires of the firetruck told Miles that it had been to someone's house somewhere off a dirt road. And considering White Wreath was rural, it could've been any of the ninety percent of the residents who lived beyond the tree line. Mr. Jenkins, the night manager, met them at the front door and threw it open for them with his prosthetic hand.

"What's going on, Mr. Jenkins?" Miles asked.

"Miles," he said. "Why don't you go back in the office, I got to talk to Gary for a minute." He looked to Gary who in turn nodded his approval. Miles did as he was told and walked past the truckers waiting for the showers. He unlocked Gary's office and plunked down in the swiveling office chair. On the desk, he found the paperwork for the contractors to install the new pumps. A few minutes passed, and Gary entered the office. Miles could tell something was wrong the way he immediately shut the door behind him and leaned against the far wall with his arms crossed instead of sitting at his desk.

"Miles, is there something you need to tell me?" Gary asked. That question is always a problem with being a teen who's always up to something. Whenever someone asks you if there's something you need to tell them, you never know which bit of trouble they're referring to.

"Well, you look upset and I have no idea what you're referring to, so I'm going to say…no,"

"Don't get smart with me, I'm being serious."

"What are we being serious about?"

"You went for a drive last night, didn't you?"

"You know I did. You were watching Jeopardy! remember?"

"Where did you go?"

"Just out an about. I'm still enjoying the new freedom of getting out and going somewhere without someone driving me."

"Did you go anywhere near the old Crabtree farm?"

"No. There's nothing over there but old rusty farm equipment."

"You're telling me the truth?"

"Yes! I went out, rode around and came home. I took out the trash and dishes like you asked. You were in the shower when I got home. It couldn't have been 8:30."

"And you didn't sneak out of the house and go anywhere?"

"Gary, no. I was home all night reading the new Stephen King book. Now, what's going on?" Gary's expression lightened up a bit since he knew it to be true that he was in the shower around eight p.m.

"Mr. Jenkins spoke with all the emergency crew fellas out there and they told him that somebody went over to the old Crabtree farm, busted up a field party and blew up what looks like a homemade crank lab. Two people about your age got minor burns and cuts from flying debris. The sheriff says it looks like a damn bomb went off, just blew it all to shit."

"That's messed up."

"It gets worse."

"What's worse than that?"

"There was another sighting of the blonde girl with the shotgun…" His eyebrows furrowed again. "The same one wearing a maroon Transylvania University sweatshirt. Tell me who she is, Miles. And no more lies. I know you bought the sweatshirt for her. No boy your age who pumps gas just goes out on a whim and buys a girl he doesn't like a twenty-five-dollar sweatshirt. It just doesn't happen."

"Her name is Annabelle."

"Right, Annabelle Booth. The same name everybody in this town knows belongs to a girl who died a hundred years ago in a distillery fire. Does she have a sister named Betty Crocker?"

"Hey, I'm just telling you what she told me."

"Does she go to your school?"

"No."

"Then how did you meet Miss Annabelle Booth?"

"She was the one who helped me get to the road after I fell into the distillery ruins."

"She helped you out of there?"

"Yeah, the last thing I remember before I woke up in the hospital. I was lying at the bottom of the old distillery. She was there."

"How much do you weigh?"

"About a hundred and sixty-five pounds. What does that have to do with anything?"

"The sheriff and the others are describing a girl about five foot four and a hundred pounds. Now I'm no mathematician, but a girl that small isn't going to be able to carry someone your size out of the ruins, up the hill and eighty yards to the road. I don't buy it. Also, you never mentioned her before, why not?"

"Because I didn't know who she was then."

"Miles," his voice became a little less upset. "Whoever this girl is, she isn't Annabelle Booth. She's some reckless thief who stole a gun from the library exhibit, and now she's out blowing up people's homes and she assaulted some hunter named Dale who buys gas from us. He described her to the letter. She tortured him and another fella with poisonous snakes. What kind of a sick messed up person does something like that?"

"I don't know. She seemed nice."

"I know she was nice to you. That's what she wanted you to think. Boy, she took advantage of you to get what she wanted and then she went tearing ass across the county. She even attacked JoJo."

"She attacked JoJo?"

"Yup. He was partying with his friends at that abandoned house when she showed up and beat him in the face with something. I'm paying the doctor bill because I know his momma can't. I'm going to say this once, so I want you to listen and listen good. Miles, she beat in my nephew's eye left eye so bad the doctors don't know if they can fix it. He could go through the rest of his life half-blind. And I'll tell you this, boy. I've never wanted to hurt another person on this Earth. I got drafted for Vietnam, I didn't want to go. I didn't want to shoot anyone. But if that little blonde monster steps foot one on our property, I will kill her myself and bury the body in the back yard. So, if you see her, you tell her to stay away if she knows what's good for her. I don't care if she thinks she's Annabelle Booth or Susan B. frickin' Anthony, if I see her, she's done. She's just done. Now you got a heart bigger than anyone I know, but sometimes you let your heart lead when you should be thinking. And that's why this time I gotta do the thinking for you."

"What does that mean?"

"It means you're grounded."

"Grounded? What did I do? I've never been grounded!"

"You're going to stay close to me until Miss Booth is in handcuffs."

"You can't ground me!"

293

"I just did. That means your car sits put too."

"You're taking my car? How am I supposed to get to work?"

"Same way you always have. You'll ride with me."

"And when school starts?"

"We'll talk about that when it happens. For now, the Caddy stays parked and if you take it out to go joyriding behind my back, you will not like the consequences."

"You're punishing me for things I haven't done."

"No, I'm punishing you for the things you have done."

"What did I do?"

"You're not telling me the truth, Miles," he said, the brow furrowing again. "And half-truth is not the same as the whole truth. I've raised you almost every year you've been alive. You've never hidden anything from me until now. We used to be friends, what happened to that? What happened to the relationship we had where you'd tell me nothing but the truth? I can see it in your eyes. You know something about this girl but for some reason, you refuse to tell me what it is. And that right there hurts me more than anything. You're seventeen now and you'll be eighteen at the end of October. When Halloween rolls around you'll be a man, and I legally won't be able to tell you what to do with your life anymore. If this is going to be the way it is between us, after all we've been through, then I don't know what to do if I know if I can't trust you. I love you more than you know, but if the situation between us isn't remedied by then, well, I just don't think I want to know a person who lies to me." Miles hung his head.

"I'm sorry," he said.

"I don't want you to be sorry, I want you to be as honest with me as I've been with you. Having said that, are you going to work today, or do you want me to drive you home?"

"No, I'm working," Miles said, standing up and handing Gary the keys to Monster as he walked out of the office. "I've got shit to do."

"That's a start." Gary nodded. "By the way, try and keep Mary out of the store. Ever since I locked the doors to her favorite place to hide on the back of the lot, she's been sneaking in and hiding in the supply room and my office. I don't mind having her around, but I can't have her getting into trouble in the store."

"Fine." Miles left the office and headed outside through the front door to check on the trash bins. It had already started to rain. *Wonderful.* The two bins between the pumps weren't half full yet so he left them alone for now. They'd be full around lunchtime. The sky was overcast, that would make the sunrise later than usual.

As he stared off high into the distance, he could almost see the cemetery. What was Annabelle thinking in attacking the others? Then it hit him; the black eye. Of course. It all made sense now. She'd gotten angry for JoJo hitting him, so she returned the favor. He couldn't say he was upset about JoJo getting what had been coming to him for a long time but almost blinding him? That took it too far. More people could've been hurt or worse killed in the explosion.

The whole sky was red that morning like the edges around an infected wound. What was the old saying about red skies in the morning? He was about to walk around the building and check on the other fuel island trashcans when he heard a splash and giggling to somewhere out of view. He peered around the side of the building to find Mary splashing in a pothole, wearing an over-sized, Disney Little Mermaid shirt that covered her down to the knees. Someone, most likely Dennis, had cut small holes all the way around the shirt at the waist and laced a piece of nylon cord through it and tied it off to make it harder for her to peel off and run around naked. The shirt was soaked through and covered in mud. Her wet hair lay in twisted, tangled, strands around her shoulders. The indentation was in direct path of a downspout spewing rainwater towards the main road so every time she scooped or stomped the water out it filled right back up.

For a moment, Miles leaned against the corner of the building and watched her splash and sing songs only Mary knew the words to. There was something pure about it. The girl was out of her mind and more content than anyone in White Wreath.

"Hey, Mary." He called out to her. "Whatcha doing?"

"Hey Mills," she waved a hand in his direction without looking up. "Splashan."

"Having fun?"

"Havachicken?"

"No, the chicken won't be ready until lunchtime. Are you hungry?"

"Havachicken, havachicken lunge time." She stomped in a circle.

"Ok. You have fun splashing."

"Splashan," she said before letting out a huge sneeze. "Blesshoo," she told herself. The pothole was out of the path of the moving vehicles, so he thought nothing of leaving her to play in the puddles as she always did.

It was around nine a.m. while Miles was scooping out the last of the garbage that had fallen between the can and bag on diesel island number two that a familiar voice hit his ear.

"What's up, stranger?" Miles turned to find Dennis peering out the window of Pearl's Oldsmobile. "You hiding from the rest of us?"

"Look who it is." Miles managed a smile for the first time in a while. Dennis got out of the car and they met in a passionate hug. "How's it going, man? How's the new boy toy?"

"It's not like that. He's really sweet."

"That's cool."

"He can hold his end of a conversation, but he also knows when to shut up too. Holy shit. I spoke with Lucifer. Did you hear about that crank house that caught fire?"

"You did? What did she say?"

"Some messed up shit, man. She says she was partying at that house when the whole thing went south. She says a blonde girl with a freaking sawed-off lured JoJo out of the house, beat the shit out of him, and then when everybody came outside to check on him she started taking potshots at Danny Mitchell's Monte Carlo."

"That is messed up."

"That's not the half of it. She says the girl opened her mouth and locusts poured out of it like some 'old testament Sodom and Gomorrah' shit before setting the house on fire."

"That sounds like someone's been reading too many Stephen King novels."

"You're right, that would sound far-fetched except for one thing."

"What's that?"

"She says she saw the same girl at your place yesterday She said she was naked and called you by name."

"She did?"

"Yeah, she did. Lucifer may be a lot of things, but she's not a liar. Is it true?"

"Is what true?"

"The girl, you dipstick! Have you got some psycho chick shacking up with you?"

"No," Miles told him, pretending to go back to gather up trash. "There's nobody staying with me."

"Dude, you've got to work on your lying because you downright suck at trying to hide things from me."

"Yeah, that's Gary told me before he grounded me and took my car."

"Holy hell, Gary took your wheels AND grounded you? He's never grounded you!"

"I know."

"Then you must've done something really dangerous or stupid or something that's a combination of the two to piss him off enough to ground you."

"You could say that."

"So now you're going to give me the short answer treatment too?" Dennis asked, looking hurt. Miles tied up the ends of the trash bag and slung it at Dennis' feet. "What do you want from me?"

"For starters, you can lose the attitude because I'm your best friend in the whole world and I'm concerned about what's going on with you. Who's the girl? It's got to be a girl, right? You were all about Lucifer at the mausoleum party and the time after until the whole distillery accident happened. Since then, the rest of us never see you. So, cut the bullshit. Who's the girl Lucifer saw at your house? I know it happened. Lucifer gave me the inside scoop about what she was doing to you on the floor of your room before the pale blonde girl decided to stand over you two and watch."

"Lucifer told you about that?"

"Every filthy, nasty, disgusting, little detail. I have to admit it was kinda hot."

"You're not helping."

"Come onnnnnn." Dennis gave his signature sly grin. "I won't tell a living soul."

"Fine, the girl is Annabelle Booth."

"The girl who died in a distillery fire in 1880."

"Actually, it was 1890."

"So that would make Annabelle how old?"

"Like, a hundred and twenty years old."

"A hundred and twenty-year-old woman is walking around White Wreath. Ok, that's a lot to accept at face value. Lucifer said she looked like a high school freshman. Is she a time traveler?"

"No, she's not a time traveler. Well, sort of, maybe."

"Ok. If she's not a time traveler, then how did she get from 1890 to now without aging? Is she some kind of spirit? Ghost? Vampire?"

"Vampire."

"Okay, now we're getting somewhere. So, if she's a vampire from the 1890s what does she need with a shotgun?"

"She stole it from a library exhibit. Everything else she once owned burned up in the distillery fire."

"Someone <u>did</u> break into the library and steal a gun." He nodded. "Ok, she's a vampire. She can do anything she wants. Why would she blow up a drug house?"

"She wasn't there for the drug house; she was there for JoJo."

"JoJo got his eye knocked in. Why wouldn't she just kill him, or feed on him?"

"She doesn't want to kill people, and she was getting him back for giving me a black eye."

"But you don't have a black eye."

"I did. JoJo hit me yesterday and gave me a black eye. When I got home, Annabelle was staying at my place. She was there because she got trapped out in the open before dawn. She slept in my room because there's no windows. It was her that put some of her blood on my eye and healed it. When I told her who hit me, she must've gone after him." Dennis's smile withered, and like Gary, he too crossed his arms.

"Well, now I'm disappointed."

"Why?"

"Because that's the flimsiest string of bullshit I've ever heard in my life. Did I offend you somehow? Are you mad at me for some reason?"

"Dennis, I'm not lying."

"Yeah, sure, a gun-toting, time-traveling vampire is wandering around blowing up meth labs. If you didn't want to tell me what you're hiding or doing with this new chick then at least have the balls to say 'none of your fucking business' instead of wasting the breath to fabricate a heap of horseshit like that." Miles paused as he considered actually revealing Annabelle to him. If there was anyone in the world he could tell, it would be Dennis. But what if something went wrong? Annabelle only trusted him. In the end, the time it took for him to consider if it was the right thing was just enough to piss off Dennis. "You know what, Miles? Fuck it. Just fuck it. I'm out of here. And you know what else? Until you're ready to stop lying to me, don't bother calling me if this is how it going to be. Later," he said, turning on his heel to get back in the car.

The Cutlass cranked over and spat gravel in its wake as it sped out of sight. Miles continued staring at the spot where the car vanished out of sight as though refusing to blink might beckon his best friend to return. The rain increased. Miles opened the storage shed and donned his rain gear just as three semi-truck sized tow trucks emerged around the corner. A man rolled down the driver's side window of the first one and yelled to him.

"Hey, you! Are you Gary Burkich? I'm here to pick up those three old cabs!" He pointed towards the old trucks in the back where Mary liked to hide. Miles quickly peered around the closest corner to find the girl already wandering off across the field towards town. Good. She wasn't in one of them.

"Yeah!" He gave the man a thumbs' up sign. "That's them! Take them away!" The tow truck lurched into gear and the others followed it to the far side of the lot where they turned about in synchronized unison and began hooking them up for transport. He wanted to watch them work but the overflowing trash cans on the remaining fueling islands needed his attention more. As he grabbed a fistful of trash bags from the supply closet, the sky opened, and a terrible deluge sent truckers scattering for cover.

As if this day couldn't get any worse.

Nightfall:

The overcast sky darkened, and Annabelle awoke in her mother's coffin. Even after attempting to clean her father's, it still smelled too much of urine to continue using it. Before sunrise, she'd lined the befouled vessel with black trash bags and swapped her parent's remains into it before sealing them inside her mother's plot with the jewelry she'd exhumed from the distillery. Sleeping in her mother's coffin left her with an acute sensation of nostalgia. She wondered if somewhere in the ancient lining of the vessel that a faded sliver of her essence or scent remained. There was nothing. No hint of pheromone or perfume. The only parts of Mae Booth that ended up in the crypt were what the hundred-proof whiskey blaze failed to destroy. Flowers she'd pilfered from a stranger's grave diminished the smell of ashes but didn't get rid of all of it. The aroma of cheap carnations and gunpowder nauseated her. She hadn't fed, and her stomach churned in protest. Scratching sounds filled the mausoleum as the coffin lid slid away. Annabelle sat up, stretching and yawning to greet the night. The smells and sounds of a dwindling rainstorm seeped in through the cracks.

Not wanting to get her clothes wet, she disrobed, pulled the chains free of the doors and stepped out into the night. Raindrops fell here and there at the tail end of a storm. The smell of summer rain and wet grass permeated everything, the purest smell in White Wreath. A wave of hunger found her and she almost swooned. Her knees wobbled, and Annabelle leaned against a headstone to steady herself before continuing on. She didn't kill when she needed blood. Why hadn't she? JoJo or any one of the other deviants at the farm could've quenched her hunger. She could have killed them all and no one would have been able to stop her. She could've hidden the bodies, and no one would ever have known.

It doesn't matter now. There's plenty of deer in the forest. I can find a doe, even a small one will do.

Annabelle stumbled her way past the rows of graves and into the tree line. Her vision doubled and blurred so erratically that she stepped face-first into a tree and fell backward on her ass. It wasn't graceful, but she pushed herself vertical and moved ahead, following the scent of fresh blood. Another wave came, faster, more overwhelming. She lost her footing, slipping on wet moss and tumbled down a hill, rolling through undergrowth and brambles.

Feet over head she rolled. A rock stabbed her between the shoulder blades. Further, she tumbled, until the hill leveled off and pitched her into a tree. The fall she could endure, but a new pain was finding her, one that was as much on the inside as it was on the inside. Every part of her being began to ache, even her bones. *Oh god, it hurts.* Her stomach cramped. She might've vomited if there were anything inside to expel. But through nausea and pain, through the cloud of confusion accosting her senses, her nose didn't betray her. It was close, very close. Annabelle righted herself and stood again. Frazzled and desperate, she stumbled lock-kneed, one step after another towards one thing she couldn't live without…precious blood.

Ahead of her, she laid eyes upon the silhouette of an animal framed by plants in a clearing. Feral thoughts found Annabelle and took hold. Her pace quickened, fangs elongating, pushing their way through her gums. The beastly side of the distiller's daughter devoured the rest to push it down deep where it wouldn't interfere.

Annabelle burst through the bushes to find a wild-eyed adolescent girl with stringy black hair playing in the mud. She wore only a dirt-covered shirt with the drawing of a smiling mermaid on the front. The two collided, blonde bowling over brunette. Annabelle pulled the girl close. As weak as she was, her prey wasn't strong enough to fight her off. She rolled the girl over so that her victim to pin her arms and torso to the ground. The girl grimaced and made strange noises as she spoke.

"Dun't," the girl grunted as she tried to get free. "Stap, dun't, dun't t-touch me-ee." The way she spoke, distressed or not, wasn't right. Something wasn't right with her. Even though the cloud of hunger Annabelle looked into her eyes and saw that something was abnormal with the girl. She looked into the girls' mind and found noise and the simple expressions of a small child. Was she simple? An imbecile? A loon from an asylum? Loon or not, her blood would be warm just the same.

Annabelle's fangs sank into the flesh of the girl's neck and she drank deep. The blood flowed and vermillion euphoria came just as fast as the sickness fled. The girl got weaker by the second, her life force beginning to fade. She'd managed to work on hand free, swinging weakly at her attacker's head, whimpering in between strikes. But the words she used were no longer that of "stop" or "don't".

"Mills, hep," she sobbed, tears pouring down the outsides of her eyes. "Mills, help." Hearing this, Annabelle froze. The garbled visions in the girl's head changed from blurs and nonsense to images she could recognize; a flood of visions emerged of a scarecrow-thin boy with a sheaf of black hair in his eyes and a kind smile carrying her across a parking lot.

She's not saying 'Mills,' she's saying 'Miles.' Annabelle gasped, withdrawing her fangs to pull back and look upon the girl as her name sounded in her mind.

"Mary!" Annabelle said as she climbed off and cradled the girl. "Oh my god, I didn't mean to bite you! I'm so sorry!" Mary choked as she writhed, coughing and wheezing for breath. "Hold still, let me help."

Mary continued to flail and swing to keep Annabelle at bay with one hand while holding her neck with the other. Annabelle acted the only way she knew how. As before, she bit her thumb, pushed away Mary's hand and let a trickle of blood fall upon the wound to heal her. But the blood didn't flow as fast as before. She squeezed her thumb like fruit to get the liquid free, but there wasn't much to spare. The lightheadedness returned, her vision falling out of focus. Her balanced faltered and when Mary bucked, Annabelle fell dazed onto her back. She tried to rise again but every muscle resisted to the point of paralysis. Mary stood over her and bellowed long, awkward, screech. She kicked at Annabelle, both hands still clutched to the neck. Blood dripped down to her collar, staining the muddy shirt with the smiling mermaid upon the chest. When the screech ended, Mary kicked her again before turning away and running out of sight.

"Wait…" Annabelle croaked; her words were almost inaudible. She tried to get up but felt as helpless as a toppled turtle. "Mary, don't…"

The sound of Mary's footsteps faded in the distance, leaving Annabelle to lay sprawled alone. Unable to keep her eyes open, she closed them to lay at the edge of dreamless sleep. The sky above churned all night until rumblings of thunder echoed high over the trees to rouse her. Hours past midnight the wind began to pick up, forcing branches overhead to shift in a rhythmic dance as before a shower fell upon the woods. Annabelle awoke to the rain washing over her. For hours she watched the clouds swirl and twist, wisps of grey, white and clouds intermixing in a dance over the treetops.

Lying there, weak and alone, she wondered what it would be like if she couldn't find a way to get back to her feet and return to her tomb. She'd been exposed before. What if there was no shelter? Would she lay here, slowly burning to a crisp until only a human-shaped pile of ashes dotted the ground? Would any part of her remain in those scattered fragments? She imagined the rains washing the particles down the gullies to sink in the soil where the insects made their nests and the moss blossomed into lush green tufts. What would mean to be reborn in the soil and become part of another thing in nature besides a young girl? Being a girl is all she knew. Could mother nature reclaim a part of her? If she nurtured a plant to grow from her remains, would she become part of the vines? Would the miniature feet of aphids tickle her stems and leaves?

The possibilities made her head hurt. She didn't want to be a plant or waste away in the burning light of the coming sun. But if her plan was to survive, she'd have to be smart and think fast. Overcast or not, the sun would rise and bring death with it.

Annabelle Booth closed her eyes and let her mind reach out in every direction. It wasn't hard to find the other creatures of the night cowering from the storm in their burrows; things with horns and wings, things with teeth and claws. The forest bristled with life. Insects in numbers uncountable clung to the undersides of leaves and limbs to escape the deluge. In her current state, none of these would suffice and there were no deer close enough for to find. Eventually, she found what she required. Not two hundred yards to the East, Kentucky grey wolves sniffed the air from their den. A male, a female, and three pups populated the lair.

"Come to me," she commanded. In her mind's eye, she watched the male rise from its place to leave the female and the pups and step out into the storm. Minutes passed. The hiss of the rain covered the sound of its approach. If she hadn't rolled her head to the side, she wouldn't have witnessed the hundred and five pounds of furred lethality poke its head past through the underbrush.

"I'm hurt," she said. The wolf smelled the air and trotted in a half-circle around her feet. It moved close but stayed out of reach, never taking its eyes off her. "I need your help. I need blood."

The wolf paused near her left hand before trotting another half circle past her feet to come to her right side. It moved a little further this time to maneuver over her head before emitting a series of low growls. Annabelle felt a very real shiver of fear. If the wolf decided to attack and try to devour her, she wouldn't have the strength to fight it off. "I bet you're hungry, huh? Me too." Seeing the animal's face so close it reminded her of a story her mother used to read to her when she was little. "Why grandma, what big eyes you have." Bared fangs dripped with saliva as it inched closer, it's low growl close enough for her to feel its rasp on her crown. "Why grandma," she said, trying to keep her fear at bay a moment longer. "What large, sharp teeth you have." The growl intensified, and it snapped at her. "Now don't be like that. What do you say we make a deal? I could make it worth your while."

She managed to lift a finger and point it at the wolf's head as she imagined the large buck she'd encountered a few days past. "I can get you ten adult deer." The wolf raised its head to look around as though expecting to see a deer before looking back to her. "I bet the mama of your pups would like that so that she doesn't run low on milk," she said. "What do you say? Are you going to eat stringy old me for one meal and wonder where your next meal is or are you going to find me a few rabbits or muskrats in exchange for enough meat to fill your family's tummies for over a month? You'll have to bring them to me alive. They're no good to me dead."

The wolf edged closer, still baring its teeth, its breath close enough to be felt on her forehead. Thinking the beast had made its decision to take the meal already in front of it, Annabelle closed her eyes and waited for the fangs to sink into her face.

But only silence followed.

She opened her eyes to find the predator's tail swinging left to right and vanishing into the dense undergrowth as it started the hunt for smaller game. Annabelle let out a huge sigh of relief.

"Good boy." She whispered before closing her eyes. "I may survive my stupidity after all."

CHAPTER SEVENTEEN

Two days after getting grounded, Miles was in the middle of a busy shift—checking in vendors and taking a turn behind the register when Dennis came in through the front door. The usual devilish smile wasn't there, but considering how he'd reacted to Miles's supposedly false story about a vampire, he hadn't expected to see him anytime soon.

"Hey, can I talk to you a minute?" he asked Miles, who still had three customers in line.

"The pumps take credit cards, you know," Miles said without breaking eye contact with a customer as he took their payment. "You don't have to come inside."

"This is important. I need to talk to you."

"I've got people waiting. Get in line if you want." Dennis rolled his eyes and groaned before stomping over and taking a place behind a trucker with a bag of potato chips and a coke in his hand. One by one the customers paid for their items and left. Dennis stepped to the counter and slammed down a stack of photocopies with an enlarged picture on them. They were upside down, so Miles couldn't tell who was on them.

"What are those, band flyers? You know you can post in the window if you need to. You don't have to talk to me."

"No, I need to talk to you right now. We can't find Mary." Dennis flipped the stack around to show Miles the flyer. It read: "MISSING!" in huge letters at the top. In the middle of the page, a grainy picture of Mary's smiling face stared back at him. The information below the photo was her full name, height and weight and the number for Grandma Pearl's house and the sheriff's department.

"Holy shit. Are you serious? I saw her recently."

"Where?" Dennis asked. "Where did you see her?"

"She was here at the Imperial."

"When?"

"During the rainstorm. She was splashing around in her favorite pothole."

"Over on the side of the building?"

"Yeah, by the old broken air pump."

"Do you remember what she was wearing?"

"Yeah, it was that cartoon mermaid shirt that covers her like a dress and has the string running through it. Is she really missing? She runs off all the time. Has old man Stevens seen her? You know how much she loves climbing into his chicken coops and petting the chicks. Remember when she fell asleep there last year and didn't come out for a day and a half? If I were a betting man that's where I'd think she is."

"That's what I've been telling people. I knew I put that mermaid shirt on her. You gotta help me look. Pearl is so upset she's about to eat her hat."

"I'll definitely help you put up some flyers, but Gary grounded me, so I can't leave the house."

"I need you, man. If I don't get her home safe, Pearl is going to fucking die of grief. Sweeney's parents are even letting him drive to help us comb the county."

"If you can convince Gary to give me my wheels back then I'll do whatever I can."

"Cool. You leave Gary to me."

"Leave me to you for what?" said a voice just out of sight. Both looked to find the mustached man rounding the aisle endcap.

"Gary, I need Miles's help to find Mary. She's gone missing and Pearl is worried sick."

"Mary always runs off," he said. "That girl has had the entire county for a playground since she was tiny."

"I know that, but she's been gone for two whole days. Usually, she wanders home after a long day of being out of the house or she ends up here." He showed him one of the flyers. "You haven't seen her, have you?"

"No, can't say I have. Has she really never been out this long?"

"Everyone is worried. She loves Miles more than anyone, and I know he's grounded for whatever, but I want your permission to let him help us look." Dennis got down on both knees. "This is no joke. I'm begging you, please let Miles help us. My little sister is missing, and I think something really might've happened to her." Gary's eyes shifted to Miles behind the register. He was thinking it over.

"This isn't some kind of distraction to go to some field party or something?" he asked.

"No!" Dennis said, getting to his feet again. "Gary, I swear to god I've got half the county looking for her! I need everyone I can get and the sound of Miles's voice calling out for her might be just the thing needed to get her to come out. Come on, it's been two days." Gary blinked and nodded.

"I love Mary to death, so I hate to think something's happened to that little lamb. Miles? Go ahead and take off. I'll hold down the register till Darla gets back. You can take your car out to help them look for Mary, but I don't want you out gallivanting all over. You're still grounded. These, however, are extenuating circumstances. You go on now."

"Thanks, Gary," the boys said in unison.

"Come on," Dennis said. "I'll take you home so you can get your car."

The two exited the building and were halfway to the blue Oldsmobile when a small black pickup came barreling off the main road and rolled up fast towards them. The driver yelled something and waved his arm out of the window to get their attention. "Hey, it's that Clay guy that changes the oil on Pearl's car." The pickup stopped quick and the driver in his camouflage hunting coat leaped from the vehicle.

"Dennis! Dennis! You gotta come quick!"

"What is it?"

"The sheriff and his deputies with the coon dogs found something down near the back of the ridge off Button Road."

"Ridge off Button Road?" Dennis wrinkled his nose with confusion. "That's just a dead- end court that wraps around behind the cemetery."

"Behind the cemetery?" Miles asked with surprise. "Are you sure?"

"Yeah, I'm sure! They think they found the shirt you said she was wearing!"

"Shit. She took her clothes off again," Dennis said. "Come on, Miles. I'll run you to get your car and we'll meet at Button road."

The two piled into Pearl's car and raced up the road to the Burkich homestead. Dennis barely stopped the car from rolling when Miles jumped out, ran into the house, retrieved his keys and got behind the wheel of the Caddy. Monster kicked over and powered its way over the hills chasing the Oldsmobile across White Wreath. They sped the whole way there and once parked at the end of Button Road; they followed the deputies who were waiting to escort them past the tree line lined with yellow caution tape. As they walked, Miles's couldn't help but think about Annabelle's "Christmas dinner" comment and their current proximity to the cemetery. Surely, she wouldn't go against her own word and deviate from feeding upon deer, right?

They walked for a good ten minutes before they came upon the discarded garment near a group of trees. Sure enough, it was the same oversized shirt with the cartoon mermaid, crab and fish all smiling on the front. Mary had littered the hills of White Wreath with her clothes since either of them could remember. The disconcerting part that sent a cold chill down the spines of the boys was the sizeable bloodstain about the collar of the garment as it lay crumpled on the ground. Miles had to avert his eyes and keep them away to push down the feelings of suspicion.

"There's blood all over it," Dennis said to the deputy. "But they haven't found her yet?"

"Nothing here." The man pointed east through the woods. "But they found some more blood and all kinds of footprints and tracks about a hundred yards over that way. The sheriff and some other folks from Pikeville looking at things. I'd take you over, but they said they wanted me to keep everyone clear."

"What did they find?"

"I overheard the sheriff telling someone that they found a couple different-sized footprints and a punch of animal tracks."

"What kind of animals?" Miles asked.

"The usual shit, deer and wolves."

"Wolves?" Dennis said with a horrified expression. "Fucking grey wolves?"

"I don't know, that's just what I heard."

"Oh, Jesus," Dennis said as he began to breathe fast. "Oh my god, if Mary got cornered by wolves."

"Take it easy." Miles tried to comfort him. "There are wolves and deer all over the county, that's nothing new and

316

the wolves usually keep to themselves and only come out at night."

"But she was out during the night!" Dennis shouted.

"I know, but look, all they found was a shirt. If she's not here she must be somewhere else, right? We should spread out and keep looking. C'mon. Let's get back to the cars. Tell me where you've looked so we can split up and cover more ground."

"Yeah, yeah, that's a good idea. Nothing is happening here. Let's go." The two returned to the Oldsmobile and Dennis produced a map which he laid on the hood of the car." Dennis pointed out the different areas that hadn't been combed. "The area near your house and the distillery ruins haven't been covered. You know that area fairly well, why don't you start there? If there are wolves out hunting, then we might not want to be out long after sundown. If you find anything call Pearl. She's going to be at home waiting by the phone."

"Ok. I'll park at the house, work my way east on one side and then come back on the distillery side of the road."

"Sounds good, man. I'm going to head north and look behind all the business and keep putting up flyers."

"All right. I'll grab some food at home and start walking. Talk to you later," Miles said, walking back to his car.

"Hey," Dennis called after him and Miles turned about. "It's good to see you."

"You too." Monster came to life and carried Miles past the Imperial and home again. Once there, he grabbed a bit of food and filled an old army canteen with cold water. Both were shoved in a backpack before setting out across the hills. All afternoon he walked, calling out for Mary. He walked so far that he ended up in the area at the end of the winding road where the coal mines began. Dump trucks and semis blew past him, whipping the tall wild grass in violent gusts. Every two hundred yards or so he walked through the shadows of the coal belts; long conveyors twenty feet off the ground that stretched to the horizon in both directions.

They hummed and thrummed as they transported the dirty black gold, a ton a minute, to the rail cars waiting to carry it away. Every hundred paces Miles called out for the girl before listening for a reply. Too many times his imagination got the better of him and he thought he heard her broken speech calling back. When he got to the end of the road, the only thing there was a pair of guard shacks for the mining site. The two men in the prefab booths shook their heads and told him that neither of them or anyone on the other shifts had seen anyone like in the flyer's picture.

Miles started back, walking the shoreline of the water, keeping an eye out for foot tracks in the mud. Here and there he found the occasional bit of trash left by fisherman but no signs of Mary. He hadn't noticed the position of the sun until he passed a small group of trees and came upon the remains of the Booth distillery blocking out the last rays of the sun in the west. As the last of the beams vanished, the color scheme of the whole woods shifted from brilliant golds and yellows to greens and greys—the colors of the evening.

His stomach rumbled, reminding him to eat. There was still one peanut butter and jelly sandwich and a few mouthfuls of water in his pack. If he returned to the house for dinner, Gary would likely give him grief about going outdoors again, so he made himself comfortable atop the retaining wall with his feet hanging over the edge of the retaining wall of the rickhouse.

Shadows grew and stretched. Miles tried to justify a way to not suspect Annabelle in being responsible for Mary's disappearance, but the notion didn't shake easily. The clues were there if you knew what to look for. Her clothes were found in Annabelle's backyard with a bloodstain near the neck. There was a chance that it was something else. No one else suspected because no one else knew a vampire was in their midst. Miles ate his sandwich and lingered to looked out upon the shifting surface of the lake. An hour had passed since sundown and the approaching nightfall made him think of Annabelle. What if her super vampire senses could help find Mary? Why didn't he think of this sooner? So many questions came to mind. What had she been doing with all her time alone? Was she alone? Had she come to the house and shadowed him without his knowledge? At a whim, she could make herself practically disappear. Who's to say she wasn't close to him at this very moment?

The strangest notion came to mind. The idea stuck, and he entertained it. Certainly, he and Annabelle were on good terms, but curiosity got the best of him. If he was wrong, well, no one would know.

"Hello, Annabelle," he said loud enough that anyone within ten feet would hear him. "You don't have to hide, we're alone." He patted the top of the wall as though inviting an imaginary person to sit down. He waited for several moments before…

Silence.

Convinced he'd been stupid. He shoved the last corner of sandwich in his mouth and chewed the thick mush back before throwing back the last swig of water in the canteen. He closed his eyes and tilted his head back to swallow it all.

"How did you know I was here?" Annabelle's voice said. It took a strong gut check to not jump out of his skin as he opened his eyes to find Annabelle seated in the exact spot he'd invited her to sit in.

"I had a feeling."

"That's amazing. I've been all over this town following people and not one person sees me if I don't want them to."

"You're not sleeping here, again are you?"

"Oh, no. But I came straight here after I woke up. I was hoping you'd be here. You haven't been coming to the Mausoleum."

"No, I haven't. Gary grounded me."

"Grounded? What does that mean?"

"It's punishment. I'm not allowed to leave the house except for work and eventually school after school begins.

The idea is that if I'm not able to interact with my friends and have fun then I'll do whatever it is he wants me to do."

"What does he want you to do? Why would he punish you?"

"Because he knows I recently purchased a Transylvania hoodie and now there's a blonde girl running about town stealing firearms and blowing up property wearing one. Gary isn't stupid and when he asked me about you, and I didn't give you up, so he punished me. But that's not what's important right now."

"It isn't?"

"No. Now listen, because I have something very important to ask you. My friend, Dennis's younger sister, went missing two days ago and everyone is worried. She's a little simple-minded but she's a good girl, kind of what you might call a 'free spirit.' You haven't seen a thirteen-year-old girl running around the woods, have you?" The whites of her eyes doubled in size and she gasped before jumping up and walking away from him.

"Annabelle?" She didn't answer, and he too stood up. "Annabelle, if you've seen Mary, I need to know. Her family and everyone else is worried sick." She turned away and she covered her mouth with her hands.

"Annabelle, what's the matter? Are-are you crying?" Annabelle turned to face him, the last bit of light in the sky, revealing the dark crimson stains coming from the corners of her eyes.

"I'm sorry," she sobbed.

"Sorry for what?" The hair on his neck stood on end. "What are you sorry for?" She didn't answer but continued to sniffle as she stared back at him.

"Annabelle? Answer me! What are you sorry for?"

"I was…"

"You were what?!"

"I was…hungry." Miles recoiled in disgust as a deep fear took hold of him. He didn't realize it, but he was already backing away from her.

"I'm so sorry!" she said, moving closer. "I didn't want to hurt her, but I couldn't help myself!"

"Don't come near me, Annabelle. You killed an innocent girl who wouldn't hurt someone if they asked her to! Why? Why on earth would you go and do such a thing? What is wrong with you that you can't keep feeding on the animals? There's more than enough deer and wolves. You said you didn't want to kill anybody so why would you start now? Why would you start with the sweetest girl on the planet? What am I going to tell Dennis? What am I going to tell Pearl? Do you realize what this going to do? This news is going to kill an old woman, Annabelle! It's going to break her heart and there is nothing you or anyone can do to undo that kind of heartbreak." Miles felt like he was going to pull his hair out by the roots.

The anguish came so fast he bent at the waist and put his hands on his knees. "Oh god!" He groaned. "God…fucking…dammit!" Annabelle reached her hand out but kept her distance. "No, no, you don't get to touch me. Stay away from me. You've done enough, more than enough. Oh, god. Oh, Jesus. He sniffled and snotted. "Tell me this, Annabelle," he said, straightening himself. "What did you do with her? Where is Mary's body? I gotta take it home to Pearl. It's gonna kill her, but I gotta at least do that? The police found the blood-covered shirt so she's probably somewhere near the cemetery, right?"

"I don't know where she is."

"What do you mean you don't know? You were the last one to see her! You killed her, right? That's what you said, right? That's what you said you're sorry for, right?"

"I bit her to drink her blood, but I only took a tiny amount. I don't think I killed her."

"You don't think, or you don't know?"

"I-I don't know. I called for the wolves to help me."

"What? Wolves? Are you saying it was wolves now? Why are you playing with me like this?" Miles began to shake with rage at the idea of Mary's last moments being killed by Annabelle. Panic wrapped about him like an anaconda and squeezed. "Why, Annabelle? At every turn of the way so far I've helped you as much as I possibly can and how do you repay me? You take things that don't belong to you, you destroy other people's property and now you kill a young girl and when you've been discovered you try and deny it was you after you confessed to doing it?"

Miles' heart thumped like it was going to jump out of his chest as it broke. His knees buckled and he caught himself in the grass when his legs no longer hold him. "Oh god, Jesus god. You killed an innocent girl. She was innocent." Miles's arms gave out too and he collapsed in the grass to lay panting and grieving. He watched her face as the crimson flowed from the corners of her eyes making steaks down her pale face.

"I'm so sorry, Miles," she said, weeping blood. "I think that…"

"I don't care what you think." He cut her off. "Save those tears. They're not for anyone you know or love." He waved his hand in the direction of the cemetery. "Go be miserable alone because I don't want to know you, Annabelle Booth. You might've been a distiller's daughter a long time ago but now you're just…a murderer now." The sound of thousands of angry cicadas filled the trees around them, and one flew directly into his right temple. It hissed and clawed at him for only a second with tiny legs, causing him to flinch and swat at it. When he opened his eyes, Annabelle was gone.

CHAPTER EIGHTEEN

The days blurred together, seamless and identical, one into the next. Miles watched from afar as the rescue efforts failed to produce any results. A vigil was held at the Imperial and Gary moved all the tables and chairs from the eating area into one corner for a memorial area. Dennis mounted an enlarged picture of Mary stapled to a big piece of cardboard. He set up the picture on one of the tables and people came from across the county to lay flowers and letters of comfort to the grieving family beneath it.

Miles hated himself for knowing the truth and not being able to tell a soul. But what good would it do to tell him? If Dennis learned what really happened flew into a rage and stormed the Booth Mausoleum in the middle of the day to confront or kill Annabelle, there was no guarantee that she would be there. After their falling out, it wouldn't be smart to sleep in the cemetery any longer.

If someone came looking for her, didn't find her, and she discovered who raided her home, she might trace the person's scent to their home and kill them for the trespass that night. No, this was the time to say nothing. But what if he said nothing and she killed again? How long could he be complicit in silence? If it came to it, would a mob of people descend upon the Booth tomb with torches and guns to hunt her down? Too many questions.

Around 7:45 in the morning on the fourth day, Pearl's blue Oldsmobile pulled up to the side of pump number one in front of the store. Dennis got out of the driver's seat while Sweeney got out of the passenger side and put the nozzle in the tank. Dennis pulled open the front door, his shoulders sagging. He looked a little too lean from lack of sleep and appetite. Upon crossing the threshold, he paused in front of the registers to look upon the heaping flowers of the memorial before making his way to the coffee maker. After filling two cups to the top and adding the cream and sugar he set the cup upon the counter without looking up. Hands dug into dirty jeans before producing a crumpled single and an even more thrashed twenty-dollar bill.

"These coffees and twenty dollars of unleaded on pump one, please," Dennis said without looking up.

Miles stared at the top of Dennis' head waiting for him to look up at him. Miles produced his wallet from a rear pocket and put a twenty-dollar bill of his own in the register.

"Gary's giving away free coffee to everyone who's looking for Mary and the tank of gas is on me," he said. Dennis responded with a long mumble, the only recognizable words being "sheriff" and "search party" before returning the crumpled bills to his pocket and absconding with the two coffee cups. Even as he turned backward to use his shoulder blades to push the door open, the two never made eye contact. The electronic bell of the door dinged louder than usual. Sweeney finished pumping the gas just as Dennis returned and the two promptly pulled out of the spot before the car vanished out of sight.

"Poor kid," Gary said as he approached from behind. "The sheriff just held a meeting in front of the courthouse."

"About the search? What did he say?"

"It was to announce that the search was no longer a 'rescue effort' as much as it was now a 'recovery effort' to find Mary Montgomery's remains. I called to talk to Pearl. That woman has had the soul pulled out of her. Mary and Dennis are the last things keeping her on this side of the grass."

"Jesus." So, it was true. The last bit of hope that the quirky girl with "angels between the ears" would wander her way home had dwindled to the point of nothingness.

"I know you're grounded and all, but right now your best friend is going through some serious shit and you need to be there, so he has someone to talk to. When you're done with your shift go on over to his house and visit with him and Pearl. Sometimes when people don't want to talk, it's nice to know that someone is there if they wanted to. You know, I don't know if Pearl has enough money put back for a small memorial marker for that poor girl let alone a full funeral and a casket. I'll keep my ears open. If something comes up, we may be able to help them or arrange for everyone to pass the hat on getting that girl buried."

"Ok. Thanks, Gary."

"Yeah, well, yeah. It's a damn shame is what it is. Here are some more fives and singles for your drawer." He handed Miles a stack of money for the till which was then shoved in a drawer under the counter. "It's getting dirty up here," Gary said as he started walking back to his office. "When Darla comes back from her break, sweep this area with a broom and then see about hitting the edge of the property with the weedwhacker."

"I'll do it."

Darla returned soon enough, and Miles swept the floor before opening the tool shed. It had been overcast in White Wreath since Mary had gone missing. It was like even the weather was sad for them. It was so dark you could hardly call it "daytime." The upside of that would be that he wouldn't have to do the trimming in the blazing heat with no shade. The downside would be that the damp clusters of grass and weeds would be exploding as he worked, showering him with trimmings.

Miles had seated himself on a pair of stacked cinderblocks trying to spool the uncooperative trimming line of the yard tool when the strangest image planted itself in his mind's eye. The stark picture was the point of view of a person standing fifty yards to the rear of the Imperial looking at him as he sat on his makeshift stool. Humoring the notion, he glanced upwards from his tinkering confirmed that nobody was standing in the field. It came again in another flash, but not as vivid.

Just then, the spring holding the trimming line spool in place jumped free of its housing, striking him square between the eyes before bouncing away and rolling out into the parking lot. Semi-trucks arrived and departed, big wheels, a dozen at a time crunching and squelching as they spun. The spring rolled in front of and around the slabs of rubber. If anyone of the tires found it, the weed trimmer would be rendered useless and he'd get a royal ass-chewing from Gary for being careless with his equipment.

Miles pitched the tool down and leaped to his feet. Across the gravel, he sprinted to keep the metal coil from getting squashed by a glowing Peterbilt tow truck oblivious to its fragile existence.

"Hey! Hey! Hey!" He waved his arms over his head. In the dark morning light the vehicle covered in so many lights it resembled a spaceship from an alien planet. The driver saw him and the truck lurched to a stop, its air brakes emitting a piercing chirp.

"Kid, what the hell are you doing? You trying to get run over or something?"

"Hold still! Don't move! Something rolled under your truck!"

"Ok, ok, I got the brakes on." Miles waited until he let off the brake pedal. The whole vehicle shifted in place before coming to rest. The driver leaned out his window to see Miles scramble under the cab on hands and knees before backing out with the item in his hand.

"I got it, thanks!" he said, holding the item above his head. The man waved before releasing the brake and the truck rolled away. Miles turned the spring over in his hands to inspect it, thankful that it hadn't been smashed. It wasn't damaged but during the walk back to the shed another vision found him. The same as the one before, an image from the point of view from the middle of the field the Imperial. A voice whispered in his ear.

"*See me.*"

He looked to the place the vision appeared to be watching. What appeared in the field made his blood run cold. A black, shrouded form waited for him amongst the chest-high uncut grass. It beckoned by its presence alone, and Miles couldn't look away. The shroud waved and rippled like the grass on the wind. He blinked twice and shook his head, but he wasn't seeing things. A cloaked visitor had come to visit. A dark reaper.

"*See me*," it said again. Its voice as faint as the rustling of the grass

"I see you," he said.

"*Come to me*,"

As afraid as he was of the specter, his feet carried him across the gravel and into the grass. The blades of wild grass shifted and swayed in waves in a hypnotic fashion as he pressed his way further in. Then, like Moses before the Red Sea, the grass began to part for him to reveal a path to where the dark visitor waited. Closer he moved, closer as the wind picked up. One step after the next he shoved the blades aside as they pushed back upon him. The distance between them dwindled and Miles stopped ten paces short of standing before it.

"*There's not much time*," it told him without speaking aloud.

The phantasmal black shroud fluttered with the breeze as it floated above the ground. There were no legs between the bottom of the flapping material and the ground. For all the supernatural things he'd witnessed to suspend his disbelief, only one person he knew had a tendency to levitate. Upon closer inspection, the supposed reaper's cloak looked to be made of shiny plastic, like 50-gallon industrial trash bags held together with duct tape.

"Annabelle?" he asked. "Is that you? What are you doing out during the day?"

"*I can't stay.*" The specter spoke a whisper inside his head. "*I hope you can help her.*"

"Help who? Do you know where Mary is? Tell me what you know, please." As he said this, the wind picked up in a violent gust and the grass at his feet parted to reveal the body of Mary Montgomery at his feet. She lay there, naked, pale, covered in mud up to the knees and elbows, emaciated from hunger, but still breathing.

"Mary!" Miles pitched the weed trimmer and knelt at her side. The stringy black hair fought his fingers as he moved in close to lift her head and look her in the face. Her eyes weren't open. "Mary, honey, look at me. Can you open your eyes?" She didn't reply directly but let out an almost inaudible whimper. "Come on, baby girl."

Miles snaked his arms under her back and knees to cradle her and lifted her from the ground. He got to his feet but when he looked up to thank the shrouded form, the head could be seen gliding across the field and out of sight. Miles wasted no time in forcing a path through the grass back to the Imperial. With no supernatural power to keep them parted, he had to fight and kick against the thick blades to reach the edge of the gravel. In the distance he found Gary inspecting the half-dissected weed trimmer.

"Gary, get the truck! I found Mary! She's still breathing, but just barely!" Miles yelled. Gary realized who Miles was carrying in his arms and dropped the trimmer. The plastic casing around the motor struck the curb, sending pieces of plastic in every direction. The man ran faster than Miles had ever seen him run before to get his keys ready with one hand while opening the passenger side door of the suburban with the other.

"It's really her?" Gary asked. "Where was she?"

"She was lying out in the tall grass." No sooner had he shut the door, Darla the cashier poked her head around the corner from where she was taking a smoke break next to the fried oil receptacle.

"Gary? Is everything ok? Where are you going in such a hurry?"

"No time to talk, Darla! Call Pearl to get the hospital now!

"What?" She strained to hear.

"I said, call Pearl now at her house and tell her to meet us at the damn hospital!"

"All right, all right, I'll do it!" She flicked her cigarette butt into a coffee can before heading indoors. The Suburban's engine revved up and Gary piloted it out onto the main road, almost cutting off a pickup truck heading the same way. The driver blared his horn and stuck his hand high out of the driver's side window to give them the middle finger.

The truck sped down the road, through the center of White Wreath, and past the diner. Gary didn't touch the brake pedal to navigate the traffic between them. Thank God there weren't any cops on the road. Mary's eyes didn't open during the entire ride. No matter how much Miles begged or pleaded, the only part that moved was the shallow rise and fall of her chest. Mile over mile the scenery blurred past them, the suburban barreling around cars already doing the speed limit.

"I have never seen shit like this before in all my life," Gary remarked as he took to the shoulder of the highway to get around a tractor that was traveling way too slow. Gravel sprayed up and the tank-like vehicle didn't slow a bit as it took out a speed limit sign.

"Jesus, Gary!" Miles yelled, leaning away from the window as the ruined sign tumbled past a foot from the passenger window. "We're all going to need a doctor if you keep driving like this!"

"The sheriff can bill me for the sign. I'm good for it. Hold on, we're here."

Gary yanked the wheel again and the truck careened off the main road to climb the long incline the hospital. Out of the side-view mirror, Miles caught a glimpse of the lights of police cars in the distance. Underneath the cover of the emergency room's overhang, the truck skidded to a forceful stop. Miles had to plant one knee on the glove box to keep himself and Mary from being thrown through the windshield. Gary threw the vehicle into park, opened his door and rushed around to open the one on the passenger side. Miles swiveled his feet out, planting them on the concrete before moving as fast as his legs would carry him inside. The "swish" of the automatic doors heralded the arrival of a wash of cool air within the breezeway.

"Help me!" Miles yelled over the people milling about. "Somebody help me!"

A doctor's head popped up from behind the corner of an adjacent corridor. A tall woman approached them, already applying a pair of blue latex medical gloves.

"What's going on here?" she asked. "What's happened to her?"

"This is Mary Montgomery." He pointed to her picture, staring back from a flyer on the bulletin board next to the vending machines. "She's been missing for several days and I don't know if she's eaten or if she's sick. Please, you have to help me I think she's dying."

Police sirens grew louder behind them and a pair of squad cars appeared around the suburban. The blaring became unbearable as the sound echoed off the platform and overhang. Gary patted Miles on the shoulder.

"You go on inside," he told him. "I'll straighten things out with the cops."

"Let's get Mary on a gurney." The doctor said. "Follow me. Are you her brother?"

"Me? No. Her brother is my best friend. I've known her my whole life."

"Ok, does Mary have any allergies to shots or medication?"

"Um, I don't know. Her grandma Pearl knows all of that. She's on her way here now."

"All right, start from the beginning." Mary was laid upon a stainless-steel gurney with a thin mattress. The doctor pulled a small flashlight from the chest pocket of her lab coat and lifted each of Mary's eyelids to shine its light into each eye.

"Mary!" The doctor called out trying to rouse the girl. "Mary, I need you to open your eyes for me!" She patted the cheeks trying to get a response before putting her stethoscope in her ears and placing the other end on different parts of Mary's torso. "Mary, girl, I need you to wake up!"

"She might not answer you, doc," he told her. "Mary doesn't talk much. She's a little simple-minded and doesn't do things the same way as everyone else. She'll talk but not in full sentences. Is she going to be ok?"

"I don't know yet, too soon to tell." With that, the tall woman pushed the gurney down the hallway and slammed it through the double doors at the end. The other doctor was already standing by with a reflective silver blanket. Both the doors swung together to obscure the view of what happened next. To the rear, the sounds of excited talking echoed in through the automatic doors. Miles looked to find Gary leading three peace officers in through the door.

"Here he is, officers!" Gary said. "Miles? Where's Mary?"

"The doctors took her to the room at the end of the hall."

"You found the girl? Where was she?" asked the officer, whose bulking physique barely fit into his uniform.

"She was lying in the tall grass behind the truck stop, sir," Miles said.

"You think it might've been some kind of assault?" one officer asked the other.

"I dunno. We'll talk to the doctor and get a report," said the bulky one before glaring down at Miles. "Behind the truck stop huh? We'll see about that. You stay here and watch these two," he said to the other officers. Seeing the "missing person" flyer pinned on the bulletin board, the officer removed it and walked to the end of the hall. Everyone watched as he paused at the doors of the far room and peered in through the plexiglass windows before looking at the flyer and back again. He turned and walked back, examining the picture on the paper before bringing it along with him.

"That's her, all right. I gotta call this into the station. It's a miracle that you found her and managed to get her here quickly in one piece. That must've taken some pretty fancy driving. Which of you did that?"

"That'd be me." Gary grinned with pride.

"Then it's going to be you that's under arrest," said the officer. Gary's smirk vanished when the officer pulled a pair of handcuffs from his utility belt and snapped the first cuff upon Gary's wrist.

"Now, now, wait a minute." Gary stammered. "What's all this for?"

"Well let's see—you ran three red lights and a stop sign, broke the double yellow at least four times to swerve into oncoming traffic, and you did all of this while driving at speeds in excess of at least twenty miles over the speed limit the whole way. I admire what you did, Gary but you'll be lucky old Judge Thompson doesn't revoke your license for good and have you serving time as well." The officer spun Gary around and put the other cuff on. Without missing a beat, Gary looked at Miles and the grin spread from ear to ear.

"Good thing he doesn't know about the sign. Eh, kiddo?" Miles gawked in awe.

"Sign?" 'Officer McMuscles asked him with scrutinizing eyes. "What sign?"

"He was born under a bad sign, officer," Miles said with the same crooked grin. "Something about being a Libra when his mother was a Sagittarius."

"What the hell does that mean?"

"Beats me." Miles stared at his shoes. "I wasn't driving."

"Are you double-talking me, boy? You want to go with him down to the station?"

"No, sir." He feigned to cower as he snuck a wink at Gary.

"Then watch that lip or it's going to get you in trouble." He pointed a finger. "You're free to stay here, but Mr. Burkich is coming with me." With no way out of the situation, Gary appeared to be making the best of it as one of the other officers took him into custody.

"Holy shit. Now that I think about it, I've never been arrested before. Hey officer, do you mind playing the siren on the way back?"

"Gary, shut up," the deputy Ed told him. "You're already in a heap of trouble."

"Miles!" He yelled over his shoulder. "Call Mr. Jenkins and have him get money from the safe so he can bail me out!"

"Okay!" He waved. "Have fun in jail! Don't drop the soap!" When the doors parted to let one group of people out, another came flooding into view. Dennis, Christian, Nora, and Sweeney followed by Pearl with her walker moving at such a hurried pace she looked like she might topple at any second. Love and worry kept that woman on her feet.

"Mary!" Mary!" She called out until she saw him. "Miles! Where's my little angel?"

"The doctors have her in the back."

"Which room?" Her head swiveled about in a frantic fashion hoping to catch a glimpse, the others also craning their necks. "I need to see my little girl!"

"You'll have to wait until they're done, Pearl. She's alive but she looked pretty weak so they're checking her out." He corralled her towards some seats in the waiting room. "Come on and have a seat. We'll wait together until the doctors tell us what's going on."

"My baby," Pearl said dabbing at the corner of one eye with a handkerchief that had more make-up on it than clean spots. It took a full ten minutes to get her to quit crying and stop looking down the hallway.

"How did you find her?" Dennis asked. Miles stretched the story to say that he was trying to take a leak in the tall grass when he found her lying on the ground. He explained how Gary had been arrested for tearing ass across White Wreath to get her as fast as possible.

"That's just shameful that the sheriff couldn't see he was trying to do the right thing."

"I guess we'll see when he gets his court date. Whether the judge sees it the same way. That reminds me, I need to call Mr. Jenkins to go bail him out." He excused himself to use the payphone and managed to convey the message over a static-filled line before hanging up. When he sat down across from Pearl, Dennis sat next to him and wrapped both arms around him.

"You're amazing. Only you would be lucky enough to take a leak and find her."

"Yeah," Miles said, thinking about Annabelle. Pearl filled out a sheet concerning Mary's medical history and gave it to the nurse. After that, they all sat in the waiting room for over an hour taking turns holding an old woman's hand. The doctor finally emerged and offered to take her into the back room. When Pearl emerged, she was as pale as a ghost. The tall doctor held her hand the whole way back to the waiting room. Her mouth hung open with shock and her eyes bugged like she'd seen the revelation.

"Pearl?" Dennis asked. "Pearl, what's the matter? Is something wrong?"

"No." She shook her head. "Dennis, I've just seen the damnedest thing."

"What did you see?" Dennis asked.

"That girl opened her eyes, put her hand on my cheek and called me grandma! She's never done that a day in her life!"

"You're kidding!"

"Swear to god she did!"

"Would you like to come back?" the doctor asked Dennis. He, in turn, sprinted down the hall, almost knocking over an orderly carrying laundry to get to the room. Five minutes later he returned with the same amazed expression. Gobsmacked.

"Well?" Everyone asked in unison.

"She knew exactly who I was. She said 'Dennis' and said she loved me."

"That's amazing!" Christian hugged him.

"Miles?" Dennis asked. "Do you want to see her?"

"Yeah, of course."

"Ok, just you," said the doctor. "I'll give you a few minutes to visit but no more for right now. Mary needs to get some bed rest to recuperate from the effects of malnutrition, dehydration, as well as some slight anemia. She'll make a full recovery but if you hadn't found her when you did, it might be a different story altogether."

"Ok. I'll go." Miles walked the hallway and entered the room Mary lay wrapped in blankets with an IV in one arm and monitors all over her body.

"Hey, Mary," he said, brushing stray strands of hair back from her brow.

"Miles," she said. Not 'Mills', but Miles.

"Yeah, yeah, I'm here," he said in a soothing voice.

"My body hurts," she said, her words neither slurred or truncated.

"It's going to hurt. You had us all so worried. We found your clothes. We thought the wolves had gotten you."

"The wolves helped to find Mary."

"How did the wolves help?"

"They combed the forests during the daylight hours when I'm at my weakest. Otherwise, Mary would never have been found."

"When you're at your weakest?" A shiver fell over Miles as this scenario felt a little too familiar. "Wait a minute... He leaned closer to her. "Annabelle?" Mary came to life and turned her head to look him in the eye.

"Couldn't fool you a second time, huh?"

"What, what are you doing? Annabelle, you can't be here."

"I'm not here. I'm in my coffin where it's safe."

"Have you been with her the whole time?"

"I wanted to make sure Mary got safely to the hospital. It looks like she did. I'm glad."

"You have to leave. You can't hang around possessing Mary's body."

"Some gratitude. I suffered a lot of pain to deliver her to you at the truck stop and you repay me by being coarse."

"The only reason this happened his because you tried to kill her."

"I only did it because I was out of my head with hunger. I would never intentionally hurt anyone, especially someone as sweet as Mary. Being inside her body like this I see why she acts the way she does."

"You do?"

"Her head is always full of static like there are a hundred thoughts crossing each other at the same time. It's like a puzzle with the pieces all jumbled. I'd think it would be enough to drive a person mad."

"We've always wondered. What did you do to her?"

"I bit her but not in the way that Dracula did in that book. I even fixed the wound, see?" She reached up with her right arm to pull the cheap gown away from her neck. Short of being a little dirty, the flesh was pink and perfect. "She was frightened and ran off on her own and got lost. I know I caused a problem, but I also fixed it. The makeshift suit might not have held, and I could have died to be out during daylight hours, overcast or not. Either way, I'm sorry for what happened, and I don't want you to hate me."

"I don't hate you. I just think you're reckless when you don't have to be."

"I don't wish to be. I'd like you to visit me when you have the time."

"Yeah, well, I'm still grounded, and school is about to start so until I can get Gary to let me off the hook, you're on your own."

"Then I hope it's soon. I should leave so Mary can get better."

"Maybe that's for the best." Mary's eyes shut and she returned to a state of rest. Seeing this, he excused himself and turned to walk away. He was reaching for the door when she spoke again.

"Mills?" She croaked. Miles rushed back to her side and the girl looked up at him with the same blissful, spacey gaze that told him she had no idea what was going on around her. Mary tugged and pulled at the tubes. "No. Dun't want. Ow, No. Ow."

"Mary, calm down, you'll pull your needles out and hurt yourself. Doctor!" The doctor returned and administered restraints to keep Mary from hurting herself or removing the monitors. The more straps they added, the more Mary fought to get free. In the end, she was sedated with the contents of a needle slipped straight into her IV. When Mary appeared to doze off, Miles returned to the eager faces of the others in the waiting room.

"What did she say to you?" Dennis asked.

"Not much." He lied. "She acted tired more than anything."

"God bless you, Miles." Pearl continued to weep. "You found my baby angel."

"It was luck, Pearl. That reminds me, I better move the truck out of the emergency room parking area, so the ambulances can get in. I hate to go, but I'm going to head back to the Imperial. With Gary in jail until he gets bailed, I'm going to have to check in all the vendors." Dennis let go of Pearl's hand and embraced Miles with a hug so strong it almost crushed the air out of him.

"You did it. You got her back," Dennis said loud enough for him to hear. "I love you, man."

"You too. Take care of Pearl and Mary. Call me later at home, huh?"

"I'll do it." He let go. "Get out of here. Take care of your business." Miles waved to the others and returned to the covered area where the suburban sat waiting. Lucky for him, the keys were still in the ignition. The truck fired up and rumbled out of the parking lot underneath beneath the parting clouds.

CHAPTER NINETEEN

A fella who regularly bought gas at the Imperial offered his legal services so that Gary didn't have to face the laundry list of charges without a lawyer. For the collective charges of: three counts of running a red light, two counts of running a stop sign, speeding, reckless driving, failure to yield, the endangerment of the lives of two minors, the destruction of a posted speed limit sign, any other judge might've locked Gary in a cell underneath the courthouse and thrown away the key. But with the extenuating circumstances of saving a missing girl's life as the root cause for all of it, being a first-time offender, and Pearl's five-minute rant about how he should have been given a medal for saving her granddaughter's life, and Gary pleading guilty in exchange for leniency, the judge couldn't throw the book at him.

When the gavel fell, the punishment was traffic school, a five thousand dollar fine, and a year of probation. Gary had a smile from ear to ear as he and Miles left the courthouse.

After that, things went back to normal, so to speak. The school year started, and Miles traded his shovel for schoolbooks and homework. When he was no longer grounded, Miles took Monster across the county to the cemetery after closing time. The interaction was always the same. He'd knock on the door of Annabelle's family tomb, and there would be no answer. Once a week, he left a care package of different clothes and books for Annabelle behind the tomb in a large plastic resealable bin where the elements wouldn't get to them. He'd even gone so far as to leave cassette tapes, a Walkman, instructions on how to use it, and batteries.

When he opened the container, there was always a new scrap of paper with the words "Thank you." written in elegant cursive atop the items being returned. Other than this, they didn't speak.

September came and went without a single sighting of Annabelle. Although, a few local hunters reported finding the carcasses of dead deer suspended by the antlers in the limbs of trees forty feet off the ground.

The arrival of October brought chillier nights.

Saturday, October 29, 1994

A brisk breeze made Miles huddle his arms around himself as climbed the hill of the cemetery. The crunch of the leaves made it impossible to be quiet when he banged on the door of the mausoleum. Like the other time, he didn't expect an answer. This time, however, things were different.

"Hello, Miles," said a voice.

"Annabelle?" he said looking left and right.

"Up here." Miles clicked his flashlight and aimed it upwards to find Annabelle in her crimson sweatshirt crouched down on hands and knees over the door like a gargoyle. "Can you turn off that light?"

No sooner than the light clicked off, she stood up and stepped off the edge of the eaves, floating down like a swimmer in the water to land before him. "You're cold, she said, opening the door to her tomb. "I don't know if it's warmer indoors, but there's no wind." She stepped inside and held the door open. Miles accepted her offer and crossed the threshold, laughing to himself that a vampire had invited him inside. Annabelle's possessions lay in her open coffin; a shotgun, some clothes and the music he'd lent her.

"It's a bit dark, don't you think?" Miles marveled as a quick breeze filled the room and a dozen candles positioned evenly spaced around the edges of the floor sparked to life to illuminate the room.

"Wow. Learned how to channel into the dark magic of the undead, huh?" he said.

"No, I used a match," she said, waving smoking matchsticks. "Why don't you have a seat?"

Miles took a place on the floor, leaning against the section of the wall beside the coffin. Annabelle stepped into the coffin next to him and pulled her knees to her chest before placing her cheek atop them. Her eyes looked sad as the orange candlelight reflected back.

"What's the matter?" he asked. She said nothing for a few moments but continued to stare at him.

"I have to leave you," she finally said.

"Leave? To go where?"

"Away. Somewhere far from White Wreath. People are beginning to suspect. I can't risk drawing any more attention than I already have."

"You don't have to leave. You can just lay low, and no one will notice."

"That's another thing. I'm a person, not an animal. I can't slink around the shadows for eternity," Her voice took a turn for the sinister as she held her hands up like creepy claws. "Sssstealing blood from the innocent."

"You're not an animal. You're just…different. At least you're learning how to adapt to your environment."

"I can't let this be my environment. And…" She gestured at the space where her parents were entombed. "And I'm too old to be living with my parents." She gave him a pleasant smile.

"That's fair. But if you're not going to stay here where will you go?"

"I've been reading the books you've given me. So many of them point to New Orleans as a place where vampires tend to congregate. I think it's the first place I should look."

"New Orleans? You mean those Anne Rice novels I gave you? Annabelle, those are stories, fiction."

"Am I not fiction, Miles?" she asked. "Am I not the thing that should not be?"

"That's different! Your arrival means that…that… you know what I mean."

"It means that somewhere along the line, the truth got out just enough for people to make up stories about us. That funeral coach came from New Orleans, Miles. And that thing that bit me in Pikeville wasn't fiction either. We're real." She reached out with a finger and prodded his arm strong enough to nudge him. "I'm really here and it's the truth. The rest of the world has the choice to believe or not believe. A long time ago I might've been able to dismiss it all. I don't have that luxury anymore. I can't pretend. As much as I want to believe this is all fantastic and terrible dream and that I'll wake up tomorrow in my own bed with my mother and father still alive, I can't pretend. I would be sad though."

"Why?" he asked. Annabelle reached out again and touched the back of her hand to his cheek. The flesh was cold, but he didn't pull away.

"Because that would mean that you're not real and that all the time we've spent together has all been the makings of an imagination run wild. I'd wake up in 1890 and no one would believe a word of what I told them. They'd call me a loon if I told them about your cars and moving picture movies. They'd likely lock me up in an insane asylum where they keep simpletons and geeks for rich people to go and gawk at."

"I'd hate to see you go. How will you get to New Orleans? That's eight hundred miles from here. It's too far to travel in one night."

"Isn't the rear section of cars dark all the time?"

"You mean the trunk?"

"Yes, the trunk. Isn't it pitch dark in there?"

"Sure, but it would be hot and uncomfortable."

"I can be uncomfortable for a little while if it gets me where I want to go."

"So that's it? You're going to hitchhike in the trunks of cars of strangers? How will you know which ones are going to New Orleans?" The question stumped Annabelle. She thought a moment, staring at her surroundings before looking at Miles.

"Would you take me?"

"Me? You want me to drive you?"

"The trunk of your car is far larger than most of the others I've seen, and I trust you to get me there safely." Miles mulled the idea over.

"You know, I've always wanted to see New Orleans. I suppose anything is possible, but it won't be anytime soon. I've got school and work and gasoline doesn't grow on trees. It would take several full tanks to get there and back."

"You wouldn't stay in New Orleans with me?"

"Annabelle, I have to get back to finish school. Besides, I-"

"I understand, White Wreath is your world."

"Yeah, for now. Look, I'd be happy to take you, but I need a few days to gather some money, that's all."

"I'm not sure I can wait, Miles."

"You can't?"

"Something is pulling me away from here. I'd love to have you with me, but I'm leaving soon to find what it is. It sounds like tiny whispers on the wind. They speak so softly I can almost make out what they're saying. Sometimes it sounds like clockwork, little wheels turning a tiny bit at a time somewhere I can't see." Miles recalled how he heard her voice in his head.

"Is it other vampires? Do they speak in whispers the way you did to me before we met?"

"Perhaps. Or something else altogether. Either way, I won't find the answers I'm looking for sleeping here." With that, Annabelle scooted the coffin a little closer to Miles and leaned over to put her head on his shoulder. "I can't thank you enough for your hospitality. I was a stranger and you helped me."

"We're both strange." He lifted an arm and put it around her. "So, it evens out."

"But you're still scared of me…" she whispered. "Just a little bit. I can feel it."

"I'd be stupid not to be. Just a little bit."

"Thanks for all the music you've let me listen to. It's taken me some time to get used to music that's made with electric instruments, but I think I like it.

"You do? Do you have a favorite?"

"I like Mr. David Bowie."

"Really. You like Bowie?"

"It makes the most sense to me. He sings love songs and loneliness and about strange things that come from other worlds. That's how I feel most of the time these days." Miles stared at her, trying to imagine his life without her.

"So, when do you think you'll leave?"

"Sundown on Halloween. I thought I might at least stick around to wish you a happy birthday. I'll leave the tomb unlocked so you and your friends can still come here as long as you take care of it."

"That's awfully nice of you. The others have been talking about coming here for a Halloween party. I was running out of excuses to keep them away from your home."

"Now you don't have to. I really don't mind. I'll move my things out so that no one messes with them."

"Gary says I'm not grounded as long as I keep my grades up, but once Halloween rolls around and I'm eighteen, he doesn't have much input after that on what I have and don't have to do."

"Of course, you'll do as he asks. He's raised you to be a proper gentleman. I can attest to that. I may not know much but I know a gentleman when I meet one."

"You think so?"

"I know so." Annabelle let go of his arm and sat up. "I hope I find ladies and gentlemen in New Orleans."

"What do you think you'll find when you get there? Do you even know what you're looking for?"

"I still remember the smell of the one that bit me. It might've been a person at one time but by the time we crossed paths, it had become something else. Something like that couldn't have wandered around for a hundred years and not raised attention or left a trail of clues."

"Just be careful, okay?"

"Okay, Miles."

"Well, I'd better be on my way. It's getting late and I promised Gary I'd stop by the Imperial and make sure the lot is clear. The construction crews arrived on Friday to start tearing up the lot so that they can remove the old fuel tanks in the ground. He's been telling everyone that he's closing late Halloween and that as of November first, The Imperial is going to be closed for a week. Oh, I wanted to tell you that Mary has taken a turn for the better since you were in her head."

"How's that?"

"She doesn't run off as often and began taking an interest in reading aloud the pages of children's books and words on signs or food wrappers. Best of all, she managed to stay dressed without having her clothes tied to her. She'd even scribble in coloring books if you gave her crayons."

"That's wonderful! I can't say I did anything, but if the encounter has left her better off then I'm glad."

"She's not cured by any means. She still climbs into places she shouldn't be. Since we had the old trucks behind the Imperial towed away, Gary's run her out of the store half a dozen times already for hiding out in the corners of the storeroom."

"Not everything can be as perfect as we want it to be."

"That's the damn truth." Annabelle got up from the coffin and stood over him.

"Miles? Would you like to see something?"

"Like what?"

"It's a surprise."

"Is it a good surprise?"

"Yes, I think you'll enjoy it."

"All right." Annabelle gripped his hand tight and hoisted him from a seated position all the way to his feet. She led him over to the door of the tomb and stopped.

"Close your eyes." He did as she asked and listened as she threw the doors wide and led him out into the cool night air. Even with the hoodie and jacket, goosebumps pushed their way to the surface of his skin. "Ok," she said. "Open them." Miles opened them to find a vision, unlike anything he'd known to be possible.

Deer. All the deer of the nearby forests had arrived and congregated around the entrance of the tomb in masse. Some lay on their stomachs as others stood over them. Thirty, forty at least, crowded around to block the view of anything around them. The stacked racks of the bucks creating a miniature forest on their own. Great Horned owls perched themselves upon the expansive antlers by the hundreds, their eyes piercing and unblinking

"Isn't it something?" she asked, looking back with a smile on her face.

"It's the most beautiful thing I've ever seen. How are you getting them to do this?"

"I asked them to come, and they came."

"Annabelle, it's breathtaking."

"Then maybe you're ready for something else."

"Like what?"

"Would you like to see things as I see them?"

"What do you mean?"

"How things look when you're on my side of the heartbeat? I could give you a taste of my blood. I know you wouldn't want to be in my place, but I know you're curious what it's like."

"Is it safe?"

"I wouldn't ask if I thought it would hurt you. The choice is entirely yours and I wouldn't be offended if you declined. I want you to see things as I do now. All the pieces are the same, but they arrange and move in ways I don't think I could ever describe in words. We're going to part ways soon and there's a chance we might never see each other again. Something like this is too special not to share and you're the only one I can show. Just a small taste."

"Sure," he nodded. "Why not?"

Annabelle held her left palm up to her mouth and sunk a canine fang into the meat below the thumb. Once pierced, she cupped her other hand under it and held it over Miles's mouth where she dibbled a few drops onto his tongue.

"There, that's enough." She grimaced as she pulled her hand away and shook the pain out.

"It's bitter," Miles remarked, smacking his lips.

"It's not sweet unless you get it from the living."

"And it…it burns."

"Feel anything yet?"

"No, not really. Wait." What started as a small tingle spread as a rush in a matter of seconds. His thoughts blurred in a cloud of sensations and Miles found himself struck deaf by a thick silence.

Annabelle?...Annabelle?...Annabelle?... The words echoed in the nothingness. His eyes fell upon the menagerie. To see it move made Miles forget himself and where he was. Everything felt fuzzy and disconnected. Looking at his hands, the fingers duplicated and waved back with tracers so intense that made his experience on MDMA pale in comparison. The meshed faces of the animals morphed together creating the image of an otherworldly beast with two hundred eyes. Beauty and horror, marvel and fear kaleidoscoping and melting together.

The eyes of the owls stared into deep into him, showed him the gaze of a void Miles could not begin to imagine the depth. The entity began emitting pronounced rasps and hums thick enough to vibrate the skin. "Annabelle?" he asked. "What is this? Is this real?"

"It's real." Annabelle stepped in front of him and controlled them with the wave of her hands. A simple gesture of moving her arm from her left to her right caused the vision to blink and ripple as the wind moves the trees before a storm. Following her lead, Miles raised his arms out in wide angles and brought them together and then apart. They mimicked his movements in the form of ripples, a living mirror casting its bent reflection back at him.

"I always wondered," he said. Then, just as fast as the rush had found him, the eyes and antlers began to collapse upon themselves. he felt lightheaded, his sight tunneling. "Annabelle...I..." The spirit came apart at the seams, the eyes and racks fading from their peacock brilliance to become like a big black nothing. Seconds later, Miles awoke with a start, lying on the front step of the mausoleum, his head cradled in Annabelle's hands.

"Welcome back," she said looking down at him. Miles shifted to look past his feet. The animals, gone, all of them. There was only darkness and headstones.

"Annabelle? What was that? What was-?"

"Everything that's hidden. Things beyond mortal sight."

"It was..." Miles paused to collect his thoughts as though it was a fading dream. "It was terrible...and beautiful."

"It is, and it has a different face every time it appears. This is the third time I've seen it in the last month."

"Three times, you can call it to you?"

"No. I was going to show you the deer and the owls, but I've noticed that whatever it is, it has a tendency to show up when I move things in an unnatural manner like calling large amounts of animals to me. It could be God, it could be the devil."

"Then maybe it's better I don't see."

"How do you feel?" she asked

"I feel better now. Help me up." As before, Annabelle stood and gave a strong pull, yanking him vertical. Miles involuntarily rubbed his arms.

"You're cold, come back inside."

"It's getting late. I should get home."

"All right." She flashed a smile to hide her disappointment. "Be safe. Sweet dreams."

"I'll do it. Are you feeding tonight?"

"I am. I'll feed tonight and Halloween. Those deer couldn't have gotten too far. I'll move my belongings and then find a meal before dawn."

"Goodnight, Annabelle."

"Goodnight, Miles." The doors of the tomb clicked shut behind her, leaving Miles to start down the hill. Leaves of every autumn color crunched beneath every step below. Above him, the limbs of the trees rustled, strangling the night air.

The ride home was uneventful but the phone call he made to Dennis was not. His friend's elation erupted through the phone when he learned the party on Halloween was still a go. After all, the party's meaning would be two-fold in that it doubled as a birthday party for Miles.

"It's gonna be sick, man! Sweeney scored some acid and Lucifer says she managed to score a bottle of some super rare kind of bourbon."

"That sounds great. I hope things aren't too weird between Lucifer and me."

"Things should be okay. She's mellowed out some since that explosion over at the abandoned farm. She asked me if the 'the blonde girl' was going to be at the party. She wouldn't happen to be talking about that supposed time-traveling vampire chick with a shotgun, would she?"

"No, there won't be any time-traveling vampires at the party."

"Are you sure about that? I wouldn't mind meeting a vampire and Lucifer seems to think she's real."

"Nope, just me."

"Well, that's a bit of a disappointment." Dennis sighed.

"Dude. You know what? Fuck you."

"In your dreams, hetero. See you at the tomb. Later."

"Later."

The line went dead and the receiver went back into its place on the wall. It was getting late and Gary wasn't home from the Imperial yet, so he plopped down in the recliner in front of the television. Flipping the lever on the side caused the two-decade-old undercarriage of metal and wood to groan its protest in articulating the footrest to rise. Once laid flat, the broken-in stuffing and leather felt like a miniature cloud gathering close to hug him. *Good God, this is comfortable. No wonder Gary never shares it.*

Gary monopolized the chair whenever he wasn't at work. With the fuel tank construction looming so close, he'd stayed progressively later and later each night. He said he wanted to be sure all the paperwork and permits were in order. The sound of the suburban could be heard rolling up into the driveway, the V-8 engine louder than anything else in the house. Gary entered with car keys in one hand and a fresh pizza box in the other. The room immediately flooded with wafts of pepperoni.

"Come and get it!" he called out. "I'm starving. Get some trays so we can eat and watch Alex Trebek."

Miles leaped from the spot and unfolded the dinner trays. Gary flipped on the VCR and they watched the whole show. Other than Gary yelling out answers and "Aw, shit! I knew that!" not a word passed between them. It felt good to have nothing going on outside of the mundane. During the final question that Miles looked across at the man that had raised him. Thinking of how Annabelle was alone in the world, it reminded him of how fortunate he was to have someone looking out for him. Dennis didn't have either of his parents, but Pearl and Mary were undoubtedly family enough.

Sometimes family isn't who you start with, but who you collect along the way.

"How is it that none of you three knows what the Towering Inferno is?" Gary barked at the screen, almost losing a mouthful of pizza into his lap. "You know what?

I'm done. I'm done for the night! Do you want this last piece of pizza?"

"No, thanks. I'm full," Miles told him.

"I'm going to bed," Gary grumbled, pushing his tray back and walking to the kitchen to put the pizza box in the fridge.

"Calm down, it's just a game show."

"I know it is, but they should have known the answer. Those eggheads got eight damn degrees between them but can't Steve McQueen and Paul Newman together to win a damn game show. Night, kiddo. I'm getting a shower and hitting the sack."

"G'night, Gary." The whirlwind ended with the bedroom door shutting behind him to leave Miles in the living room alone to finish his last slice. A minute later, the door opened up just enough for Gary's shirtless torso to be seen in the gap.

"Hey, you, it's your big day tomorrow, right. Any special thing you want to do?"

"Not really. I'm going to a party on Halloween with Dennis and the others so that's going to be my big thing. Why do you ask?"

"No big reason. I thought you and I might go somewhere nice and get a bite to eat. You're not too big for cake and ice cream, are you? I got some for the house because I thought you might still like some."

"Yes, I like both. It's fine."

"Ok, good. I've got some stuff to do at the store tomorrow, but we can leave early and go somewhere nice for a good meal, all right?"

"Works for me."

"All right, g'night kiddo." Gary smiled before shutting the door again.

The next day, the pair drove to the Imperial bright and early. Everyone in the store wished Miles a happy birthday. Both Darla and Mr. Jenkins hugged Miles, remarking about how big he'd gotten and traded stories he'd heard a hundred times before. The whole morning was more of the same. Of course, sometime before lunch, Mr. Jenkins felt obligated to spin the yarn at full volume of the time he'd found Miles, barely five years old, behind the propane tank with his pants around his ankles taking a shit in the grass while simultaneously holding a corndog in each hand.

"I said, 'boy, whatchu doin?' and he looked me dead in the eye and said 'I'm eatin these corndogs!'"

The whole store, which was easily occupied by no less than twenty customers, erupted in laughter which in turn caused Miles to turn beet red and exit the room pretending something in another room needed to be cleaned. The storeroom and kitchen with the deep fryer seemed as good of a place as any to hide weapons-grade mortification. He lingered around the shelves that housed the condiments when the shelf moved on its own and let out a small giggle. Startled, he heard sounds above and looked up to find Mary, dirty as ever but clothed, sitting on the top shelf near the ceiling.

"Mary, get down. You know you're not supposed to be back here." He raised his arms up to her, and she jumped off, almost knocking him over.

"Havachicken," she said, looking at the buzzing fluorescent bulbs in the ceiling instead of him.

"It's too early for chicken. Come here." He took her by the hand and led her out to the snack aisle where he grabbed a "quarter cake" from the snackcake shelf. No one was at Darla's register, so he reached over the counter, scanned the item and threw some change on the counter before leading Mary outdoors.

"Havachicken," she said again.

"Not chicken, jelly roll." The cellophane peeled away exposing the red and white swirled, sugary goodness beneath. Mary took one sniff and grabbed the whole thing and shoved it in her mouth, plastic and all. "Honey, don't. Stop, here, take the plastic off first." She fought him for a moment before realizing the slip of cardboard on the underside impeded her ability to eat it. Ultimately, he had to fight her to pull the plastic and cardboard out of her mouth while the rest was still in there. Once free, she raised both hands and forced everything outside her lips inside them. Her cheeks puffed out like a squirrel. "Girl, I love you to death, but you're a fucking hot mess."

"Fuckahotmess," she mumbled, slapping both of her cheeks with her hands. The dessert exploded out of her mouth, painting his pant leg with red and white goo. Before he could react, she was already off and running across the field in the direction of home, laughing the whole way. He considered giving chase. In seeing Mary leaping through

363

the tall grass, blissfully ignorant of the rest of the world, it would've been useless to try and scold her for being herself.

"Such a hot mess."

Not long afterward he and Gary drove north to Pikeville where they shared lunch in the quiet corner of a café. Halfway through the meal, Gary reached inside his jacket producing a small rectangular present wrapped in birthday-themed paper and placed it between them on the table. The paper had race cars and rockets ships on it like something designed for a five-year-old.

"What's that?" Miles asked.

"It's a gift, happy birthday."

"No 'kiddo'?"

"Not anymore. Shit, you're a man now. If you go out and get in trouble with the authorities now, they'll throw the book at you, so keep your nose clean."

"Like speeding through red lights and taking out speed limit signs?"

"That's exactly what I mean. They could've carted me off to jail if they wanted to."

"They did cart you off to jail, you just didn't stay long because we had bail money."

"You know what I mean. Those were extenuating circumstances."

"I know what you mean." Gary pushed his plate away from him, kicked back a little in his chair and crossed his arms

"So, what are your plans for the future?" Gary asked. He'd been asking this a lot lately. Miles needed a good answer.

"College, I guess."

"That doesn't sound too enthusiastic."

"Something to do with music. The last time we spoke about this you said I have more records than anyone. It makes sense I should try and find a career that has something to do with what I love, and that's music. But I can't play an instrument."

"Neither can those dipshits in the rap music who run around in circles yelling 'motherfucker' every other word, but they're still getting paid."

"I don't want to be a rapper and I don't want to go into the military for college money. I figure there are enough colleges and trade schools around Lexington, so I'll probably head that way."

"Then maybe you should open your gift," Gary said, pointing a finger at the package. Miles dropped his utensils and began peeling away the paper. It was wrapped tight like a brick. Even with the first layer pulled to shreds, there were still more beneath, He pulled and tore and unrolled until four stacks of bills with paper bands around the middle fell onto the table between them. Five bands marked "$1000" each.

"Five grand?" He looked up at Gary in awe. "Are you serious?"

"That's about what you paid for your car, right? If I was in your shoes, I'd have snatched it up too. You got lucky and came away with a real find. Also, this way you'll have some money in your pocket when you take off for the big city. You'll need funds for your first and last month's rent and down payments on utilities and the like. It's not cheap."

"Wow, I don't know what to say other than thank you."

"You don't have to say anything. If you need a little more for books and the like down the road, we'll see what we can do about a few bucks here and there. Otherwise, you're on your own, but you just make sure you call home every now and then. And once you get your own place, you're going to be having all kinds of half-naked ladies wanting to stay over. So, you be a gentleman and keep your hands to yourself and don't go messing around with some girl half out of her head on wine coolers. You'll get more than you bargained for."

"I got it. Thanks so much, Gary."

"You're welcome. Just make sure you keep moving forward in the direction of your choosing. Don't let others tell you what you need or don't need to be doing to live your own life. You done eating?"

"Yeah, I'm done."

"Good, let's get out of here." The two stood at the same time and Miles almost crushed Gary with the biggest hug. "Ok, ok." Gary patted him back. "All right knock it off, you're a grown-ass man now. I'll get the check. Pick up that stack of cash or the waitress will think it's a damn tip. The coffee was good, but it wasn't that good."

October 31, 1994

Monday. Miles skipped school to drive to the county clerk's office and put the Cadillac in his own name. Gary met him there and each one signed the certificate to transfer possession. Once printed anew, Monster was finally all his, lock stock and barrel. He kissed the title when no one was looking. The rest of the school day went without a single noteworthy incident. It wasn't until after the last bell when he met the others out in the parking lot that things got interesting.

"So, we're still doing this thing at the Booth tomb, right?" asked Nora in her torn up, Edward Scissorhands t-shirt.

"Woo-hoo! Hell yes, we are!" Sweeney shouted, throwing up a pair of middle fingers in the air.

"Don't get too wild, party boy." Lucifer sulked as she lit a cigarette. "We don't want you horking on the floor like you did last time."

"Shut up, Lucifer." He flashed middle finger towards her. "That was an accident."

"I'll say what I want, I can hold my booze and drugs. And speaking of which, I've got a special treat for everyone."

"I hope it's wicked special because I scored at least two hits of blotter acid for everyone."

"Now that's a party," Dennis commented. "Everyone's made up their alibi about coming to my place for a sleepover to celebrate Miles's birthday, right?" Everyone nodded in agreement. "Good. See everybody there at 10 pm sharp. Call me or Miles if you need a ride. Let's get out of here. The teachers are glaring at us again."

9:00 P.M.

Night had fallen, and Miles sat on the floor of his room staring in a mirror as he applied the last of his makeup. For a big occasion like this he wanted to go all out and truly look like the 'space vampire' Gary jokingly accused him of being. The clothing ensemble started at his feet with a pair of leather army boots, followed by torn and "spiderwebbed" black tights. Above that, a black pair of soccer shorts were just big enough to cover his ass. Above that, yup, even more black in the form of an oversized stretched out black sweater with a large homemade white skull painted across the body. The fact that the skull looked 'janky' and poorly drawn made it look more sinister than a store-bought print. The outfit ended around his neck with a black band sporting chrome spikes in alternating half-inch and full inch length all the way around.

If you're going to dance with the dead, dress up for the occasion.

"Broken Hearts are for Assholes" blared through the speakers of his stereo at such a volume that the faux wood paneling covering the walls vibrated and made the posters tacked to them dance. Gary might've complained if he wasn't still working late at the Imperial. As for makeup, Miles had slathered 'ghost white' on everything at the base of his neck, all the way up to his forehead before painting a thick black horizontal band across his eyes and nose as a tribute. "I've seen things you people wouldn't believe," he said to his own reflection.

Surprisingly, no one had called him for a ride to the party, not even Lucifer. Where things stood with her was impossible to tell from one minute to the next. The last notes of the song played before he pressed the 'power' button. Although the weatherman said it would be a mild night, he snatched his leather jacket from its hook on his way out of the house. On the way out the front door, Miles flipped off the switch to extinguish the porch light. He didn't need it to see where he was going. The real reason wasn't to see the ordinary, but for something special instead. Monster waited for him in the darkness, the two fresh coats of carnauba wax he'd applied by hand to its black paint mirroring every star in the night sky.

"Hellllooooo, gorgeous." The jacket found its place across the middle of the front seat and the cool leather cradled Miles as he sat down and closed the door. A turn of the key awoke the beast and the car sped off, gliding over and across the winding Kentucky hills. There were no cars on the road. It was Halloween, sure, but far too late for parents to drive their children across White Wreath in search of tricks and treats. It wasn't until he passed in front of the Imperial until he saw anyone at all. In the fleeting seconds Miles could take his eyes off the road, he caught glimpses of both Gary and Mr. Jenkins through the big window by the front register. The huge hand-painted sign in the middle of the gravel entrance reading "CLOSED ONE WEEK FOR REPAIRS, THANK YOU FOR YOUR BUSINESS" said everything anyone needed to know.

It wasn't long after that Miles pulled the Caddy into the lot across from the cemetery and killed the ignition. The night held unexpected surprises to be sure. It'd be an unforgettable night for friends, music, dancing, and maybe even lust and visions. How fitting to be in a cemetery when you're ready to bury your childhood. Time to grow up.

He parked Monster in the lot across from the cemetery. No cars were coming from either direction, so he hopped out, crossed the two-lane road and scaled the stone wall. Boots scraped and skidded to push him up before he got his leverage and pushed himself over the top. Walking up the long hill like he'd done so many times before, a fair breeze followed, carrying stray leaves and smoky smells that someone was still burning an autumn bonfire. A waxing crescent moon above kept things nice and dark. No one else appeared to be around when he arrived at the Booth tomb. The chain was on the outside of the door again, the links hanging limply from the handles.

With the push of his hand, the door swung inward. Miles entered, listening for signs of life, or the undead. "Hello?" He wasn't a step past the threshold when his foot struck something small and metallic, knocking it over. He reached blindly down and found the flashlight he'd given Annabelle. It came to life in his hands, the wide beam illuminating all corners of the crypt. He didn't see anyone. But if he'd learned anything, in the past few months, just because you can't see something doesn't mean it's not there.

"Hello? Annabelle?" There came no reply but echoes of his own voice. Her father's coffin had been shoved back into its spot in the wall and the splintered masonry cleaned away. He found a small bouquet of freshly picked wildflowers laid atop the coffin as well as one on the ground in front of Mrs. Booth's tomb marker. Annabelle had said her goodbyes. All the lights and electrical cords sat in the corner, all the candles collected and placed in a pile nearby, the blankets folded and stacked.

The others would be arriving soon, so he hefted the coils of extension cords over one shoulder and made his way to the groundkeeper's shed. Like the times before, it didn't take long to find the electrical plug in the workshop and run the cable. As he approached the tomb, footsteps sounded in the tall grass to herald the faint silhouettes.

"Who goes there?" he asked in a faux Shakespearian accent. "Who approaches from the shadows black to haunt my front step?"

"It is we," Dennis said with a laugh as he appeared, a flashlight pointed under his chin to look sinister. "The mirthful spirits of youth and boiling blood. Might you invite us inside your home so that we might entertain thee?"

"Entrance to my home, you say? Then surely you have wares to trade for the shelter of my home for the night."

"That we do," said a feminine voice as another silhouette emerged. Lucifer took Dennis' flashlight and held it under her own face. Her hair had been teased and styled up into a mohawk and 'Siouxsie Sioux' makeup framing her eyes. "Strong drink and drugs for the senses, and pleasures of the flesh to trade, we have." The others stepped out of the shadows, Sweeney, Nora, Christian and Kate each one dressed in costume or club gear.

"Then you are all very welcome spirits, indeed." He bowed, waving them inside. When they started walking in, Miles grabbed Dennis' sleeve to hold him close. "Hey man, what's Lucifer doing here? She was mad as hell last time I saw her, and I thought she was hanging out with JoJo's crowd."

"You didn't hear? Lucifer told me that after the whole farm fire incident happened that JoJo was continually fucked up on some kind of pills or whatever and getting super aggressive with people, even his own crew. And mad or not, she's smart enough to know to be pleasant if it gets her into a get-together like this. You should see the bottle of rare bourbon she brought. I've never seen anything like it before. Oh, and Sweeney brought enough acid for everyone."

"Everyone is tripping tonight?"

"That's right! Alien invasions and unholy resurrections from wall to wall! Nora brought a cooler, jugs of orange juice and all kinds of stuff to mess with when we're blitzed out of our gourds."

"Wait, if we're all getting blitzed then who's the designated babysitter?"

"Nobody, cowboy. The training wheels are off for this one. No seat belts, no safety nets, no more parental advisories. It's you, me, five individuals of questionable moral fiber and fourteen hits of high-quality blotter acid to pit our imaginations against one another in a no holds barred battle-royale in the freaking fourth dimension! Come on, let's get inside and rig the lights." He smiled wide. "Sweeney says he's going to absolve us of our sins."

It didn't take long to get everything up and running. Once the lights were squared away, Sweeney surprised everyone by pulling a costume catholic priests robe and a tall pointed white hat out of a duffle bag and donning the whole outfit. He had no intentions of playing the role of a snake-oil salesman, not on a night like this. He cued up a track on the CD in the boombox and had everyone kneel side by side in front of him. After that, he produced a clear baggie with small squares of paper within it from behind his back and held it aloft. With grand gestures Sweeney raised his arms full above his head and spoke;

"Unclean souls, before you are granted access to the next world, you must be pure. Will you all receive communion so that you might enter that sacred land?"

"We will!" The rest said in unison.

"Then let us begin." Sweeney put on a latex glove and began to stick his fingers in the bag to get the blotter paper as Lucifer produced a round metal pizza pan and lined up shot glasses upon like a communion tray. With a twist the cap from a tall light green, glass bottle bearing a huge label upon it, she filled each of the vessels to the top with bourbon before lifting it like a serving tray. Sweeney started on the right side of the row with Kate as each person raised their hands up in prayer. He held the tabs high, saying: "The body of Albert Hoffman," before placing two tabs on her tongue. When he stepped to the side, Lucifer stood over her and held out the shot glass.

"The blood of the barrel," Lucifer said. Kate took the shot and crossed herself. Down the row they went, Kate, Nora, Christian. "The body of Albert Hoffman, the blood of the barrel, the body of Albert Hoffman…". The closer it got to Miles, the more an uneasy feeling found him. It seemed like a bad idea not to have at least one of them stay sober in the event of someone having a "bad trip" or accidentally hurting themselves and needing a ride home or to the hospital. Sweeney stepped in front of Dennis and he received his tabs. Lucifer gave him his shot. Sweeney stepped in front of Miles.

This is it. No turning back now.

"The body of Albert Hoffman," Sweeney said. Miles received the tabs. Lucifer stood over him as Sweeney dosed himself.

"Blood of the barrel, handsome," she said with a breathy voice and wink. Miles took the shot, the super smooth whiskey burning its way down his throat. Lucifer gave Sweeney a shot to chase his hits and she knelt before him to receive her own. When Sweeney was done with his shot, he made the sign of the cross over them all and shouted;

"I pronounce you all sinners and commit your beautiful souls to the technicolor void! HALLELUJAH!"

"HALLELUJAH!" Everyone yelled in return. Sweeney hit play on the boombox and a man's voice went off like a bomb.

"Kick out the jams, motherfuckers!" Blaring rock music filled the air. The costumes and props were pitched aside, and everyone began to dance. People bounced and slammed to the song as the bottle of fine bourbon passed from one mouth to the next. When the bottle came around to Miles, he took a single shot to taste the smoothness everyone was already talking about. It was the best he'd ever tasted, truly the blood of the barrel. But for every subsequent time it came back to him he merely held the bottle's opening against pursed lips before passing it on. Around and around it went, underneath flashing lights and strobes, vanishing fast until Sweeney took the last drops and passed Miles the empty vessel.

When the next song started, and he thought no one was looking, he slipped outside for a moment alone with the empty bottle still in his hand. Away from prying eyes he reached into his waistband and pulled out the tabs of acid he'd hidden instead of taking with the others. The time was right, the people were right, the place was right. Why didn't it feel right? From the sound of laughter and shouts coming from inside, everyone else was having a blast. The tabs looked so tiny and innocent between his fingers.

If he took the magical tabs now, he could rejoin the others in their enthusiastic cloud and ride the next nine hours throwing wide the doors of perception. If he left them out, he'd be sober but might regret never taking this moment to feel the hallucinogenic winds fill his sails. He thought twice and finally decided to fish out his wallet, fold the tabs up in a dollar bill and put it back in his pocket. *Maybe another time.* Here it was that he was surrounded with the people most like him, but upon turning over the empty bourbon bottle in his hand, he felt the same hollowness. Miles eyed the label in the moonlight depicting an old man with large ears lighting the cigar in his mouth. Above and below him, the words "Pappy Van Winkle" and "Family Reserve."

He had no idea who the man on the label was, but the twenty-year-old bourbon with his name on it was a thing of beauty. It was then that a feeling somewhere between a twinge and a shiver found him.

"I gotta get out of this place," he said aloud as he set the bottle atop the closest headstone and leaned against the huge oak tree. "If I were to leave tonight, some company might be nice. Do you still want to go to New Orleans?"

"More than anything," said Annabelle, perched a few branches above his head. "But I still haven't fed yet."

"Leave the people in the tomb alone."

"I wouldn't dream of eating your friends. Besides," she stopped to smell the wind, "There's a huge musky buck not far to the south from here. Have you told your friend Dennis you're leaving?"

"No, but I think he'll understand. If he doesn't, then, oh well. I'm going to go. Take your time and find your buck. I'm going to run home and leave a note for Gary so he doesn't worry and then come back to pick you up here at the front gates. Does that work for you?"

"I'll be waiting," she said.

Down the hill, past the rows of graves, he walked. A crunchy dirge played beneath his boots from the layers of leaves covering the paths. Monster appeared as a welcome sight when he scaled the wall. A stillness came as he paused to stand at the top. He looked back from his vantage point and could no longer see the tomb. Dennis, maybe someone else, would soon notice he was absent and try to find him. To be honest, Miles couldn't bring himself to care and leaped off.

His watch said ten minutes to midnight as Monster carried him home. As it came into view through the left side of the windshield, the Imperial looked unusual with all its external lights turned off. The front fuel island and tanks would be removed in the morning. At a glance, nothing else looked out place until ambient light from inside the building framed the profile of JoJo's Ford Explorer parked next to the building.

Monster lurched as he stomped the brakes to keep from overshooting the driveway. The car pulled onto the property just far enough to get off the main road and rolled to a stop. Like he said he would, Gary had held over the cash drops from over the weekend to make payouts for the coal mine truckers who'd want to cash their payday checks. Of course, JoJo would magically reappear when there's an abundance of cash in the drawer to ask for a handout.

Miles stepped out of the car; the smell of gasoline reeked enough to make him pull the neck of his sweater over his nose. Bright yellow caution tape decorated the front door of the building, so he headed around back. A passing glance into JoJo's vehicle showed it to be vacant of knuckleheads. When he reached the back door, it was already open a crack, and he pushed it wide. To his surprise, the smell of gasoline was inside as well. Five steps inside, the scrawny knucklehead with the neck tattoo stepped into view at the other end of the hall. In his hands, a red gas can emptied its contents onto the tiled floor. The words jumped from his mouth without a second thought.

"What the hell are you doing?" Miles shouted. Not hearing Miles's approach, the thug almost jumped out of his skin before slipping and knocking over a display of candy bars. The can clattered across the floor, the last of its contents dribbling out. As this happened, the Samoan stepped out of the men's room, a stockless black shotgun with a 'wrist breaker' pistol grip in his hands. Shocked by the sight of one another, he and fat kid froze before the weapon leveled at Miles's chest.

"The fuck are you doing here, faggot?"

"What's going on out there?" JoJo's voice sounded from somewhere out of sight.

"It's your cousin," said the other one, climbing back to his feet and pulling a 9mm from the waistband of his jean shorts. "The spooky queer one."

"Then what are you waiting for? Get him in here!" Both knuckleheads waved their guns at Miles to move him towards the front of the store. With their direction he passed the showers he turned left and then left again. Looking at the back of the building, he stood at the crossroads of the corridor with Gary's office on the left, the storeroom ahead and the small kitchen with the chicken fryers on the right. The hot bins hissed as they churned their chicken oil at volcanic temperatures. "Neck tattoo" shoved him into the office. A chilling scene unfolded as Miles found Gary and Mr. Jenkins on their knees with hands zip-tied behind their backs while JoJo and the third knucklehead held them at gunpoint.

As disturbing as this was, it paled in comparison to JoJo's emaciated appearance and ruined left eye. He hadn't seen him since the night of the meth lab fire, but he looked like whatever "mountain crank" his was shooting in his veins had made him lose another fifteen pounds he didn't look like he could spare. His pale and pockmarked skin looked like it was shrink-wrapped to his skeleton. As for the eye, it had turned completely white, covered in an unnatural milky film.

"The fuck are you staring at faggot. Don't you think I'm pretty anymore?" He used his right middle finger and pulled down the lower lid to show more of the ruined orb. "Jesus, you look like a fucking girl dressed like that. Yo, what are you waiting for? Tie his hands, dipshit." The hefty guy kept the shotgun on him as the smaller one pulled Miles's hands behind his back and tied them together. They didn't put him on his knees but held him close.

"Gary, what's happening?" Miles asked.

"What does it look like?" Mr. Jenkins answered for him. "He's robbing us."

"Just take the money," Gary told JoJo. "But please don't hurt anyone. Just take the money."

"I'm going to. What's the combination to the safe?"

"36-24-36," Gary said.

"Really?" JoJo laughed. "You old pervert." He set to work turning the dial on the angry-looking safe and a few seconds later, the door flew open. The knuckleheads hooted and whistled at the sight of the huge stacks of cash within. "God damn, Uncle Gary," he said as 'tattoo neck' pitched him a small red and white canvas bag. JoJo used the barrel of his pistol to scoop the money into the bag.

"How much is that?" Asked the smaller one.

"Sixty-three thousand," Gary said in a defeated tone.

"That's not your damn money!" Mr. Jenkins shouted. "What you gonna do with that money? You gonna party for a few days before the cops catch up to you and put you in jail for twenty years?" JoJo's lip wrinkled into a snarl and he straightened to his full height.

"The cops won't find me if there's no witnesses to tell them to look for me." JoJo raised his brushed chrome pistol and pressed the end of the barrel against Mr. Jenkin's forehead.

"You don't scare me, punk." He started past the gun, defiance in his eyes. "I've seen what real horror looks like. You think I lost my arm being afraid of guns. I've seen-"

The gun went off and Mr. Jenkin's head flew back, painting the faux wood paneling of the office wall with brains and blood. The small space of the office made the 9mm sounded like a magnum. Gary cried out in terror as the body hit the floor. JoJo then turned the gun on Miles. It was hard to make out the words with his ears ringing, but he could still read lips and facial expressions.

"Don't!" Gary shouted. "Don't do it! Don't hurt my boy!"

"Are you kidding me? I can't wait to do the world a favor and wax this little homo." Miles's heart stopped as JoJo's finger wrapped tight around the trigger. Seeing the gun drawn on him was too much for Gary. A primal scream jumped from his mouth and he leaped from his knees to his feet to ram his shoulder into JoJo's ribs. JoJo fell sideways onto the work desk and the shot went wild, missing Miles by inches but striking the smaller thug in the shoulder. He jumped in fright and knocked the Samoan guy backward and off balance.

"Get off me!" JoJo yelled, shoving Gary back with one hand while the pistol came up again in the other.

Rapid-fire shots went off one after another and in JoJo's panic, he managed to empty the entire gun into Gary's chest. It was almost enough to split the eardrums. There was no time to think. Miles made a break for it. The smaller thug was still stunned and gave no resistance when Miles battered him aside and bolted for the door. The floor remained slick with gasoline. A turn to the right brought the front of the store into view. Two more quick turns got him a clear path to the back door. Muscle memory carried him as the sight of witnessing Gary's body crumple into the corner played over and over in his mind.

He slipped and slid as he hurried past the showers, but he didn't go down. It was when he dashed by the payphones that more shots filled the air. He was almost out the door. *Omigodomigodomigodomigod.* The 12-gauge "wristbreaker" went off like a cannon behind him, its pellets peppering his left shoulder as the majority of the shot hit the exposed fuse box next to him. The voltage short blinded Miles a little with its purple and blue colored arc as the resulting explosion showered over him like 4th of July fireworks going off indoors.

He'd be a sitting duck if the door opened inwards like most buildings, but the Imperial's back door swung out. There was no slowing down, his head and burning shoulder struck the door at full force to create another loud bang and release him out into the cool night air. There was hardly any time to notice much around him as he ran, but the light from the spreading fire within the doorway began to light his way in the darkness. Around the corner he bolted, sounds of yells and shouts coming from within. The Cadillac came within view.

Not much further, not much further.

He didn't know how he was going to get the keys out of his back pocket but that's something he'd deal with when he reached the car. There was still a chance to get away. But for all his agility and balance displayed in his escape of the building, the loose laces of his boots betrayed Miles and tripped him ten feet short of Monster. He flailed weightless for a split second. With no free hands to catch himself, gravity became a cruel master. It took hold of Miles and combined with the velocity he'd been running, slammed his body chest and headfirst upon the unforgiving surface of the gravel.

Blinded, deafened, and struck dumb from the fall, he writhed to get up. Limbs felt useless. The ability to stand was so far from him that he might as well have been asked to sprout wings and fly.

Licking flames continued to grow in the Imperial's front windows, lighting the front of the lot where he lay. The fire spread and light from within began to illuminate the lot. Plumes of black smoke continued to fill the store until it began seeping out of the eaves and vents. From where he lay in the middle of the lot, Miles watched his whole world go up in flames. The pain that welled in his eyes were not for his own wounds, but for the man who'd raised him, now dead from the gun of a junkie. Any remaining strands of innocence and security he might've been clinging to burned with the Imperial. He wanted to cry out for Gary, scream into the night if only to scream. It never came as the shock of hitting the ground left him limp and mute. Only simple words and phrases appeared through the wooziness: *Get up. Danger. Fire. Guns.*

He tugged at his restraints a second and third time, the zip-ties refusing to relent. Cries and shouting appeared at the far corner of the building as the thugs came pouring out of the building. Some of their clothes and shoes were on fire and they danced and cursed to put them out as they ran. The big one stomped and waved the shotgun trying to extinguish a flaming pant leg. The smaller one and "tattoo neck" swatted at each other, dropping their guns to pat out the last of the fire. JoJo emerged last, the weighty, red and white bag hanging from one hand.

"Let's go!" he yelled at them. "Put that shit out and get in the truck!" They did as they were told and ran over to the vehicle where the bigger thug looked directly where Miles lay on the ground.

"Check it!" said one of the thugs. "Is he dead?"

"You shot him, didn't you?" Said another.

"Yeah, I capped him!"

"Naw, he's still moving, look!" said the other

"It's cool, I've got this," JoJo told them. "Get in the truck. I've got this." The four climbed into the vehicle and it came to life. Tires squelched and spat gravel, the Ford Explorer driving twenty yards to the rear of the building before turning around. Past his feet, Miles watched the light of the vehicles 'high beams' filled everything as the engine revved higher and began its high-speed approach. JoJo wasn't going to shoot him, he was getting a running start to run him over. The lowered suspension and small tires didn't allow for enough room for a cat to get under let alone a human being. If the impact didn't kill him instantly, being trapped beneath the undercarriage would break every bone in his body before it reached the end of the lot.

It was coming, fast.

The thought of being mangled to death by the cracker wagon was motivation enough for an adrenaline shot to help clear the mind. Miles squirmed for leverage to get his feet under him, but it wasn't happening fast enough.

The truck was past the back of the store.

The lights got brighter, the engine louder.

The horn began to blast, yelling heads sticking out the windows sounded as shrill as anything.

At ten yards, Miles couldn't look away. If this was the end, if this was death coming to collect him, he wanted to see it. Then, a flash of vermillion and gold passing overhead from the opposite direction followed by a violent collision and the crumpling of metal. It sounded like a bomb going off. The lights of the Explorer went black as it came to dead stop…two feet short of him. And there, with her shoulder buried in the radiator and engine block, a girl out of time, a girl named Annabelle had delivered him from death. He tried to speak but it came out as a barely audible croak of "help".

"Don't move," she said as she pulled herself out of the crushed engine block. Someone inside the vehicle yelled and guns fired from within. Bullets began to fly through the broken windshield, one striking Annabelle in the chest. It knocked her back but didn't put her down. She, in turn, leveled her sawed-off shotgun at the windshield and unleashed two blasts through the windshield.

Then, faster than the eye can follow, she broke the barrels open, pitched the spent shells, reloaded new ones, and emptied those rounds into the interior. All four blasts sounded like they went off at once.

When the sound of the shots finally echoed away, she shouldered the scattergun and stepped around the drivers' side of the vehicle peering within. The front door was jammed behind the ruined quarter panel, so she broke the window and yanked the whole door free of its hinges. Inside, she found JoJo slumped over the steering wheel, his face almost unrecognizable as it bled into a bag full of money. The ruined seats and headrests looked like Swiss cheese.

Past him, the big thug wheezed and gurgled. His chest, neck, and head oozed from where the steel shot had penetrated. Upon seeing Annabelle, he convulsed in a bizarre death rattle and he became motionless. She took a step to the right and pulled the rear drivers' side door off its hinges as well. More shots rang out from the rear passenger seat. She ducked to let the rounds pass her by, reaching down to grab the Explorer by its frame. The opposite rear door opened and a voice yelled out.

"Stay away from me!"

Annabelle hefted the weight of the vehicle and flipped it away from her. A wet crunch sounded as the Ford landed on its side, pinning the last living person of the crew in the door frame. Convinced that the situation was resolved, Annabelle rushed to Miles's side and broke the zip ties.

"Are you all right?" she asked.

"Gary." Miles croaked.

"Gary? Where's Gary?"

"He's in there." Miles panted to get his breath. "Don't go. Everyone is dead." His ears rang less as the blaze began eating its way through the roof. "I thought you were waiting at the cemetery."

"I heard shots," she said, seeing the shot holes in his sweater. "Oh my god, you've been shot! We have to get you out of here, get you to a hospital. It's not safe here with all this fire. We need to get you home at least."

"Home is gone," Miles said as he sat up. "Look, my home is burning, Gary is dead."

"Then what will you do?"

"I don't know. It's all gone. Jesus, Gary is dead, Mr. Jenkins." Annabelle stood and watched the fire.

"MILLS!" A voice called out from the darkness. Annabelle's stance went rigid. Both Miles and Annabelle looked to see Mary materialize from the tall grass. Wearing only a t-shirt, underwear, and one ruined sock that once was white, she ran across the gravel to where he sat. She knelt down next to him, throwing her arms around his neck.

"Mills," she said.

"Honey, it's ok. Get off. You're going to get-" It was too late. As she pulled back, the front her new t-shirt with the smiling face of a big purple dinosaur was already soaked with the blood from his shoulder. "Mary, you can't stay here. It's not safe. Run home. Run home to Grandma Pearl."

"Gramma!" she said with a big smile. "Gramma, havachicken!"

"Yes! Run home to grandma for chicken!"

"Havachicken!" she said with a wide grin. Mary peeled her remaining sock off and threw it at Annabelle, striking her in the face. She then took off like a shot, running wobbly legged back across the lot, vanishing into the tall grass again, singing about chicken and giggling all the way.

"The police and fire trucks will be here soon," Miles said, standing to look upon the fire.

"What will you do? What will you say?" Asked Annabelle.

"I can't explain that." He pointed to the ruined truck lying on its side.

"Then don't. Remember our plan? We leave this behind and go to New Orleans."

"New Orleans?"

"For a short time if you want. I can't stay here, and you have a car."

"How will we live when we get there? I have <u>some</u> money but neither you or I know anyone, and it costs a lot of money to live in a big city like that."

"How much would it take?"

"A lot." He waved towards the burning building. "And I don't have a job anymore." A terrible headrush hit Miles and he bent at the waist, putting his hands upon his knees for balance.

"Wait here." Annabelle walked over to the Ford, put her hands on the roof and shoved it back over onto its wheels. Upon walking around the driver's side, she reached in and came back with the red and white canvas bag. "There." She dropped the bag at his feet. "Is that enough for you to at least take me to New Orleans?" Tens of thousands of dollars in cash practically overflowed from the open bag.

"Yeah, that would probably be enough."

"Then we should go now. It's not safe for me to stay here." Miles looked at the stacks of cash spritzed with blood across them again before snatching it all up by the handles.

"Fine. New Orleans it is. There's nothing for me here anymore." The two turned away and started for the Cadillac. Annabelle motioned to the rear of the car and he used his keys to open the trunk.

"What about your shoulder?" she asked.

"It hurts but we have to get out of here now before others show up. Can you put some of your blood on it later to fix it?"

"Of course." Annabelle laid her shotgun inside and had one foot in when they both heard another voice behind them.

"Help." It said again. Both Miles and Annabelle looked back to see "tattoo neck" rolling in the gravel, trying to crawl his way away from the vehicle. "I can't… I can't feel my legs," he said.

"If we leave him, he'll just lie and say we attacked him. Then the sheriff will try and hunt us down," she said. "We can't afford to leave any witnesses."

"No, no we can't." Annabelle stepped out and closed the distance between herself and the thug. Miles expected her to crush his neck with her boot or slam his head into the gravel to end him. Curiously, she walked over, grabbed his shirt by the scruff of the neck, and dragged him back to the car like a bag of potatoes. She rounded the back of the car and lifted him by the arms and legs before setting him inside the trunk. Once situated, she stepped up and climbed in with him.

"We're taking him with us?" he groaned in pain

"Of course, we are." She flashed him a sly smile. "It's a long way to New Orleans, and he owes me a meal." Annabelle grabbed the trunk door and pulled it down.

"Wait!" said the thug. "Don't leave me in here with-" The 'ka-chunk' of the trunk shutting silenced him.

Miles still felt woozy and his shoulder burned like the devil, but Annabelle was right. It wasn't safe to stay here any longer. He looked to the now raging fire and then off into the distance where the trees and sky shared the darkness as one. White Wreath held no more secrets or ties for him. Somewhere out on a distant hill, Dennis and the others were having the times of their lives. Maybe they'd have visions or fantastic escapes. Maybe they were clinging to something familiar because they didn't know how to let go and search out something else. *Lucky them.*

The bag of cash went behind the driver's seat and Monster roared to life. No cars or passersby had happened upon the scene yet. Miles considered the Imperial to be Gary's funeral pyre and left it to burn. The gravel lot crunched beneath the tires as he pulled out of the lot and onto the main road. His head began to clear as the tires spit gravel.

Half a mile down the road, something caught his eye in the tree line along the highway. It was Mary running through the woods on her way home to a woman who would hold and love her. At that moment she was as wild and free as anything could be. As the car passed, he caught a snippet of the song she sang, a riddle of nonsense as sweet as honey on the wind. Miles pressed the gas pedal harder and the car swept him away towards a place he'd never been, somewhere unknown, beyond what he knew.

Monster sped into the darkness, the winding and dipping slopes of the Kentucky blacktop as smooth as twenty-year bourbon.

He drove all night. No radio, just the windows down to let the night breeze dry his eyes when the tears came.

END.

The following playlist is a sampling of the music that influenced the creation of the scenes, characters, and overall world of White Wreath. I hope you'll take the time to listen to the tracks as well as pursue the other works by the artists listed. Thanx. AJC.

Bourbon and Blood Soundtrack:
OR
"Annabelle's secret audio mash bill"

1: A Forest- The Cure
2: Mary- Oingo Boingo
3: Pretend We're Dead- L7
4: Voodoo People-The Prodigy
5: Ignore the machine- Alien Sex Fiend
6: Bloodletting- Concrete Blonde
7. Stigmata Martyr- Bauhaus
8. Naïve- KMFDM
9: the passenger-Iggy Pop
10: Do you fear for your child? - My Life with the Thrill Kill Kult
11: Love will tear us apart- Joy Division
12: Black sunshine- White Zombie
13: Running up that hill- Kate Bush
14: The Killing Moon-Echo and the Bunnymen
15: Heaven Knows I'm Miserable Now- The Smiths
16: Just One Fix- Ministry
17: She's in Parties- Bauhaus
18: World in my eyes- Depeche Mode
19: Burn-Nine Inch nails

The author hails from Nonesuch, Kentucky (Woodford County) but currently lives in Lexington where he plays spooky music for the black clad creatures of the night.

He's worked a variety of jobs to include: a gas station attendant, an army special operations paratrooper, a Halloween costume store clerk, a roadie, an artist's model, and a bourbon salesman.

This is his debut novel.

Follow Andrew on Twitter @ajcoleofficial
For news and updates about future releases.

Copyright © 2020 Andrew J Cole
All rights reserved.

CPSIA information can be obtained
at www.ICGtesting.com
Printed in the USA
BVHW040958020320
573816BV00014B/562